RISING LEVIATHAN

THE AFTER EDEN SERIES: BOOK THREE

AUSTIN DRAGON

Published by Well-Tailored Books, California

Rising Leviathan / After Eden Series: Book Three

978-0-9887235-8-0 (ebook)
978-0-9887235-6-6 (paperback)

http://www.austindragon.com

Book cover design by Leslie K.

Formatting by Polgarus Studio

Printed in the United States of America

"After Eden, Thy Kingdom Fall.
All Kingdoms Fall, New Kingdoms Rise."

World War III. It was inevitably going to be one of religion, this great, grim, evil war of humans, machines, and *other things* in the shadows that have never existed before. Unfortunately, neither the cause nor the outcome was within our perception, though the former should have been. No one could ever have imagined that it would not just be the third of the world wars, as that is unremarkable, but the explosion of the first global war of the Technological Age, the Tek Age—a hell we had never seen before.

Net-Dictionary

Wolf 359

1. A red dwarf star located in the Leo constellation, approximately 7.8 light-years from Earth, making it one of the stars nearest to our solar system.

2. A fictional space battle in the Star Trek Universe between the United Federation of Planets and the Borg Collective in the year 2367.

3. The opening battle of World War III in New York City on September 11, 2125. Over sixty percent of the United States of America Atlantic Oceanic Battle Fleet was destroyed by the Supreme Islamic Caliphate Battle Group on the first day.

Other terms:

Pagan:
1. (universal or American usage) a non-believer of god or gods; one that doesn't believe in religion, often negative to, hostile to, or hateful of religion.
2. (Russian Bloc) a member of the Wicca, Druid, or Old Pagan religions.

Jew-Christian: (American usage [by non-religious people]) a religious person, other than Muslim.

Faither: (global usage [by religious people]) a religious person, other than Muslim.

Tek World: common slang for tek-cities, tek-metropolises, or general tek-society.

Resistance: (pre-World War III)
1. [by non-religious people] government term for the network of Jew-Christian domestic "terrorists" in America.
2. [by religious people] the civilian resistance force against the militant, anti-religious American government.

Continuum:
1. (general usage) the parallel society created by and controlled exclusively by Faithers outside of Tek World.
2. (formal usage) the formal alliance of the New Protestant Order, New Jewish Continuum, New Catholic Order, African Collective, Shogun, and the Magi.

Transmission Intercept #114790 (World War III)

[Date tag: 13 September 2125] Rube, please respond. I'll keep resending. Pro-Caliphate Muslims have seized the Canadian government, no doubt triggered by the Caliphate attack on New York City. Canada has erupted in civil war. The Quebecois are fighting Muslim forces in the East, and all sects of the Star Trek have joined with Jedis to fight the Muslims in the West. Not a single Canadian soldier has yet responded to Caliphate invasion forces. Sources say the Canadian military has instead taken up fortified positions on the border to protect America. Sources also say that the Canadian President and his entire Cabinet have already fled the country. {Unintelligible expletives; not English} It burst on the Net—Russian Bloc forces have invaded! That means they're either completely ignoring their Witch Wars or have already dealt with it. Canada can't stop the Russian Bloc military, so this isn't to invade Canada, but America! Rube, I have to go now; it's total chaos in country. I hear gunfire and mortar explosions, and I see fire, smoke, and looting everywhere around me. Rube, get as far away from America as possible. This is it. This must be World War Three. See you at checkpoint Charlie. Live long and prosper.

Department of Homeland Defense and Intelligence Agency Security Dispatch / 13 September 2125: Sender is identified as Lorian Denak, a journalist of Vulcan, Alberta, Canada. Recipient (called "Rube") has been identified as anti-American journalist and activist named Sprocket. Canada has fallen and the entire Canadian government has fled the country for America. Confirmed: Russian Bloc military invaded Canada at 00:10 hours. Threat Matrix projects that Muslim forces now in control of Canada will fall to the Russians within the hour. Russian Bloc invasion of America via the northwestern states is imminent. No additional military forces will be redeployed to the northern border. All American military forces are committed to the battlefront against the Caliphate's Northeastern Atlantic invasion (designated: War of the Three Towers or "Wolf 359"). Threat Matrix predicts that PERFECT STORM Scenario is a ninety percent probability, with projected attacks from CHIN forces via the Pacific and Brazilian forces from the southern border. If projections become reality, the President will formally declare the commencement of World War Three.

Table of Contents

THE WICCAN MATRIARCH

(The Rise of the Leviathan King)
Russian Bloc

The Black Dinner

"All things are subject to interpretation. Whichever interpretation prevails at a given time is a function of power and not truth." — *Friedrich Nietzsche, late 19th century German philosopher*

Twenty-nine years earlier…

Tsarskoye Selo, Russia
7:30 a.m., 27 May 2096

Did video really kill the radio star? Tek (technology) advancement killed many industries, but has created many more and transformed others. Robots now come in so many varieties. If it is humanoid with its bare metallic or polymer skin visible, it's a robot. If it is made to look as human as possible, it's an android; in any other form, it's called a bot. Very popular among business executive types, academia, and the speaking circuit, are robots one can *link* into, called surrogates. Two people, or more, at different locations can conduct a meeting with a much more personal touch than any vid-screen or audio-only interaction could provide.

They both sit across from one another at a half-moon table in the man's private study. The surrogate has an oval vid-screen—filled by a human face—as its head. The face is that of Madame Aura, her eyes closed. "I am in a deep cyber-trance state," she has told many people when asked what exactly she is doing. The robot's slim bluish-silver body rapidly shuffles the over-sized, glowing, green-backed cards with its extra long, double-jointed fingers. It flips a card and lays it on the center of the table—a green, dancing female clothed in a toga over the image of the globe.

"The World," the Madame Aura surrogate announces. "As I fly through the cosmic currents in my mind's eye, all of the psychic energy of the Net speaks to me with one voice. Russia *will* rise. Ascendance, as the decaying empire of old will be replaced by a new empire with a blaze of fire. You, President Krutikov, are both the catalyst and the king of that new empire. You will live forever."

He smiles.

Volgograd, Russia
9:55 a.m., 27 May 2096

The Motherland Calls statue looms into view. The entire cityscape below is covered by a thick layer of synthetic clouds, with the statue, nearly ninety meters of it, towering through them. Historically, the monument commemorated Russia's fallen soldiers—all war heroes—in their victorious Battle of Stalingrad against Nazi Germany in World War Two. Nowadays, it is the national symbol of the Russian Bloc.

The Emperor admires the view. The Russians always do this. Foreign dignitaries that attend any official state function, no matter where in-country the meeting is to be held, are flown over the Statue. The aircraft even go so far as to pass just above the Statue's imposing sword pointing into the heavens.

Visibility of the ground is restored as the synthetic clouds dissipate. As they near Tsarskoye Selo (Pushkin), the skies seem to glow a light neon green. For a fifty-mile radius, all airspace has been cleared, except for the dozens of saucer-shaped surveillance drones hovering a mile or more in the air or flying about, covered in green lights.

The opulent Catherine Palace is an architectural jewel of Russia and a testament not to its namesake, Catherine the First, but her daughter, Elizabeth, and was built over three centuries ago. Five massive hybrid helicopters begin their final descent to the western landing area of the palace grounds. The helicopter in the group's center touches down first and the other four, in diamond formation, hover for a moment before also landing. Aircraft doors open and dozens of well-dressed men exit the center rotocraft. They move awkwardly, as if unaccustomed to wearing suits or, more likely, because of the amount of concealed weapons on their bodies. The security escort detail forms two lines about three paces apart, one man behind the other. Their ruler exits with two large bodyguards following closely behind on either side.

Emperor Al-Siddiq of the Supreme Islamic Caliphate walks between the two lines of his escort detail. All of the men are dressed in expensive black suits and wear no headgear. He, however, wears traditional attire: a bright white robe (*galabiyya*) and white *keffiyeh*, with a golden agal flowing down to his waist.

A well-dressed young man in a flashy blue suit jogs to him. "Welcome, Emperor Al-Siddiq, to the United Federation of Russia and Europa and to the Great Catherine Palace."

The Emperor nods. The man returns the gesture.

"I will take you inside, Emperor."

"Thank you," the Emperor answers. He looks in the distance at two other, separate groups of hybrid-helicopters on the grounds over thirty meters away. "My *comrades* are already here I see."

The young man smiles. "Yes, Emperor, they are waiting in the lobby."

He leads them down the marble walkway to the western entrance of the Annex. The entire palace grounds are circled by magnificent greenery and, on this day, enough ground security personnel to constitute an army—human and robotic guards, manned vehicles, and AI- (artificial intelligence) controlled vehicles.

As they near the entrance, the Emperor admires the exterior blue and white facades with its combination of basic columns and sculpted male and female figures—any nude female sculptures should, of course, be covered, and the large arched windows on the two bottom stories. The secure section of the Palace is a comparatively modern construction. Two Arabic men walk out and hold the door open as the Emperor and his security detail enters. The escort detail waits outside.

The entire room is a giant elevator and it descends one level to an automated moving walkway. The wall is covered in great works of Russian art. The Emperor suspects that the whole purpose of this entrance is not to show off beautiful art, but to thoroughly bio-scan all guests. The walkway quickly transports them to another platform elevator to be lifted up to the ground floor of Palace. As they ascend, they can hear the classical music.

"The Royal Russian Symphony Orchestra," the Russian man says.

"Here in person?" the Emperor asks.

"Unfortunately, no."

"That is unfortunate. I could have gotten autographs for my grandchildren."

"It is live though. Our very own master conductor, Natan Chekhov, is directing."

"Splendid."

The platform elevator arrives.

"Emperor, our Great Hall," the Russian man announces.

The golden room has massive windows all along its walls on both sides, running the entire length of the more than forty-five meter chamber. The Emperor's gaze moves to the ceiling paintings.

The Russian man chimes in, "Three separate compositions. An Allegory of Russia, an Allegory of Peace, and an Allegory of Victory. They are the original forms from when the Palace was completed three hundred and forty years ago."

The Emperor nods in acknowledgement.

The vibrant sound of music fills the Great Hall. A holo-screen lies on the ground, and everyone can look down as if the Royal Russian Symphony is actually there. Maestro Chekhov, with his shoulder-length green hair, looks up occasionally as he conducts the orchestra, wincing, grimacing, smiling, and frowning. His right hand jerks all around while holding a light-conducting baton.

A crowd of men is watching too, waiting, but the Emperor's eyes move to only two men. President Ri Wen, the premier of China and the leader of the Chinese-Indian Alliance (CHIN). The American intelligence community always refer to him as a vulture (obviously mimicking the American President's pet description of the man), but he has always felt Ri Wen to be the human embodiment of a snake. Two-thirds of the world's population is under his leadership—or dictatorship. It was only seven years ago that his father, President Fu Wen, died. It was during the long reign of his father that the alliance with India was created. His son is equally vicious and calculating. Ri Wen has continued to stop all rogue Muslim incursions into CHIN territory as effectively, and ruthlessly, as his late father.

"President Wen, it is an honor to meet you in person, on behalf of all Islamic people."

The Emperor noticed the moment he entered the lobby that the man had been studying his every move. Wen is dressed in an all-black royal "kung-fu suit" (*chao fu*) and only now notices the images of vultures stitched into patterns all over the fabric—probably as close to making a joke as this Chinese killer will ever come.

"No, it is my honor, Emperor Al-Siddiq. I, on behalf of the people of China and the peoples of India, humbly make your acquaintance for the first time since the untimely death of my father, Fu Wen. I will work very hard to gain the trust and respect that you had for him."

The Emperor nods and then looks over to the other man.

President T. Wilson of America starts to walk to him as if on cue. The man is above average in height and looks—most people would wrongly guess that he is a movie actor with a muscular build. His perfectly-placed brown hair and clean-shaven face compliment his black suit with the standard (and annoying) American flag lapel pin on the left.

"Emperor." Wilson extends his right hand to the Emperor and shakes it firmly. "I, too, am honored to meet you on behalf of the United States of America."

The Emperor has ruled the Supreme Islamic Caliphate for about the same length of time as T. Wilson has been the American President. It was Al-Siddiq's father who was the chief architect of the Fall of Western Europe over a quarter century ago. In a matter of weeks, the Muslim Middle East seized twenty European countries to form the Caliphate. All of remaining Eastern Europe frantically merged with Russia to form the Russian Bloc. Al-Siddiq continued their conquests with the Fall of Jewish Israel, the invasion of non-Muslim Africa with the Islamic-Christian War, and issued the order to have the Caliphate totally destroy Palestine Israel.

"Mr. President, I thought Americans don't shake hands. Your

people view it as a religious custom. Please don't tell me that you're breaking your own traditions for me."

American President T. Wilson, the man who drove Jews and Christians into segregated regions far away from every American tek-city and had every other religion, including Islam, cowering in the shadows to his "pure," godless government.

"No, Emperor. For special and important occasions, such as this, we believe to not greet a guest by shaking the person's hand as…blasphemy."

The Emperor starts to laugh.

The young Russian man steps forward. "Presidents, Emperor, may I give you a quick tour of the Palace before we begin the official proceedings? We can start in the western wing with Arabesque Hall and the Antechambers. Then we can backtrack to see what we Russians call the 'good part.'" He smiles. "Portrait Hall, the Amber Room, Picture Hall, the Chinese Drawing Room and the Dining Rooms."

"Thank you, sir," President T. Wilson says. He glances at the other two leaders. "Have either of you been here before? My aides showed me the pictures on my tab (tablet). Looking at this building makes me wish you Muslims had destroyed the White House back on Nine-Eleven. We would have used this as the model for the new one."

The Emperor laughs. President Wen simply watches him.

President T. Wilson laughs. "President Wen, I'm joking, I'm joking. Let's have our Russian host—" he turns to him, "What's your name?"

"Serge, Mr. President."

"Let's have Mr. Serge give us the dollar tour and enjoy each other's company. We're all enemies so let's be friends as long as we can."

President Wen now smiles. "Yes, we are going to be good enemies together."

President's Private Residence, Catherine Palace
11:05 a.m., 27 May 2096

A dozen federal security agents stand in front of the Russian President Krutikov dressed in his silver suit. His long hair and bushy eyebrows grayed white many years before.

"Everything must be perfect," he says.

"Yes, Mr. President," they answer.

He walks over to one of the men and puts his hand on shoulder. "I know some of you object to my son being here." He squeezes the shoulder of the muscular, bald-headed man with a goatee and then turns to face everyone. "All of you would lay down your life to protect me. He would lay down his soul. I'm not some religious believer, but you know of what I mean. He may see things from his experience that you may not notice and vice versa. I need all that expertise today."

"Understood, Mr. President," the head security chief, Vasily says. "No one will bring it up again."

"Good. This is a historic day for us. The worst thing for Mother Russia was the Fall of Western Europe. We were the dominant force in all of Europe and the Middle East, then the Muslims created the Caliphate and we became a second-rate nation overnight. They became an empire; China and India aligned to increase theirs, and we became invisible. No more. By year's end, no one will talk of only three 'Lords of Earth,' but four. Mother Russia will rise again to its natural superpower stature on the world stage, equal with the Caliphate, Chinese, and Americans. No longer will we be ignored."

"Yes, Mr. President," the men say in unison.

"Make sure we are not disturbed when we close the doors and

the formal talks begin. Watch their security people closely." The man is happy as he stands to take stock of his men again. He nods. "All is happening according to my plans."

New Green Dining Room, Catherine Palace
11:26 a.m., 27 May 2096

"Thank you. I'm glad you enjoyed the tour. I know so much about it because I used to come here every weekend as a child. I lived just ten miles away," Serge continues. He stands at the front of the dinner table with the three leaders already seated. Each of them has his own security guard standing quietly against the wall behind him. "Surprisingly, it was all women—from Catherine the First, to Empress Anna, to Empress Elizabeth—who had the genius to create such a building that even today, less than a decade away from the twenty-second century, we can still be in awe of."

"Is the originality of the building authentic?" President T. Wilson asks.

"Oh yes, Mr. President, it is. Obviously, there was substantial damage from World War Two, but everything, as you saw on our tour, is in the exact neoclassical,"—he smiles—"well neoclassical for the 1700s, not the 2050s. Only the exterior grounds have been touched in modern years and only the most noninvasive of interior security tek."

"Very much like the District in America." President T. Wilson drinks from his glass.

"Much like the Supreme Caliphate has done for centuries," the Emperor says.

"Much like China has done for millennia," President Wen adds.

"But this isn't the real Green Dining Room," President T. Wilson says.

"No," Serge acknowledges. "It was created by our President a few years ago to be a special place for hosting leaders and dignitaries from around the world."

"Russia has been a good place for neutral talks," the Emperor says.

"Yes, it has, Emperor. To your point, Mr. President, this room was created because the original Green Dining Room is kind of…boring."

The men laugh.

President Krutikov enters the room with his entourage of staff and security. "Presidents, Emperor." He smiles as he raises his hands. The leaders rise from their seats.

The Emperor steps forward first. "President Krutikov, I and the entire Islamic people are honored by your gracious open hand and this historic day, all under the great eyes of Almighty Allah."

"President Krutikov, I, on behalf of the people of China and the peoples of India, humbly make your acquaintance."

"On behalf of the people of the United States of America, I also am honored to meet you, President Krutikov."

"Thank you, thank you." Krutikov shakes each man's hand.

"How did you get the Palace empty of the tourists? Isn't this prime tourist season for Russia?" President Wilson asks. "If I ever tried this at the White House, I'd have massive demonstrations and they'd try to impeach me."

Krutikov laughs. "I did as all good presidents do; I lied. We had to close temporarily for this summit. Get everything final and perfect. We told the people we've been *remodeling* for a month and will have a special reopening. It's basic psychology. You deny people something they want for a little while and then they want it even more. We'll double tourism revenues when it reopens. Once the secret construction is done and we can ensure total security, we'll be able to do both without the subterfuge. We needed a special place for our summit.

"Gentlemen, there will be no fancy military honor guards or excruciating ceremonies for our historic talks, but you will have the best five-star, four-course Russian meal you will ever have the pleasure of eating in your entire life!"

2:05 p.m.

The outside hallway is as ornate as the rest of the palace, but here modern interior design tastes are more visible with the almost neon-green color scheme. They can hear no sounds from within the room anymore. Igor thinks it's strange not to hear even a low murmur of voices and that none of the security detail inside has given a check-in signal.

"We should peek in," Igor says.

"Are you crazy, Igor?" Vasily says. "This isn't one of your underworld, crime rendezvous. This is the debut summit of the most powerful men in the world on Russian soil. Stay at your post or I'll bounce you off the detail. If not for your father—"

"Yes, I know."

"You're a criminal."

"I'm a businessman who provides services the people want."

"Do what I say and stay at your post. We have men inside. We will not break protocol."

2:16 p.m.

President Wen continues, "President Krutikov, I am puzzled as to your fixation on this phrase 'Lords of Earth,' an infantile term invented by infantile reporters. It is why my country carefully regulates our media so they speak as adults and not children. The Australians and the Spanish Americas also seem to be fixated on these words.

"You must understand that there can only be three on this planet. There was a Cold War between America and your country over a century ago. There were threats, maneuvers, counter-maneuvers, and unfortunate violence, but there was never a war. The reason there was a World War One was that there were too many 'Lords of Earth' at the time. One spark and all were engulfed. Today's global balance of power must be carefully maintained and there can never be a threat to that order."

4:17 p.m.

The Russian security detail stand at their wall posts, but all are now looking at each other nervously. Igor has been simmering in anger for over two hours. He moves from the wall.

"Igor! Get back to your post," Vasily yells.

Igor ignores him and continues down the hallway to the Green Room door. The security teams of the other countries move towards the Russian team.

"Igor! If you open that door, you will be neutralized!" Vasily yells.

The head security man looks at his team and they draw their weapons. Igor opens the door. A pale, red-eyed Serge stands in front of them. Igor notices something else in horror.

"Erik!" Igor yells as he runs in.

President Krutikov is lying on his back, his eyes staring out, and a white soupy discharge is pooled at his open mouth.

Vasily yells, "Get the doctor! The President is down! He's choking! The President is down!"

"The President is dead, sir," says a junior agent quietly as he kneels down to the body. He checks for a pulse, holding back tears.

"The President is alive until the doctors say otherwise," Vasily snaps. "Get the medics in here now!"

Igor looks up at the other leaders at the table. The Emperor pays no attention, not even looking at him. He continues to eat his food. President Wen stares at him without emotion, his hands clasped together resting on the table. President T. Wilson turns around in his chair to look at them; he is also unemotional.

"What happened?!" Igor stands up from the body.

He looks at the world leaders and then at Serge. He looks at the other Russian security man who was in the room with Serge. The young agent is at his post at the wall, crying, but just standing there. Igor looks back at Serge.

"What happened?! Why didn't you call us?!" He yells the questions over and over.

Security men from the other countries gather in the room. Half surround their leaders and the others surround Igor.

"Calm down, sir," one of them says.

"Calm down, Igor," Vasily says and grabs him. Igor violently shakes off his hand.

"They killed him!"

"Calm down, Igor!"

Igor pushes him away. The foreign security men rush him and drop him to the ground. "Get off of me!" Igor yells. First in English, then Russian, then he explodes in tirade of curses.

Security swarms in and President T. Wilson is whisked out the room. He is followed by President Wen, and then the Emperor.

"No one leaves!" Vasily yells.

Medics burst into the room and surround President Krutikov on the floor.

One physically shakes his head. "Mr. President, Mr. President, can you hear me?"

Others scan him with devices. One of the medics sadly looks at the others and shakes his head. The team of medics lifts him onto a hover-gurney as one of them places a disk right on his chest above his heart and race him out of the room.

A foreign security agent for the Emperor steps back into the room. "You don't honestly expect His Excellency to wait here like a commoner," he says to Vasily. "Your man choked on his own food. Learn to chew your food properly like the rest of the world, Russian."

They are angered by his comments, but say nothing as he leaves the room to join his detail. Other Russian security men start to appear in the room in a panic.

With their leaders safely out of the room, the remaining foreign security agents allow Igor to stand to his feet. He begins to lunge at them in rage but is immediately knocked down by his own Russian security team and pinned back to the ground. The foreign security quickly leave the room as even more Russian security arrive, including many in military uniforms.

"Do not let him up until they are in the air," Vasily yells.

Igor cannot move his body, but he manages to turn his head to look up at Serge.

He looks back with fear. Vasily also glares at Serge.

"Nothing happened," Serge says. "He choked. The President choked and…I panicked. I tried to save him but…it was too late."

"Serge, do you have any idea what you've allowed to happen in this room? This is our President! Ours! The people love him." Vasily shakes his head; an expression of panic starts to creep onto his face. "You killed us, killed us. People will blame you. People will blame us. And when they're done with us, they'll blame the world."

The White Circle

"Though the sex to which I belong is considered weak, you will nevertheless find me a rock that bends to no wind." — Elizabeth I, the "Virgin Queen," fifth and last monarch of the Tudor Dynasty, pre-Islamic England and Ireland (1558-1603)

"Look at the feminization of our country. We were once a masculine Mother Russia and we were great. We are now a mama's boy Mother Russia and we are laughed at. And who elects these men? The older I get the more I am convinced women should never have gotten the right to vote." — First Lady Magda Krutikov, wife of former President of the Russian Bloc

Bucharest, Romania
9:55 a.m., 17 May 2096

Athena looks on from behind her desk. At twenty-eight, the fair-skinned blonde is the leader of Romanian Sanctuary. She wears a sheer white scarf covering her necklace of purple stones. The office is on the small side, but it is well organized and homey with its holo-pictures, plants, and a cat scratching post tower in the corner.

"We're all part of the Sisterhood," she says to the woman. "We have to help each other."

"Is it not all make-believe, a higher power of some deity?"

"That's one point of view, but we don't believe the universe spontaneously and randomly and inexplicably appeared and created all of this for a few billion years or so and then will go back to nothingness. We believe there's so much more to the life than we can mentally or physically perceive in our current state."

"How do you know there's more to life than just this?"

"We call it *knowing*. I just know that there is. We believe there is a higher deity—"

"Not a God or Allah, but a Goddess," the woman interrupts. "All the same difference to me."

"The sisters that make up the Matriarch believe we and all living things are created by a power we call the Goddess, others call it Mother Earth or Mother Nature. We each have a responsibility to each other, to the planet, and to all living things."

"Please don't use that word *goddess*. A goddess who creates men to control women? Your cosmic logic breaks down there for me. As one who has been abused by men, all you do when you say that word is make me angry."

"Many sisters here have been victimized in one form or another. The sanctuary is a place to go for safety, counseling, fellowship, to reflect on life, get away from it all, have a meal, to talk if you want to, or to just be left alone. There's no tek and no men allowed, just supportive sisters. Our spirituality is very important to us and helping others is an integral part of that."

"I've never been a fan of organized religion."

"We're spiritual but not religious."

"Different words that mean the same thing. You are recognized as a religion by the government."

"True, but that's politics. They consider yoga a religion."

"You're organized, aren't you?"

"Obviously. We're here. It's kind of like political parties.

Everyone says they hate them, but without them you can't get anything done. I was raised that spiritual was the personal, inner journey, and religion was boring rituals, big temples, and out-of-touch organizations. I still believe that, but if everyone is on their own private journey, how do you know you're on the right road? How do you grow? How are you challenged? How do you know you're doing good or bad?"

"I can't say that I'm a fan of morality either."

"You're not? So those men who abused you, was it immoral, bad, evil? If there's no such thing as objective morality and all is relative, who's to say your subjective, anguished view of what happened is superior to their happy view of what happened?"

The woman pauses before she responds, "Point made."

"Our organization is to strengthen our sanctuaries, nothing more. We need a safe-zone and structure. We provide that. It's all very informal and casual. You won't see a stuffy, office-suit of the executive over-class anywhere in sight. Only casual suits when we need to be more formal, but very casual otherwise."

"More like a women's club than anything else."

"It's much more than that, but I take your meaning."

"What about the sanctuary or your supportive sisters telling people what to do?"

"I knew you weren't done with the morality question. Yes, we do that. We have principles and values. If we don't have that, then why exist? We'd be like everything that you're trying to escape from. Rules and boundaries don't limit life; they make it possible."

"You're a philosopher too. Is this your full-time job?"

"It has been for the last few years, yes."

"What's your story? How did you become the Priestess of the Romanian Sanctuary of the Wiccan Matriarch?"

Athena grins. "We never say all that. No one says Eastern

Europe, especially with there no longer being a Western Europe anymore. We say Europa. We also don't say Chinese-Indian Alliance. We say CHINs. My story?"

"Yes, how did you come to all this?"

"I was there. The Fall of Jewish Israel. I was thirteen years old. We called each other, my friends and I, and we said: 'Let's go.' We wanted to see dead bodies in the street. We got there to see the end of a country. We saw dead bodies, all right. Women, children, and men. We were sick to our stomachs. My best friend Zee couldn't stop throwing up. My other best friend, Tie, was catatonic for six months. Charred bodies, bodies blown apart.

"I was disgusted by myself. I hated myself. What a horrible person I was. To go to a country to see death because I thought it would be fun. You see it all the time. Kids killing someone because it's fun, or kids committing suicide because they're bored, or vice versa, but to be one of them. I hated myself so deeply. I put a curse on myself for the horrible person I had become. At thirteen years old, you're an adult. The law says you are. Then I heard them—millions of screaming voices in the streets. I thought it was people, or children, but it was the cats, cats left behind in the city. They were everywhere, screaming and crying. This was my punishment for being such a horrible person. I was the embodiment of what becomes of a society without the laws of good and evil. Adults killing cities and their children going to those cities to laugh at the dead bodies. I realized that a Tek-World without spirituality, morality, and logical compassion leads to the end of everything. Our own human advancement is an illusion without belief in something greater than ourselves, because if it is just ourselves, we are monsters and our children are little monsters."

The woman is very moved as Athena continues.

"I had to atone, so I dedicated myself to helping my fellow woman. And animals too, especially cats, which I know seems strange to some to single them out for special charity." She smiles. "I always hated cats before. Cats are not pets; they're more like people and I realized that's the reason I didn't like them. I really didn't like people. Another thing I had to change about my horrible self. So I made it one of our principles when I became part of our leadership. Who would have thought it would lead the way in our conflict with the witches. But evil must be confronted. They kill cats for their sick rituals. We protect cats and all the animals, but especially people."

The woman nods. "What's that up there?"

Athena looks to the bookshelf behind her. "Oh, my winged helmet." She stands and takes it down. "When I was a little girl, I wore it all the time. I was inspired by an old American movie and my hero was this little girl Sara Anderson, because *her* hero was Thor of Old Nordic mythology. My friends and I played imaginary war games all day long. We were fighting our Great Witch Wars. Fighting the evil witches with my winged helmet on my head and my special spiked hammer, we defeated them every time. Simpler times." She returns it to the shelf.

"Thanks for sharing."

"My pleasure," Athena says as she sits back down. "Can I answer anything else for you?"

"No, I have my answers. You do a good job."

"We'd love to have you as a member. Don't hesitate to call again. We live in a world with all our advanced tek gadgets and systems, and connectivity, but people are as alone, aimless, unhappy, and depressed as they have ever been in history. All the drugs, sex, and vid-games will never drown it all away."

"And spirituality is the great answer."

"For some, yes. Others it's not. For me, it is."

"I'm glad I came. At the very least, I found a place for yoga classes without being ogled by men and lesbians. Living in misogynist Russia and next to the anti-woman Caliphate, it would be nice to belong to something pro-woman and woman-centric."

The woman stands to shake her hand.

"We believe in hugs too." Athena hugs her goodbye.

The woman walks to the door and stops. "You all don't wear any kind pointy hats or carry wands?"

"No hats, no wands, no broomsticks. We're not the witches."

The woman laughs. "Good."

Moscow, Russia
2:55 p.m., 17 June 2096

Two policemen in light body-armor uniforms run after three suspects through the busy streets. One of the policemen looks back and sees that there are almost a dozen people running with them—"cop-groupies" who feel it's their duty to help the police, even including shooting at criminals; "vigilante avengers" who, whether the police are there or not, "go after" the criminals; reporters ever looking for a story; and random people who started running with the crowd just because they saw other people running.

"Get back!" one of the policemen yells.

Some stare at him, some laugh at him, others ignore him. One of them points. "Look!"

The policeman returns his attention to the fleeing Anarchists they are chasing.

One of the Anarchists has stopped and is trying to grab a random woman simply standing on the street. She struggles with him. The policemen shoot at him with nonlethal bullets. The man pushes the woman away as he draws a weapon. The policeman's weapons switch to lethal and the man is struck in his chest by bullets. The woman pulls a gun from her own purse and starts firing as well, shooting him in the head. Half of the people running with the group start firing at the man too. The man is riddled with bullets as he crashes to the ground.

"Stop shooting everyone!" a policeman yells angrily.

The police try to grab some of them, but the people with guns scatter while others stand, filming with their e-pads.

"Forget the civilians!" a voice yells in their ear-sets. "Get the other two!"

The policemen resume chase and so do their "groupies." The woman who was almost kidnapped and a couple of children join the pack. It is futile to say anything; this is what regular police (regulars) have to deal with on Russian streets.

Police speed past them on motorcycles, followed by a police car.

"Break off pursuit!" a voice says in the ear-set of the driver. "Terrorist suspects identified."

Vasily and five of his men exit the bar. They wear civilian jackets, but have on their body armor and boots.

"Vasily, why are they shipping us off to Siberia? It's not right. If they're going to treat us like garbage after Catherine Palace when it wasn't our fault—"

"We follow orders, we don't make them. But we better all think about resigning our commissions and getting out of Russia."

A police car stops first and then the motorcycle police. Police exit the car and immediately start firing. Vasily and his men instinctively fire back, shooting and killing all of the police in less than a minute.

"What was that?!" one of Vasily's men yells.

Vasily talks into his wrist-comm. "This is 009. We were just fired on by regulars! What the hell is going on—?"

The police on foot appear from around the corner with their "groupies" and start shooting. It is nothing short of a wild shootout. Vasily and his men take positions and return fire cutting down the police and attacking civilians with ease.

Vasily yells into his wrist-comm again. "This is 009 again. Respond now!"

The explosion is so fast there is only a puff of black smoke as Vasily and his men are blown to bits. The striking saucer drones hover above with all their indicator lights glowing red.

Bucharest, Romania
12:47 p.m., 17 May 2096

Athena sits at her desk reading notes from her desk tablet. There is a slight knock and two women enter. Czarina is tall and dark-skinned with long braided hair down her back. Her scarf is black and her necklace stones are cream colored. Titania has a light brown, Asiatic complexion and features with long black hair. Her scarf is yellow and her necklace stones are white. They sit down in front of Athena's desk.

Athena touches the screen to advance to the next page on her tablet. "I'm glad that the scheduler is at least spreading my appointments equally on my calendar. Before, I had no time to eat or go to the toilet."

Czarina and Titania watch her, giddy like two adolescent girls.

"Are you going to let me in on the secret?" Athena asks.

Czarina remembers something else. "Oh, I forgot to tell you that there's going to be a top-secret summit in Moscow courtesy of the President."

"Top secret? And you know about it?"

"I have my sources."

"I thought you swore off boyfriends in the government."

"Oh, not him. This is a new one. The President is hosting the Americans, Muslims, and Chinese all together."

"Great. So instead of plotting the end of the world separately, they'll be plotting its end together in the same room. Makes me wish I was a witch so I could put a disappearance spell on the whole lot of them."

Titania interjects, "What about you, Athena?"

"Huh? What about me?"

"When will you find yourself your wonderful new man? It's not like back in Russia where they're all bastards. Zee and I can find you one."

"Please, leave my love life to me."

"You're like a wiccan monk," Czarina says.

"Nun," Athena corrects. "Thank you. No broken hearts, no drama, no diseases for me."

The women laugh.

Czarina remembers again. "Oh stop talking, Athena. You're making us forget why we came in."

"Me? You're the ones talking."

"You won't believe it," Titania says.

"What?" Athena asks.

"The Matriarch is sending a representative."

They smile at her. She scratches her head thinking.

"I wonder what they want."

"It has to be," Titania says.

"They're probably just visiting. That's all."

"Visiting?" Czarina laughs. "Russia visiting Europa? To them we're just the backcountry, not their superior tek-city metropolis Russia."

Most people who lived in Europa felt that those who lived in the Ukraine, and especially Russia, looked down on the rest of them.

Russia is the "real" Russian Bloc. Russia is a "real" tek-city. Everywhere else might as well be some archaic non-tek wasteland where the primitives (Europans) lived, and if they did have any tek it was from centuries ago.

"This is it, Athena. The rumors are true," Titania says. "They're going to ask you to join the Matriarch Governing Circle."

"You two are too much into the religious politics."

"That's why you love us," Czarina says.

"Okay, just in case, let's get the cleaning-bots to work for when she arrives."

"They're already hard at work as we speak," Titania says, smiling.

Streets of Moscow
11:26 a.m., 17 June 2096

Athena sidesteps a hole in the cobblestone sidewalk as she walks up the incline with her hands in her light coat. She moves her long blond hair to the left side of her face. Her white scarf is wrapped snuggly around her head, covering her face below the eyes.

Moscow streets are always packed with people from all walks of life, some in stiff business suits, some in casual suits and jeans, like her, and some partly naked. It seems no one in this country has their natural hair color. It is purples, pinks, silvers, bright whites, glossy blacks—all the colors of the rainbow, and every synthetic one in between. Lots of tattoos and lots of facial and body piercings are also common. Everyone smokes, from the oldest person to the youngest child; psychogenic, hallucinogenic, and stimulagenic ciggs, cigars, "sticks" or blunts. And like every tek-city in the world, every man, woman, hermaphrodite, and neuter is connected to the Net with their e-pad, tablet, Net-interface eyeglasses, ear-set device in one or both ears, or wristband.

Real dogs are Russia's perennial favorite pet. "Real" dogs include hybrids, like the chi-poodle (Chihuahua and poodle) the woman in front of her has on a leash. It's not crossbreeding; it is the genetic splicing of two species. Believers, like Athena, have been unsuccessfully lobbying the government to ban the practice, but the public wants what it wants. At least having robotic pets and humanoid robots outside the home was banned by the government many years ago, but always there is someone disobeying the law. A Goth-looking woman walks past her, with a half-dozen "cute" robotic lizards, all following behind her on their hind legs.

Ever-flashing, ever-changing digital billboards hang on every commercial building in the city. The advids (vid-advertisements) are all related to shopping, sex, drugs, or entertainment. Hovering advid drones are everywhere too. With so many commercial drones in the air, police drones blend in without notice. The Russian Bloc is still a quasi-police state, even if the people demand it to be so. *Argus*, the government's ever-watching vid-surveillance system, monitors Moscow and every tek-city in the nation. The border with the Islamic Caliphate is less than seven hundred miles from the capitol and only fifty-five miles from closest northwestern border city. With the Caliphate on the western border and the CHINs on the southern border, the nation is always on "alert."

It is the reason the government did nothing about another "accessory" of the people—concealed weapons. Handguns were also everywhere. They were banned at one time, but that was before the Fall of Western Europe. Both Russia and Europa were afraid of the Muslims or CHINs marching over the border. "An armed people are far less likely people to be a conquered people," a former Russian president had once said. It was always amusing to see someone in their shiny late twenty-first century clothes with an ancient Smith and Wesson in their belt or pocketbook. Only the rich or criminals can afford the latest tek-guns.

Though Argus vid-cameras can "see" through most materials and recognizes millions of faces per second, she touches her face scarf to make sure it's in place. It makes her feel better.

She continues through the crowds. Besides her native Russian in all its many dialects, she hears Ukrainian, Polish, Arabic, Greek, Romanian, Czech, and probably a dozen more before making it to her destination. There are no signs or markings on the nondescript brown building at all. It doesn't even have auto-open; she manually pulls the door and enters.

The interior is dimly lit and looks like the first floor lobby of a small one-star hotel. She notices a figure behind the counter about three meters from the door.

"Athena?" the woman asks.

"Yes."

"Please, follow me."

Athena now takes full notice of her. She is a middle-aged woman, well over six feet tall, long flowing gray hair, no makeup except for flesh-toned lipstick, and wearing a simple black dress. The pink scarf wrapped around her neck seems an odd color choice considering her very masculine physique.

The hulking woman leads her to the building elevator. It opens and they both walk in.

"I'm Yana."

"Nice to meet you. Your accent is Serbian?"

"Very good ear. You live nearby?"

"Yes, I moved back into town last weekend."

"From Romania?"

"Yes."

"Infested with Vampires," Yana scoffs. "A chaos religion made up of fang implant wearers."

"They stay mostly in Transylvania but they are the majority."

"How do they treat us there?"

"I never had any problems."

The door opens and a younger woman waits in the hallway. She is also in a black dress; long, silky, black hair, and a ring of green stones around her neck, and a green scarf.

"Athena," the woman extends her hand. Some believers shake hands, others don't. "I am Hilda, nice to meet you. We have some time before Mother Sister is ready for us."

It may be an unremarkable three-story building on the outside, especially the first-floor lobby, but this floor is very modern. She leads Athena down the hall with Yana following a few paces behind.

"Did you fly or take the metro?" Hilda asks.

"Fly. I prefer flying to the metro. I only have to put up with one stranger sitting next to me rather who knows how many on the train."

"Isn't that the truth? I've never been on a plane myself. Let's go in here."

She opens the door.

"Is this building really a hotel?"

"It's a private one. Run by Matriarch, for sisters only."

The room is a medium-sized conference room. Three women sit at a table facing them, each in a different colored dress, different colored scarf, and each with colored stones around their necks.

Hilda joins the women at the table as she gestures for Athena to sit. The chair in front of them seems deliberately small. Yana closes the door and stands back against the wall behind her.

Athena smirks briefly as she sits. *Let the "interrogation" begin.*

"We have heard many things about you, Athena," Hilda says.

"Nothing good I hope."

"Born in Saint Petersburg, grew up all over Russia. Your bio-parents moved you many times, probably to every country in Europa."

"I prefer the non-politically-delicate term: parents. Most parents are biological parents."

"You spent the last seven years in Transylvania…"

"You mean Romania proper."

"Where you rose to become priestess of not one but two sanctuaries. To people who don't like you, you are known as Athena the Witch-bitch, or, if they're feeling diplomatic, Athena the Traditionalist."

Athena smiles. "The Europan sanctuaries I took charge of had degenerated into not much more than brothels. Men were very eager to 'find' spirituality by joining the sanctuary and join with numerous partners during the witching hours. It's quite impossible to help women in need, and those with children, in such an environment. Men were lining up to get in the front door and women were escaping out the back door. The sanctuaries had become debasements of our spirituality and the Matriarch. I could not help women—victims of abuse or violence, running from the sex trade or drugs. So I kicked out all the men. I told those who didn't like my methods that they could follow them. I also ruffled feminine feathers because I reject atheism, relativism, nihilism, hedonism, anarchy, and, most importantly, stupid women."

Hilda holds back a smile. Her fellow sisters at the table are stone-faced.

"Athena, in Europa people are more homogeneous. Even the biggest tek-city there is but a tiny village when compared to the tek-cities of Mother Russia."

"Meaning?"

"Meaning, to run a sanctuary here is like herding cats, not sheep."

"Europan Sisters can be very cat-like in their stubbornness and independence. I do know something of the Moscow Sanctuary."

"I can assure you that you don't. We require all sisters here to behave a certain way. It requires us all to act as a single entity."

"Of course."

"What works in Bucharest doesn't work in Moscow. With all due respect to our Europan Sisters, Moscow is the center of the nation. We lead, they follow."

Athena remains quiet.

"Many will be very upset with Mother Sister for choosing you for the priestess-ship."

Athena is caught off-guard. *The priestess-ship?* "What? I thought you were considering me to join the Moscow Governing Circle."

"With your selection as the Moscow Sanctuary's new priestess, it is my duty to convince the entire membership to unanimously support the Mother Sister's decision, despite your opposing views to the Governing Circle in the past. For example, you publicly opposed the Matriarch's plan to try to overturn the government's mandatory bio-switch plan."

Athena's mind is racing, but refocuses on Hilda's statement. "It was an act of utter stupidity—and evil."

In 2061, an American veterinarian-turned-medical scientist introduced the breakthrough bioengineering medical procedure to the world. Virtually all babies would have the neonatal operation. Instantly, all unwanted pregnancies vanished from most of the world; both the male and female party would have to have their reproductive abilities "switched on" to have a child. Only in the last decade had it been made mandatory in the Russian Bloc.

"In your opinion."

"In everyone's opinion outside Moscow. Sixty-percent of the country is women and ninety-percent of them favor the bio-switch. Explain to me how reverting back to the time of women having unwanted babies and women going so far as destroying them furthers the standing of woman-kind and the Matriarch."

"Patriarchal government imposing its will on women's bodies…"

"If nearly one hundred percent of women favor something, it's not patriarchy."

"Nearly the majority of women outside of the Matriarch support the sex industry, but you have the opposite position on that matter."

"I'm going to let you think about that for a moment because those are two very separate issues. The Matriarch defends the life of all living things. We're the ones fighting the epidemic of cat-killings in this country. Are you telling me you want the Matriarch to be against cat-killing, but pro-baby killing? With so much of the nation, and the world, indifferent to life, it's our spiritual obligation to be the loudest voices in favor of *all* life and *all* human things. We're women. We weren't given the cosmic power to bring life into the world through birth to turn our backs and not fight with our lives to defend that life." Athena laughs. "As I said, I reject stupid women. A bunch of bored intellectuals sitting around a table looking for causes to get into."

"Did you really expel all the men from your sanctuaries?"

"Yes. Sanctuary is for fellowship and counsel. Want to sex around? Go get a room, go out in the alley, go elsewhere."

"Sex does come from the goddess."

Athena leans forward. "Sanctuary is for fellowship and counsel. It's not a sex club. You can have all the sex you want before or afterwards."

"And no men should be allowed."

"We're called the Matriarch, so that would be a no." Athena can't tell if they are serious or purposely trying to get a rise out of her.

Athena continues, "We have women leaving for America all the time for greater women's freedom. That country doesn't have a Matriarch, only an anti-spiritual, anti-religion bigoted government.

Every other religion, Vampires, Vulcans, Jedi, we even have a growing Klingon population in Rozhenko; witches, Warlocks, Hedonists, Anarchists, Nihilists, Goths, Arthurians, Foundationalists; all of them growing. And us? The funny women with long hair, wearing scarves and colored necklaces, and a dozen cats in their homes. If this continues, I'll break the Matriarch in half myself."

"Athena, you are a radical."

"Why am I here then?"

Hilda ignores her. "Exactly what Mother Sister wants for the Matriarch." She smiles.

Athena hears the door behind her open and turns. Yana has it wide open and another woman enters.

"There she is. *Prima inter pares*, our very own 'first among equals.' Hello Athena." She walks to her beaming. "I'm Mother Sister." Athena stands and instinctively extends her hand. "Oh no, I believe in hugs." The woman gives a firm hug.

Mother Sister's graying hair is almost to her knees. She wears a blue dress and jacket, a necklace of blue stones around her neck, and a navy blue scarf.

"I hope my daughter wasn't too hard on you," she says.

"Daughter? She looks like your twin sister."

Mother Sister nods. "Very good. Brown-nosing the right people, right from the start. Actually, I had Hilda when I was ten so we are almost bio-sisters. She's the opposite of me when it comes to vanity. She dyes her hair, but then everyone in Russia does."

She turns to everyone else. "Leave me alone with Athena, please."

Hilda and the women at the conference table rise and leave the room with Yana.

"Let's sit together, Athena."

They both sit and get comfortable.

"Mother Sister, I wasn't told you were considering me for the priestess-ship."

"Yes. Surprised?"

"Very."

"You'll be part of the Matriarch Circle so please, call me by first name, Delphine."

"Yes."

"When the people I talk to say bad things about someone then I know they are doing something good." A Russian Blue cat jumps on the table out of nowhere, startling Athena for a moment. Delphine strokes the cat's head and neck. "A recurring description by both your supporters and detractors is that Athena the Traditionalist is on a short list of women most likely to run the Matriarch within the next twenty years."

"No one even knows who I am."

"Athena, you took over two failing sanctuaries in countries where the power of sisters has been declining, transformed them, significantly grew their memberships, and made them centers of power. Of course people know who you are."

"Hilda's interrogation of me…"

"It's important that we know how you think, not just what you think, and that you can defend those positions in the face of very opinionated, vocal, and opposing sisters. We want to bring you in to run the main sanctuary of the Matriarch, our Moscow Sanctuary, the largest Sisterhood in the world. I am creating a new Circle—every sister a true leader, a visionary thinker, a solid administrator, and solid planner. I always laugh to myself that Russia, arguably the most misogynistic place in the world, the last original country of the West, with lots of female flesh on display and lots of submissive womankind, will be the matriarchal spiritual center of the world."

"Women made in Her own image. What exactly is the agenda you have for me?"

"Do for Moscow what you did in Europa. I am bringing all the Europa leaders in the Sisterhood to Moscow. They accepted my invitation only because of you. It's time for us to be a real Matriarch. End the division between our Russian-Ukrainian factions and our Europan ones. When will your circle be here?"

"Next week."

"Good. I'll assign a few key people to your circle with your approval. We need everything to look just right for your priestess-ship appointment."

"That's fine, but despite what others say, I do hate politics so."

"They say that because you're good at it, but leave the politics to me."

"What happened to the last priestess?"

Delphine pauses as she takes her cat in her arms. "She's dead."

"You mean she crossed over?"

"She's dead."

Athena has a concerned look on her face. "Who?"

Delphine shrugs her shoulders.

"The government?"

Delphine shrugs.

"Witches?"

Delphine simply stares at her.

"Are you going to tell me?"

"We're at war."

3:06 p.m.

Moscow, like all major tek-cities in the world, only allows auto-drive. Yana sits up front as the smart-car drives. Delphine talks to Athena in the back. Their car is in one of the many twelve-car queues, nearly bumper to bumper speeding down the freeway at over one hundred and sixty kilometers an hour.

"I have also assigned Yana to your circle for security. You're Russian-born, but she knows the current climate."

Yana turns around to look at her and smiles. Athena nods.

"She will oversee the arrangements to have you moved into one of our Matriarch hotels."

"I happen to like where I'm living now."

"You say that because you haven't seen your new lodgings. We will spend the next days and weeks briefing you on your new duties, your daily schedule, and our new security measures. When we feel you're ready, we'll have your appointment ceremony to the Moscow priestess-ship and the Governing Circle."

"Do I have any say in my life as the new priestess?"

"No."

Catherine Palace, Tsarskoye Selo, Russia
4:10 p.m., 17 June 2096

The limo arrives at the main gate and is waved through by security. It drives to the main entrance and stops. A soldier exits the passenger side and opens the back door. The Colonel exits and looks over the building and the grounds.

A soldier runs to him from the main steps. "Colonel. We're ready."

"Who has control of the site?"

"The presidential office. They won't let us in, sir."

An agent in a black suit walks to him from inside the main entrance. He tries to remain calm but as he nears them his nervousness is clear.

"Colonel."

"Why haven't we been given access?"

"That must be cleared by the Kremlin?"

"Who in the Kremlin?"

"The President would have to do so."

"Isn't the Palace open to the public?"

"It is closed for remodeling."

"Yes, the supposed remodeling for months on end. Tell me boy, is it your intention to insult my intelligence with this continued charade? Who is in control of the Palace vid-surveillance?"

"The Head of Security, of course."

"Where is he?"

"He is…not here."

"Really?"

"Yes, he is at the Kremlin."

"Who is in charge when he's at the Kremlin?"

"I am." The man now realizes his predicament.

"I want all vid-surveillance for the date of twenty-seven May."

"We only keep the current month's surveillance available on the grounds, sir."

"Do you know what one of the jobs my eldest son held? Head of Security,"—he deliberately pauses for a while—"For the Catherine Palace. He would tell me how he could access any second of any day for any location internal or external for the Palace going back fifty years."

The agent is sweating even more now. The Colonel stares at him.

"Lieutenant," the Colonel says to the soldier next to him.

"Yes sir."

"Take out your side weapon and shoot this man."

Moscow Matriarch Sanctuary
4:10 p.m., 17 June 2096

The building is beautiful. The Matriarch is the polar opposite of Islam, but both have one thing in common: the religious center is also the center of life for their believers. Athena notices everything about the exquisite interior. She walks to a massive circular railing in the center of the first floor, looks down, and sees the giant pool on the basement level. She looks up and sees the glass-domed roof. The entire center of the building is constructed to be an open, oval hole from the third floor to the basement level, cutting through the first through third floors.

The sanctuary is quite impressive as Athena is given a quick tour. The interior is also very active with sisters everywhere, going to or coming from some activity.

Delpine walks into the massive town hall room with a big smile and open arms. "Sisters, here she is."

The room is filled with about a hundred women of all ages, some dressed formally, others casual, but all wearing some type of scarf around their necks over colored-stone necklaces. Athena stands behind her as the crowd of women draw near; all eyes on her.

"Athena will be joining the Matriarch Circle as our new priestess for the Moscow Sanctuary. She comes to us from Romania," Delphine announces. "But she was born here in Russia."

The last comment seems to please the crowd.

"Romania?" asks one of the sisters.

"The land of the Vampires," says another. "Did you see any ghosts or goblins when you were there?"

The women laugh.

"I hear the Star Wars religions are on the march there. They tried to come here but once we outlawed their stupid lightsabers they stopped coming."

"I didn't know that," Athena says only to join in with the crowd.

"You see, one of them made a 'real' lightsaber and apparently,"— she laughs—"it sliced off his arms, blew up in his face, and sliced off his head…"

"Sounds like something a man would do."

"There are plenty of women in that religion."

"…there were even a few bystanders who were maimed by this flying lightsaber blade. The government rounded up all the Jedis and took away their phallic-sabers."

The women laugh louder.

"Where in Russia are you from, Athena?"

"I was born in St. Petersburg."

"Good, right in Moscow. Russia is not like the rest of the Russian Bloc, and Moscow is not like the rest of Russia."

"We heard you ran two different sanctuaries before."

"Yes, I did."

"We hear you're quite unorthodox in your views. Is it true you are strong proponent of marriage?"

"Hetero-marriages, yes."

"And other marriages?"

"I could care less. They can advocate for themselves. We must advocate for ourselves."

"Women don't need husbands. That's a shockingly retrogressive position."

"Why would a sister advocate for such a patriarchal construct?"

"Despite the global pan-sexual movement, every society is abandoning it."

Athena answers, "Maybe because women feel complete when they have a family, which includes a man and children. We were made that way as a species. I thought that was a good thing, following Nature. The goddess did create men too. Bad men are bad. Bad women are bad. Everything else is good. Your attitude suggests that you champion the high ideals of femininity and womanhood, but when women do, you look down at them. A woman is a woman, not a man with female parts."

The sisters are offended but stay quiet.

Athena tries to change the subject. "I've noticed that no one uses the word Wicca here. It's still common in Europa. Is that word out of fashion here?"

"The misinformation campaign of the witches has been quite good. We no longer use the word."

"A war always starts with language first. In America, the atheists seized the word Pagan to call themselves. Now the entire world does."

"Just like how the Nazis co-opted the swastika from the Hindus."

"Athena doesn't know of the special challenges we have here with the witches."

"She will know thoroughly soon," Delphine says.

"Athena, what encounters have you had with them?"

"None so far."

"What do you think we should do about them?"

"A little extermination would be nice."

Every woman stares at her in total silence, looking for any sign that she is making a joke.

Athena continues, "Look at the patriarchal religions. Islam allowed their evil to grow unchallenged and it became the normal majority. Non-Islamic religions dealt with theirs so that there was only the good to chart their spiritual path."

"How do you know all this? Non-Islamic religions? You mean Christians and Jews? Are there even any left? No one even says those words anymore here."

"There are some in America."

"Lots in America and the Spanish Americas."

"Aren't the Orthodox here Christians?"

"I think so."

"No they're Russian Orthodox."

"Athena, we can learn nothing from the study of patriarchal religions. I'm actually quite shocked that you would even mention their names in the presence of the goddess in this sanctuary. We had heard you had some unconventional ideas."

"People with very little in their empty skulls always say that me." Athena says to the woman. "I ran two sanctuaries and increased our membership by a factor of ten. Do you know why? They said: finally we have someone to inject some testosterone into the Matriarch."

Some women laugh.

"The Matriarch doesn't need any man-juice to be strong," the woman counters.

"Then why aren't we?" Athena asks.

"Sisters," Delphine interjects. "Let's at least give Athena her obligatory honeymoon period before we start the real cat-fighting, please."

The Mother Priestess has broken the tension. Athena grins and the other women smile too.

"Athena, as you can see, we have a tough crowd here, but you're tough too. Let some of the sisters get you some food and have you personally meet everyone," Delphine says.

A small group of women walk Athena to the food tables as the crowds of women follow. Delphine waits with several other women.

"When are you going to explain to us why you've appointed a radical to run our sanctuary?"

"The days of living in the shadows is over," Delphine answers. "The circle of life is always about change. We need her to take us through this part of journey."

"We couldn't more strongly disagree."

"I've listened to all of you before and was willing to continue. But that was when we had a president in the Kremlin who was not pro-Wicca, but was definitely anti-witch. The circle of life has turned again and that time is over."

"There is no evidence that the President is dead or incapacitated."

"You're right. He hasn't been seen in person by anyone in four weeks and anyone who asks about him disappears. Yes, no rational conclusions can be drawn from that. I'm no longer listening to any of you. Your counsel has outlived any usefulness to me."

Delphine walks away from them to the food tables.

The Red Riots

"It is impossible to predict the time and progress of revolution. It is governed by its own more or less mysterious laws." — *Vladimir Lenin, Russian communist revolutionary and first premier of the Old Soviet Union (now Russian Bloc)*

Somewhere in Moscow
11:44 p.m., 20 June 2096

Serge waits in the alley with a small suitcase. It reminds him of a bad spy movie. He hears running footsteps. Several men appear from around the corner.

"No!" he shouts as the men open fire. He fires back.

The gun battle is as violent as its short. Bodies fall to ground dead, including Serge.

The Black Russian, Moscow, Russia
10:10 p.m., 22 June 2096

Igor enters the club in a shiny black suit. A dozen men follow him in a straight line. The loud music inside can be heard long before you even enter the establishment—you're not supposed to listen to it; you're supposed to feel it. The walls, ceiling, and even the floors are giant holo-panels with ever-flashing, ever-changing images of people dancing, kissing, wrestling, fighting, or having sex. Inside, throngs of people dance wildly everywhere. The club is fitted with plumes, meter-high poles ever blowing out "samples," so you can leave your drugs at home. Clouds of drug vapor saturate the room—orange, yellow, and purple clouds.

In the center of dance floor are single-person platforms, each with wild dancers, all half-naked. Igor is grabbed along the way by women and men trying to get him to join them. He pushes them away. Past the dance floor is the drinking area. People stand at the edge of the floor watching like zombies, smoking or drinking, or both. There are lines of people to the bar, but no one waits long. It is a kiosk wall. People yell their order into an audio node and instantly their computer-made drink in a disposable glass pops up through an opening. A loud beep follows; the person's digi-card has been auto-debited. The very dimly lit sitting area is filled with cozy booths and, from the noises, people are doing more than just sitting and smoking.

Club security gestures Igor to walk through the scanning archway, but has his men wait outside the room. He follows three large men inside and is pointed to an empty facing chair.

"Here he is. Do you know I offered Igor the chance to be my right hand?" the Controller says. The silver-haired man with a black mustache and beard sits in a plush leather chair. He only wears black suits with frilly black shirts. His artificially enhanced purple eyes watch Igor coldly. His hands, with very long black-painted fingernails, rest in his lap.

Drugs and prostitution are all legal but organized crime still controls all of it as well as all the illegal aspects of the industries. The Controller has run Moscow's crime world for decades.

"You spat in my face," he continues.

"I decided to stay in my own territory."

"Why? You're Russian, not one of those East Europan inbreeds. You belong to Russia. East Europan crime bosses only live because we allow them to. It's like Mexico. Crime bosses care about the major tek-cities, not the million backwater villages."

"I didn't come here to fight with you."

"Why then? You come here like a frightened little animal."

Igor ignores the insult. "I need transport out of Russia."

"Why don't you call your own people?"

"I have my reasons. I'm not asking for charity. I'll pay you, of course."

The Controller doesn't hesitate. "No."

"That's it? You're turning away a paying customer?"

"You aren't a paying customer. You're the walking dead."

"What does that mean?" Igor looks around at the crime boss's six large bodyguards. Three stand behind Igor, the other three behind the crime boss.

"You insult me," the Controller says. "When a person comes into my establishment, friend or enemy, they are beyond harm. If I wanted to kill you, I could have done so before you entered my place, in the street."

"What is it you're not telling me?"

"Igor, let me save you the time. No one will help you flee the country, no one. The government has put the word out on the street that anyone who fingers the whereabouts of one Igor Aleyek will get more rubles than they can spend in a lifetime."

"Then I'll be leaving." Igor stands.

"What happened at Catherine Palace?"

Igor turns to him. "Half the government is on your payroll. Why ask me?"

"That's just the point. My informants are not able to find out. There hasn't been even one leak. This kind of efficiency of keeping secrets is impossible for a government, any government in the world. But they're doing it."

"Is there anyone you can recommend to help me then?"

"Igor, you are never going to escape the country."

"Thank you and good night."

"Why isn't your guardian protecting you?"

"There are people in government preventing it."

"The Russian President, the most powerful man in all of the Russian Bloc, who is not shy to make people disappear, is being prevented from keeping his little son from harm. Igor, I will figure out what's going on soon. The government wants you and it will have you. And there's nothing you can do to stop them."

"Good night." Igor brushes past the bodyguards and leaves the room.

The bodyguards look back to the Controller. The man waits a few moments before speaking.

"Kill him and collect the money from the government."

"That will break our truce with the Europan mobs," one of the bodyguards says.

The Controller looks at him angrily. "Go get my money."

The bodyguards leave the room.

Streets of Moscow
10:56 a.m., 17 June 2096

A little girl eats her ice cream and looks up at her. Athena smiles back as she places her digi-card—a tiny plastic combination credit card-debit card-identity card—back into her inside jacket pocket. Nowadays most people, especially in Russia, can keep it digitally on their device too.

"Oh." The girl realizes. "You can have mine." She reaches into her own little satchel and hands Athena an apple wrapped in a cloth napkin.

"Fruits and vegetables are good for you," Athena says.

The girl laughs as she takes another bite of the ice cream cone. "No, you take it in trade."

Athena puts the apple in her satchel. "I didn't know Moscow had little girls wandering the streets."

"*We are legion*." She says with special emphasis and smiles as she licks more of the ice cream. "I didn't know the world still had good people. They say there is no good and evil. It's all relative, but I know different. The good buy me ice cream."

Athena watches her closely. "Before I go and leave you to do your mischief, just promise me that you will keep safe, never allow yourself to be harmed by anyone, and don't be too proud to ask for help when you need to."

She eats the last of the ice cream cone and rubs her lips with her fingers, satisfied. "I can definitely promise the first. The other two—who cares? Moscow is the safest, friendliest tek-city in the world."

The Black Russian, Moscow, Russia
1:00 p.m., 23 June 2096

Except for his briefs, a naked Igor returns, riding an antique bicycle down the street. Crowds gawk at his nakedness, stare at his body tattoo, or stare at his manual pedi-bike—you only see them in a museum. He stops at the club entrance with ten guards dressed in black suits, smiling and laughing.

"Igor, you're not going to do us right here?" one of the guards says as the others laugh.

Igor grins. *Crack!* He punches him in the nose and the man careens backward.

Inside the club, guards stop what they're doing. The alarm sounds in their ear-sets and they all run to the front door en-masse. With the blaring music, no one hears the machine-gun fire outside.

Igor drops the weapon before he enters and walks under the arch—a deadly piece of tek that automatically stun blasts anyone carrying any kind of shooting weapon, hidden or otherwise. He marches past people, most are oblivious to him, but some proposition him or try to grab his body. Another guard runs over.

"Stop right there, Igor."

"Did the Controller really believe I'd let him put me in the morgue?!"

Igor stabs him multiple times in the abdomen with a hard plastic shank. Igor allows him to drop to the floor. The remaining six guards charge at him. As the men fight, people all around them continue as if nothing is happening: dancing, sucking in the drug vapor, drinking, sexing. The psychedelic flashing lights makes the fight seem surreal, and blinds the guards. Igor is wearing infrared corneal pieces and only sees the thermal images of his attackers.

It's over. Igor wipes the blood off his shank and grabs one of the guns from the bodies. He walks into the inner chamber.

"How many men?" Igor asks into his ear-set.

"There's no one else in there but him," a voice answers. "But that room is supposed to be an arsenal."

Igor cautiously enters. The Controller sits, seemingly lifeless, in his chair. Igor moves closer. The Controller is already dead.

"A man is running in," the voice says in his ear-set.

Igor turns and aims his gun as the man appears.

"Stop Igor! I have nothing in my hands!" The man in a yellow suit ducks down to the ground with his hands in the air and his eyes closed.

Another man in a black suit enters the room and points his gun at him. "I got him, Igor."

The man in yellow opens his eyes slowly and ignores Igor's man. "He's been dead for at least an hour."

All three men notice the pounding, pulsing of the outside music has stopped.

"How do you know that? Was it you?" Igor asks.

"No."

"Who?" Igor asks.

"I'll tell you everything but we have to get out of here."

"You will tell me now or I'll kill you too."

"I'm with the Ukrainian mob."

"So? I've never seen you before."

"Our boss was killed yesterday."

"So?"

"You haven't heard yet but same with the Czechs, Transcausia, the Central, the Southeast. Do I have to spell it out to you? We're being set up!"

"Set up for what?"

"What's wrong with you?! As being behind the assassination of President Kritokov! They're saying you were the trigger man."

"What! I was there! The foreigners killed him! I was there! And he wasn't shot."

"You killed him."

"He was my father! They killed him!"

"We know it wasn't you, but they have a kill-on-sight warrant on you."

"They'll never catch me."

"Do you hear any music?" Igor's henchman asks.

Igor and the Ukrainian look towards the door. Igor runs to the Controller's main desk. He pushes the dead man away in his chair and touches the desk's table tablet. The vid-cam feed displays—the club is empty!

Ten minutes pass. The missile hits and the club explodes.

Secret Hospital, Moscow, Russia
7:12 a.m., 24 June 2096

The Russian Prime Minister stares at the bodies on the gurneys—the dead bodies of Serge and the other Russian guard in the New Green Room at the time of the Kritokov's death. He stands with a half dozen aides.

"Both men were present in the room when the President was killed," the aide says.

"How did they die?"

"Suicide, sir."

The Prime Minister says, "They realized their gross failure in protecting the President."

"Yes, sir."

"What is the story?"

"Organized crime managed to get a man on the security detail and managed to kill the President. The men were so overcome by grief and love for the President that they took their own lives."

"The mobster?"

"Located and a killed by drone-strike."

"Good. Now that everything is wrapped up, we can break the news to the people about the President."

"Yes sir. We have all media standing by."

"Make sure they know not to ask any questions at the press conference, none at all, no surprises."

"Yes sir, they know."

Moscow Matriarch Sanctuary
8:16 a.m., 25 June 2096

Dozens of sisters watch the vid-screen, some seated, some standing, all around the room's long oval table.

"This twenty-fifth day of June, 2096, President Erik Krutikov is dead," the announcer says. "It happened at a secret world-summit here in Russia hosted by the President. The plot was hatched within Russian and Europan organized crime and authorities tell us that military forces have already begun taking swift action. The primary assassin of the President was this man"—the picture flashes on the screen—"one Igor Aleyev who died in a violent gun battle with authorities."

Athena maintains her blank, unemotional stare.

"Off," Delphine says and the vid-screen goes blank.

No one speaks for a while.

"Now we have the confirmation for what many of us already suspected. I think we should all stay here for the next few days as things to settle," Delphine says. "There are few things more dangerous than getting caught in a civil disturbance in a major metropolitan tek-city. It's nothing like you've ever seen."

"Maybe we should leave the Sanctuary then," a sister says.

"No, we'd have to risk open travel and we shouldn't leave the building unattended. We should be fine as long as we stay inside, even if there is an upswing in terrorist attacks. Any government reprisals won't be here. We need to keep any attention away from us and we need to stay away from the chaos and instability that always come from these kinds of events. Contact the other sanctuaries and inform them to stay inside their sanctuaries. Use landlines only."

One of the sisters nods and exits the room with two others.

"I hate this," another sister says. "Now we have to hide like mice."

"Better this than getting caught in some random government sweep or an attack," Delphine says.

"At least they're not blaming us."

"Give it time," Hilda adds.

"Sisters, we still have our work to complete. Athena, let's continue with the briefing," Delphine says.

A sister stands. "We left off with our Polish leadership."

Athena's eye catches a face on the tablet in Delphine's hands. "Who's that?"

"Who?"

Athena points to Delphine's tab, then reaches over and points to one face on a list of faces on the screen—a girl with shiny black hair.

"Do you know her?" Delphine asks.

"Who is she?"

"That witch is the leader of all Russian Bloc Dark Wicca," a sister says. "The witches."

Athena jumps up from the table. "*That's* Morgana?"

"Yes, what's wrong?" the sister asks.

"What is it, Athena? Tell me," Delphine says.

Athena walks to her satchel and takes out the apple.

It takes almost a half hour. Everyone is waiting and finally Yana returns to the room holding the apple.

"It's poisoned," Yana announces.

There are gasps and sisters look at each other in shock. Athena sits back down next to Delphine at the table.

"When is the succession ceremony?" a sister asks.

"We planned for the end of the month," Delphine answers. "But with the current events we should postpone it."

"This shouldn't change our plans," a sister counters.

"They tried to kill Athena so it does change things," Delphine says. "Athena?"

She sits in her chair, brooding.

"You don't have anything to say?" Hilda asks.

"Maybe we should skip the *pointless* presentation and instead get me up to speed on the faces of every last one of those witches!"

"We'll continue with the pointless presentation as scheduled," Delphine says.

Athena jumps up from her chair. "If we're at war, then let's talk war!"

"Athena, you're not in Europa anymore," Delphine says. "You're in the largest and most powerful tek-city in the Russia. Everything is bigger, faster, and more dangerous here. Not everyone can thrive here. The question to ask yourself is: are you ready to fly or fall?"

"The only way the witch could have known about me is from someone in the Matriarch."

Hilda says, "What you are suggesting is offensive."

"The White Wicca and Dark Wicca are at war, Athena."

"That's nothing new," Athena says.

Delphine says. "Athena, they have killed people here in Russia. They have infiltrated all the mobs, have taken over the Russia sex trade, and supply even the Caliphate and CHIN territories. They have used that wealth to buy up Russian government officials. We believe they plan to seize control of the Kremlin, have us purged from our own Matriarch, and then set up the first matriarchal theocracy."

Athena bursts out in laughter. "That will never happen."

Delphine continues, "Which part? They are quite serious and quite insane."

"Why did you really pick me for the priestess-ship?"

"I told you already."

Athena is unconvinced.

"Athena, people trying to kill you in Russia is not unheard of."

"Well obviously the Wild, Wild West stereotypes of the country are true after all and now I'm stuck. They've already tried to kill me once." A thought enters her mind. "Why would the witch leader of the Dark Wicca *personally* try to kill me?"

"She does it all the time," a sister says.

"No," Athena says shaking her head. "There must be more."

Delphine says to everyone, "We have a job to do and we must keep the Sanctuary secure."

"I'm out of here. I'm going back home. I don't want to be involved anymore."

"You are involved," Delphine says, standing from her chair.

Athena ignores her and leaves the room. Yana runs after her.

"Athena!"

"Leave me alone."

"Athena, you can't go. It's too dangerous out there."

Athena ignores her and walks to the front door.

Red Square, Moscow
12 noon, 25 June 2096

Red Square is the political, military, commercial, tourist, and transportation center of Russia. It is even considered the religious center of the entire Russian Bloc, though ninety percent of the Moscow population is nonreligious. Every building is a historic landmark, despite their function, and every brick of the ground pavement is dark red in color.

The Square is a daily tourist bonanza for Russia and the place to showcase military parades (annually Victory Day, Russia Day, and Unity Day), massive concerts, special sporting events, public ceremonies, and one former president even used it for a "running of the bulls" as was the annual pastime in pre-Islamic Spain. The Square, all three hundred thirty meters by seventy meters, is also used by the people for demonstrations and protests, both peaceful and violent. But it is also used for show-of-force action by the government.

Green tanks race towards the Kremlin. Gunships and drones fill the airspace above the presidential residence. People are filling the streets.

Inside one of the tanks, the Colonel watches the dashboard vid-screen as they near the Kremlin building.

"Colonel, there is no way that they will allow us walk into the Kremlin without presidential authorization," a soldier says.

"Open gun ports."

"Excuse me, Colonel?"

"Open gun ports."

"Are we starting a civil war?"

The Colonel turns to him. "Then we better win." He turns to the tank driver. "Stop."

"Colonel?"

"Am I speaking Swahili?! Why am I having to repeat every order?!"

"Yes, Colonel."

The tank stops and all the other tanks in the caravan stop as well. The roof door opens and the Colonel appears.

"You!" he yells at a group of young people in the crowd.

"What are you doing?" the young man asks.

"How many Net-friends do you have?"

"Me? I have maybe a thousand."

"That's all. Go away. What about you?"

"I have almost six thousand," another young man answers.

"I need more."

"I got five hundred thousand friends," a girl says walking to the tank. "All over the world and those friends have tens of thousands of friends, too."

The Colonel nods. "You are my new best friend. Tell everyone that the Prime Minister is lying. The mobsters didn't kill the President. The Prime Minister did. The Russian military is on the side of the people to take back our country."

One of the young men in the crowd says, "You mean a coup?"

"Yes."

"How do we know you're not lying? The military is never on the side of the people," a woman in the crowd yells.

"Who protects you from the Muslims, from the CHINs, from the Americans? Would you be free to walk down Russian streets without us? Stop being ungrateful! That is not the quality of a Russian citizen!" He looks at the first woman again. "What are you waiting for? All of you now, tell everyone what I said. The enemies of the President and the people are trying to steal the people's government. The Prime Minister *and* the mobsters! You are now the press for the people!"

The growing crowd takes out their e-pads and tabs to message *everyone*.

Hotel of the Dark Wicca
2:22 p.m., 25 June 2096

Little Morgana watches the images on the vid-screen. She's no longer in her innocent child disguise. She has black eyeshade, black lipstick, and her naturally long black hair hangs to one side of her face. The only non-Goth thing about her appearance is the dozen red neck rings from the bottom of her throat to under her chin.

Red Square explodes. Military tanks and airships fire at each other. Buildings are hit and so are people who scramble around like ants filming with their e-pads. A couple is run over by a tank. A group of people is blown apart as a tank takes a direct missile attack. The vid-screen newsfeed flashes from images of burning vehicles and tanks to panicking and dead people. Even drones are shot from the sky and crash to the ground.

"It's all over the Net," one of the witches says. "The military is saying the Prime Minister is involved."

Morgana smiles. "Looks like someone is trying to outsmart us. We'll salvage this, despite the men involved."

A witch enters the room. "Morgana, you won't believe who's here."

Moments later, Athena sits in the center of the couch staring at her would-be murderess. She looks at the pentagram necklace around the child-woman's neck with disgust. Morgana smiles, strokes the necklace, and plays with the pendant with her fingers.

"You forgot something." Athena reaches into her satchel and tosses it at her.

Morgana catches the apple in her hand. "Why thank you?" She doesn't hesitate to bite into it.

"It's poisoned."

"It's not the same apple I gave you."

"How do you know it's not poisoned?"

"Because you're a good witch. Glindas never do bad things. That is why Glindas will never rule the Earth." Morgana devours the apple in a less than a minute.

"I'm here to tell you I'm leaving. Going back home."

"Transylvania?"

"Romania. And I'm not a good witch. I'm not a witch at all."

"You keep telling yourself that, little Glinda."

The other witches in the room start giggling.

"I hope never to see you or any of your witches ever again."

"Just like that? Leaving Mother Russia?"

"I'm not interested in your fantasy games."

"Games? There are no games here."

Athena stands. "Don't bother me again."

"Or what?"

"You heard me."

"You know what Athena?"

"What?"

"One day you're going to wish that you had poisoned that apple."

Athena smirks. She stands and walks out the door. The other witches in the room laugh at her.

"Bye-bye Athena."

The Kremlin, Moscow
8:57 p.m., 25 June 2096

The Prime Minister sits in his secure bunker looking at the Colonel's face on the vid-screen.

"Colonel, you will stop this attack immediately!"

"Or what? You'll send the military after me? I am the military, Mr. Prime Minister."

"Why are you doing this? Why?"

"You failed to kill everyone at the Catherine Palace summit."

"I did no such thing."

"They told me what really happened in that room. So I had to ask myself, why would our Russian Prime Minister lie about the true murderer—murderers—of our President?"

"Colonel, please stop this. You are right. It wasn't the mobsters. But think about it. If we had told the people the truth, the people would have risen up against us and toppled the government."

"We have a duty to avenge the President!"

"How? Colonel, how? We have no proof. We know they did it but how can we prove it?"

"We know and that is good enough. When did you become emasculated, Mr. Prime Minister? In the sixties when the Muslims seized Western Europe, one stupid American boy sitting in a bunker used mind games to save their Americans abroad from getting slaughtered. That American boy is now their President. He faced down the Muslims and the Chinese. Are you saying that Russia is inferior to America? We can't avenge our own people against our enemies?"

"Colonel, the Caliphate sent me a communiqué three days ago. It stated that they would be conducting 'war game exercises.' Their forces are massing in Greece and Turkey on our Southwest and from within Germania on our West; they are doing the same in Sweden. Two days ago, CHIN forces began massing all along the Southern border, after, of course, sending an official communiqué that they were conducting 'routine training.' The Americans sent me a draft of a press release yesterday and asked if they should approve it. It said: 'Effective immediately the United States of America will be suspending indefinitely all domestic and commercial travel and commerce with the Russian Bloc.'"

The Colonel says nothing.

"Colonel, all I could do is make it so we could survive this disaster, and use the crisis to our advantage. Everyone thinks twice before starting a fight with Russians, but that doesn't mean they won't start it. We cannot have this Colonel. Will you please stop? Unless you can tell me what I should have done differently. Unless you can tell me why I shouldn't have used this tragedy to our advantage."

The Colonel thinks for a moment. "I will cease hostilities, but Mr. Prime Minister, I suspect neither of us will survive politically. I will give the stand-down order."

"Thank you, Colonel. All I care about is that the nation survives."

Athena's Apartment, Matriarch Hotel, Moscow, Russia
7:57 a.m., 26 June 2096

Athena packs a set of suitcases.

"We're happy to announce that there is now a formal ceasefire between the military and the Kremlin," the reporter says over her e-pad audio-only newsfeed.

"You have visitors," Yana's voice sounds in her ear-set.

"Thanks Yana." Athena walks to the door and opens it just as they are about to knock.

"Athena!" The two women hug her at the same time.

"Get inside." Athena closes the door after them. "You made it. How's Fingers?"

"She's fine," Czarina answers. "She'll arrive tonight."

"I hate Moscow," Titania says. "We haven't been in Moscow in years and when we do decide to come, they decide to have a civil war. I've never seen so many police drones in the sky."

"And does anyone have their own natural hair color in this tek-city?" Czarina opens up the third empty suitcase on the bed and they start filling it too.

"This country is supposed to be our new home." Athena returns to packing.

"I'm glad you decided not to quit after all," Czarina says.

"It'll buy us some time. The witches won't be looking for us while we increase our security. I still don't think the Matriarch is being forthcoming with us."

"Athena," Titania says. "It doesn't matter. You will be the priestess. You'll be in charge."

"What's she like?" Czarina asks.

"Mother Sister is a leader. We'll have our hands full running the Sanctuary, but she's supporting us completely. I have carte blanche."

"There you go. Everything you asked for," Titania says.

"When do the weapons arrive?"

"Yes, when will you tell us the full story?" Czarina asks. "What did the witches do?"

"It seems my life is following the same recent high-espionage intrigue of Russia. There was an assassination attempt on my life my first day here."

Armies of Chaos

"I believe, as Lenin said, that this revolutionary chaos may yet crystallize into new forms of life." — Mikhail Gorbachev, the last President of the Old Soviet Union

"Prime Minister Tolokonnikova is dead!"

Athena's Apartment, Matriarch Hotel, Moscow
6:05 a.m., 27 June 2096

Athena always goes to bed with the audio newsfeed on. After so many years, she can't sleep any other way. Her eyes are still closed, though she is semi-awake. Something jumps on her.

"Fingers, get off."

Her black polydactyl cat, two extra toes on each paw, ignores her and nuzzles her face.

"The sudden death of Prime Minister Tolokonnikova, just days after the revelation of the death of President Krutikov, has put the Kremlin and the nation in a panic," the announcer says.

Athena opens her eyes.

The Kremlin
6:30 a.m., 27 June 2096

Military personnel and tanks have completely cordoned off the presidential complex. Crowds of people, including journalists, mass around the building yelling at the soldiers for information.

The room is filled with almost two dozen senior commissioned officers and top aides.

"We must announce new elections immediately," General Mikhail says, standing at the window and watching the massing crowds in Red Square.

"What happened to the Prime Minister?" another general asks.

"We don't know."

"Died, murdered, what?"

"I said, we don't know."

"What do you suspect then?"

"General, something exploded from his stomach."

The generals look at each other.

"What does that mean?"

"Generals, I can't even begin to speculate when we have the CHINs and Caliphate on our doorstep, and so many conspiracies are in the air that even I'm sleeping with my pistol under my pillow. And who knows what the Americans are doing."

"The rumor among the military is that it was them that killed the President at the Catherine Palace Summit," says an aide.

"Them? Them who?"

"The Americans."

"Why just them? The Muslims and the CHINs were there too. No one outside of senior leadership was supposed to have known about that summit. Also, the rumor among the presidential staff is that it was us, the military, that killed both the President and the Prime Minister, so our hand-picked puppet could take control."

"Just yesterday the news-feed said it was mobsters," says a general.

"Where's the Colonel?" asks another.

"Siberia, where else?" he answers.

"What about the assassination of our President?!" a large general yells impatiently.

"Since we are in no position to do anything about it, if it were them, why discuss it? Put it on the back burner until we can do something. We must stabilize the country. Elections now, as Mikhail said."

Mikhail looks through the window again. "Where does the KGB stand on this?"

"They're with us."

"Then let's announce the emergency elections immediately, and have Orlok act as temporary president. Are we all agreed?"

The military men nod in unison.

"Tolokonnikova was trying to be too clever with all his maneuverings. He should have announced the President's death as soon as it happened. Now everything is so murky with so many different factions plotting. We may never know what really happened at Catherine Place," another general says.

"Then let's invent the best assassin to get the best political outcome for us. As you said, we may never really know. Two hundred years later we're still debating the murder of the Last Tzar," Mikhail says.

Domodedovo International Airport, Moscow
1:47 p.m., 27 June 2096

The private jet has already landed and its two passengers descend down the steps. Mrs. Lucifer covered in a fur coat and dressed in a blood-red dress and wearing white pearls, holds on to the railing with her bony, pale hand. Mr. Lucifer, in his blood-red suit, with his snow-white hair and mustache, follows.

They can see military troops sitting in slider jeeps watching them closely.

"Look at all this excitement in our new home country-to-be," she says.

One of the porters walks to them. "We so apologize for this, ma'am. The military is on high alert and all arrivals and departures are under greater scrutiny."

"We hear your country lost another leader today," Mrs. Lucifer says with a hint of sarcasm.

"It's awful. Our President, and now our Prime Minister. The nation is in chaos."

"Too bad such things don't happen in America," she says.

The porter smiles awkwardly. "The shuttle will take you to your limo."

"Wonderful. My husband and I look forward to joining the chaos. Maybe even contribute a bit, if we're lucky."

Holy Patriach's Residence, Church of the Twelve Apostles
2:41 p.m., 27 June 2096

"Where are you?" the man says as he crawls on all fours on the floor. "I am here." He stands in his long, flowing garment (*exorason*), his white hair disheveled. He runs to his bed and kneels before a shimmering green crystal ball in the covers. "Are we where we're supposed to be?" "Yes, my Lord, we are." "Good, my son. Our time is at hand."

"Holiness." A voice from outside the chamber interrupts his conversation with himself.

The man rises, snatching the crystal ball from the bed. He runs to the large dresser and a secret compartment automatically opens. He puts the ball inside and slides the door closed. The man grabs his black klobuk—the traditional fez-like head covering (*kamilavka*) with *epanokamelavkion* (veil), which hangs down over the shoulders and back.

He stands with authority; the craziness in his eyes gone—hidden. "Enter."

The doors open and a priest in black comes in. "Holiness, they await your presence."

The Pope Patriarch nods and follows. A detail of aides stand along the hallway and bow as he passes them.

Moscow Sanctuary, Moscow
6:15 p.m., 27 June 2096

"What war?" Czarina asks.

Athena's circle—herself, Czarina and Titania—sit at the long oval table at one end. Delphine's circle—the Mother Sister, her daughter, and three other senior Matriarch leaders— sit at the other. Yana stands by the entrance of the tiny conference room.

"The reality is that the Matriarch has been on the verge of dissolution," Delphine reveals. "The animosity we've had with the Dark Wicca is nothing new. It's gone on for decades. But it's different now with Morgana. Half the Matriarch wants to escalate the battle with them, the other half wants to further recede into the background and avoid any conflict at any cost."

"But what does that mean—war?" Czarina asks. "What's been happening?"

"Vandalism and sabotage of our facilities, theft, physical attacks on sisters, kidnappings. Within the government, they've pretended to be Matriarch members and took over meetings and functions. Put out press releases that Morgana ran the Matriarch," Hilda says.

"Why weren't any of the Europan Sanctuaries told about this?" Czarina asks.

"Because we knew what would have happened." Delphine says.

"Yes, we would have done something about it."

"With so many in the Matriarch opposed to my appointment as priestess, why choose me? And now there's this turmoil in the country." Athena asks.

"Yes, many in the Matriarch feel you're too traditional, too unorthodox, too radical. But I'm convinced that is what we need. You're Russian, and you're not. You're native born so Russian sisters will follow you, yet you've lived most of your life outside Russia, so you have credibility with the Europan sisters. You're the perfect bridge for our two factions.

"As you can probably guess, the Russian faction of the Matriarch is more intellectual and much more pacifistic; the Europans are more militant. The Dark Wicca has been growing in strength and influence, inspired by Islam."

Athena's circle looks at each other in disbelief.

"Murderous misogynists are their inspiration?" Czarina asks. "Witches are insane."

Hilda says, "Welcome to our New Russia in the latter part of the twenty-first century."

Athena sighs. "We must not allow this evil to engulf the Matriarch."

"Sounds so melodramatic," Hilda says.

"I'm not trying to be amusing. When a religion is engulfed by evil—you either use a little violence now to keep all of it from turning evil or have to use far, far more in future to turn it back, and most likely it would be too late. I choose the first. We should know this better than most in the world with the Muslims right across the border wanting to add us to their Caliphate. I have no interest in being a burka-wearing slave or a servant of witches."

"The Dark Wicca claims they have a million-woman secret army among those burka-wearing slaves," Delphine says.

"And you believe them?" Athena asks.

"No, of course not, but they have used the claim to build their power base here."

"What do we want to do?" asks another sister. "We will have a very difficult time getting a majority of Russian sisters to fight. Many will simply say that if there are Wicca who want to worship evil, then let them. It has nothing to do with us. Even if we have all the Europan sisters, it's not enough."

"Russia is the only quasi-superpower in the world that allows religious freedom, but that can change in the blink of an eye. We must be careful. We're the minority here," Delphine says.

"Russia will always be religiously pluralistic," a sister says. "We have the Russian Orthodox. The country may be majority atheist, but they like Russian Orthodox. They're our living history so they allow them."

Hilda says, "I wish we could be so optimistic. In the eyes of the government, there is no two separate and distinct Wicca Orders. We're all the same. Islam is outlawed. They almost outlawed those stupid Klingons even though they created their own mini-city. Vampires came close, though personally I wish they would be banned."

"Half the Matriarch will not fight. The foundation of our religion is: 'All life is sacred; do what you will, so long as it harms none, or whatever you do comes back to you threefold.' They will not go against that and ask aloud why we are so quick to do so."

"With all the unrest in the country, we shouldn't do anything against them. We should wait."

"I didn't share this information before," Delphine says. "But they plan to attack us here at the Sanctuary. Under the cover of the current chaos, they plan to take the Matriarch from us, which is what

Morgana wants. They'll use whatever violence to achieve it."

Sisters are agitated, scared, and some are on the verge of tears.

"Then it will be self-defense," Czarina declares.

"We're not talking about self-defense. You're talking about preemption," a sister corrects.

"*The* question," Delphine ponders. "Do we ignore our foundational beliefs to save the foundation?"

"I don't care what arguments we have to use to get the Matriarch to stop the witches," Athena says. "I don't care. And I don't care if most of the Russian sisters don't see the danger. If there is evil in the Sisterhood, then we have to stop it, no one else—us. Round them up and exile them. We have allies in the government. People are put on the government black-list all the time. If they use violence, we put them down with violence."

"You're not thinking things through, Athena," Delphine says.

"Meaning?"

"We have no power to have people exiled. Even if we did, then that would mean exporting our 'evil,' as you call them, to some other country or countries. If they're alive, then they'll seek revenge against us, no matter what, or how long it took. You're advocating something even more radical than you're prepared to do."

Athena looks at her. Mother Sister is right.

"Then let's go as far as we can go for now," Yana speaks up. "Self-defense is still a foundation of the Matriarch. We confront them and diminish their power."

Delphine nods and looks at her circle. Everyone nods.

"We're all in agreement," Delphine says. "I will call for a full meeting. Tomorrow morning."

Hilda looks at her. "We have another development," she says.

Outside Athena's Room
9:30 p.m., 27 June 2096

Athena's trio stands quietly in the hall. A sister walks past them and disappears into her room. Czarina takes out her device again and finishes her scan.

"We can talk."

"As of right now, none of us are to be alone," Athena says. "Both of you move into my room and we'll also take turns on guard duty."

"You can't be serious, A," Titania says to Athena. "The Sanctuary has the best security. Much better than what we have in Romania."

"I'm not worried about outsiders at the moment."

Czarina and Titania look at her.

"I don't like what you're suggesting," Czarina says.

"Let's move your things into the room."

Secret Hospital, Moscow, Russia
5:01 a.m., 28 June 2096

The Prime Minister's body lies on the gurney. The doctor steps out of the room to four men waiting for him dressed in black suits.

"Has anyone been allowed to examine the body besides yourself or your team?" one of the agents asks.

"No others," the doctor answers. "All files have been transferred and deleted. I can call the med staff for transport."

"No, we will do that."

"And when the Kremlin arrives and asks where the body of the Russian Prime Minister is?"

"Tell them to call us," the first man says. "They know the number to the KGB."

The Open Room, Moscow Sanctuary
8:31 a.m., 28 June 2096

The banquet-sized room is filled with women talking, yelling, and protesting. Delphine stands in the front trying to calm things down by raising her hands in the air. Hilda and two senior members stand behind her to one side, Athena's trio stand to the other.

"Sisters, please," Delphine says.

A shrieking whistle shatters the commotion. Everyone turns around to see the large Yana removing her fingers from her mouth. The room is silent.

"Sisters, please, one at a time."

"What are we going to do? This man, Orlok, is probably going to be the next President of the Russian Bloc."

"He's holding a press conference and every religion group will be there except us. And that evil child-woman is passing herself off as the leader of the Matriarch! What are we going to do?"

"Sisters, I will call the Kremlin directly…"

"Call who?!" a sister interrupts Delphine. "President Krutikov was our ally and he's dead. So who are you calling?"

"There are others."

"There is no one, no one not under the control of the witches."

"They're passing themselves off as the Matriarch. We have to stop them."

"Why aren't our allies saying anything? They're saying nothing. No protests."

"Mother Sister, what is our plan?"

Delphine raises her hands again. "We have a new priestess, and we should allow her to assert her authority."

The eye of every sister in the room turns to Athena.

"My circle will handle it," Athena says.

"What does that mean?" a sister asks. "The three of you alone?"

"Yes."

"What do you intend to do?"

"We expect leadership to lead and not speak in riddles."

"And that's what I'll do," Athena says.

"Sisters, Athena and I spoke before this meeting. She has the full blessing of the Governing Circle to act on our behalf for the entire Matriarch. I haven't disclosed this publicly before, but the Dark Wicca attempted to murder our new Moscow priestess."

There is shock among the sisters.

"Murder?"

"The witches have to be stopped."

"What is your plan, Athena?"

"Sisters, let me act. I'll return when we've handled things."

"Handle how?"

"What are you going to do?"

"Is there a reason you won't tell us your plans?"

"Yes." Athena says no more to them. The crowd is not satisfied with the secrecy.

Delphine walks to Athena. "Take anyone you need to help you."

"Thank you."

Presidential Offices, The Kremlin
1:42 p.m., 29 June 2096

Orlok sits at the desk with yellow-tinted clear glasses. The very skinny bald man listens to the men in his ear-set as they continue their virtual briefing.

"Sir, the press conference will not only show that you are in complete control, but you have the full support of the people throughout all government, military, business, secular, and religious circles," the holo-image of one of his staffers says.

Orlok sits as if he were nothing more than a statue, only his occasional blinking shows he's even alive.

"We'll have the Pope Patriarch of Moscow and All Russia and the High Priestess of the Wiccans on your left, General Mikhail for the military and Mr. Soon of the Government Tek-Workers Union on your right. Everyone else will stand behind them on their respective sides, four dozen each. Any overflow will sit in the front rows."

"What about the others?" Orlok asks.

One of the generals in the room with him asks, "What others, sir?"

"Our Brothers of the Flash." He smiles.

"Sir, we don't know what you mean."

"The Brothers of the Nuclear Flash."

Everyone looks at him for a moment.

"Nuclear? Sir, no one uses that word anymore. Let's keep it that way. This event is about you. Let's not confuse the world with anything else."

"Russia must be considered one the superpowers. They lump us in with Africans, Spanish Americans, and Australians. They are not Brothers of the Flash."

"Yes sir. We will talk to them and make sure that changes after you're elected."

He nods. "Continue the briefing."

"Yes, sir," the general says.

Military Conference Room, The Kremlin
8:25 p.m., 29 June 2096

The generals are in an uproar.

"What was that?! Orlok never talks. That's why he's been promoted up the ranks. He never talks, but does what he's told. Now he talks and he's talking about nuclear weapons. What in the hell?"

"No one even uses that world anymore. I don't even think the word 'nuclear' is even in the Net-dictionary anymore. Do we even have any old nuclear weapons anymore, except for our old missile stockpiles? All our ICBMs and energy plants are fusion."

One of the generals points at another. "He was your pick. You control him. Have him keep his mouth shut!"

"He'll be under control, even as President."

"I'm getting very scared here. We are all so sure that we're in control, but I wake up in the middle of the night, convinced that we're not."

"He won't even have launch codes as President."

"I'm not concerned about that."

"Well we are. Why is he so pale? Are we sure he's not a Vampire?"

"He's not."

"Is he religious? He's bald. Only those people allow themselves to be naturally bald."

"I've known him for decades. He's as atheist as any of us."

The other general continues, "I'm concerned that we're even talking about this. No one talks about nuclear anymore. We're all spending billions on advanced military robotics, bio-warfare, and biological-enhancement tek. No one talks about last century nuclear weapons anymore and suddenly he mentions it. Why is he talking about it? Don't talk about it!"

"Okay, okay, generals."

"It's all irrelevant anyway." The general gasps even before finishing his sentence.

"Meaning what?"

"Meaning nothing, sorry. He won't have the codes."

"No, you meant something else. What did you mean?"

"Nothing, I'm sorry."

All the generals look at him.

General Mikhail looks at him angrily. "What did you mean? It's obvious some of you know. What? You might as well tell us because we will find out."

The general who slipped up continues. "Russia has no nuclear weapons."

"What are you talking about?"

"Presidents Goraya and Ilyan had them all secretly destroyed."

"That's what, two, no, three decades ago. Why would they do that?"

"That was back in the sixties during the Fall of Western Europe. Why would they do that?"

"You all remember what was going on. Talk of merging the UN and EU to create a new organization called the Federation, a paradise of all mankind which needed no such weapons. It's what caused the rise of the KGB. Those Presidents left the entire Russian Bloc defenseless."

The KGB was the nation's premier security agency back before the Bloc was formed, back before Russia, when the nation was the Soviet Union. The KGB then was the internal and external security, intelligence, and secret police all in one, until its disbandment in 1991. It existed in a sense, but it was reborn after the Fall of Western Europe. It is the government within the government, a separate and independent secret police feared by all, but dedicated to the defense of the Bloc from all threats domestic and foreign, from citizens to generals—and presidents.

"Does Orlok know this?"

"No, it's not possible."

"What about the CHINs, Caliphate, or Americans?"

"No, of course not, besides the KGB made sure the country wasn't left naked. They recreated the old ones, albeit a tiny fraction of the original missile stockpile, but they had newer weapons created, lots of them."

"Gentlemen," Mikhail says. "We must focus on seeing our plan to the end. Our beloved President is dead and so is his suitable substitute in the Prime Minister. It is our duty to ensure the nation boldly steps into the next century and beyond, despite the plotting of our enemies. We must strictly manage Orlok. Let us put all thoughts of this disturbing secret history lesson out of our minds. We don't have time to be disturbed."

Streets of Moscow
3:00 p.m., 2 July 2096

The drone fired one shot from the air and blew out the entire front end of the trio's minivan. As in any tek-city, with auto-drive there are no such things as car chases. The Grid controls your car and the government controls the Grid.

The police troopers, body-armored from head to toe and heads fully encased in helmets, swarm the vehicle with weapons drawn. These are not regular police (regulars). They are black-clad *Bogatyr*—Russia's elite police. They pull them out of the vehicle. Every country has a name for their advanced police; in America, the common term is stormtroopers. They pin Athena, Czarina and Titania to the ground. Athena's mouth is bloodied from the explosion rattling her teeth, Titania is still dazed, and Czarina is boiling with rage.

The Bogatyrs find the vehicle's secret compartments and find the weapons.

"What were you planning on doing with this?"

"It's just pistols," Athena yells. "It's for protection. We're religious minorities and we have permits."

"You mean you have permits in Europa. This is Russia."

He nods to one of the other officers. "We found the terrorists," the officer says into his shoulder-comm.

"What are you talking about?!" Athena yells. "We're citizens of the Russian Bloc, not terrorists."

"We're not terrorists, you fascist!" Czarina yells.

The Bogatyrs pick them up to their feet. All around them are drones.

"What is all this?" Athena asks. "You need all this for three women?"

The trio is loaded into a police van. They sit quietly, handcuffed, ankle-cuffed and chained to the roof of the car. The van drives.

"We can't allow them to put us into the jail system," Titania says. "I'm not afraid to say it: I'm scared to death. A little target shooting once a month and a black belt that you can brag about at parties doesn't mean a damn here. It could be months at the soonest before we even get to court to respond to our arrest."

Czarina shakes her head. "They've called us terrorists. It could be years, not months."

Titania bends down as far as she can, trying to calm her panic. "We can't go to jail. I've been there. The horror stories are true unless you pay for protection. I can't go there again."

Czarina looks at Athena trying not to cry.

The police van stops. The trio looks at each other with fear.

"Oh no, here we go. The nightmare begins," Czarina says.

The door opens and a Bogatyr without his helmet looks in.

"Which one of you is Athena?"

"I am."

"Do you want to call in your favor now?"

Athena stares at him.

"What is he talking about?" Czarina asks.

"She knows," he says.

Athena hesitates.

"What's your answer?"

"Yes."

Grand Kremlin Palace
6:05 p.m., 2 July 2096

Government press conferences are always in the morning, no later than noon, but this is different. It is a big event staged specifically to calm the nation and send a message to the world. Russia is in control of the Russian Bloc.

It is an overflow, guest-list-only crowd in the Saint George's Hall. People are being directed to their places by staff. Orlok is led to the stage.

"Commander Orlok, the Patriarch of Moscow and all Russia," the aide says.

The head of the Russian Orthodox Church shakes his hand. "It is a pleasure to meet the next President of the Russian Bloc. I had a dream about you this very morning, sir. My lord told me that I must support you with all my life. That you are the one man in all the world who will raise the Russian empire above the blaze of fire."

Orlok is entranced by the man. The Patriarch's entourage of priests and Orlok's military staff are both unnerved by the words.

"Commander Orlok, let's continue," says one of the officers. The Patriarch lets go of his hand.

They turn to meet the next group.

"Commander, this is Morgana, the High Priestess of the Wiccan Matriarch."

The girl wears a provocative slinky black dress to her knees, platform shoes, and all-black makeup. She extends her hand. "The Matriarch is honored, Mr. future-President, the largest religious coalition in the Russian Bloc. I introduce my submissives: Johnny Satan of the Warlock-Vampire-Satanist Triumvirate, Candy Chaos of the Nihilist-Hedonist Punks, and Delphine of the True Pagan-Druid-Wicca Trinity."

After brief comments, Orlok is quickly led to meet with

representatives of other religionists, labor unions, science guilds, corporation coalitions, etc. The press conference is going to begin soon.

Delphine looks out into the audience as everyone is being directed to their spots to stand on the stage. She freezes—*Athena is staring back at her, sitting in the center of the front row.*

Mothers and Sisters

"It's simple. Women hate women." — Yana "the Hulkstress," the Wiccan Matriarch

Grand Kremlin Palace
6:45 p.m., 2 July 2096

The trio reaches the outside hallway but they have already been noticed by security.

"This was a mistake," Titania says. "What good is it to know what we know, if we won't even be able to get out of here?"

Athena is worried too. "All we have to do is make it to the outside press."

"If they want us bad enough, they won't care who's outside watching," Czarina says.

They exit the Kremlin building. Plainclothes security and military soldiers are stationed in the outside courtyard. Several turret-robot sentries are posted on the outer perimeter.

"Wait here," Athena says. She walks up to one of the soldiers. "Officer, I wish to make a report."

"What is it?" the soldier asks.

"I saw three suspicious women inside and I think I should report it, especially with what happened to the president and prime minister."

"Suspicious how?" he asks. Another two soldiers joins them.

"It's how they were watching Mr. Olov—"

"Mr. Olok," the soldier corrects.

"Yes, Mr. Olok. I swear they're plotting something. They were sweating and whispering to each other and were keeping to themselves. I don't think they even had security badges."

"What did they look like?"

"One Caucasian female with blond hair, one African and one Asiatic, both females with dark hair. They were near the lavatories when we left."

"Thank you. We'll investigate."

The soldier runs to the building entrance and is already calling in on his wrist-comm. The trio starts walking away as panic starts to ripple across the Kremlin security detail.

"What did you say to them?" Titania asks.

"Sisters can do Jedi mind-tricks too. I described us and said we were inside, before someone describes us and broadcasts where we really are."

"Everyone can do Jedi mind-tricks, except Jedis," Czarina adds.

"Let's hope it buys us the time we need."

The modern tek-city—the greatest achievement of humankind in all of history—is the state-of-the-art equivalent to the great pyramids of Ancient Egypt. The city protects, transports, and nourishes; but it also monitors, tracks, and detains if needed. It is the place to be, except if it explodes in mass riots or you are on the run.

The women walk into a nearby store and straight into the unisex bathroom. Their scarves go into the trash, their colored necklaces go into their pockets and they each tie up their hair so that it is no longer running down the side of their body. Their jackets are reversible so they turn them inside out. Can they fool Argus, if they are "tagged"? No, but everything helps.

They blend as best as they can into the crowds. The authorities are looking for three women together so they walk apart from each other. They can't use taxis or the metro; it'll be the first place they look. They'll stay on the main streets; more people to hide among and the side streets are probably where they'll expect them to go. It will take a while, but their only option is to never stop walking until they make it out of the tek-city.

A car coasts past them slowly. They look—Hilda is in the front passenger seat and Delphine in the back. The car speeds away. The trio runs. They have to get off the main streets now.

A bright red limousine drives up the far end of the side-street and stops. Inside Morgana is sprawled out in the back seat, her head bobs all around with the music blaring from her dual ear-sets. Two Goth Wiccans sit across from her sharing a blunt, each blowing out red smoke. Johnny Satan gets out of the driver's seat, walks back to the trunk, and opens it.

Athena, Czarina, and Titania run down the side street and stop—a bright red limo. They see Johnny Satan dragging a headless naked body on the ground. He watches them with a smile as he hoists the body up and throws it into dumpster. He waves to them.

Two cars drive up and stop behind them; blocking their way. A woman jumps out from the passenger seat of the first car; she is carrying a long dagger. Other doors open and women exit.

"Look at the Glindas." Morgana approaches the trio with her two Goth Wiccans. Johnny Satan follows.

Morgana, with her eight-inch platform shoes, looks right into Athena's face.

"I don't how you did it. Escape from the police, or how you got into the Grand Kremlin. You were supposed to be brutally tortured in the bowels of the state's prison, never to be seen again." She laughs. "But this is better. Life is a constant battle against boredom and you've brought so much excitement ever since we met."

"What did you put in the dumpster?" Czarina asks Johnny Satan.

He laughs. "My latest victim. I'm always guided by the better devils of my nature."

"How did you do it? Get the Matriarch to ally with the likes of you?" Athena asks.

Morgana laughs. "Delphine? I own Delphine. How do you think I knew where to find you now? And when you first came to Moscow?"

Athena tries to keep her anger in check.

"Release that anger," Morgana says. "Everybody knows what's really going on except you three. The Dark Wicca is at the threshold of complete domination of Greater Russia, then the Caliphate next. A new matriarchal order will engulf the world. No President or Emperors. It will be Empress Mistress Morgana, ruler of the world."

Are we supposed to laugh?

"See my slave behind you, the Arab witch with the dagger? My Chinese witch behind her? I told you that we are legion. China and the Middle East belong to Russia. And they will again."

"Okay, Morgana" Athena says. "We'll leave you to it then and catch the next plane back to Romania."

Morgana giggles for a bit. "Will you?" she asks.

"Will we what?" Athena asks.

"Let me do her and the other two," Johnny Satan says.

"The war is over Athena. There's nothing you and your two Glindas can do about it. The Matriarch is run by Morganas—hey, I just made that word up—and we are purging it of all Glindas, especially Europans who don't know their place. I am your Mother Sister now, and I must protect all my sisters, even those who don't know their true place in my world. But what do you know about futility? I'll allow you to pick."

"You are a disgrace to the religion."

Morgana laughs. "Religion, Athena? What religion?"

"You know nothing of it, which makes it so easy for you to debase it. Wiccan spirituality has been here millennia before any of the patriarchal religions were even born…"

Morgana starts laughing again.

"Athena the Traditional, this religion is as fake as all the rest created by men. There is no Goddess or God. There is only the 'me.' You hate religion, but you create your own and call it spirituality. You hate churches, but create sanctuaries. Hate God but create a Goddess. You reject organized religion, but create the Matriarch. You have existed for millennia? Ha! The modern White Wicca was started by a yoga teacher from Minsk. I should know. She was my great-grandmother!"

Morgana sticks her finger in Athena's ear. Athena smacks it away.

"I told you to pick."

"Pick what?"

"Left hand or right hand?"

"I don't know what you're talking about."

"Athena, I know you. You're fixated with this concept of reformations and eradicating supposed evil. I'm an evil witch, and I can't leave such a Glinda as you unattended. Pick."

"I don't know what you mean."

Morgana continues, "I need to break you. I need you to stop. I should kill you, but that would be too easy. I believe in chaos and that evil must leave alive that piece of pure goodness that can defeat them. It's the order of things. If not, then the universe will disintegrate, but that goodness must be utterly broken, just as I did with Delphine.

"I'm going to have my slaves cut off your right hand because, though you think it of me, you are the ones who think this is all a game. In the real world people suffer and die. There is no white maiden to ride in on a white horse and save you when all is lost."

Athena runs but is tackled to the ground by Morgana's women.

"Get the electric ax, Johnny."

7:55 p.m.

Athena lies in the ambulance staring up at the roof. She is no longer screaming, no longer crying. Her eyes are open, but she is far away. Mentally she exists in a place that she has never been before.

Czarina and Titania sit up front in the passenger compartment still crying and still in shock.

"Hang on, Athena," Titania says to her softly.

The ambulance arrives and hospital workers rush Athena to the emergency room.

9:02 p.m.

The doctor walks out to Czarina and Titania who are waiting in the lobby. The two women stand.

"She's fine," he says. "We reattached the hand with no problems."

"Is there any permanent damage?" Titania asks.

"Such injuries are simple to repair. Patients have so many options nowadays: mechanical, android, cloned. But in this case, all the tissue and nerves were easily repairable."

"Good." Titania sighs.

"However, your friend's mental state may not be fine at all. Dismemberment psychosis can be a real condition."

"We'll take care of her," Czarina says.

The doctor nods. "You can take her home. That will help with her recovery."

Lenin Hotel, Outskirts of Moscow
8:05 a.m., 3 July 2096

Czarina pushes the wheelchair. Athena sits almost comatose; her right hand is encased in a large mechanical glove with colored sensors—a metal cast. Titania follows. No one speaks as the auto-doors of the hotel swing open. They stop in the main sitting area. Czarina and Titania leave her and walk around one of the lobby columns so Athena can't hear them.

"I've very concerned about her. I'll stay with her in the lobby. Find out when the next flight is," Czarina says.

"We should never have come to Russia," Titania says sadly.

"Let's get out of here as soon as possible."

Titania looks around the column and her eyes widen. "Where's Athena?"

Czarina turns. The wheelchair is empty!

Moscow Sanctuary
2:30 p.m., 3 July 2096

Athena stares at the house, partly hidden by trees. She is sweaty from walking for hours, barely able to hold her encased hand, the drugs wearing off, and the pain naturally increasing.

"Let it go," a voice says.

Athena has no mobility and slowly turns her body. It is Yana.

"Let me help you with that," she says. Yana takes off her own neck scarf and quickly creates a sling. "You should not be walking around with that." She puts the sling over Athena's head and places it so that it holds up the encased right hand. "You definitely shouldn't be here."

"Are you one of the Morganas?"

Yana stops and looks at her. "If you mean, am I a follower of that witch-bitch, then the answer is no. Athena, revenge is not what should be on your mind now. Get on a plane and get out of Russia."

"Why are you here?"

Yana sighs. "I'm not interested in listening to my own advice."

"Why did she do this to us?"

"Athena, there is so much going on that I wouldn't even know where to start. It all doesn't matter now. The Dark Wiccas run the Matriarch and from what we've seen today, they probably were always running it. Go home. You at least have your life."

Yana is shocked by something she sees past Athena. Athena feels like an invalid as she slowly turns again. Delphine approaches them with Hilda and several armed sisters. They stop and Athena sees, from the corner of her eye, a hand holding a gun.

"The drones will hear it," Delphine says.

"You're dead!" Yana yells.

Delphine is unconcerned.

"Yana, we have you both covered," Hilda says. "Did you think we'd sit here unprotected?"

Something hits the tree where Yana and Athena stand. There is another puff of smoke.

"Put it away, Yana," Hilda commands. "You can walk away or be sent home in a coffin. We're allowing you to escape, but that charity won't last if you don't leave now. Put it down or our rifleman will shoot you dead."

Yana lowers her gun.

"Yana, the Matriarch will not only be in the center of the Kremlin," Delphine says. "But we will have the power to simply make a call, send a text, and make an enemy disappear. None of you can grasp the magnitude of what the Sisterhood will soon be."

Athena doesn't know why she came here now. She's seen enough and heard enough. She turns away from all of them. Back the way she came, holding her metal hand in the sling, she moves slowly down the sidewalk.

"Athena." It's Delphine's voice.

She stops again and slowly turns.

"I never thought I'd see you again."

Athena is in too much pain, but her stare is no less full of hate.

"You don't need to say anything. This has been in the works awhile and the window of opportunity presented itself with the President's untimely death. All of Russia's religions are unified and we'll have a president that we can control. Better us than the CHINs or the Americans. You either join the power or they exclude you from power.

"After this president, Morgana will be the next. Russia will again have an Empress. The Matriarch will run the Russian Bloc. Sisters will run the government. This is the future I have always envisioned. I did this because I could never have achieved it any other way. The Matriarch was dying anyway—fidgety, fussy old women with no place to go or fit in; bored female intellectuals just looking for someone, anyone, to pontificate to; weird animal protectors with a compulsion for stray cats. That's all we were beyond the Mother-this, Sister-that, oh most exalted goddess, protectress of the Feminine.

"Ever been to America? Religious people live as exiles outside the tek-cities under constant persecution. Exiles in the country they created. Not here. Now we'll have power. It's power that will allow us to practice our spirituality without being molested, power to rise above everyone else. We've been taken advantage of by all the atheists, non-heteros, and other religions, with women always at the bottom of the power food chain. We can't grow our religion if we can't protect it. The Matriarch will no longer be a joke and no one ever saw us coming.

"All I had to do give up those sisters who could be a threat to the Dark Wicca. To make women the dominant species on Mother Earth, why not? You were a threat to our plans. You could have unified all the sanctuaries against us before we could act. No one could be allowed to prevent us from transforming the world when we were so close. After all, we are all part of the Sisterhood."

Athena slowly turns away again. The sling is no longer helping. She hobbles away.

The Leviathan King

"Power is like being a lady…if you have to tell people you are; you aren't."
— Margaret Thatcher, Prime Minister of Pre-Islamic England

"I loved the stories they used to tell me as a child in my town. A creature Leviathan exiled to the bottom of the world by the gods, but one day rising in glory and fury, rising from the waters to seize the lands, the heavens and the stars. I so wanted to be Leviathan!"
— Igor Aleyev, Eastern Europa mobster

Unknown Location
1:38 a.m., 4 July 2096

The rooms have a bunker-like feeling with all the windows sealed and the doors reinforced. It is very dimly lit by design with two armed guards at the door, passing the time by playing inherent games on their e-pads—not only are the men's devices not Net-connected, but the very bits of tek that allow that connectivity has been removed.

In another room, Igor sits in a chair with dozens of armed men around him, crammed almost on top of each other. Some are sitting or kneeling on the floor, others are standing, and some lean against the wall.

"Igor, the only thing keeping you alive is that they think you're already dead," one of the men says. "Everyone who was at the Palace is gone, everyone—dead or disappeared. You're the only one left. You can't do this. Why do this?"

"I'm the only one who can possibly get away with it," Igor answers.

The Kremlin
11:00 a.m., 4 July 2096

Brick-and-mortar newspaper conglomerates had disappeared many decades ago due to the Net, but it was not long before a new structure arose and people, like Mr. Post, became uber-editor-publishers, overseeing a stable of freelancers all over the world. Only one net-zinc (the Source in America) had more prestige than Moscow's—his—*My Pravda*. Mr. Post even behaves like a head of state.

He stands on the stage to address the journalists—most whom work for him, government dignitaries, and business moguls. It is an audience of several hundred, including government security police.

"People of Russia and Europa, I give you Anatoly Orlok, the next President of Russia!"

Post begins the applause as Orlok steps up to the stage to join him. Everyone is on their feet and applauding. No one in the large auditorium sees the man enter the room.

Igor Aleyev enters the room from the back in nothing more than his spandex-like boxer briefs, walking to the stage. Security men at the rear and side of auditorium immediately recognize him and are shocked. The mobster—the former President's son—is supposed to be dead. He smiles at them as he pushes through the crowd with his tattooed body of muscles. He's known among the crime families as the "Leviathan King," for the giant squid creature tattoo covering his entire back and spreading out over his arms and legs, wrapping around his chest—his entire body, except for his head.

Post notices him too from the stage and his smile disappears. Orlok stares at the mobster with a blank look. Security men race to them as Igor jumps up on the stage. Post and Orlok step back.

Igor stands silent as the commotion grows in the auditorium. "Who is that?" "Isn't he dead?" "That's that mob boss." "How did he get in here?" "What's that tattooed on his body?"

His hands rest in front of him, his right wrist locked in his left hand. He remains silent and after a few moments the auditorium is silent. Now he can speak to the world.

"Good afternoon people of Great Russia and people of Europa, no less great. My name is Igor Aleyev. I am the surviving son of President Erik Kritokov. I can't say this of anyone else, but I loved that man. He raised me and despite what I became, his love for me was unconditional. He never asked for my help or any favor like so many others. He never stole. He never cheated. He rose to the presidency, gained the love of the people all on his own, his own hard work, his own ceaseless determination, his own flawless character, his deep love for this nation. I always told him: you are too good for Russia.

"Did my father die naturally? Was my father murdered? We probably will never know that question anymore than we'll know if some crazy, Cuban-loving Communist killed Kennedy all by himself. The question does not matter. My father is dead and every faction imaginable has crawled out from under the rocks to scheme and to kill. I walk into this place half-naked because if I didn't these 'honorable' police would have shot me down and 'discovered' a weapon on me. There are so many conspirators aiming to seize control of the presidency. Not one of them thinking of the people.

"Effective one hour ago, I registered as a candidate for the presidency of the Russian Bloc…"

The crowd gasps. Post almost faints and falls. Anger flashes on Orlok's face.

"I, Igor Orlok, will seek the office to become your next president. In the spirit and memory of my father, I will not cheat or steal like my opponents, despite what I am. What am I? I am a vicious mobster born in Russia and controlled the crime world for much of Europa. We have enemies, you and I, domestic and abroad. Whether it's the CHINs, the Muslims, the Americas, sometimes our own Russian military or Russian government. Who best to protect you from all of them than a mobster? I, Igor Aleyev, seek your support and your vote to return Russia and Europa to greatness."

The place is abuzz. Igor steps down from the stage and walks through the crowd with every person fawning over him. No one cares about Orlok. Everyone wants to know Igor, even if in their hearts no one expects him to be alive for very long.

Thirteen women wait for him at the edge of the crowd.

"I cast a death spell on you!" Morgana yells as she points her fingers at him. "You will burn, Mr. Igor, burn."

Igor walks to them as entire crowd moves with him.

He leans forward to Morgana and whispers, "You've just started, but I've killed many, many more people than you."

Igor leans back and returns to working the crowd. People look at him and look at her. Morgana is not smiling.

Sheremetyevo Airport
10:42 p.m., 4 July 2096

There is nothing else on the newsfeed: "Europan mobster is seeking the office of the presidency." Athena looks up from her e-pad.

"Flight 119 for Transylvania is now boarding," the male computer voice says.

Czarina and Titania stand up from their seats next to her. Athena looks at them but remains seated.

"What's wrong?" Czarina asks.

"We're not going. I'm not going."

"Athena, are you crazy? Russia is going to be a war zone for certain now. The government and military will never allow a mobster to take the presidency. They do that in Mexico and the Spanish Americas and Africa, not here. They'll never allow him to sit in the president's chair."

"I'm staying."

"Athena, you are in no condition to stay here," Titania says. "Don't do this."

Czarina asks, "Why? Tell us why."

"Do we really think we'll be able to get on that plane, get back home, and live happily ever after? Just click our heels and forget everything as if it never happened? We have to do it."

"Do what?" Czarina asks.

"Kill the Matriarch."

Night of the Cats

"Dogs never bite me—just humans." — Marilyn Monroe, Old Hollywood icon

Pacific Ocean
2:32 p.m., 4 July 2096

The private jet flies low over the blue waters. Cartel super-boss (at least he used to be) El Angel sits in a plush faux leather bean bag chair. Ten men sit around him in their moveable chairs.

"Why are we going near this man, boss? He's a dead man."

El Angel says, "Maybe, maybe not. I want to be sure. Also, we need the money." He holds up his small tablet. "How positive are we?"

"Positive beyond positive, boss. We tracked it down to the source—the Russian. But he won't ever be giving out numbers again for people to call any mass-murdering demons again."

"The Russian was ancient. A man that old doesn't take his secrets to the grave. He would have passed it on to someone else—a son or daughter or other family. We still don't know who sends them."

"We have no more money to buy those kinds of answers anymore, boss."

El Angel looks at another man. "When we arrive make the exchange. Igor doesn't want any mention of it. Give him the number

93

and his man will transfer the money to our account. When it gets there, transfer it immediately to our other accounts."

"Yes, boss."

"Boss, why wouldn't we keep it for ourselves?" another man asks.

"Never you mind. Let it run around Russia for awhile instead of our continent."

"And let the priest escape."

"The priest is going to pick next president of Mexico. That priest, as powerful as he is, has even more powerful friends than we have right now at the moment. We'll get him when the time is right. For now we need a new base and Russia sounds good to me."

"Igor might have something to say about that."

"Igor won't be around for too long. If the government doesn't kill him, his own fellow mobsters are planning to kill him. If that doesn't happen, we'll do it, one way or another. He's dead and the number seals it."

Private Net Profile Broadcast of Igor Aleyev / 13:00 hours, 5 July 2096

"People of Russia and Europa! In organized crime there is something you never do—back down. Your enemy comes to fight with knives, you bring guns; they kill two of your men, you kill twenty of theirs. But if I want to show that I am sincerely walking the path of my father then I must prove it to you. The President is dead and so are the Prime Minister and dozens of others in high office. I have no doubt that if I were to campaign like a normal politician that I would be assassinated. To prevent it I would have to surround myself with such a mob army that I would play right into my enemies' hands. There would be a showdown and many of you, innocent bystanders, would be injured or killed. So I will do what a mobster is to never do—I back down. I will stay in seclusion to the election. I will put my fate in your hands. To return us to what we had under my father and to end the chaos, you will have to vote. You will decide: the Manchurian candidate or the mobster. I'm not religious, but I pray you make the right choice for the sake of the nation. We must be my father's legacy."

Presidential Offices, Kremlin
1:42 p.m., 5 July 2096

Military, government, and intelligence men argue amongst themselves. Orlok sits quietly.

Mikhail yells to be heard. "Where was the broadcast initiated from?"

"How many people got that broadcast?" an officer asks.

"We can't trace the activation source. All we can tell is that it was definitely sent from outside the country."

"Outside? Where is he then?!"

"We don't know."

"The broadcast was sent to everyone, and I mean everyone."

"How is that possible? Only the government has access to the nation's census data."

"He's a mobster. He stole it."

"He's a presidential candidate now, and he has to follow campaign rules. Direct communication with voters is illegal and subject to stiff fines."

"So we'll fine him to death?"

"Why isn't the KGB getting involved?"

"They won't show until the new president is official."

They all look at the seated Orlok.

"Any specific instructions, sir?"

"Has Post been approved to be my new Prime Minister when I'm elected?"

"Yes, sir."

"Send him out to work the crowds and the media. Let us say that the mobster is more interested in running his criminal empire of stealing and rape. Make up lies. *He* was the one who killed his father. *He* killed the Prime Minister. Let us say that he fled from Russia because he was a child-rapist. Things like that. Get Post out there now."

"Excellent, sir. People see us and don't see him, they'll believe us."

Orlok smiles. "While we do that, find him."

"He left the country and we don't know where yet."

"Everyone has agents in our country," Orlok says. "We have ours in theirs. Use those agents, pay whatever is needed, and find him before the elections."

"Yes sir."

Private Compound, Cabo San Lucas, Mexico
2:32 p.m., 7 July 2096

"The second message went out successfully," one of Igor's men says.

Igor sits on the patio staring out at the ocean, drinking clear blue vodka from a glass. After a few moments, he hears commotion from the front of the house. He sets his glass on the side table and turns.

"There he is!" the Mexican mobster smiles at him with his arms outstretched. "The Leviathan King himself."

Igor smiles too and rises from his chair to give the man a hearty hug.

"Good to see you, Angel." The men take a seat. Igor glances inside and sees El Angel's entourage of a dozen men.

"So the Leviathan King wants to be the next President of the Russian Bloc. I can't tell you how excited that makes us, to have one of our own in charge of an entire nation. There's one problem. You'll be long dead before you set foot anywhere near Moscow again." El Angel laughs. "But you're too smart for that. You're not going back. How about we swap places? I take Russia, you take Mexico."

"What do you know about scorpions?" Igor asks.

El Angel tries to pretend. "Mexico has a lot of them. Why?"

"I'm going make this very simple. As you correctly noted, I'm not a man with lots of time to waste. My two questions are, who was your contact to the Russian and how did you find out about the Russian?"

"What you talking about, Igor? The Russian? You're the Russian." He gives a forced laugh. "All you Russians are 'the Russian.'" El Angel's smile is gone. "Igor, I would think very carefully about your next actions. You need every friend you can find on this planet with all the kill-contracts for your head."

Igor ignores him. "I have the number and you have your money so it's a clean slate. The Russian is actually dead. He was killed. I would bet it was you or one your associates. He was killed around the same time you inexplicably gave up your entire territory. You flew out last year like a dog on fire."

"Igor, why am I here? Your people made us believe that you were putting together a mob army to protect you against the Russian government, and that you were going to make serious digi-cash available to us."

"Who was your contact to the Russian?"

"I have no idea what you're talking about."

"I need that information, Angel."

"I don't know what you're talking about."

"These people you contacted for the scorpions could be the same people involved with the demon."

El Angel swallows hard. "I said I don't know what you're talking about."

"I can't allow these things to be used against me so I must find these people, either before I become president, or afterwards. If you know about them, then others do too."

El Angel stands up. "It was very nice to see you again Igor. You enjoy your day."

Igor stands and blocks him. "I need that information. I need to know how you found the Russian."

"I don't know anything."

"Why do you want to play it this way?"

El Angel smiles. "Am I supposed to be scared of you? I'm Mexican, and no one scares us."

"People always say it was the Chinese, but it was Russians who perfected the art of torture. With the tek of today, I can remove your head from your body and plug into your brain like a laptop."

"You don't scare us."

"Us?"

El Angel looks inside. All his men are gone.

6:13 p.m.

"Igor, why are we doing this? Orlok has everyone looking for us. We have to hide better than what we're doing now or get ready for all-out war."

Igor removes his blood-drenched shirt and pants. His henchmen watch him disapprovingly.

"We don't have time for this, Igor."

"In all the years you've known me, have I ever made a misstep?"

"No, but you never ran from a fight either."

"Snap out of your delusion. If we have an all-out war with the Russian government and military, we lose, period. No matter how powerful we think we are. Only nations can fight nations."

"Then what are we doing, and what do we do now?"

"We're dealing with issues that must be dealt with. We're marking time until I become President."

"Igor, we've never seen anything like this before. They've even got witches hunting you."

"What witches?"

"The one calling the plays on the street is one called Morgana and another name we keep hearing is a Johnny something. They got religions now after us. All our lives we never see a religious person, now one after another is after us. First Catholics, now them."

"They'll never let you walk into the Kremlin to sit in the chair, boss."

"We may be out of country, Igor, but that doesn't mean anything. They have every last agent hunting you and every informant looking for you. They'll find us no matter where we hide if we don't do something. You should never have let Angel in here. Any one of those Mexicans could have informed on us."

"Yes, exactly what I'd expect."

"Igor, can't we steal the election? They always count the votes and know the results before the people vote."

"No disrespect, but your father did it too."

"I know, but we'll win another way."

11:59 p.m.

A plane descends from space and slowly dives into the night sky.

At the compound, Igor sits in his chair with a tek-gun in his right hand. All of his men sit around him with an assortment of modified guns, rifles, and machetes. They all wear clear glasses, not looking at each other but the surveillance feed of outside.

"Turn off the glasses and walk now!" Igor says.

They drop everything and follow him.

"We're not taking anything with us, boss?"

He ignores the man.

They understand and follow him out the back door of the compound to the ocean. Igor kicks off his shoes as they walk on the beach sand towards the water. He walks through the water and then jumps in.

"Swim!"

The men look at each other.

"Igor, we should get to compound's bunker instead!"

"It's not deep enough."

There is a flash. *The explosion strikes before the sound even has time to catch up.* The men standing are blown back, falling or thrown deeper into the ocean as the explosion vaporizes the compound and the fire starts to envelop everything around it: greenery, land, structures, vehicles, etc. Birds and insects are incinerated, and so are Igor's men that were not fortunate to have submerged, voluntarily or involuntarily by the blast.

Igor's head rises from the ocean to stare back at what was their hideout. It is a burning inferno. Igor submerges, not waiting a second longer. He swims away with an almost inhuman speed.

Ukraine Hotel
7:38 p.m., 5 July 2096

Everyone is astonished as Athena's trio walks into the meeting room. The anti-Matriarch sisters stop their arguing. Many can't avoid looking at her encased hand. Athena is allowed to sit and at least be heard.

"Everyone knows what they did to you, Athena, but you must go home."

"The Matriarch is purging everyone. We're all escaping any way we can."

"Who's the leader of the opposition?" Athena asks.

"Athena, there is no leader. We're finished. They're purging all of Moscow of every sister as we speak. They captured Yana and beat her within an inch of her life!"

"They did that just to send a message," Athena says.

"Yes, it worked."

"So no one is left?"

"Athena, there is no one. We're beaten."

"We just allow the witches to take over?"

"There is nothing else to do, Athena. You and your sisters need to leave Russia. If they catch you again…"

"Where's Yana now?"

"Why? She's being shipped out of Russia."

"Shipped?"

"She's been designated an 'undesirable' by the government. Are you listening to us? The witches have allies right in the Kremlin to do whatever they want."

"All of our names are on that list," a sister says. "The police find us, they arrest us."

"We're not running away," Athena says.

"What do you plan to do?"

"Take back the Matriarch."

"It's not ours to take."

"We can depose Delphine."

"What about Morgana?"

"We'll take care of Morgana after we depose Delphine."

"How?"

"We need to know everything about the Moscow Sanctuary first."

"We don't know anything anymore. The witches have taken over the building."

"Then we need to find some witches who do know about everything inside, now."

"And then?"

"Take back the Matriarch, and then I'm going to do what I should have done when I had the chance."

"Athena, we are believers who value all life."

"Evildoers never put restrictions on their behavior. The good always come up with excuses to mask their cowardice and not stop evil from winning. All life isn't of equal value. When we're born? Yes. After that, people become the road they travel on. If those evil people get the presidency, we might as well commit mass-suicide, because they'll kill us and bring the Bloc into war with the world. There will be nothing left of Russia or Europa but a burning continent, because we'd lose. We'll take back the Matriarch alone. You don't have to fight, but stay out of my way or I'll kill you too," Athena says angrily as she stands.

Nightshade Café-Bar
10:33 p.m., 5 July 2096

"Athena, we're always with you, but saying the words and living those words are two different things. Do you really want to do this?" Czarina asks.

Athena enters with Czarina and Titania.

"We're going all the way this time," Athena says.

"Goodness doesn't always win in the end," Titania adds.

"I may not be fully ready now, but I promise you that when that day comes, I will be. Tonight, we do what we can win at."

The nighttime crowd is exclusively made up of Witches, Warlocks, and Hedonists dressed in neon-glow, skin-tight, shiny, spiky, dark colors or bright ones; some are practically naked. The entire establishment is filled with colored drug smoke, which hangs above tables of patrons smoking, drinking, laughing, and talking.

Three Dark Wiccans sit at table laughing hysterically, so loud that they can be heard above anyone else in the room. One of them looks up and sees them.

Athena pulls a chair to the table and sits across from the witch who is obviously the leader from the ornamentation of her clothes. A cat jumps up on the table and instinctively sits closest to Athena, licking her good hand.

"How's your other hand?" The Dark Wiccan laughs.

"We're seizing control of the Matriarch," Athena says.

"Go run away, little Glindas."

"We don't like cat-killing witch-bitches," Athena says.

"I like killing cats and dissecting them and eating their brains. That's what witches do."

"Try it with this one then," Czarina picks up a cat from the ground and throws it at the witch. *Boom!* She is knocked off her feet by the robotic cat exploding.

The two other witches stand and pull knives from their jackets. Titania is already armed and shoots both of them in the chest with a taser gun, each bullet violently shocking them unconscious.

Their witch leader leaps to her feet for the door, but Czarina hits her full-force in the face with a punch. The witch falls to the ground, out cold.

Athena walks to the fallen witch leader and kneels down. "We're going to drain every iota of intelligence from this witch-bitch if we have to find mind-benders to work on her twenty-four hours a day for months on end."

Athena stands and the sisters drag the three unconscious witches out of the establishment. No one in the cafe even cares, and continue to go about their business as if nothing is happening.

Military Offices, The Kremlin
7:35 p.m., 8 July 2096

Mikhail and the officers are gathered again in the meeting room at the conference table.

"Did we get him?" he asks.

"We can't confirm yet, but we have drones scouring the area."

"We have to find that body!"

"We'll find it."

"Do you know why they call him the Leviathan King?" an officer asks.

"All these mobsters like their nicknames, and he got his from his body tattoo of that squid-creature on his back and body."

"He's the winner of the 'Leviathan' ten years in a row."

"The 'Leviathan'?"

"It's an extreme sports competition in Europa. Think the Iron Man Triathlon but it takes place all under water."

"How do you know this?"

"I competed myself a few years back. I came in fifty-second out of over three hundred. I'm considered a weakling even though I can free-dive to sixty-one meters and stay submerged for ten minutes."

Mikhail is nervous. He looks to his other men. "Send more resources into the area."

"What about the Mexican government?"

"Ignore them."

Moscow Sanctuary
7:35 p.m., 8 July 2096

Cats have full run of the grounds—running, hiding, playing, and sleeping.

They are a block away. Athena sits in the front passenger seat of the car, Czarina and Titania in the back; Yana in the driver's seat. A line of vehicles are parked behind them.

9:01 p.m.

Delphine sits at a new triangle-shaped table with Hilda and other sisters in the colored, smoke-filled room.

"They plan to move up the election," Delphine says.

"I just want it over with," says one of the sisters.

"We all do."

A sister bursts into the room. "Mother Sister!"

"What?!"

"They're here!"

"Who?"

"Athena and the others."

"How did they get past security?!"

Several Sanctuary sisters run to the main entrance armed with pistols as the equally armed Europan sisters enter the building.

A witch guard with a rifle appears and moves to the front of the Sanctuary sisters. "What are you Glindas doing? Did you come to see the Matriarch rise to supremacy without you?"

"Don't you know that curiosity killed the cat?" says another witch who appears.

Several other witches appear from around the corner armed with swords and other blade weapons. *Suddenly one is hit by a bottle and she yells out as she is engulfed by flames. Two more witches are hit with Molotov cocktails and burst into flames.*

Yana runs right into the remaining witches, knocking them down. Her face is black and blue and filled with cuts, but she fights as she always does. She picks up the first witch and throws her through the first floor window. The witch is cut everywhere by glass as she crashes to the floor, bloodied. One of the witches tries to cut her with her an axe, but Yana grabs it from her, buries it in the chest of the first witch, pulls it out, and swings at another, hitting her, too, in the chest. Yana attacks the remaining witch women by pummeling them.

Athena has walked past the fighting and further into the Sanctuary. A sister attacks. Athena hits her with the full force of her metallic cast-hand, cutting open the woman's head as she falls to the ground. Athena steps over the body and continues inside.

Czarina, Titania, and dozens of other sisters run in with pistols and rifles. The shooting begins. Athena walks through the gun-battle to the elevator. Bullets fly as she enters. The door closes.

The door opens on the second floor and an axe comes at her. Athena blocks it with her metal-cast hand and karate kicks Hilda in the stomach to the ground. Athena walks to her and raises her metal-hand.

"No!" Hilda pleads.

Athena ignores her and slams it down on her face.

Two sisters appear and shoot at her. Athena ducks and shields her face with her metal-hand. A bullet ricochets off it. Athena lifts her left hand and fires rapidly at them with her pistol. She hears nothing more.

Athena stands and walks to them. They are dead, both killed by headshots. She stares at them, almost sick to her stomach. *The war is real.*

The elevator has returned. Czarina and Titania exit with several women.

Athena yells, "Find Delphine."

The women go from room to room as Athena looks up to the glass dome roof. She runs to the staircase, runs up as fast as she can, then kicks open the door to the roof.

Delphine stands at the ledge of the roof with a contraption on her back.

"So witches can fly," Athena says.

"You've won nothing here."

"We're going to burn this building to the ground and then we'll hunt you down."

"You forget you have Morgana to deal with. I don't think you'll be as successful with them as you've been tonight."

Athena lifts up her metal hand. "But I'm a new woman."

Athena fires with her left hand at Delphine's rocket pack. The Mother Sister launches as she throws something. Athena cannot see what it is, but dives out of its path. The explosion engulfs Athena in flames. She runs, fires again at Delphine, and then all remaining bullets at the glass dome roof before jumping.

The fire will burn her alive! Athena falls through, writhing in fire and pain. She can see the fleeing Mother Sister's rocket pack also engulfed in flames. The wind of the fall helps, but she is still on fire. Suddenly, she reaches the saving embrace of water as Athena crashes four-stories into the basement level pool.

Athena climbs out of the water to lie on the ground next to the pool. She lies there awhile with her eyes closed. *I thought I was afraid of heights.* Sisters arrive and run to her, including Yana.

"Are you okay, Athena?" Yana says, leaning down.

"I'm okay."

"Athena, I have good news and bad news."

"Please no games. Good news."

"Good news is the Sanctuary is ours and that was an amazing free-fall into the pool here to simply put out a fire."

"That's good news."

"Turn your face to me. Bad news is, I'm going to have to knock you unconscious to prevent you from going into shock because of what you're about to see."

Athena sits up. Her severed hand in the metal cast is hanging off the stump of her arm, gobs of blood dripping. She starts to scream—Yana punches her in the face.

Demons and Brothers

"I'm back!" — Wisp the demon

Election Day, Moscow, Russia
7:00 a.m., 15 July 2096

The streets of Moscow, like the rest of Russia and Europa, are filled with voters.

"Here you are," the sex worker says as she hands out a small gold disk. "Free redeemable credit for voting for Igor Aleyev for President and one whole credit for every friend you get to vote for him."

The sex workers, of all genders, are dressed in skimpy psychedelic outfits. They all wear digital billboard hats that flash VOTE FOR IGOR as they walk the streets with tablets, stopping people everywhere.

Presidential Offices, The Kremlin
7:00 p.m., 15 July 2096

Orlok sits in his chair like a human mannequin. Civilians, agents, and soldiers surround him. No one speaks.

A man enters the dimly lit room.

"Sir, I…we've confirmed it over and over and…the mobster has won the election."

"How could he win when we control it?" an officer asks.

"We must not have had as much control as we thought," an officer says.

"He's a better cheater than us," says another.

Orlok says, "The mobster is dead so I will still be president."

"Sir," the man starts. He is so nervous that his body is trembling. "Igor Aleyev walked onto the field at Luzhniki Stadium in the middle of a football match. Authorities tried to arrest him but the crowds…There was a riot and police were attacked by the crowds. They formed a million-plus human shield around him and he's walking by foot to the Kremlin."

Orlok stares out into space. "Let us see if he makes it past his swearing-in ceremony."

"Mr. Orlok," a soldier says. "It's over. We lost. He's the president now and that means everyone in this room is sworn to protect him. If he's impeached that's one thing, but if and until that happens, nothing is to happen to him. It's over."

Orlok smiles. "Yes, we must be loyal to the office of the presidency."

Secure Hotel Room, Moscow
7:00 a.m. 16 July 2096

The room is spacious but has been turned into a vault with reinforced-steel moveable walls, additional sensors, and large three-legged robots to block all the windows.

Igor sits at the desk reviewing the numbers on his tablet. A dozen fully armed men stand in front of him.

"Three hundred billion rubles, boss," the henchman says. "They're going to call it the 'Igor Baby-Boom' because so many babies are going to be conceived today. Every one of our sex workers will be on vertical duty."

The men are laughing, but Igor's mind is elsewhere.

"Good," he says. "Start thanking the families. Since I don't want to have to owe anyone anything, tell them that all profits from the workers will be split amongst them alone. I will not take a cut."

The men look at each other.

"Igor, if you don't take a cut, they'll be suspicious. No one walks away from this kind of money."

"Tell them that's how it is. Tell them I'm out of the crime business for good because I'll be too busy trying to stay alive. Tell them I expect them to understand because we are people who understand the constant threat of assassination. I'm the President, not a mobster anymore."

"We'll take care of it, Igor."

"When will the KGB meet with me?"

"They said after you're sworn in."

"I don't like how that sounds."

"None of us do."

"Who's outside waiting to see me?"

"Two Americans."

"Why am I meeting with them?"

"They paid to meet with you. A *lot* of money, boss."

7:45 a.m.

Mrs. Lucifer sits in the chair in a one-piece black dress and red pearls around her neck. "Mr. President-elect, it is our pleasure to meet you."

Igor sits quietly. Three of his security men stand against the walls, but the couple doesn't care.

"Why would American royalty in politics, responsible for the election of your last, what, six or seven presidents, be interested in a Russian president-to-be?"

"Thank you for that, but those political accomplishments go to our late son. Mr. Aleyev, we all live on the same planet."

"Please have your husband sit down. He's making me nervous."

Mr. Lucifer stands off to the side in his black suit and red tie.

"Oh don't mind him. He doesn't talk and he doesn't sit. Everything below the waist is mechanical. Isn't that right, precious?"

"Why do want to see me? Are you now looking for foreign elections to get involved in?"

"Let's just say that we are not the cheerleaders we once were for the American presidency."

"That's very intriguing. Our countries have such a rich, long history of spy and counter-spy."

"Nothing all that exciting, Mr. Aleyev, just simple revenge. What if I was to tell you that there is a plot to replace certain world leaders with doppelgangers? Not in the mythological or bad sci-fi movie sense, but some kind of scientist, ultra-secret thingy."

"Mrs. Lucifer, I would say you're watching too many of those bad movies."

"Mr. Aleyev, my husband and I have been on this Earth for almost a century, and we've seen all kinds of things that people told us were impossible to ever exist, but there they were."

"What are we talking about here, Mrs. Lucifer?"

"When they first made movies they had so many limitations."

"I don't watch any movies made before 2025," Igor says. "Don't like black-and-white movies. If you wait long enough, every movie will get remade."

Mrs. Lucifer continues, "But then came CGI and the start of the Tek-Age, but they didn't call it that back then. They could make *anything* they could imagine and put it on the screen. I wondered how long it would take for everything else to catch up."

Igor says nothing.

"Mr. Aleyev, if you want to see a real-life doppelganger, invite the Canadian and Brazilian Presidents for a visit. Or you can just walk into a room with that Orlok person of yours."

Igor pretends not to be interested. "How does telling me any of this fit in with your revenge plot against your president?"

"I'm getting to that, sir."

"Thank you for visiting, Mrs. Lucifer."

She smiles and turns her head slightly. "Precious, the president is kicking us out." She stands. "We both know more than we're saying. In any good relationship, you always have to leave something back. But you can always to do little favors for one another."

"Mobsters are not known for liking games."

"We're looking for a new place to live, Mr. Aleyev—new identities, new bank accounts, new home, everything. America is not so nice for us anymore."

"And why would I do this for you?"

"When you're as bored and wealthy as my husband and I have been for so many decades, you are in a constant search for the unusual and weird. My husband and I were Satanists in our youth. We should have been tickled red to see one of 'them' up close, but somehow it was not so funny when it bit off my husband's lower torso." She smiles. "Be careful, Leviathan King. You're not really in the control you think you are."

"I've been a mobster for decades. I know that."

"They'll be coming for you."

"I'm about to be sworn in as president. Of course they're coming for me." Igor stands. "I'm sorry, but I won't be able to grant you any favors."

"Call us when you change your mind. We are quite knowledgeable of secret things."

"Don't expect my call.'"

"My husband and I are optimists. We'll wait anyway."

"I could just have you deported. Foreigners are not too popular these days in Russia."

"We're not foreigners, Mr. Aleyev, which Russians do hate. We're tourists, which Russians love." She turns away. "Come on husband, time to go. He'll call us if he survives."

An aide opens the door and leads the Lucifers out.

Igor looks at his guards.

"If I had known what those two crazy Americans were going to say, I would have had you wait outside."

Ukraine Hospital
6:31 a.m. 9 July 2096

Athena lies in the bio-bed drifting in and out of consciousness. Her entire right arm is now encased in a mechanical cast covered with indicators.

Her eyes catch a flashing cartoon face in the distance. She stares at it for a long while, then she stops breathing.

Johnny Satan sits in the chair against the wall at the foot of the bed. The flashing face of a little devil on the center of his shirt goes dark. He jumps up and she can no longer see him.

"How are you, Athena?" She hears the voice, but doesn't see him, still too groggy to move her head.

Something round drops on her stomach area.

"I heard you and your friends visited the Sanctuary last night. You were all quite violent. Nothing like what I would have done, but marginally adequate for a bunch of Glindas. Now we have to find a new building. You seem to like playing with fire. That incendiary device on your belly can turn you into a crispy meat jerky in a matter of minutes."

Athena jerks her body to flip the disk onto the floor. She clenches her teeth, wanting to scream.

"Do you know what we're going to do to you?"

Athena snaps at him. "This will end! Pick the place! We're going to end this! Pick the place for the showdown, and I'll be there with a surprise."

"Surprise? What surprise could keep us from killing you? You can't even walk or function anymore. And you keep breaking off that right hand," he snickers.

"Are you scared? Scared I may defeat you in the end?"

"Is this another sophomoric Jedi mind trick to get me to do what you want? If you run, I'll just start with the others."

"Pick the place!"

"You pick."

"Dark Side of the Moon."

"How do you know about there? No Glinda would set foot in such a place. She might not come out with her chastity belt intact." He laughs. "I'll see you there at midnight tonight—a nice get-together for us during the witching hour. It should be a lovely full moon, or we can pretend it is, even if it's not."

Johnny's face comes into her view. He stares into her eyes.

"Be there Athena, or I'll visit your friends. I already have Yana. She's a feisty one."

"What?"

"She'll be in my trunk when I arrive. But when you show up and defeat us, then you'll get her out or, as I suspect, you'll join her."

The warlock skips out of the room.

6:38 a.m.

The sisters are in a panic.

"How did he get through security?" Titania yells. "How did he get by all of us?"

Czarina paces back and forth furiously.

Three sisters exit the elevator and run into the room.

"He's right," one of the sisters says. "Yana is gone. She's disappeared. No one saw anything."

"Yana can beat up any man, even that puny warlock."

Czarina stops her pacing and takes the pistol from her jacket. "Well I'm not waiting here."

"No, Zee!" Athena yells. "Look at me, look at me! Promise me that you will not go after him."

"I can't make that promise."

"Zee, promise me. I will have it handled."

"How are you going to do that?" asks one of the Europan sisters. "Look at you."

"Just put me in the wheelchair."

"And then what?"

"I'll handle it. It ends. If someone were to ask how we got here, I couldn't even tell them. But I will be able to tell them how we ended it."

"Athena, you don't have to do anything. We're sisters. We help ourselves," Czarina says. "We'll finish this."

"No, it must be me. I could have ended it with Morgana when I had the chance. I could have stopped it all before it ever started, but I won't repeat the mistake. We know how dangerous and evil they are. I must end it for good."

"I can get all our sisters together, fully armed," says an Europan sister.

"You are not listening!" Athena writhes around in her bed and then attempts to get up.

"Athena!" Everyone grabs her.

"Athena, you have to stay calm," Titania says. "You can't agitate your hand. Remember what the doctor said. If you damage it again, they may have to amputate your whole right arm."

"You all have to listen to me! They want you to do what you're planning. They're counting on it. They took Yana because she's the strongest one of us. That evil warlock walked right into my room, sat at the foot of my bed. We can't defeat them. They know us too well, all about us, everything. Delphine and the others was one thing, but them. They're pure evil. We've never fought pure evil before. We don't even know what to do and they know that."

"Then what are you going to do?" Czarina asks.

"I'm going to get help, something that can defeat pure evil."

"What would that be?" Titania asks.

"Greater evil."

The Sisters can't believe what she's saying.

"We've known you a long time, A. You don't know anyone like that, and you don't know anyone who knows someone like that," Czarina says.

"Igor Aleyev is my father."

Unknown Location
1:30 p.m. 9 July 2096

There was a time when a wheelchair was simply a chair with wheels. Today they can walk, climb stairs and, for those with money, come in hover-mode versions. Athena sits in her hover-chair, now resting on the floor, her entire right arm encased in a metallic cast. She manually dials the number for the vid-phone call. In this part of town, no one uses voice command for fear of drone surveillance. It connects after a few rings.

Igor Aleyev sits in his chair with a smirk.

The two of them just stare at each other for a moment.

"I didn't know the President of all Russia and Europa answers his own calls. Is it a new 'save the taxpayers money' directive?"

Igor doesn't respond to her.

"How's the female sex-slave business?" she asks.

"I'm a businessman. That's all I've been all my life."

"You must be so proud getting women to degrade themselves for men."

"No one forces anyone to do anything in my business, and anyone can leave at any time. And it's all genders, not just female. When will you moralists realize that if no one wants something, then it will simply go away? But it isn't going away. It's always growing. It even has a name. Free-market economics."

"When will you amoral degenerates realize that a person that's sexually and psychologically abused doesn't have the ability to make those kinds of decisions for themselves?"

"Yes, you religious moralists would make the decisions for them. I can see everyone fighting to line up on your side of the futile argument. How's the witch thing working out for you?"

"I'm not a witch."

"Please, I don't want another history lesson. How's the wiccan thing working out for you?"

Athena stops. She closes her eyes and counts to ten. She opens her eyes and gives a deep sigh.

"Does that yoga meditation thing you wiccans do really work?"

"It does."

"I'll stick to my blue vodka."

"I'm calling in my blood favor."

Igor smiles. "I thought your religion doesn't take anything from men. I thought, you especially, what did you tell me? You'd rather be tortured and dead than take anything from me."

"I want that number."

"What?"

"I want the number now and then we are even for the rest of our lives. You will never hear from me again, which is what you've always wanted."

"I don't know what you're talking about."

"I'm not leaving until you give me the number. I saved your evil life and you owe me. I'm here to collect!"

"The only thing you did was make a vid-call to my people."

"I called your people and if I didn't, you wouldn't be alive today. The great mob boss that people fear, lying on the floor helpless, like an infant, dying from a heart attack. My vid-call allowed your people to get you to the hospital, get you a synthetic heart, and allowed you to go on living your degenerate life."

"How long ago was that? You were a child."

"That's the code with you criminals, and it applies to everyone and there is no time limit. It's for life. Give me the number."

"No."

"Give me the number."

"No."

"Then I'll call every mobster in Europa. Someone else has to know what you know."

"You will not do that!"

Athena can hear a door bursting open on the other end.

"Get out of here!" Igor yells at someone off-screen.

"If you don't give me the number, I'm dead."

"I give you the number you're dead."

"Why do you care? This is the only solution for me."

"Whatever you think you know, you don't."

"I know more about your exploits than you think."

"What, hacking into my systems as a little girl? Go and don't call me again."

"Okay, I'll start dialing the others."

Igor is angry. "What do you hope to accomplish?"

"The only thing that can kill evil is greater evil. Isn't that what you told me as a child? Isn't that how you *acquired* your first criminal clan? A man who made even your skin crawl and you're not scared of anything."

"I thought you moralists say the only thing that can kill evil is greater good."

"Greater good is not available to me now, so this is my only solution."

Igor shakes his head. "What trouble could my good-witch offspring possibly get into? What enemies could you possibly make that would lead you to this?"

"Have your men look up the names Morgana and Johnny Satan."

Comrade Café, Ukraine
2:30 p.m., 9 July 2096

Athena sits in her chair, motionless. Outside the café, a man sitting on a bench watches her closely. Another man walks through the door. He approaches her slowly and takes one knee in front of her.

"At least the Russian Orthodox is a legitimate form of nonsense, a real religion, part of a real history, Russia's history. He says: here's your number. Do you know what this really means?"

"Yes, I do. End of discussion."

"He says: the money is already in your account. He says: he's sure he's going to regret this for many years to come, but at least he won't owe a witch a damn thing anymore. It's worth it just for that."

"Tell him, then this is, as they say, it."

"Yes. He says, the end and for you in more ways than just one. Bye, witch."

The man stands and leaves.

She wonders if her father is watching her, maybe through the glasses of the man on the bench. He can't meet her in person, but talks through one of his henchmen via ear-set. He wanted to be President, but can't even go out in public.

Athena holds the paper card he left on the table in her hand. No one uses paper anymore.

2:41 p.m.

The number rings and then connects. Athena waits for someone to answer but no one does.

"Hello," Athena says.

"Name?"

"Athena Asgard."

"Target?"

"Johnny Satan, Morgana…"

"Only one name."

Athena hesitates. "Why can't it be more?"

"One name."

Athena is frustrated. "Johnny Satan."

"Who gave you this number?"

"He called himself Dmitry."

The line disconnects.

"What!" Athena panics. She dials. It connects.

"You lie this time and the number will be permanently disconnected."

"Who gave you this number?"

She hesitates. "Igor Aleyev."

"Do you know the terms of this contract?"

"Yes."

"Invoice sent. Payment must be made in thirty minutes. Mercy on your soul."

The line disconnects.

Hotel Room, Moscow
7:07 p.m., 18 July 2096

Igor lies in bed staring up at the ceiling. He won the election but the danger is far from over. He's president and will have no life for the next six or twelve years—meetings, briefings, ceremonies, press conferences, events, over and over. It is the price of power. If he does what President T. Wilson did in America by rescinding presidential term limits, he could be president for life, too.

"President-elect!" His guards enter his bedroom.

Igor sits up in his bed with a tek-gun in his right hand.

A tall man comes in behind the guards.

"President-elect, I'm a truly sorry for this intrusion. I am Mr. Yanov with the KGB."

Igor is surprised. The KGB only meets with a new president after they are sworn in.

"I am here to inform you that the swearing-in ceremony will be tomorrow morning instead."

"Why? Why is it being moved up?"

"Sir, there is a confirmed, credible assassination threat against you. We must get you sworn in immediately."

The Mad Pope

"Don't discount the 'gossip network' of nuns. You hear things. Nothing you can put your finger on, but the whispers and rumors are based on something tangible. Something is not right there in Russia and everyone knows it." — Sister Maria, the New Catholic Order, Mexico

The Church of the Roman Empire—the East Orthodox Church and Catholic Church of the West—formally split in 1054. When Western Europe fell to Islam in 2065, practically overnight the new Supreme Islamic Caliphate became a world superpower, and the Orthodox lost two-thirds of its followers. The Russian Orthodox Church stepped up to be the leadership of all Eastern Orthodox Christians worldwide, which meant only the Eastern Europe that merged with Russia.

Seraphim I, the Pope Patriarch of Moscow and all Russia, is a major leader in Russian Bloc politics. So much so that he spends most of his time these days politicking rather than any religious duties. However, he is revered by the nation's Orthodox Christian followers as its religious leader, including a small community of Jews who live with the Orthodox for safety reasons.

The Secret "Behemoth" Complex
7:03 a.m., 19 July 2096

Today is a special day for the Orthodox. For decades, it's been the ceremony for the Pope Patriarch to stand at the side of newly elected Russian Presidents as they are sworn in. Though an atheistic nation, the Orthodox are viewed as part of the intrinsic historical heritage of Mother Russia. No other religion can make such a boast.

The official residence of the Pope Patriarch and the headquarters of the Russian Orthodox Church is still Moscow's Danilov Monastery. However, for the last couple of decades they have been building a massive city for its five hundred thousand Orthodox, including the fifty thousand Jews who live with them. The "city" is actually level after level of underground large apartment-style complexes for families and smaller ones for individuals. They call it Behemoth.

All the hallways are bustling with activity, preparing for the day's ceremonies or simply going about the normal daily duties of life. The Pope Patriarch's personal secretary, Father Vladimir, briskly walks through the hall and glances at his wristwatch.

"Father."

He stops to see one of the nuns walking to him. All Orthodox nuns wear black habits, the long, ankle-length dress with close-fitting hood. "Yes, Sister Nika."

"Are you not accompanying His Holiness today?"

"He had us remain here."

"And go to the Presidential Ceremony alone?"

"Yes."

She gives him a confused look but continues. "Father, I'd like to bring my concerns directly to the council's attention."

"Sister, I've told you before that I will do so, but after the new president is sworn in. Obviously, you can understand why I've waited with the crisis and turmoil in the country."

"Oh course, Father, but the sisters and I have been trying to bring these issues to the council's attention for at least a year now."

"Please be patient, sister."

"Yes."

"I do have to go to a meeting."

"Father, if one of the priests had brought this up instead of one of the nuns or maids, would he still have been waiting for almost a year?"

"Sister, I'm going to ignore what you're insinuating. And the answer is yes. As the priest of the floor, I can promise you that I take the concerns of any person very seriously. God does not care about your gender or nationality, and neither do I. We are all equals. It would be the same as if I heard these things from one of the other floor priests."

"I'm sorry, Father."

"Sister Nika, all there is, is unsubstantiated suspicion. We need more. He is our High Holy Pope Patriarch. I am protecting your reputation as well as mine."

"Yes, you're right. I'm sorry."

7:14 a.m.

He runs to the conference room and slowly opens the door to enter.

"Father Vladimir, you're late."

"I'm sorry. I was delayed."

He sits down at the oval table where several other priests and bishops are already seated.

"It actually had to do with this meeting."

"Yes. Go on," says a bishop.

"The suspicions are growing. We can't hide it from the general community much longer."

"We're going to have to. The Complex becomes fully functional by year's end. His Holiness will be living here permanently then."

"What is it that we really have?" asks another priest. "Just stories. After three years of watching him, all we have are stories. I feel like Judas."

"The High Holiness is revered by the people, but he's not Jesus. He's every bit flesh and blood as are we."

"He believes he's Jesus," the secretary-priest says. He pauses knowing he should not have said what he did—such a provocative statement. The priests and bishops all look at him.

"You're not serious?" one of them asks.

"I heard him once say that he was the…true Messiah."

Another priest says, "I heard it myself too, one of the workers was with me. His Holiness was…talking to himself, looking in the mirror."

"He was teasing you, both of you. He knew you were there," defends one of the priests.

"I don't believe so."

"When was this?"

"Last year."

"Why didn't you tell us?"

"We already have claims of him talking to himself, having whole conversations with himself."

"And this supposed crystal ball that so far only one person has seen," adds a bishop.

"Yes, the maid."

"Yes, but no one else has seen the same thing."

The secretary continues, "Gentleman, why are we having this meeting now? Nothing has changed. We have no concrete proof. Has he harmed anyone? Is he not performing his duties with dignity and efficiency? Not at all. Why this meeting?"

One of the bishops leans forward. "There is a possibility—please, do not tell anyone what I'm about to say, not your mother, your wife, sibling, a counselor, no one, because we don't have a shred of proof—the Resistance has been trying to contact us."

"The Christians and Jews in America?"

"And in Africa," the bishop adds.

"Contact us how?"

"Danilov and even at Saint Basilica."

"There are some of us, bishop, who feel that maybe this is divine providence, that we've been separated from them for so long. We have a unique position here in Russia, unlike the rest of the world. It's Russia that is the nation of religious tolerance, not America. We're allowed to live and participate in public life unmolested. The ones in Africa are fighting the Muslims. The ones in America are fighting for survival."

"The bishop's views represent only a small minority of us," the other bishop says. "We should be part of the greater Faither community. Why shouldn't we? I hear they have even formed a unified alliance together."

"Yes, the Continuum is what they call it," the secretary says.

"We've been told that the American government has blocked all their attempts to contact us all these past decades."

"One of their representatives says that's a lie," the bishop says. "That representative told me personally that the Resistance has been smuggling Christians and Jews, sex slaves and political refugees out of the Russian Bloc for the last five years."

"They have people in-country?" The other bishop is as surprised as all the other men at the table.

"Yes, five years."

"Who did they say they talked to then, if they tried to contact us?"

"His Holiness himself."

"That's impossible."

"You believe him, a stranger? I don't care if he's a believer like us. That's taking the word of a stranger over our own religious leader, a man you've known for the last forty-five years of your life?"

"I have to be truthful. I believe the stranger."

St. Basil's Cathedral, Moscow
8:02 a.m., 19 July 2096

In Russian architecture, there is nothing similar. St. Basil's Cathedral was built to symbolize a fire rising into the sky. The vivid colors and its unusual layout—a cluster of small and larger pointed domes—make it stand out from any other building in Red Square.

The Presidential Swearing-In Ceremony will begin within the hour. The Cathedral, also known as the Cathedral of the Protection of Most Holy, was commissioned to be built in the middle sixteenth century by Ivan the Terrible. It is the geometric center of Moscow, which is why it has served as the place for important political events for decades.

The Pope Patriarch of Moscow and all of Russia stands in his ceremonial white dress. His aides, three bishops, stand on each side of him. The entourage of the new president appears through the waiting crowd. President Igor is dressed in a white suit that almost matches the Pope Patriarch's attire.

"Pope," Igor says as he walks to him.

"Your Holiness," one of his staffer corrects.

"Sorry, I'm still getting used to these formalities, but I'm not a believer so to use that word would be insincere, and in my mind, disrespectful. However, I do respect the Orthodox as the original theological ideology of Russia and I respect its leader. I know that no matter how nonreligious we naturally become, Russia will always be an Eastern Orthodox country."

"Thank you for that, Mr. President," the Pope Patriarch says. "Before we start, the Church has a gift for you."

President Igor is intrigued. "A gift? That's unprecedented, isn't it?"

The Pope Patriarch holds up a shiny greenish sphere from his robe. "I am commanded to present this to you."

Igor takes the sphere and examines it.

"Hold it up to the light, Mr. President. You will see it then," the Pope Patriarch tells him.

Igor holds it up in the air to study it with the ceiling lights shining through.

The Pope Patriarch yells out as he plunges a dagger into Igor's chest. Guards are in shock and freeze as Igor stumbles back. The Pope Patriarch grabs the bishop closest to him and shoves him at the President and his guards.

Igor stands, grabs the knife and slowly pulls it out of his heart— the white chest area of his suit is a spot of blood red and it grows in size. Igor presses the spot with his left hand as he grabs the gun from one of his guards and runs after the man.

The Pope Patriarch is already at the end of the banquet room and disappears onto the balcony patio. Igor gets there, but the Pope Patriarch is gone. *Did the man jump to his death?* Igor looks over the balcony to the ground and at all the near-by buildings. He notices a moving blur from the corner of his eye. He looks up the Savior Tower to see the Pope Patriarch in the distance, scurrying up side of the building like a squirrel. The man climbs over and is gone. Igor continues to stare.

"Sir, we must get you to the hospital."

Igor angrily looks at the guard, then to the army of guards now on the balcony with him, and then looks out across the sky to see the arriving saucer drones.

Almost killed. Assassin escapes. Now the cavalry is here.

The Secret "Behemoth" Complex
8:33 a.m., 19 July 2096

The Pope Patriarch exits the underground elevator.

"Holiness, you're back so soon?" the secretary-priest says, waiting with staff.

The Pope Patriarch ignores him as he walks past. "I have failed in my mission. Our enemies will seek to engulf us. This day was foretold. The Leviathan will rise and try to devour the Behemoth."

"Holiness, what are talking about?"

The Pope Patriarch has the look of a wild animal in his eyes. "Istanbul, Antioch, Alexandria, Jewish Israel, Rome. They have arrived in Russia! Orlok would have turned over the presidency to me! He failed and self-terminated. They come to engulf us all, and I failed God's mission."

"Holiness, what is wrong? You're scaring us."

The Pope Patriarch pushes him away and runs. The priest runs after him with the other staff following.

Their leader runs up a spiral staircase and onto the upper level of his apartment where his bedchambers are. He runs to the large dresser and the secret compartment opens automatically for him. He lifts another crystal ball in the air.

"God! I have failed! We must be punished to atone for that failure! It was no coincidence that a man called Leviathan arrives just at the ascendancy of Behemoth! Leviathan is the Antichrist! We must escape in Behemoth to receive punishment!"

The bedchambers are filled with other people, both men and women, frightened at the ramblings of their leader.

"Holiness, what are you saying?" the secretary asks.

"Silence!"

The priest looks at everyone. They have no idea what to do either.

"We must all go down in Behemoth to hell, the only place the Leviathan cannot get us!"

The secretary-priest yells. "Your Holiness, what are you saying?!"

The man steps forward with an expression of hate. "I am not Your Holiness! I am the Messiah!" He looks up and yells, "Activate!!"

The floor starts to shake. People look all around, panicking.

"What are you doing!" the secretary-priest shouts.

"We must go to hell for punishment and sanctuary!"

People start running.

"No one will escape!"

"Computer, deactivate!" the secretary yells. "Deactivate!"

"Invalid user," the computer says. "Invalid user."

Everyone gasps as they feel the entire structure start to fall.

People run and realize in horror what is happening. Their entire underground city is sinking downward! People scream.

A woman runs into the room. "Father, it's me! Please do not do this! It's your daughter, Father! Your family is here!"

The Pope Patriarch stares at her wildly with the crystal ball held up high. "Liars! Imposters! I know you are all plotting against me! I will not let you crucify me again, Roman whores and bastards! Your Messiah is all-powerful! None of you can stop our fall and ascendance in hell!"

The city falls.

The Blackest Dark

"It may be necessary temporarily to accept a lesser evil, but one must never label a necessary evil as good." — Margaret Mead, 20th century cultural anthropologist and author

Restricted Area, The Kremlin
5:30 a.m., 20 July 2096

The hallway is very badly lit. A lone Igor walks to an elevator. The door opens and he enters without turning around. The door closes and it descends.

6:37 a.m.

An army of federal agents congregate in front of the elevator. The chief agent is angry.

"At 5:30 hours the President entered and descended to the presidential bunker. At 5:41 hours he reset all control passwords and disabled all overrides."

"How did the President get out of the hospital without his security detail?"

"Sir, he ordered us to remain behind," an agent answers.

"The President cannot give that order."

"We followed his orders, sir."

"We need to get down there and secure the president."

"It's thirty stories down, sir, a completely self-sufficient, underground complex."

"Get him on the line."

"I'm here." Igor's voice booms throughout the hallway, startling everyone.

One of the agents whispers to the chief agent. "Embedded audio systems in the walls and ceiling."

"Mr. President," the chief agent says. "What are you doing? You abandoned your security detail. You are prohibited by law from doing that. These are laws that even you must follow as president. When are you coming back to the surface, sir?"

"I'm going to remain down here for a while by myself. I feel safer this way."

"Mr. President, either you have to come back up or allow us to send your detail down."

"I prefer this way best."

"Mr. President, your security detail must stay with you at all times."

"Security? That is an interesting concept in Russia these days. It's former President dead. It's former Prime Minister dead. No one can say who, why, or how. The KGB burst into my room, told me of an assassination plot against me, and replaced my entire personal security with their handpicked agents. The next day, the Pope Patriarch walks up to me and stabs me in the chest with a metal blade—a blade that even the most basic of scanning tek would have detected. The man runs away with my entire security detail standing there, not even one shot fired at him. I run after him myself, and find the man way across on the Tower, climbing up a building like a human spider. A man, I was always told, who was practically a cripple. No one can tell me where he is? Or where any of his followers are? His entourage of bishops fake, a group of actors he hired as stand-ins the day before, yet they got past security."

"Mr. President, you have every reason to be outraged. I have personally taken charge and every one of the men on your security detail has been relieved of duty. They've already been shipped off to Siberia. Everything else is under investigation, but I promise you, you will have answers."

"Thank you, but I'll stay down here until then."

"Mr. President, we have to transfer all missile codes to you immediately."

"It's okay. You hold on to them. If the Muslims or CHINs invade the country I'm confident you know what to do."

"Sir, that is your presidential responsibility. No one can make such decisions other than you."

"Hold on to it for me. I'll come up when I'm needed."

"Mr. President, you have briefings to attend. The KGB also demands to speak with you—matters of national security. Many people have to speak with you."

"Just tell me when the KGB arrives."

"We are here now, Mr. President." A man in black walks through the crowd with five other men. Except for him, all of them carry tablet cases. "My name is Meier, Mr. President. My predecessor was demoted over his bungling of the assassination attempt. We must speak with you urgently—and confidentially."

The elevator door opens. "Come down."

The KGB men enter the elevator and it closes. Everyone else looks around, wondering what to do. The chief agent gestures for his men to follow him outside the main chamber. "How long can he stay down there?"

"Sir, there are listening nodes everywhere in this building. The

President can hear anything we say anywhere in the building. He can hear us now."

"I know that. What's the answer to my question?"

"The bunker was designed to withstand any kind of external earth-penetrating weapon and internally the place is a self-contained ecosystem. It has the latest replicator systems."

"Replicator? We really can do that? Materialize food and things?"

The agent stares at him. "Sir, a replicator is a robot. The bunker has its own animal farms, fish farms, and fruit-vegetable farms. The replicators manage the farms, pick the produce, butcher the animals, and cook the food. He can stay down there for…forever."

"Water?"

"Secret access to the city's water supply."

Inside the elevator, the KGB men stand quietly. It stops suddenly.

"Mr. President, the elevator has stopped," the KGB man says.

"I stopped it," Igor's voice says. "We can have your briefing this way."

"Sir, I understand, truly I do, your paranoia. You must, however, trust your people."

"I don't. What is your briefing, Meier?"

"Mr. President, my superiors will be very angry with us if we don't resolve this situation and return the country to normalcy. You must at least make public appearances throughout the nation to assure the people you are alive and well and in control."

"Yes, more opportunities for assassination."

"Sir, no one will assassinate you. We will ensure that."

"Your assurances don't carry much weight with me when I have to pull knives out of my own chest and chase down would-be assassins by myself as my predecessors lie in coffins. Coffins, I learned, that were seized by none other than you, the KGB."

The KGB man is very frustrated. "We took control of the bodies for a full autopsy by trusted doctors. Sir, there is nothing for me to say. Everyone—sworn to protect you, has botched this. The conduct has been appalling. There is nothing for me to defend. Tell me what you want us to do? At some point you will need to trust us. Ultimately, we are here to defend our nation with our lives, and that means defending you with our lives."

"Who are the people with you, Meier? I'm trying to run their profiles through Argus and they all have security clearances higher than yours, and their files are restricted. I thought as president I could access any and all files."

"No, you can't sir," says another KGB man. "KGB files are not enabled to be Net-accessed by anyone. But I'd be happy to personally take you to the data bank though, Mr. President. I am Zukov, the director of the KGB."

"Always the games."

The elevator reverses, moving back up.

"Sir, we must talk personally."

"I need to think for a moment."

"Mr. President this is the presidential doctor next to me. Doctor, tell him."

The elevator stops.

The doctor looks at the vid-cam. "Mr. President, you do remember who I am? We met before. I'm not part of the KGB, but the Kremlin Medical Corps. You know I was also Erik's friend, longtime friend, before he was ever in government."

"I remember you."

"Erik—I mean, the President just died. That's it."

"He just spontaneously died?"

"Yes, he had a seizure from an aneurism and died. It looked like he was choking on food but it was the seizure."

"The Russian Bloc is melting down before our eyes and you're saying it just happened. No one believes that."

"I can't help the imagination of people. One man shot America's Kennedy but most people believe it was some kind of grand conspiracy. I can't help if people want to believe fantasy rather than boring or grossly unfair, random reality. People look up at the sky and see all kinds of things in the clouds. Sometimes a cloud is just a cloud and not two rabbits screwing in a field."

"People don't just die of aneurysms and heart attacks anymore."

"Says who, sir? Why? Because we're living in the 'future'? Mr. President, people die of heart attacks all the time. Ninety-nine percent of the people on the planet, with the notable exception of Japan, have their own natural organs and those organs can fail. Yes, after they get new ones, either cybernetic or bio-replacements, they will certainly outlast the person, but again that is after they fail or are failing. As for the brain, we might as well be back in the stone ages. We can't grow them yet or repair them fully and any kind of brain-machine connectivity is, at best, rudimentary. If the brain fails, there is nothing we can do to stop it. Erik just died."

"No one believes you, doctor. I don't."

"I didn't say that after the death all kinds of people conspired in all kinds of plots. That is obviously true. The Prime Minister was murdered. That is for sure. The evidence is being gathered against the culprits. Mr. President, I'm telling you the truth."

"Mr. President, it is imperative we talk now," Zukov says. "You must take charge. Do you know that the Parliament is closed, both houses? They are leaving or refusing to come into to work. People are in the streets. Irresponsible media says you were killed or you're in a coma, despite our press conferences. People need to see you. The very state of the Russia Bloc, running the country, is at risk, sir. We must talk now, sir."

The elevator begins moving upwards again.

"Mr. President, Mr. Orlok was also found dead today," Meier says. "That's what touched off the panic."

The elevator stops again.

"And you want me to leave the bunker? You can't protect anyone!"

The Dark Side of the Moon, Moscow
12 midnight, 10 July 2096

The crowd of people gathered outside its doors is smoking much more powerful drugs than inside. Other than Witches and Warlocks, there are Anarchists, Nihilists and Dark Druids. Whether religionists or not, outside or inside the club, they are all part of the criminal world. They are dangerous and on every government watch list there is. But so is half the Moscow population.

Athena sits in her hover-chair in the corner of the open second floor of the social club and bar. Her heart is racing. She has never known so much fear.

Outside the building, Morgana waits, casually watching the people in the streets. She's dressed head to toe in black, with a large pentagram around her neck. In her ear-set, she hears the voices of her fellow witches stationed on every corner, every block, spiraling out from the center of the club. She glances at the trunk of Johnny Satan's red limo parked at the curb and starts to laugh.

She starts to hear the giggling of a little girl and turns. She is surprised to see the seven-foot, snake-like lean figure standing at the other end of the club in the shadows. There is a wide-brimmed floppy hat on its head.

"What are you supposed to be?" Morgana asks. "I have my own natural little girl voice, but let me use yours. It sounds cool. Say something."

"Umm…You do know I'm a demon, right?" Wisp says.

"That voice is great with how you look!" Morgana walks over to it. "You're perfect for our evil darkness and death cult."

The second floor is empty except for Athena. She paid the club owner to "rent" the floor for the night. He could have named any amount and she would have paid it.

"A dead animal for your thoughts." Johnny Satan's smiling face appears from the stairs. "Athena, Athena. You did show after all. When you flew in on your chair—aren't we supposed to fly brooms?—Morgana and I couldn't stop laughing. This Glinda shows up just to prove she's brave, when all it means is she's going to end up in my trunk with the other one."

Johnny jumps from the steps onto the upstairs floor. Athena is so numb with fear that she doesn't flinch.

"Here's Johnny!"

The warlock starts laughing and starts to do a little dance in front of her. He stops and looks her over.

"You're scared alright. How were you planning to defeat me? Another Glinda? Sweet as honey, but with superhuman strength? A goodness spell where you give me a soul, and I'm so horrified by all my evil deeds I just kill myself?" He leans over and whispers, "I'm going to rape, torture, then kill you, then do it again. That is your future. I kill one or two people at random a week, just for fun."

She remains quiet, but he notices something in her eyes. She's different. Not from her appearance, but from her eyes—her soul is darker. She's waiting for something.

"Speak, Glinda. You are such a disappointment. I was expecting something unexpected. Not this. You sitting in the corner waiting to die. What a disappointment! But what can one expect from Glindas? You won't even get to see Morgana become the Supreme Empress of Russia, Europa, the Caliphate, and the rest of the world.

Come here, Athena. Let me put you in my trunk."

They hear the first step to the second floor almost break in two, then the splintering of the next step. Johnny stops, looks in the direction of the sound, and then back at her.

"Athena, what did you do?"

Something walks up the stairs. Whatever it is, it weighs so much that each step cracks. A massive figure appears—its barrel-chest is huge, almost five feet across. It wears a long raincoat and a fedora on its relatively small head, compared to the size of its body. Its legs are thick, and its shoes are massive. They cannot see its face.

"Well hello stranger," Johnny says smiling. "Are you Athena's surprise? I'm not impressed by the Halloween getup. You should see what we witches and warlocks wear at our parties. Only the homos can come close to our outrageousness. Hey watch this."

Johnny pulls out a sawed-off shotgun from his jacket and fires point-blank into its chest.

The thing doesn't flinch. Johnny doesn't quite know how to react. It walks to him and grabs his gun hand with its massive right hand. Athena cringes as she hears bones cracking. Johnny yells out. She never heard someone yell so loud. The thing covers Johnny's face with its massive left hand to silence him.

Athena now realizes why she couldn't see its face. It has none, just shimmering black skin. It opens its mouth, which seems to widen and widen more, a circle of ridged teeth. It slowly lifts Johnny and places his head in its mouth. The Warlock's wide eyes watch in horror. He fights with every ounce of energy he has, kicking wildly with his legs.

Athena turns her head and closes her eyes. His screams are muffled. She hears a snap and the screams stop. Something falls to the ground—she knows it's his body.

She opens her eyes slowly and looks. The thing stands there

watching her. It coughs and something falls from its mouth—a head. It smiles with its ridged teeth.

"What is your name?" Athena asks.

The thing seems caught off guard by her question. It thinks for a moment.

"No stranger has ever asked me that." The voice is a sickening high-pitched, cartoonish one like someone who has sucked in helium. "You are so kind. My name is Lothario."

"Lothario, is this the end of my contract?"

"Brave, too," the demon says. "We almost always have to chase after our clients. But to have one so brave as to wait near the target. Or are you mentally unbalanced? No, Athena Asgard, this is not the end of your contract. The one who hires us must join the victims. Those are the terms."

"But I have a way out, don't I?"

Lothario starts to chuckle.

"That's what I was told. If there is even a chance that I could personally defeat you, then you would give me time to prepare, right? A short time, but time. A final meet, a showdown. I can't run, so why not?"

It continues to chuckle louder. "Who told you that?"

"That's what I was told. Make the offer."

Lothario raises its massive arms and claps. "I'll play. A final showdown. Yes, that would be…wonderful."

The thing turns and starts to walk down the steps, once again splintering each landing.

"How much time do I have, Lothario?"

"I'll ask my brothers, but no more than the end of the July moon. Let's say that."

It chuckles.

Athena waits without moving. She glances quickly at the corpse pieces that used to be the warlock. The thundering sounds of the demon walking down the steps stop and then nothing. The downstairs door closes.

She nods her head and the hover-chair activates. She descends down the steps and immediately is horrified by what she sees—dead bodies everywhere.

How did I not hear this?!

Athena realizes that the bottom of the stairs has a sound-screen blocking all sounds, one side from the other. That's why it was so quiet on the second level. She didn't even think of it.

She starts to cry as she nears the main door and can see them closely. All ages, all genders, everyone dead—crushed, mangled by the demon, but Lothario didn't do this.

I did this. I'm responsible.

She increases gears, flies out the club, and stops. Lying off to the side of the door is Morgana. The Witch leader is drenched in blood and looks like she's—half-eaten! Morgana stares up, her right side is practically gone—right arm, right leg, part of the right side of her face—all gone. They stare at each other. Athena can feel the food she ate from hours before wanting to come up. She drives away.

Athena yells out as she sees more dead innocent people in the streets.

"What did I do?!"

African Collective Keyhole Dispatch / 10 July 2096

Continuum: Confirmed. Demon: Wisp has been sighted in Moscow Russia. Confirmed: Unknown Demon #2 (Code name: Hulk) also sighted. Confirmed: Unknown Demon #3: (Code name: Hydra) also sighted. Forty-five fatalities confirmed; one survivor. Magi are already in-country.

Presidential Bunker, The Kremlin
3:30 a.m., 26 July 2096

Is this how it starts—the madness?

Igor sits in darkness. The main lobby in front of the elevator is completely lit, every second, twenty-four hours a day, no interruption. He sits in the room facing the elevator, never moving from the chair. The large bucket and bottles nearby are his only bathroom.

Every sound he hears sets off an internal panic. *Is someone trying to drill into the bunker?* His heightened awareness makes him watch for even something as small as a bug, even though, unlike the rest of Russia, none could get in here.

They finally relented and told him, "Mr. President, okay, we will pass an order in Parliament to allow you to use your own bodyguards instead of the Federal Police."

Really? They relented. *Now* they will send my own men down. *No!*

He knew the Pope Patriarch since he was a boy. What he saw stabbing him and crawling up the Tower was inhuman. *They must have done something similar to my men.*

Igor grabs his ears and shakes himself.

He used to laugh at religious believers. They always felt they were being watched, that the government was out to get them, and were infiltrating their ranks. It was, of course, true, but he still laughed at them. Now, here he is, sitting in a tomb of his own making.

I leave this bunker and I'm dead.

The phone rings on his presidential tablet.

"Answer." The line connects.

He first hears coughing, then low breathing.

"Who is it?"

"You're dead, Mr. President, like your father."

Igor crushes the tablet by slamming his fist into it. He picks it up and throws it at the wall.

He sits back down and touches all the guns on the side table, dozens of them.

12:02 p.m.

He has finally fallen asleep after so many hours of watching for "them" to come. His head stirs for a moment. His eyes start to open. *What has woken me?*

He hears the noise and sits up straight in his chair. The elevator door opens and a man exits, the KGB Director.

"Lights on," Zukov says.

Igor squints like he is some kind of vampire allergic to daylight. He raises his hand to shield his eyes as they adjust. Zukov stands back and waits. Igor reaches for his table of guns, but stops. His eyes look left at the bucket and dozens of urine-filled bottles. He looks back at Zukov.

"Mr. President, I'm not here to judge you."

Igor seems to shrink in his chair. *You don't have to because I do. I've gone insane.*

"Mr. President, you are not a mobster anymore. You are the President of one of the superpowers of the world. You escaped your enemies many times bent on killing you. You outsmarted them at the ballot box to take the presidency. You survived assassination. However, you seem powerless to defeat your final enemy: your own paranoia. Is this how you want to end your presidency?"

Igor doesn't look at him. He realizes he is also naked except for his soiled boxer briefs. He's ashamed.

"How did you get down here? I changed all the codes."

"Mr. President, we always retain master access. You need to

understand, sir, that it would be a simple matter for them to call a special session in Parliament and have you removed from office due to dereliction of presidential duties."

"Let them try. The people elected me."

"And? If we remove you, what would they do about it? A small fraction would take to the streets? A small fraction would hold protest rallies in Red Square for a day or two? The exalted people that all elected officials worship in public? They may live in a state-of-the-art, living, breathing, shiny tek-city, but they are still no more than sheep…to be managed. They are too busy with their lives for you. They have important things to occupy their time: work, tek toys, drugs, sex, movies, sports, some vacation. Their lists have no room for you. For the hardcore ones, all we have to do is cut off their Net connection, have a drug supply stoppage, close the sex quarters of the city for a short time. They're sheep too, all of them, even the ones with the big mouths who like to talk back to the government.

"Do you know why the KGB was reactivated years ago? We had too many crazy presidents in office. There is no more dangerous a president than a pacifist. We had this president. He and his successor secretly dismantled the nation's entire nuclear defense system. No one thought such a thing was possible, but they did it. There was such a shock that a mere two men could leave a nation-empire of hundreds of millions completely defenseless to the CHINs and the Muslims that we were brought back into existence with a new mandate. Protect the president from our global enemies, but also protect the nation from its presidents, if and when needed. So I will ask you again. Do you want the Parliament to remove you from office? Is that what you want? You need to answer me because I'm trying to help you."

"No."

"Then you need pull yourself together and be our president. This bunker that you have convinced yourself you can be safe in…that only holds if you remain as president. You can be removed."

"I bet none of you wanted me here. I know the entire government is against me."

"Why do you say that? You're the boss of the government now. I voted for you. All the KGB did. The people who count wanted you, not Orlok. However, we all now know that there were, and are, many more actors in this game than just us. We must be unified going forward."

Igor smiles. "So the KGB wanted me to win the election."

"Yes. Have you seen how that man looked on the vid-screen? Orlok. I've never seen a human being so pale. This time, the good guy was the bad guy and the bad guy was the good guy for us."

"Only in Russia."

"Will you pull yourself together?"

"Yes."

"Good. We have the preliminaries out of the way. Now, may I ask what could have possibly possessed you to give your bio-daughter that number?"

Igor looks up, surprised.

"Sixteen days ago over forty people dead in a bar and on the streets of Moscow. The lengths we had to engage in to achieve a complete media blackout."

"How could you possibly know?"

"We tapped your communications, Mr. President. I'm sorry, but what in your mind makes you believe that the duties and responsibilities of the President make you the sole authority? It's like any corporation. The President isn't in charge. The Board of Directors is. And if that President doesn't do what they want or make the company money, they throw him or her out. Is it any different with your mob clans? You sit in the seat as long as, to quote the old phrase, 'keep the trains running on time.' If you can't do that, then you're out. You are the boss, Mr. President, but we Russia have not returned to the monarchy. No kings and queens here. We are part of a club of people who run the country, Mr. President, and we are melded to the interests of this country and will be so, long after you're gone from the seat.

"Mr. President, why did you give that civilian that number?"

"How long have you known about them?"

"Since '65. One of them attacked in a northern Mexican city. Their government did an impressive job of spreading misinformation, but we have agents in their inner circle, like I'm sure every other nation does."

"That's thirty years ago?"

"Yes, Mr. President. Did you think the first incident was the '81 incident? Everyone has been watching for them. I'm sure the CHINs, Americans, and Muslims probably already heard what happened here. They're monitoring our country so closely I can feel their breath on my neck. It's one thing to allow these demons to wander around bush-countries like the Spanish Americas or Africa, but the middle of a major tek-city with populations in the millions? Tell me, Mr. President, why you would do that? Why would you jeopardize the safety of the people of this country? It is the act of a juvenile mobster. You are supposed to be our President."

Igor's swallows hard. *What did I do?*

"They were going to kill her, these witches. My people told me they were the ones directing the first round of assassination attempts on me…before I was president. There have been rumors for years, no proof, of them making some of our mob clan-bosses disappear so they could take over parts of our business. I didn't do it for her. I did it for me. I wanted them dead. These witches, they're killers, always plotting something."

"These 'hit men,' they're animals, sir. Animals may or may not do things the way you want them. They killed a lot of witches that night, one leader dead and another survived, barely, and have disappeared again. Are these deaths worth the innocent lives?"

"You know my answer. What else do you want me to say? Hunt them down and destroy them."

"We will do no such thing, Mr. President. They're not stupid and neither are their handlers. We don't know enough yet. What happens if they appear and decide to walk through the streets of Moscow to get you? How many innocents will we sacrifice then?"

"It's just one skinny snake creature."

"No, Mr. President. There are at least three of them."

"What?"

"Yes sir. We do nothing. We've already put their description in Argus and will treat their sighting as an imminent terrorist attack. Drones will be directed to use whatever means necessary to kill them. That will include missile strikes, if necessary."

"What are they? Who owns them?"

"We don't know, but they are kept here."

"What do you mean?"

"We believe they are being housed here in Russia."

"Housed here? I don't understand. That's impossible. I know every inch of this country. If they were here, we'd know."

"There is one place you don't know every inch of. 1996 was the date."

"I don't what that is."

"You don't know Russian history, Mr. President. It was the Old Chernobyl nuclear plant meltdown. We quarantined an entire Ukrainian city. The plan was to keep it closed for a century. We are now in 2096."

"The Zone."

"Yes."

"We used to sneak in there as children. People still make jokes. Drink Chernobyl water and you'll grow an extra arm. Or for us boys back then, if we were really lucky, a second and bigger one in your pants. Is it even radioactive anymore?"

"I think every Russian child has snuck in there or wanted to at some point; spurred on by horror and alien movies and vid-games about the ghosts of power plant workers wandering about or radioactive zombies."

"We snuck in there to see some six-legged dogs or two-headed birds, maybe a ghost or two. We never saw any, of course, but we sure looked hard for them. I don't think we even saw any Zone police."

"Most of it is not radioactive anymore and hasn't been for fifty years. But Chernobyl was a Level Seven event, the highest you can go. There used to be Red and Blue Zones. The entire Zone used to reach into Russia and Belarus too. Now it's only the Ukraine part and most of it is safe for humans. But there's still a Black Zone that's still completed restricted, one of the most contaminated places on the planet that can kill any biological organism, even today. That means people."

"I don't know what you are telling me. Are you saying they are in the Zone? The Zone is a tourist attraction, an amusement park almost. People are always in there now."

"On guided tours. And not in the Black Zone."

"They're in this Black Zone? How?"

"We know where they are."

"You know where they are? Then strike. Why haven't we before? You're the one who's reminded me that I'm a president and not a mobster anymore. Forget what I as the mobster did. As president, I'm telling you to strike it."

"And spread a radioactive cloud, dust and debris over Russia and the Ukraine? Over the entire Russian Bloc potentially?"

"How can they be in the Black Zone then? How?"

"Mr. President, do you know that Russia has some of the best biosphere tek in the world? Use it for rebuilding after a nuclear Armageddon. Use it to protect your cities from any global climate disaster: floods, continental earthquakes, a new ice age, or solar flare catastrophe. Use them for terraforming by building a colony on the moon, Mars or another planet, should we ever figure out how to do light-travel. More likely, it would be a trans-generation spaceship. That biosphere tek has been tested in the Zone for decades. And certain scientific interests have used it for their own *extracurricular* testing."

"Irrelevant, strike. Any radioactive fallout could be managed. Even I know that."

"Strike what, Mr. President? Do you think we're the only ones developing bio-organic weapons? In America it's called Project New People. In China, I believe the code name is Pangu. The Caliphate views bio-org weapons as evil according to their religion, but then they have no shortage of people to be human-bombs. I suspect they will always be ahead of everyone else in that regard."

"All this time, they've been right here. You said they weren't ours when I asked. Now you're saying they are."

"Neither the government nor the military controls them, sir."

"Then who?"

"We don't know who they are. All we know is they're here and have been here for a long time. But until we do know, no one, not me, not you, the military, the KGB, nor our secret forces, is going to enter the Black Zone."

"Your solution is to do nothing?"

"Mr. President, the nation is in chaos. People think you were assassinated by the Patriarch. That's why we need to get you into the public's eye. We are in no position to take on anything else. We must stabilize the nation first. Then, later, gather the intelligence we need. We also have to recognize that elements within our own government are allied with them and have been protecting them. However, we must never forget that the Caliphate and CHINs are our primary enemies. The Americans, our secondary enemy. We monitor the Zone, nothing else for now."

"What about the demon, the demons?"

"Mr. President, that is my point exactly. We'd have to wipe out entire cities to stop them. You must take charge, stabilize the country, and we can manage the level of surveillance we need to watch for them and deploy attack defenses if needed."

"I'm not going to the surface."

"That's fine, sir, but you must lead."

Igor nods.

"I will get it started, Mr. President."

"Who killed the Prime Minister?"

"The Witches."

"Who killed Orlok?"

"No one. With the disappearance of the Russian Orthodox and his defeat to you in the election, he committed suicide."

"How convenient."

"Speaking of which, Mr. President, you will keep all weapon system codes with you at all times. Not me, not your men, no one else. The military were his primary backers, but Orlok had everyone in the KGB terrified with his constant use of the word 'nuclear' and his 'brotherhood of the flash' talk. Your possession of those codes is what really makes you the president in the eyes of the world."

"Okay."

"I will have the case sent down then. And, Mr. President, where is that number?"

"I destroyed it."

"Do you think your bio-daughter told them it was you who gave her the number?"

"No, why?"

"Let's hope so."

"Why? What if she did?"

"The demons consider both parties, the one who calls the hit and the one who gives that person the number, as the one entity who hired them. Meaning they will kill both parties."

"That is not true. I know all about the number and its use."

"You didn't know about the '65 event, and your mob enemies would, of course, be motivated to make sure you had the wrong information. How did you get the number?"

"A mobster known as Angel, but he's dead."

"Your previous criminal experience may know better than our intel. If you know that to be true, then it is. I will get everything started now, Mr. President. We have prepared your daily packet. Your first senior staff meeting is at six hundred hours. We can keep them virtual for now. No one will see that as unusual. See you in the morning, sir. Get a good night's rest, and I will have your presidential suits sent down. And I know I don't need to say this, but be presentable for meeting."

Zukov leaves and Igor watches him disappear into the elevator. He stares around and can feel the growing fear.

"Lights off!"

Igor sits in the dark again.

Angel set me up!

Witch Hunt

"I was a believer, before I was an atheist, when I was a child. I stopped believing because God was conspiring against me along with all my enemies. Godlessness is so much better. I can't deal with an ethereal being, so I chose to believe it doesn't exist. I can deal with the earthly. The earthly I can let live or wipe from existence." — President Igor Aleyev of the Russian Bloc

Cyberspace
12:00 a.m., 28 July 2096

There is darkness. A flashing green dot appears first, then dozens, hundreds of thousands, and millions, then billions and more. The secret holographic Net-meeting in Freespace—the corner of the Net not created, run or monitored by governments—begins. The code becomes a room, and in the room are several people standing in a circle. One of the figures is glowing.

"I will commence the meeting of the Continuum. Moses Atticus for the New Protestant Order. Present: Tova Ben-Hurion for the New Jewish Continuum, Father Marcos for the New Catholic Order, Archbishop Masai for the African Collective, and Kanji for the Shogun Order."

The next figure is now glowing.

"We are in total agreement with the recommendations," Father

Marcos says. "The Russian Bloc is too unstable for any of our activities—assassinations, multiple disappearances, possible civil war, and there is reason to expect greater religious persecution. We need to shut down the Underground Railroad there sooner than planned and pull all resources out of the country. Cyclops and Gemini are executing Operation Last Departure. God be with those we can't save."

The figure of Tova is now glowing. "The Russian Orthodox was the hub of all Faithers in the Bloc. Both our Arab and Persian Jewish contacts there have been getting disturbing reports for years but we never believed it. We just attributed it to typical anti-Faither bigoted propaganda. Nine days ago, their leader, the Pope Patriarch of the Russian Orthodox, attempted to assassinate their new President."

There are gasps.

Tova continues, "That's the reason we believe the religious persecution will be significant. Also, every Faither under their auspices of the Russian Orthodox has disappeared, completely."

As each image speaks, it glows.

"Killed? Detained?" Moses asks.

"Disappeared without a trace, over half a million people. We haven't confirmed if it was the Russian Orthodox themselves, the government, or other forces."

"Were the Orthodox Christians read into any part of the Project?" Kanji asks.

"Absolutely not," Moses answers. "It took us five years to finally make contact with their leadership after more than a decade of trying. Russia is very different place. Faithers there seem content with being slaves of the government and believe that being a collaborator goes hand-in-hand with their citizenry. We never fully trusted them."

"The Catholics concurred," Father Marcos adds. "No one was comfortable with them. We always tried to give them the benefit of the doubt because of everything that happened to them, being trapped in their own country, but still."

"I know many of you have been concerned regarding the absence of the Magi at this critical time," Masai says. "*It's* back."

"What?" "What's back?" they ask.

"*It.*"

Father Marcos knows. "In Russia?"

"Yes, the Magi informed us. It's back along with its *brothers*," Masai answers.

As they are talking, Moses, Tova, and Kanji's holo-identities are slightly out of phase for a moment. The images return. They know now too.

"The Magi are in country to intervene," Archbishop Masai says.

"The Russian Orthodox has disappeared. Russia is on verge of civil war, and now demons. None of us believe in coincidences," Moses says.

Kanji begins, "The Shogun Council has been concerned with the Mormon Order. We have been suspicious since they initially ceased communications after the dissolution of the Resistance. We still don't know what's happening, but it is something."

"What would be the impact of their non-involvement?" Tova asks.

"Our entire Russian-Asiatic operations could be at risk," Kanji continues. "The Project must be accelerated."

The Kremlin
7:00 a.m., 29 July 2096

The entire senior Kremlin, military, and KGB staff watch President Igor on the vid-screen. The President sits quietly in his official white suit. He is cleaned up and well-groomed.

"Times are so fickle in politics," he says. "When Orlok seemed to be our inevitable president, the Kremlin was about to create the first-ever parliamentary system in our country, based not on geography but religion—Orlok's Plan. Maintaining our ban of Islam, nearly half of the directly elected Assembly would be set aside for all the many religions in Russia and Europa. The Orthodox would make up fifty percent of those new religious seats. Only a small minority wanted to follow the path of our enemies, like America and China, and ban all religions.

"But I'm the one who is president now. Even a broken military timepiece is right once a day. Effective thirteen hundred hours tomorrow, based on their complicity in the events that have had this nation in chaos these past months, I will issue an executive order to outlaw all religion, punishable by immediate expulsion from the country. Further, the KGB uncovered the chief orchestrators of a plot to seize control of the presidency and create their own theocracy—the Witches. We've always had names for these women, these 'black widows,' these terrorist women, plotting the death of Russians from the shadows. As a result of their treason they will be targeted for immediate resettlement to Siberia. Don't announce it officially until one hour before we begin so we can catch as many as we can for public trials before they go underground.

"Finally, those members of the government who supported Orlok's Plan will be purged from my government. They will never be able to serve in any position in government, never be able to vote, and never be able to comment politically in any way, or in any form, for as long as I remain President. All designated mobsters in Russia and Europa will have a one-week grace period to register all activities with the government and end all activities not sanctioned by the government. After that grace period, any mobster engaging in unsanctioned activities will be summarily executed.

"Does anyone have any objections to my new directives?"

No says a word.

"One more thing," Igor says. "Yoga will also be outlawed in the country."

"But Mr. President, yoga is an exercise, it's not a religion. It's meditation."

"Finding inner peace, tapping the power of the universe, one with nature's aura. It is a religion, and its practitioners are either witches or witch sympathizers," President Aleyev answers back. "Close down all yoga clubs. And gentlemen, I'm sure no one in the government or military engages in such religious activities."

Matriarch Sanctuary, Temporary HQ, Ukraine
11:55 a.m., 30 July 2096

Sisters greet a returning Czarina, Titania, and Yana like rock-stars. Large glasses of vodka are thrust into their hands.

"Isn't this ethnic stereotyping?" Yana jokes.

"Vodka! Vodka! Vodka!"

Yana stops, puts the glass to her lips and drinks it down without hesitation. Sisters cheer her on. She gulps down the last of it and throws the glass against the wall, smashing it. The women cheer. Czarina and Titania follow suit and also receive rounds of applause.

"Where's Athena?" Yana asks.

"She's inside recovering, but she's fine," Czarina answers.

"He's really dead?"

"Yes."

"Where's the witch-bitch high priestess?"

"She's…worse than dead."

"I don't go for 'worse than dead.' I want dead-dead. Europans are not interested in Russian high ideals. That witch must be dead or she'll be back."

"You were more important," a voice says.

Everyone turns to see a frazzled Athena sitting in her hover-chair.

A frantic sister runs into the chamber with an e-pad in her hand.

"What's wrong?" a sister asks.

The sister reads: "Newly elected President Igor Aleyev has banned all religions in Russia and Europa. All citizens will have to cease all religious practices or be deported from the country. A general federal warrant has been issued for the arrest and deportation of all Witches; due to their complicity in trying to take seize the government."

There is shock in room. Everyone instinctively take out their e-pads and tabs to view the breaking story on the newsfeed themselves.

"This can't be happening. He said nothing of this when he campaigned."

"All politicians do is lie. His silence was lying."

"Russia is back to Stalin times. Soon it'll be the Gulag again. History always repeats."

"We already have the Gulag. What do think 'sending someone off to Siberia' means?"

"They mean witches, not us, right?"

"He's dead," Athena says, looking up from her e-pad.

"Who?" Titania asks.

"An old ex-boyfriend. He was the one who had the police let us go after they caught us and were taking us to prison that time. I called him a few days ago to watch for any of our names on the arrest rolls as a favor, just in case. I've always been paranoid about random police arrests of believers in Russia."

"If you hadn't, we would have been among the disappeared too," Czarina says. "He must have been high-up in the government. What happened? How do you know?"

"His name is on the police obituary list. Clashes with the public. No other details. He wasn't very happy that I called him for the favor, but he did it anyway. Never forget a contact. You never know when you'll need them."

Titania starts, "Athena, there is someone else you can call in a favor—"

Athena shoots a dirty look. "There's nothing more I can do. Believe me when I say if I try to intervene, I will disappear and it will be worse for all of you. I can do nothing."

"Who killed the warlock?" Yana asks. "Mangled the witch-bitch? Killed all those people?"

"We have to escape as quickly as possible," Athena says, ignoring her.

"They can't mean us," the sister says again. "The government knows we're not witches."

Yana doesn't relent. "Athena, we have to know."

Athena's eyes start to tear up. "I made a horrible mistake. I did something I'm going to have to pay for. That's why I can't go with any of you."

"What do you mean?" Czarina asks.

"I may not make it to next month."

"Nothing will happen to you, Athena. We take care of our own."

Athena is almost crying. "You wouldn't say that if you knew what I hired to save us. Save us because we weren't strong enough to do it for ourselves."

Everyone is quiet for a moment. No one knows what to say.

"We need to leave Russia," Athena says. "Pack only what you can carry and get out of here now. We have to assume the entire Russian government is already on their way here for us."

"But Wicca are not Witches—"

"Stop it!" Athena yells out, interrupting the sister. "I told you what happened to me because I didn't take this seriously. My hand cut from my body, innocent people dead because of my actions. Atheists don't make distinctions when it comes to believers. They mean to kill us all. We have to leave now."

"And go where?" one of the sisters asks.

"We'll be relatively safe in Europa," Yana says. "Eastern Europe is part of Russia, but they don't own it."

"Then we hide there. But I will stay behind."

"No, Athena," Czarina says. "That's unacceptable."

"Sisters, the New Matriarch must survive. Whether I survive cannot matter more than that. If I'm alive next month, I'll join you. If not, then this will be the last time I see any of you."

The sisters evacuate the building with satchels, suitcases, bags, boxes, cases, and finally kennel cages full of cats. Cars and minivans are loaded up. Athena watches from her hover-chair.

One of the sisters gets a call on her e-pad. She talks, then hangs up, and runs to the others. Yana walks to Czarina and Titania. They all walk to Athena.

"We found Delphine," Yana says.

"We don't have time for revenge," Athena says.

"Yes, we do," Yana says. "But actually, the call was from Delphine herself."

"Look!" one of the sisters yells.

In the distance, they can see them—saucer drones approaching. Everyone runs to the vehicles.

Streets of Russia
1:00 p.m., 30 July 2096

Police soldiers in heavy black body armor run into hotels, apartment complexes, homes, and businesses, breaking down doors, pushing onlookers out of the way, grabbing people, and making arrests.

Onlookers and vehicles are kept away by police and foot-patrol robots. Drones blanket the sky above the police raids like locusts. In the distance, tanks roll through the streets.

Streets of Moscow
1:00 p.m., 30 July 2096

It is commonplace now; the streets filled with the panic and protests of the people.

A car stops in front of a parked van. A Goth witch exits the driver side and the woman, Sacarri, exits the passenger side. They open the back door—lying across the seat is the mangled Morgana. Sicarri grins.

"Isn't amazing how fates can change? Yesterday you were destined to be the Witch Empress of all Russia and Europa; soon in a position to take on the Caliphate itself, and I was your lowly servant. You were no different than any man, despite all your talk and show. The lives of women determined not by woman-power but sex for men's bodies and physicality for men's eyes. You're just another pale-faced infidel. If I didn't owe you, we would have tossed you in the refuse bin as I'm sure you planned to do to me when I served my purpose for you." Sicarri looks at the other two. "How long will it take us?"

"We have to take the long way, but we can get across the border in forty-five minutes."

"Well Morgana, we will be in Islamic Caliphate territory, soon and there I am the secret Empress. There my Sicarri Order grows slowly and patiently until the day we will strike at the Saudi Arabian heart of the Caliphate and create our first female theocracy. I never understood your ridiculous plan to turn infidel, Godless Russia into a matriarchal theocracy. Is it not easier to turn a patriarchal theocracy into matriarchal one?"

Morgana looks at her with her one good eye, without emotion or reacting in any way.

"It is time to retire your whore clothes, Morgana. You'll look quite nice in your new burka," Sicarri yells to the others in Arabic as she closes the back door.

They all get into the van and drive off, leaving the car behind.

Nameless Ukraine Hospital-Clinic
1:22 p.m., 30 July 2096

When they arrive, it is obvious this is one of the many Matriarch mini-hospitals scattered across Russian and Ukraine for sisters only. The attendants are all sisters, though they have already gotten rid of their scarves and colored necklaces; some even have cut their long hair short.

"We don't time for this," Titania says to the group. "This is foolish and dangerous."

"The government is on the streets, breaking into houses and businesses and arresting people everywhere," a sister says.

"They have tank road-blocks on almost every corner. How are we going to get out now?" asks another.

"Why did we come here?" Athena asks angrily. "We may have lost our chance to escape the country."

"I know none of you want to hear this, but the Matriarch still has allies in the government," a sister says. "They'll get us out."

"You mean Morgana's allies?" Yana challenges.

"Our allies. Morgana is gone. Delphine knows who they are and will contact them for us."

"Are you demented?" Czarina asks. "They tried to kill us! They were going to kill us!"

"Just talk to her. That's all. We're already here."

"The only thing we should do when it comes to Delphine is dump her out the window," Yana says. "Maybe I should call the police myself and give them an anonymous tip on the whereabouts of an evil witch."

"Please don't do that now. Just talk to her," the sister pleads.

"There is another matter we need to discuss," says another sister. "With this new government decree, there are many sisters who weren't part of the Matriarch who want to join us."

"No. They aren't sisters."

"Not all sisters were part of the Matriarch. They're every bit a part of Wicca as us."

"No they're not. Some believe in multiple goddesses, other worship a Goddess and God. Some don't even care about nature or protecting animals—"

"I can't believe that we're standing here having theological debates in the hallway. The government is searching for us to kill us," Athena says angrily.

"What about those who call themselves 'good witches'? The Matriarch repudiates witches."

"We don't have time for this. We must get to Europa," Athena says.

"Talk to Delphine first."

In the recovery room, Delphine lies in the bio-bed. Half her face, under her chin, her neck, arms, and legs have third-degree burns. Most of her formerly long, flowing beautiful hair is matted or burnt off. A sheepish female nurse stands at her bedside, a worrisome expression on her face.

"Don't mind my appearance," Delphine says. "They've already replaced my broken bones. I never knew there were so many in the legs and hip. My new skin will be put on Friday, and I'll look more radiant than ever."

Despite her situation, Delphine is happy and smiling. The Europan sisters curse at her in many languages: Bulgarian, Hungarian, Slovenian, Czech, Polish, Bulgarian, etc. Yana goes into a long angry tirade in Serbian. The Russian sisters, Athena, and her circle, just stare at her.

"Don't think, Delphine, that because we're not cursing you, too, that we want you dead any less than them," one of the Russian sisters says.

"I know where I stand. Thanks for coming anyway."

"You tried to kill us," Athena says.

"I tried to save the Matriarch. It was never personal. I told you, we were a dying Order and I couldn't allow that to happen after a lifetime of work. So-called religions based on nothing were thriving, while we, where women are the foundation, the center of life and protectors of nature, animals, and flora, were dying. A matriarchal theocracy would have made us strong. All of Russia and Europa would have been our sanctuary."

"Evil always can find excuses for its evil," Athena says. "Theocracy is evil whether female or male. Only a fool or intellectual would think otherwise."

"This is Russia, Athena, the land of revolutionary movements. I know my history. You win and you rule. You lose and off to the Gulag for you. I lost. I accept the consequences. Our plan failed, but that doesn't stop me from not wanting the Matriarch destroyed."

"No one will listen to you Delphine," Yana says. "You showed your true colors."

"You all will have plenty of time to exact your revenge on me. What's important is we don't allow ourselves to be destroyed. I still have allies left in the Kremlin."

Sisters laugh at her.

"The same people trying to round us up now?" asks a sister.

"Not them," Dephine says. "We leave Russia, stay in Europa, it doesn't matter which country, and fly under the radar. The government will ignore us. Stay away from politics, the press, anything public, and they will ignore us. We can create a virtual safe haven."

"I wish I'd be alive to see your deserved end," Athena says coldly.

"Athena, you have to live. If Morgana returns, who will stop her? You let her live twice now, so you have to survive. You're her arch-nemesis and only you can stop her."

"I hate you Delphine!" Athena yells. "You did this to us."

"I only accelerated what would have happened anyway. The Matriarch needed to rise, despite its women."

"So that's the motivation?" Athena says. "The great Delphine hates women?"

"I don't hate my kind. There's a difference between hating and knowing. Know your kind."

"Yes, Delphine, we know your kind," Yana says.

"The sister who tried to kill all sisters." Athena is trying with all her might not to attack the woman, or simply walk out of the room.

Delphine reflects. "But the Matriarch will go on. I am already dead inside. You killed my daughter, remember, so again, you all won. I accept it without bitterness. But the Matriarch will go on. This could all be a godsend for us in the end. Women have too many choices. Limit those choices and you increase their power."

All the sisters are sick of listening, sick of the very sight of her.

"We can all see why you and Morgana got along so well together," a sister adds.

Delphine's face is now sad. She turns slightly and reaches her arm out to her personal nurse. She hands Delphine the folded piece of paper.

"Call this number. It's one of the largest private charter jet companies in Russia. The owner is a secret sister. While the streets are in chaos, you will simply fly above it all to safety. I'll find my own way out."

Outside Hospital
3:01 p.m., 30 July 2096

The caravan of vehicles speeds away. Sisters look back at her through the vehicle windows, Czarina and Titania among them. There is only sadness in their eyes.

Athena watches, crying. She stands up from her hover-chair,

holding herself up despite the off-balancing weight of her metallic, cast-encased right arm. No more sitting. She has to get used to running.

In the Shadows

"Fear and anxiety will either evolve you into a far superior version of yourself or it will devolve you into whimpering primate. You may never know which until 'it' happens. Personally, I've never cared much for being a monkey." — Shoshana Israela, the "Iron Rose, leader of the Jewish Wolf Pack.

Presidential Bunker
4:06 p.m., 30 July 2096

Igor sits in front of his table vid-screen as the number dials. It connects; both parties are on audio only.

"Mr. President," Mrs. Lucifer's voice says. "You're causing all kinds of trouble in your country, but still have time to make personal calls. Are you ready to grant our request?"

"You have nothing to bargain with," President Igor says.

"Then hang up."

There is a long pause. She breaks the silence.

"Do you know where my husband and I were earlier today? That Chernobyl Exclusion Zone in Ukraine. The Zone, I think everyone calls it. The site of a nuclear meltdown, but now an amusement park with daily guided tours. Only in Russia. We especially liked the Red Forest— red is my husband's and my favorite color—it looked so real, though it's just an artist's recreation of the pine forest outside the reactor that turned red-brown, withered and died. Wish we could have gotten closer. The Zone is a splendid ghost city, all those empty vehicles and buildings. The things people used to drive in the past and they still called them cars. Our tour guide said the Zone is the largest vehicle and ship port graveyard in the world. I wish we had seen some ghosts though."

"What do you have to bargain with?"

"Mr. President, there are people in this world who believe in nation-states—patriotism, duty, loyalty—and then there are those who believe in internationalism—no nations, but one world, a world of the strong and the weak masses. My husband and I achieved our power and wealth as patriots, but with that we have explored the internationalists for the last few decades to occupy our time."

"Will this be a long story?"

"Not at all, Mr. President. We'd like to introduce you to some scientist friends, actually friends of friends…of friends. We think you'll really want to become their friend too."

"Why would I want them as friends?"

"They live in that great wasteland."

"What wasteland?"

"The Zone."

Igor pauses again.

"The Zone, or more precisely the Black Zone, is owned by these internationalists, some of them just happen to live in your country."

"No one lives there."

"As President, I'm sure you've been told about them. I hear your father was starting to ask too many questions about them with requests for forensic audits. A very dangerous thing to do in dictatorial government."

"What are you insinuating?"

"Mr. President, we should introduce you to our friends before someone comes after you too."

President Igor laughs. "No one can get me where I am."

"You do know the Russia Bloc is considered a global joke. You want to be a superpower. How funny. What civilized power allows its leaders to be so arbitrarily killed so frequently as in Russia? Believe me, Mr. President, they can get to you. The assassin could be human…or not."

"Meaning what? Robots can't get to me either."

"You're going to great lengths, Mr. President, to pretend you don't know what you know. You already know what assassin is coming for you."

"I don't know—"

"But our scientist friends can help you get ready."

"Why are you doing this, American, so interested in my affairs? My people tell me that your own American President had your only son killed. You do this for petty revenge? So American."

"We are Americans, Mr. President. And Russians are no different."

"How does this fulfill your thirst for revenge?"

Mrs. Lucifer laughs a bit. "I can't give you all the answers to the universe all at once, Mr. President. Let's just say you'll be motivated by petty revenge too when you figure it all out. So do we have an agreement, Mr. President? New identities and asylum for us, the 'who' and 'where' information for you."

"Yes, you have an agreement."

10:46 p.m.

Their black hoods are taken off their heads and they are pushed into the elevators by security. Igor watches from the vid-screen monitors.

Dozens of handcuffed scientists descend in the elevator. The doors open. Only the lights outside the elevator are on. Everywhere else is dark.

"Please, come out," the voice of President Igor commands.

The scientists reluctantly comply.

"Mr. President, why have you had us kidnapped?"

"I had to call in quite a number of favors to find you."

"Mr. President, why are we here?"

"This is your new home."

The scientists look at each other.

"What do you mean, Mr. President? Why are we here?"

"You don't have to pretend. I know who you really are, what you've done, what you've done before that, what you can do. You will work for me now. You will stay in this place until I am satisfied."

"Mr. President, we don't know what you mean. You must have us mistaken with others. We are simple doctors."

"Don't you all live in the Zone?

The scientists hesitate.

"The Zone? What Zone, Mr. President?"

"The place where you live. Where you make things."

"Mr. President, you are mistaken in what you believe you know about us. We are simple doctors. You need to let us leave now."

"The only way to stop a monster is to become one. That's what you will do for me and you will never leave this place until you do."

"Please Mr. President. We don't know what you mean. We swear."

"The creature Leviathan was exiled to the bottom of the world by the gods, but one day rose in glory and fury, rising from the waters to seize the lands, the heavens, and the stars. I will be Leviathan."

The scientists look all around in the darkness for any sign of an escape. They will never leave this bunker.

Streets of Ukraine
July 2083

Athena hated her father. It never did become a hatred of men, though many would say it did based on her chosen religion. Anything he said, she ignored. Anything he wanted, she would do the opposite. Any advice from him, she dismissed—except for one.

She remembered her father speaking to some man, not sure who the man was.

Igor says, "Power isn't obtained by brute force. It's information. It's building a network of contacts everywhere, the network can never too big, people with knowledge, knowledge on anything and everything. It's that database of people that will make you powerful or, even better, help you survive the powerful. It could be next month, next year, next decade that their seemingly useless information at the time becomes the most important commodity in the world to you, at precisely the time you need it most."

Athena walks up to the man, Boris. His hair is naturally graying. She's only fifteen, but almost taller than him. He stands at the corner waiting for his son to come home from school.

"Hello, Mr. Boris," she says.

He glances at her. "Hello, Ms. Athena."

She stands near him and looks down at the ground thinking.

"Is there something else you want?"

"I'm sorry."

"You're sorry about what?"

"What happened in Israel."

He swallows hard as he stares at her. She can see the deep emotions start to well up within him, but he contains it. He looks away.

"You're not Muslim. You didn't do it."

"I was such a bad person though. Maybe I can help you one day.

I don't know what, but maybe I can."

"Thank you Athena. Maybe I can do the same."

"Maybe you can tell me about when you lived in America. I always wanted to know all about those rumors about Kansas. The people who made the weather make lightning and tornadoes. Was it real?"

Mr. Boris smiles. "I was there. I was part of the Resistance."

Boris and Son Ships, Shipping Center, Moscow
5:11 p.m., 30 July 2096

The streets are still chaotic. The interior alarm beeps as soon as Athena enters the shipping store. She wears a surgical mask—common for someone from the Asian Consortium territories—and dark glasses. Her hair is tied into a ponytail and hidden under her collar.

The store can ship anything via ground, air, or sea. One can even send data files anonymously from the center. A couple is behind the counter and there is only one other person inside; a man looking at the various shipping containers on shelves. A hydraulic robot stands inactive in the corner.

"No cyborgs allowed in my store," the owner says to her from behind the counter.

"It's an arm cast, not a cybernetic arm."

The owner walks up to her, grabs the arm, and looks at it.

"There are laws protecting the free access rights of cyborgs in this country," Athena says.

The owner looks at her with anger. "I don't care about laws. A cyborg thief ripped up my store and crushed my dog trying to steal, so no cyborgs in my shop! In fact, you can leave."

"No, I need to talk to the owner."

"I am the owner."

"Where's Mr. Boris?"

"I'm Mr. Boris, the son. Why?"

"I'm trying to find the Orthodox. No one can tell me where they are."

"They're gone. They disappeared. No one knows where, and why should I care anyway?"

"Are there any unaffiliated Orthodox anywhere?"

"Why are you asking me these questions?"

"Wasn't your father Orthodox?"

"Yes, he was. But he's dead and I'm not. Not dead and not Orthodox."

"You must know some Orthodox somewhere, other Jews or Christians."

The shopkeeper laughs. "Those are words I haven't heard in a long time. Hitler and Stalin got rid of all the Jews, and Christians live in America. There are no more here now that those bastard Orthodox are gone. Bastards tried to kill the new president."

"I need help."

"What's wrong with you?"

"I think you know more than you're pretending to know. I swear I'm not with the government."

"I don't know anything and I don't care if you believe me or not."

"I need to find that religious Order that can control the elements," Athena continues. "I need to find them! I just don't know their name, but if I could find an Orthodox or another affiliated religious Order, they could help me. This is a matter of life and death!"

"They're gone, I told you."

"I'm being hunted by these things, and the only ones who can stop them is this religious Order."

"I'll tell you again, I don't know them."

"It's my only chance."

"I won't tell you again. Get out or I'll call the police!"

Athena turns away and walks out of the store.

The man walks to the window and watches her disappear into the crowds. He returns to the counter. His wife is helping the other customer.

"There are crazy people everywhere," he says to her.

"I don't know why you even let her talk," she says. "Throw them out. I'm glad the government is banning religions. Should have thrown them all out at the same time we threw out the Muslims. Finally we'll get some peace in the country. The symbol of Russia is the Motherland Monument with sword in hand, not the Statue of Liberty with its stone candle and stupid religious holy book. Let them go there. It's good to see that Russia is back. Like our glory days of Lenin and Stalin."

He looks at the containers the man is buying.

"Did you find everything you need?" he asks.

"Yes, I did," the customer answers. "I didn't know I'd be in the middle of a war zone today."

"Oh no, this is nothing. This is just a simple government crackdown. Just go about your business as if nothing is happening. Watch out for drones in the sky because they sometimes shoot by mistake, and watch the roads so you don't get run down by government vehicles."

"Where are you from, sir?" his wife asks. "Your Russian is very good but I hear the accent. Are you a tourist?"

"Yes," he answers with smile. "America."

Magik

Jerusalem, Israel
2:58 p.m., 3 July 2059

The Holy Land Tour bus is driving its twenty-something passengers back to their Galilee kibbutz lodgings—a Muslim driver, a Jewish tour guide and forty students—Christian, Jewish, Mormon, and one Sikh.

"I think great things are going to come out of this group," Moses says to them.

The young man sits next to his fiancée Emma, with his brother Sam right behind, the Tovas in the adjacent seat, and Vincent in front of them.

"Divine providence," Vincent says.

Vladivostok Seaport, Primorsky Krai, Russia
7:03 a.m., 31 July 2096

"Vincent," a voice calls from outside his door.

Vincent sits up in his bunk. "Yes."

The door opens and a man peeks in. "They're ready for you on the dock."

The cabin is small but space is used efficiently. Next to the bunk is the fully-equipped work station, the door to the small latrine, and tiny shower on the other side.

Vincent follows him from below to the main deck.

The commercial port is filled with boats, ships, hydrofoils, and sea crafts of all sizes and makes, including a few massive cruise liners. The nation may be in turmoil, but it is normal business here. Sea workers are everywhere, along with a variety of wheeled and flying robots moving gear and cargo.

Vincent goes down the starboard stepladder of the *Divine Providence*, the sleek, seven-meter sea craft is a hybrid catamaran-submersible and is able to sail on top of the water or dive and operate like a submarine under water.

Three of his crewmembers wait as the Russian officer continues his inspection of their manifest, checking off items with his finger on his tablet. Vincent joins them.

"You are the captain?" the inspector asks.

"Yes," Vincent answers.

"You are scientists? What kind?"

"Marine biologists."

"You study fishes then?"

"Yes, all sea life, both animal and plant."

"Ever see any kind of sea serpent down there?"

Vincent smiles a bit. "The closest we've come is a giant squid, maybe six meters in length. We got pictures."

"Everything seems in order. Be sure to follow all boundary restrictions. These are very dangerous waters. There's the border with the CHINs, the Asian Consortium say they're neutral, but go into their waters and you'll find out that they have a different definition of neutral."

"We'll stay in Russian waters at all times."

"Good luck with your expedition. If you see any sea monsters, please send me a photo. My kids would love it."

"Yes, we'll do that."

The inspector walks to the next boat. Vincent and his crew begin to board their sea craft again when another inspector runs to them.

"Wait," he says.

Vincent and his team stop and wait for him to reach them.

"Have you passed your inspection?"

"Yes, we're approved for departure."

"Not yet."

The new inspector looks at the name of their craft and views the list on his tablet.

"You have to pay your crisis fees."

"Crisis fees?"

"Yes, the nation is in crisis with all the assassinations, street demonstrations, and military action. Foreigners are required to pay an additional fee as a result."

"We were already approved."

"And I can 'un-approve' unless you pay."

Vincent stares at the man.

One of his crewmembers leans over to him. "Captain, we need to depart. Let's just pay the money."

"What's your name Inspector?" Vincent asks.

"I'm not required to give my name, foreigner, for you to pay the fee you owe."

"You will properly identify yourself or I'll call the police."

"The police?"

"Our parent company informed all our boats that anti-Aleyev forces were stealing money from foreigners by pretending to be inspectors and to notify the police of anyone refusing to present their ID."

The inspector smirks at him. He reaches into his pocket and shows his ID. "I'm going to impose an additional tax on top of the fee. Do you want to keep talking or do you want to pay what you owe?"

Vincent is angry. He takes out an e-pad and authorizes payment. The inspector hears the beep on his tablet and touches the screen with his finger.

"Have a safe trip, foreigner." The smiling inspector walks away from them.

One of the crewmembers steps in front of his view. "Captain, let's go. This is their country."

It only takes moments for them get aboard. Vincent and the three crewmembers enter bridge control.

"Prepare to disembark," Vincent says. Two crew members take seats at their individual control stations; the third walks through to go below. Three other scientists—two female and one male—are already at their stations.

"Glad we're on water. This country is a mess. Their new president is kicking out all religions. He and T. Wilson 'Boggs' must be related," one of the men says.

"Docking systems are disengaging," says one of the women. "Witches and Vampires. Can't say I have much sympathy, especially the Vampires. We are free for sailing, Captain."

"Take her out and dive at preset marker," Vincent says as he sits in his chair at the captain's station.

"Our captain almost started an international incident," one of the men says.

"What happened?"

"Government shakedown, what else."

They notice that Vincent is almost in a trance.

"What's wrong captain?" a woman asks.

"You know." He looks at his console.

"There's a good explanation," the woman says.

"We've had no contact whatsoever from any of the others. It's not possible that the Continuum would be out of touch with us for so long," Vincent says.

"Preparing to dive," one of the men says.

"Vincent, you worry too much."

"That's exactly why I'm in charge. I think I'll use my personal line and call them directly."

They look at him.

"Vincent, you can't do that."

"All communications must go through the Apostles. Vincent, you can't circumvent that."

"Captain, this is not the time to time to be 'independent.'"

"I see my wife has been busy recruiting my crew."

The crew starts to chuckle.

"We're just keeping our captain honest."

"Don't worry I won't do anything radical—today."

The crew glances at each other before returning attention back to their consoles.

"Diving," one of the men says.

Presidential Bunker, The Kremlin
8:03 a.m., 31 July 2096

Igor sits at his main desk talking to his KGB staff on audio-only from the in-desk tablet.

"Mr. President, we are putting in place your directives and we are getting maximum compliance," the KGB director says. "Non-compliants are exiting the country. You'll be amused to know that the CHINs have offered sanctuary for all our religious emigrants."

"They've exterminated more religious people than any nation in the history of the world," one of the staffers scoffs.

"People are taking them up on it, along with the Asian Consortium, Australia is of course closing its borders; some are going to Canada and the Spanish Americas."

The President looks at his tablet. "I've gotten reports on all the items of the directives except number thirteen. Why?"

"Excuse me, Mr. President. Can you repeat what you asked?"

"You heard me."

"I can't hear you now, sir."

"You can hear me. What's going on?"

The line suddenly disconnects. Igor checks the system. *They manually shut off the line.*

"Michele," Igor says and the system dials the number.

The man's face pops up on his vid-screen. "Boss. Oh, sorry, Mr. President."

"Michele, where is KGB man?"

"What do mean, boss? I mean—"

"Call me President Boss, Boss, President, I don't care."

The man smiles. "I can do that."

"Where is KGB man?"

"He's in the hospital, President."

"What?"

"Yes. Oh not him. His son is ill."

"Who was I just talking to?"

"What do you mean?"

"I was talking to Zukov on the secure line."

"He hasn't been in since last week."

"What?"

"Boss, I can send down some teks. I said it yesterday: those systems are not working properly for whatever reason. You must have disconnected something by mistake."

"Do so now." He sees him talking to others. "Michele, what's happening with directive thirteen?"

"What's that, boss?"

"I added another provision. Foreigners are not allowed to own Russian land or in-country businesses."

"Half of the nation is owned by foreigners, boss."

"Then half of the nation will return to Russian hands. If we didn't have so many greedy Russians, this would not be necessary. The Europans don't sell all their lands to foreigners. They won't even sell to Russians."

"They all remember what happened to Western Europe. They're obsessed with holding on to every last piece of dirt. Okay, I will find out now, Boss."

"I need to know what's going on up there."

"I don't know, boss, but I'll find out. The teks should be there. They'll fix everything like magic."

He hears the proximity hum of the elevator as it descends to the bunker main floor.

"Boss, what should—"

Igor shuts off the screen and rises from his chair. He grabs a tek-rifle from the side desk and runs in front of the elevator with the gun pointing. The door isn't even fully open before he fires a pulse inside. The lights are blasted out as bodies are thrown against the inside walls of the elevator. The doors fully open.

Five of the scientists appear with hard hats on. They run to the elevator and drag the bodies out.

One of the scientists looks up. "This is good, sir. They did exactly as we expected. We have the genetic material we need."

Igor looks down at the four bodies of the fake teks and smiles.

9:05 a.m.

Zukov storms in and confronts a staff in panic.

"Is your son okay?" one of the staffers whispers to him.

He waves him off with his hand. "Who were the teks that went down? How did they get past security?"

"They had authorization."

"How could they have authorization to the bunker?"

"We don't know, sir. They walked right in."

"From where?"

"We don't know yet."

Zukov shakes his head. "I stood in front of the President just days ago and assured him that we would protect him and we have this breach—another breach."

"They must have hacked into the presidential Grid."

"We monitor the presidential Grid so how is that impossible?"

"There could be several explanations."

Zukov raises his fist in the air as if he wants to smack them all.

"Let's be very clear here, gentleman. He won't just send me to Siberia. I will have all of you as company with your families." His ear-set rings. "Zukov."

"Sir," the voice of the man says. "Sensors did pick up gunfire in the bunker."

"This can't be happening. Priority red," Zukov yells out. "We must get to the President!"

Another agent runs to them. "Zukov, we know exactly who gave the tek imposters the clearance into the bunker."

"Who?"

"It was the President himself."

Everyone looks at each other.

"Why would he do that?"

"I don't know."

"Were they carrying anything?"

"We reviewed all the sensor data and they weren't, but…"

Zukov waits for the end of his sentence. "But what?"

"What is disturbing is that the system can't determine if the four men were even human."

"What do you mean?"

Secure Conference Room, The Kremlin
11:00 a.m., 31 July 2096

Zukov enters the room with a squad of Spetsnaz—Russia's elite Special Forces. He touches the table tablet.

"Mr. President, if you don't answer me right now, I am prepared to meet directly with Parliament to have you removed from office. I also am prepared to authorize multiple Spetsnaz teams to use all means necessary, backed up by the military, to gain access to your bunker."

"That would be unwise," Igor's voice comes through loudly over the overhead speakers.

"What are you doing down there, Mr. President?"

"I am ready to perform all duties now. However, I will not be leaving the bunker at any time, for any reason, due to my safety concerns. I was able to circumvent the Kremlin security measures twice and bring down two groups without proper checks. I have already been in contact with the Parliament and they agree with me. We will not have another president assassinated."

"Mr. President, what were the two groups you brought down to you?"

"The first were scientists from the Zone that we had talked about. The second were subjects from the Zone."

Zukov is very concerned. "*Subjects*? Why would you do that, Mr. President?"

"I need to be able to protect myself."

"Mr. President, I don't know what that means exactly. What are you planning on doing?"

"Zukov, I've re-enabled all KGB access codes. You can come

down at any time. You can come down now, Zukov, and convince me."

Zukov swallows hard. "I don't think I'll come down just yet, sir. My duties require me to remain here. I can send down others."

"How is your son?"

"He's fine, sir. Thanks for asking. We thought initially he was poisoned but the only poison it turned out to be was food poisoning. Mr. President, will you tell me what you are planning on doing?"

"I'm not planning anymore. I'm doing it. Come down and I'll show you."

"Mr. President, I will send down my number two man."

Igor laughs a bit. "Why not you?"

"I won't be doing that, Mr. President, even if you order me to."

"Why?"

"I think I know what you're doing and no one will be going down there."

"Zukov, I have to tell you the truth about something."

"What's that Mr. President?"

"I lied about the protocol for the number."

"The demon, sir."

"Yes."

"So your mob colleagues set you up."

"They did, you were right. It does kill all involved. So many of us these days have been caught in one double-cross or another. If only we could be assured of whom we could trust in our own ranks. We are the top leaders and we can't even trust all our people. Zukov, from now on, no one is to be allowed into the presidential residence, including the entrance to the bunker. Am I clear?"

"It will be done immediately, sir."

"Good."

"This is not what I envisioned for you, sir."

"Not what I envisioned either, but no one forced me to be president. I wanted this and despite it all, I will stabilize the country and I have every intention of still being the best president the nation has ever had."

"Mr. President, did it ever occur to you that besides assassination or an accident that your father could have…committed suicide to set all of this in motion? He so wanted to make Russia great that he might have thought he could enrage the people to greatness."

There is a long pause. "I suppose it's as plausible as all the other possibilities. The theories will never end as to what happened that day. And I was there, right outside the door. We'll never know."

"Will you ever come out from the bunker, sir?"

"No, I don't think I ever will. The darkness makes me feel…safe. As time goes on I suspect I will become more and more a part of it."

"I'm sorry I never got to shake your hand, sir."

"It's okay, Zukov. I wish I'd had a chance to spend more time at the beach. I love the water so. But we must never think about regrets."

Victory Park, Moscow
11:00 a.m., 31 July 2096

Athena sits in the park with tears in her eyes looking at the geysers from the pool. She can't be in a public place when it comes. But she doesn't know what to do or where else to go. She is alone and mentally blocks out all the pandemonium of protests and police activity around her.

"Do you speak English?"

Athena looks up. A man with dark tan skin, short, curly black hair, dressed in a white suit and white leather slip-on shoes is before her. Standing at his side is a woman with a fair complexion, blond hair tied in a ponytail, in a black suit, black heeled boots, and a black top hat on her head.

"Yes, I do."

"We're tourists," the man says.

"Americans?"

"Continental Europeans are so gifted at identifying the national origin of others."

"How can I help?"

"You've been crying. Maybe we can help you?"

Athena looks at the couple more closely.

"How can you help me?"

"Maybe we can help?" the man repeats.

Athena says, "Do your words have another meaning?"

"Would you like them to?

"I would. But I don't think we're talking about the same thing."

"You shouldn't be here."

"Why?"

"You have a train to catch to Romania, Athena."

Is it them?

"Who are you?"

"The answer is already known to you. Go join your people. The next metro will arrive when you arrive."

Athena stands. "How do you know me? How did you find me? Are you really them?"

The couple smiles but say nothing more to her. They walk away. Athena wants to run after them, but she can't. They walk right into a mob of protestors with the police advancing. She glances at the time on her ring-watch for a second. She looks away from it fast, but the couple is gone. She's angry that she was distracted so easily. There is nothing else to do but go.

Athena starts to run but stops and turns to look in the opposite direction that the couple went. She sees them. The couple is watching her from across the park. If only she could have talked with them. She waves and they wave back. She runs to the metro station.

Athena's Apartment Building
1:00 p.m., 31 July 2096

The building is deserted. Athena walks up the stairs, four flights up, to her hotel room rather than using the elevator. She reaches her room, the biosensor unlocks the door automatically and she closes it behind her.

11:59 p.m.

The massive figure of Lothario walks up the steps in its long raincoat and fedora on his small head. When it reaches Athena's door it doesn't wait; it punches the door off its hinges to crash to the floor.

It walks in to see Athena huddled in the far corner. She is a woman waiting to die.

"Oh Athena," it says with its helium voice. The shiny black skin of its face smiles wide, showing its metallic-looking ridged teeth. "Please don't tell me you've given up. Or did you trick me? You told me that you'd give me a good challenge. Before I eat you, I want a good challenge."

"Are your brothers here too?" Athena starts to sob.

"Oh no, Athena. They thought they'd be bored so they stayed home."

"How many of you demons are there?"

"I'm not tellin', Athena."

"Where do you demons live now?"

"I'm not tellin'. Athena, you seem to be more interested in getting me to tell secrets than preparing to die. Athena, I don't think you really are Athena."

"I'm not Athena."

"Who are you?"

"The answer is already known to you."

Lothario laughs. "One of my brothers suspected this. Tell me

Magi, when I destroy you, what will your people say? Will they mourn you? Will they bury your scraps in a pocket? Will they try to hide deeper in the ground with the worms?"

Athena seems to levitate to her feet. "That's a nice hat. We like that hat."

Lothario starts to laugh hysterically.

Athena's entire body starts to shake and starts to split in half. Each half falls away to either side and starts to change in shape, size, and color. Within moments, it is the Magi couple standing before the demon.

Lothario is still laughing. "How do you do that? It's magic. What are your names?"

"My name is Wings. My wife is Top Hat."

"You think you are so clever. You will never defeat me. All you did was bring me another body to eat."

"But Lothario, we are clever."

"You know my name." The demon is giddy with joy. "This is going to be the best challenge I ever had."

1:37 p.m., 1 August 2096

The building begins to shake and contort. All the lights on the street surrounding the building are glowing red. Lothario's broken body crashes through the walls and tumbles through the air as the building implodes.

THE MORMON ORDER

(Prelude to Project Leviathan)

North Pacific Ocean

The Big Blue

"The sea, once it casts its spell, holds one in its net of wonders forever."
– Jacques-Yves Cousteau, Pre-Islamic French oceanic explorer,
scientist, and filmmaker (1910-1997)

"Be careful of its allure, as with any wild expanse, the oceans can
become a very cold and lonely grave." — Wings, co-herald, House of
Pi, the Magi Order

Vladivostok Seaport, Primorsky Krai, Russia
7:52 a.m., 31 July 2096

"If you see any sea monsters, please send me a photo." That's what the
"nice" Russian inspector said.

One doesn't have to leave the planet to see another world.
Vincent looks like an outer space astronaut with the large mirrored
front of his helmet. His clear blue diving suit, however, makes him
look like a merman (the male version of a mermaid) with the large
fins of his feet. Only his legs move, in unison, as he descends deeper
through a school of mackerel into the "big blue." Closer to the
surface, it is like a magical realm teeming with aquatic wildlife and
plants, but below that is the void of hydrospace—the sea life gets
scarcer as the depths seem more endless. The ocean gradually gets
darker and so does his camo diving suit, which mimics its

surroundings or can be made to appear as any color, pattern, or texture.

The Sea of Japan is its own ecosystem, partially separated from the Pacific Ocean by the Korean peninsula, Japan, and its islands. It's the home of virtually an endless variety of fish and sea life, despite the busyness of sea craft traffic. But many of the larger sea animals like seals and dolphins are extinct here, and whales are long extinct. When Western Europe fell to the Caliphate thirty-plus years ago, the animal conservation movement to protect them, both intellectual and radical, disappeared overnight.

The *Divine Providence* above will remain anchored for as long as his mission takes. Being in the waters of another sovereign country is a double-edged sword. There is the governmental protection of that nation, going through whatever steps or inconveniences necessary to get permission to conduct their undersea scientific work, in this case paying double the bribes to Russian officials. But it also means the nation knows your exact location at all times, and can, and does, monitor all activities closely. The alternative is not an option in this case. Without official permission, they could be designated an "invading power," not a mere group of scientists. Elements of the Russian Fleet, based out of the Crimean peninsula, are not shy to deploy for any reason. Without official permission, they would have no state protection, and be at the mercy of any other power or, worse, criminal pirates. Everyone knows about the cyber versions on the Net, some human, some independent programs, endlessly trying to hack into people's devices or systems, but the flesh and bone ones still do exist on the high seas. They steal sea crafts, their cargos, and sometimes even its people for ransom or sex slavery—if they don't decide to just kill everyone instead.

The *Divine Providence* is primarily here for scientific study— exactly what they've reported to the authorities, but it is also the military flagship of the Order. Three members of his crew are conducting "decoy" surveys for the benefit of Russian military monitors while Vincent goes about the Order's real mission.

Vincent glances up, and with the enhanced vision of his helmet, can see his three divers above in bright yellow diving suits swimming in another direction near their craft. He continues his descent. In moments, neither his divers nor the craft will be visible, and, due to the tek of his camo-suit, he is already invisible to all detection surveillance. The Russian Bloc is more unstable than he's ever seen. They'll be on the lookout for Caliphate, CHIN, and even American subs and aquatic drones, not a lone diver.

The oceans take up two thirds of Earth's surface, but in 2096, most of the oceans are still uncharted. More is known about the surface of the moon or Mars, than the Earth's hydrosphere. People remain fixated with other worlds in the universe, ready and waiting for their "imminent" colonization or maybe even alien worlds filled with friendly extraterrestrials—all we need to do is find some kind of wormhole. No one made it clear to the general public that warp drive is actually quite impossible.

Far down in the distance, the natural illumination—bioluminescence—of the thousands of deep sea animals and flora becomes more visible. Who's to know what is indigenous to the region or what was transplanted here by marine scientists years or decades ago for legitimate conservation—or because it would make the area "look nice." Artificial external illumination of any kind is not wise here, even if you wanted to be seen or didn't care. The danger wouldn't be from a Russian or foreign sub in the vicinity, but the primitive underwater surveillance of a pirate craft that doesn't "see" with sonar, but line-of-sight. Down here artificial light can be picked up from more than fifty miles away. Vincent relies on the night-sight of his helmet.

The view is both breathtaking and frightening. As far as the mind is concerned, the ocean has no bottom. Here, as in space, the human being is infinitesimally insignificant. It's a grand canyon many times more massive than *the* Grand Canyon and is able to swallow up mountains higher than the Himalayas.

The signal is getting stronger.

Vincent has been in or on the water all his life—expert diver, boatman, seafarer, navigator, and even submariner. He has driven every kind of sea craft ever made. He's been in deep, dark water so many times that he lost count decades ago; all alone, or surrounded by sea life, even including great white sharks a few times. It's all second-nature to him.

I feel as if I'm being watched.

Faithers never ignore such feelings, especially in this Tek World. Vincent switches to thermal view and swims in a small circle as he scans the entire area. Nothing.

He touches his wrist control, and a fin rises out of the center of his back and his helmet elongates. From afar, he'd look like a hammerhead shark, though very few sharks come to this area anymore. He scans the area again, but more slowly. Nothing.

The mind can play tricks on anyone, even a seasoned pro like himself. In a massive, black expanse, all alone, it's a wonder it doesn't happen more often. Some people play music or listen to an audiobook in their ear-set, but that's against protocols.

Keep focused. Here, unfocused people become dead people.

Down he goes. The signal is stronger—the pauses between beeps in his ear-set are getting shorter and shorter. There it is.

Paranoia goes hand in hand with being a Faither. Mormons were part of the Separatist Movement before the movement even had a name. Faithers abandoned American tek-cities for the "safety" of Faith-World, far past the Outlands and Trogland. Mormons went further—they left America all together.

The "fish" lies at the edge of the precipice; a machine identical to a real fish in every way. If the bot had not embedded itself into the ground before its power malfunctioned, it would have fallen into the ocean depths, never to be seen again. "Fish" are used for vid-surveillance and data gathering. Now that the Order is a seafaring people, these small robots are essential to Mormon external security, which is why finding out what happened is a high-priority matter. An entire company of Fish are gone without any clue as to the reason for their malfunction or loss of contact. The recovery signal for all of them fell out of range, except for this one.

He touches his wrist control and his faceplate does a rear view—showing him what's behind him from the vid-cam in the back of his helmet. A giant manta glides away in the distance. *This is a bit far down for him. Maybe that's my undersea watcher.*

Vincent pulls the Fish out of the floor sediment and loose rocks. It must have been the very last one in the formation. The crewman who gave the unique signal to the fish-bot to bury itself in the ground deserves a commendation for his quick thinking. Only one remains to be recovered out of the total twenty-six.

As his hand rests on the Fish, his proximity alarms start screaming in his ear-set. His motions are instinctive; he spins in a 360-degree circle, scanning up and down. Nothing. The alarm doesn't sound for nothing.

He switches to thermal view as he spins around again. Nothing. He looks up.

In a split second, he jerks backwards with his body, aided by his arms and legs. The boat fills his entire view as it falls past him, only inches from his helmet. He straightens as stiff as a board fast, but the falling object scrapes his left knee.

"Back!" he calls out.

A blast from his diving suit's chest propulsion nozzle moves him back further. If the palm of his gloves hadn't auto-clamped on the Fish, it would have been gone.

The boat is some kind of submersible and the wake of its rapid descent pushes him away, but he opens his chest pouch, puts the Fish inside, seals it, and dives after it. Once past the ledge of the precipice, he turns sharply to the left and swims away.

For any aquatic mission, preparation is key. No matter how long the mission, the prep time for that mission takes even longer. The sea life for the region is known, any potential predators are known, territorial ones are identified; any sunken crafts are identified to avoid any treasure hunters or recovery teams. Lost-and-found reports of missing weapons, equipment, or devices from other sea craft are culled over; all weather and current sea maps are known; the international political climate of neighboring countries is known; pirates are accounted for; underwater, surface, air, drone, and sat-surveillance is known. What takes the most time is a detailed study of side-sonar maps of every square inch the sea mission will take them to. Not only to find the best routes to and from, but if needed, the best points to launch defensive attacks from, or to simply hide. In submariner language: "They can't destroy you if they can't find you."

He swims for about thirty feet. Into the cave he goes. The cave is big enough for three people to fit in comfortably. Fortunately for him, no other critters are home. Vincent quickly pulls his camo-poncho from another chest pouch. Its nickname is an "invisibility cloak." He covers the entrance to the cave in front of him with it. The camo-poncho, like his diving suit, mimics surroundings in color and texture. It now looks like a solid rockface. He pulls an Eyeball from his waist pouch, extends it, and pushes it through a small hole in the poncho as he props his body against the cave wall and some rocks. He can comfortably wait as long as he wants to and see outside via the Eyeball vid-cam.

His boat will not leave without him. They will be worried, but they won't leave. The diving suit itself will send out a special pulse signal, if the diver expires.

That submersible was purposely dropped on him. He views all the sensor logs now on his virtual display. His diving suit records all images in a 360-degree view from nodes on every major section on the suit. The recording storage is the last four hours. Accidents can happen on the sea, especially in and around such a busy port. He's seen cranes drop submersibles into the water before, robots drop cargo containers on people; the list is endless. But this was different. It followed him from the surface, moved ahead to just above the location of the Fish, and when he found it, down it came.

Even without the data, Faithers don't believe in coincidences. Fish-bots on patrol malfunctioning and disappearing, feeling of being watched, submersible "falling" out of nowhere. If it had hit him, it could have crushed him, ruptured his suit, or taken him down to the bottom of the sea, killing him. In this part of the ocean, the bottom is over two miles down. His eardrums, lungs, and blood vessels would all explode long before he'd have the "pleasure" of the pressure of sea crushing his entire body into nothingness.

Not moving a muscle, breathing as slowly as possible, all systems powered down to the absolute minimal settings; he waits. And he watches the horizontal split screen of the Eyeball—night view and infrared view.

What are Miri and the kids doing right now?

Random thoughts on just about anything to pass the time. A blur passes from top to bottom of his view, about ten feet away.

What was that?

He can stay in the same spot for only thirty minutes more without powering up fully to allow his suit to create air to breath. He's already been submerged for a full hour, though it seems like much shorter. He waits. Five minutes. Ten minutes. He plays games in his mind to stay focused. Ten minutes. Fifteen minutes.

An apparition-like figure floats into view.

Vincent watches the white-headed black figure stop. The strange diver has an upside-down, whitish, oval helmet with pointy ears. He looks more closely and realizes they are actually antennas made to look like pointy ears. It has a visor running from one "ear" to another, and in the mouth area it has what looks to be three clawed teeth. Its entire body is like a long ragged robe, no arms or legs are visible. The bottom part of the "robe" initially looks all ripped up, but they are actually dozens of tiny fins.

The figure scans all around. Its eyes "turn on" and it continues its search with the blue-light beams from its eyes. It shines the beams all along the sea cliff side. There! It swims forward as its clawed arms appear from its robe suit. It cautiously circles the outside of the cave shining the light inside. Nothing.

It sticks its head in. The cave is empty. It swims away quickly as it flips from back to front and throws an object inside. There is a sonic explosion! A cloud of debris envelops the immediate area and then disperses. The cave is no more.

The diver looks downward, noticing a faint light falling. The diver waits. The manta-bot appears again and descends after it. The diver links with the bot's night-vision vid-screen and can see it's the Fish. A robotic arm pops out of the belly of the manta-bot and grabs it.

The diver watches the bot do a 180-degree arc to swim back up towards him as its robotic arm retracts with the Fish back into its belly compartment.

Boom!

The sonic explosion violently blows the diver away as the bot disintegrates into pieces. The strange diver recovers. The manta-bot is gone, its debris on the way to the seafloor. It snaps its head back to what used to be the little cave.

I saw something.

He swims up above the precipice and scans the area. He sees a light in the distance, moving away fast. The multi-fin design of its diving suit is equivalent to dozens of powerful finned tails. It streaks out after the light, quickly closing the gap. The diver stops. The light is moving away from the *Divine Providence*.

He wouldn't be swimming away from the craft. This is another trick.

The strange diver turns around immediately like an eel, and swims in the opposite direction.

Vincent surfaces alongside the *Divine Providence*.

"Captain, where were you?" one of his crewmen says and helps him up the sea-ladder. "What happened?"

Vincent takes off his helmet and hands it to him. He moves quickly into the deck bridge command center; the two men follow.

"Captain, are you okay?" asks one of the female crew.

"Do an immediate sweep for any low-band, P2P communications," he directs.

"Yes, Captain," another crewman answers.

"Prepare for a full spread of sonic charges now."

"Yes, Captain," a female crewman says.

Vincent takes something out of his chest pouch and hands it to one of the men. "Download all the data from this asap."

The man takes it. "Yes, sir." He walks past everyone and disappears down the steps below.

The strange diver nears the ship.

"This is Channa," he says into his comm. "They may have recovered the surveillance."

"Are you able to destroy the craft?" a voice asks in his ear-set.

"Are there any other vessels in the area?"

"Yes, two private ones and the Russians have three heavy boats nearby."

"We'll have to risk it. I'll destroy the craft, but I will need immediate evac. I need another Manta."

"A replacement is on its way to you now."

Channa continues swimming towards the catamaran ship, but the *Divine Providence* powers up and jets away along the water's surface.

An underwater explosion flashes fifteen feet away from him. A second explosion follows ten feet away. A third explosion blows up something behind him—must be his replacement Manta. He dives as fast as he can. Explosion after explosion blankets the entire area. All he can do is dive as fast as possible. So far all of the sonic charges are near the surface.

An explosion nearly on top of him stops his dive and tumbles him around and around, knocking out his suit's controls. He falls.

"Very good, Jew-Christians," he says aloud. They must be listening.

Wolf Point

"For me… that is a really difficult question, Dr. Laurenson, because the world around me is shrinking and the Four Horsemen of the Apocalypse are comin' to see me today, and they're not bringing flowers which… just makes it real difficult to get organized." — Rudy Mackenzie, the Jacket, 2005

"If someone made a movie about how we got here, they would have demanded their money back and said it was stupid and unbelievable. But here we are. I'm a German Jew suddenly finding himself in 1930s Third Reich Germany." — Prophet Jedidiah Clay, the Mormon Order

Elizabeth Center, Anacostia, Southeast Washington DC
11:02 a.m., 5 April 2070

Homeland Deputy Director Anita McDunn walks out of her office to the executive assistant area. Her eyes are dark and her short blond hair is angled to her chin. She and all her executive staff wears black suits.

"Ms. Crabtree."

One of the executive assistants, all busy at work on their laptops, turns to her. "Yes, ma'am."

McDunn hands her a tablet. "The President wants this new directive blasted out on all media channels immediately."

"Yes, ma'am."

Americans work long hours already, but if you work in the District (Washington, DC)—the White House, the Capitol, Homeland, and any one the many auxiliary agencies, divisions, or private firms—you work even longer.

Voice-typing is forbidden in most of the District for obvious confidentiality reasons. The executive assistant quickly types the directive and will spend the rest of the day ensuring all domestic and international media know that the President of the United States has mandated a new word to be used going forward to describe all non-Muslim religious people: Jew-Christian.

At 11:02 at night, Ms. Crabtree finishes her day's work, locks up her desk and files with the touch of a biometric button, grabs her purse, and leaves for home. But she never gets there—ever.

Salt Lake City, Utah
6:29 a.m., 17 May 2076 (Six years later)

The impromptu meeting is held in an underground bunker of a room. Fifteen men sit at an old oak table; dozens of men and women are crammed into the room. The men at the table are the leadership of the Mormon Order. They are known as Apostles or Elders (they no longer use the title of Presidents) and the one known as their First Elder, the leader of the Order, is called the Prophet. Two other Apostles are his Counselors. Informally, among the people in everyday dealings, all the men are simply addressed as "sir" or "mister."

"It happened yesterday, in Kansas City. Two pastors were killed by government police," the man says nervously. Another young man and woman stand with him for the briefing. "Eighty people are dead, including at least a dozen government police. The city is in revolt and major sections of it are in flames. The Kansas governor is supposed to be launching a final ground and air assault. The civilian city is making their stand right there, thousands of Faithers."

"If we go, how long will it take for us to get there?" one of the Apostles asks.

The woman says, "We can be there in fifteen minutes, sir." It is Ms. Crabtree.

"Prophet, we can't get involved," another Apostle says. "I know that's harsh, but we can't, not now. It could jeopardize our Exodus project. That's the priority. Get our own people to safety first, especially now, before it's too late." He looks around at the other fourteen men. "Gentlemen, are we in agreement?" The men start to raise their hands slowly to approve.

"Ever been to the Grand Africa Reserve?" Apostle Simon begins. "One of the last few remaining places left on Earth where wildlife can live free of people and all their technological garbage. You have giraffes, zebras, gnus, yaks, ostriches, etc. All different, but always hanging out together, for mutual safety. That's the Faither community."

He is dressed more casually than the other men at the table, but unlike when the other men were talking, no one is saying anything. Everyone is listening closely to him.

Apostle Simon speaks up louder. "Gentlemen, I know Apostle Thomas only has the best interests of the Order in mind, but as my father used to say, when your friends need ya, you come runnin.' Are we honestly going to sit here and allow the Boggs government to slaughter our friends while we hide in a hole?"

Why Faithers hated the government could be summed up by one phrase: President T. Wilson. Christians called him Galerius, after the ancient Roman Emperor who was the most vicious murderer of Christians. Jews called him Haman after Haman the Evil, who was a fifth-century-BC noble of the Persian Empire that instigated a plot to kill all of the Jews of ancient Persia, only to be foiled by Queen Esther. Mormons called him President Boggs, after the Missouri Governor who issued an extermination order of all Mormons in 1838 America, and forcibly expelled thousands from the state.

"That is not what we're doing, and you know that," Apostle Thomas Sr. says. "Our primary responsibility must always be the safety of the Order. Should we be slaughtered with them?"

"Gentlemen, you can vote any way you want, but I'm going," Apostle Simon says. He looks at the trio of officers again. "So who's flying and who's going to put some wicked guns in my hands?"

"I'm flying, sir," the woman once known as Ms. Crabtree says with a smile.

"I'll put all the wicked weapons in your hand that you need," a young Vincent answers.

Apostle Simon stands. "Okay gentlemen, you can stay while I and these three youngsters go into battle. No one, and I mean no one, is going to ever say Mormons were 'not present.' I'm not abandoning my friends. That's what we formed the Faither alliance for."

Thomas Sr. stands too, angry. "The interfaith alliance was formed so we could have monthly discussions about protocol and other niceties, so we wouldn't offend each other at gatherings. It was never to be some blood pact for Mormon men and women to get killed in someone else's battle."

"Martin Niemöller, that Christian pastor in Nazi Germany, said it best. I'll paraphrase for you. First, they came for the Jews, and I did not speak out—because I was not a Jew. Then they came for my friends, and I did not speak out—because I was not them. Then they came for us, and there was no one left to speak out for me.

"Gentlemen, I'll either see you soon—or on the other side. But I don't hide in holes when my friends need me." He looks at the trio again. "Lead on youngsters."

Apostle Simon follows the civilian officers. Three other Apostles immediately stand and run after him, then the remaining ones. Only Apostle Thomas Sr., the Prophet, and the two Counselors remain.

"Let us provide whatever air support they need," the Prophet says.

"Yes, Prophet," Apostle Thomas Sr. says.

"We'll do whatever we can do from here. Have all our medical people standing by too."

"Prophet, my words were not said out of cowardice as Simon was suggesting."

"Thomas, let me be blunt,"—he looks at the other two men—"and I also mean you. Simon returns and he'll be running the Order. The Separatist Movement is splintering every single Faither group in the country, whole denominations are collapsing. And the government is trying to chase us out of our own state."

"Prophet, the logic of the Resistance is flawed. Confrontation will lead to extermination," Apostle Thomas Sr. says. "Warmongers never see that."

"Simon knows that and he isn't a warmonger. The Exodus project came from him. You didn't know that did you?"

"No, I didn't."

"Thomas, you…we have to have the respect of the people to lead, to remain united as one people. The Christians have their own internal civil war going on and so do the Jews. Mormons don't do that. We must never allow it. You need that respect of the people. Simon returns and he'll be running the Order."

"Prophet, he's going to his death."

"Have you become Pagan on us, Thomas?"

"No, sir."

"Miracles do still happen for believers. God isn't dead, despite what the Pagans say. Even in the devil's playpen."

"Of course, sir."

The Prophet's eyes seem to tear up. Thomas Sr. is unsure of the source of the emotion in the man. Is it desperate hope? Is it deep-rooted hopelessness, or something else? Their leader walks out of the room and they follow.

Secret Stronghold, Wolf Point, Montana
8:00 a.m., March 2081

Utah is still the "homeland" of the Mormon Order, but now there's also Wolf Point. Their leadership is here now. It is here that Exodus is being finalized.

Three men sit casually in the private room with their notepads and cups of water in hand. It is where the men meet daily in the temple stronghold.

"They say it's those significant events in history that make the men of significance in history," the Second Counselor says.

"I would never engage in such a boast," says Simon. "The Order is so morbidly cautious on all matters, ever since the marriage wars, that we needed to take another path."

"At least it's the Christians, and not us, that are associated with the marriage wars," the First Counselor interjects.

"What does it matter? All the culture wars are long over, and we're the losers," Simon counters. "My Father used to tell me that there were communities with churches on every block, but it wasn't a sign of the proliferation of faith or glory of God, but proof positive of the utter disunity and pettiness of the faith community. We're their descendants and this is our curse to bear. But that's not why we're here."

"Since you became Prophet after the Kansas Event, you've been leading us through one critical mission after another," the First Counselor says.

"Like the Jews," says the Second Counselor. "We can both now relate to the loss of a homeland. And here we live on the land of pre-Americans, who also lost a homeland."

"It's the biblical story of Lot living in the Cities of the Plain, all over again. He was not exactly the epitome of a man of wise decisions. No matter how genuinely righteous he and his family were, they could never have remained. Their personal exodus was inevitable, as it is with us."

"My children always ask me how we got to this place," the First Counselor says. "My religious answers don't seem to be adequate for them."

"Tell them that people will always vote for Santa Claus. They want to remain the child, always selfishly receiving the gifts, never being the adult with the responsibility of selflessly making those gifts for others."

"Yes, indeed. The lost world."

"The soul of the world disintegrates. First comes the persecution, tyranny, and violence, then the final physical disintegration. We can get all comfy here in Wolf Point, but Exodus is not over."

"What are you saying?"

Private Residence, Moscow
11:34 a.m., March 2086

"Simple. Most of our men were dead. The government drove us out of the North—New York, Ohio, Illinois, and Missouri. The directives were to exterminate us. Kill us or drive us out. Polygamy was a necessity. Men were assigned to women and families. Repopulation of our people, with so many men dead, was the focus. Though, even back then, only around five percent practiced it. It didn't happen before the Great Persecution and it stopped after it. This, Father, is a very sensitive issue for us. As any married man knows, you can barely handle one."

The Father smiles. "Yes, true. I'm so sorry, Mr. Simon, for my indelicate questions. The Russian Orthodox has been cut off from much of the world for some time now. Being within the Russian Bloc has been both a blessing and a burden for us. We did not suffer the same fate of our Orthodox brothers and sisters in Western Europe and Israel, but we have been so isolated. Again I'm sorry for my insensitivity."

"Your point is well taken. You and I, your people and mine, can't complain when so many Faithers were lost."

"Yes, true."

"Father Vladimir, may I ask what prompted the question since polygamy hasn't been practiced or allowed in my Order for almost two centuries? It's somewhat surprising to even hear the word in the same sentence from another Faither, especially when both Pagans and Muslims are the only ones who practice it today."

"The Russian Orthodox is a tolerant people, but we are uniformly committed to our faith and its customs and practices. Our concern is not your Mormonism, but your Americanism."

Prophet Simon laughs. "Is that the problem? Why didn't you say so?"

"America is so anti-religious that we've found some of its religious people hate religion."

"So true, Father. We have dealt with one Great Persecution in America. We're not about to wait for the second one."

"Our Pope Patriarch will help your people in any way. We have a small community of Jews who live with our community."

"Yes, we heard that."

"But this is a very dramatic move for your people, to just leave your home country. I'm told you have an entire state, and completely control its government to protect your people."

"We have to, and the Fall of Jewish Israel only strengthened our decision. Israel didn't have a buffer zone with its enemies, neither do we."

Father Vladimir nods. "You should see the streets of Russian and Eastern Europe. We're just like Korea and Southern Africa; everyone carries a weapon waiting for 'invasion'—Caliphate or CHIN. I just realized why you're not looking at Africa."

"The Christian-Islamic War on the continent is not our idea of an ideal safe haven."

"Australia?"

"We don't feel it's secure enough for our needs."

"It's a shame the Spanish Americas are so dominated by criminal cartels. If only the Catholic Church did there what we have done here in the Russian Bloc. Become integral to the government and integral to helping the people solve their daily problems, serve their needs."

"Have the Russian Orthodox made any contact with any Faithers outside the Russian Bloc?"

"Our Pope Patriarch is handling those communications directly. It must be handled carefully. We may be part of the government, unofficially, and beloved by the people, but we're monitored like every other citizen."

"Yes, this former American can relate to that. You seem to have more drones in the sky than we do. When can we get started?"

"All government permits and approvals are in order. Your city-ships can enter Russian Bloc waters as soon as your people are ready. Your people know far more about sailing and oceanography than mine, so I don't know how much use our advisors will be."

They stand from their chairs and shake hands.

Wolf Point, Montana
2:32 p.m., June 2086

There was a time when this city was sparsely populated with a sole pre-American Indian reservation. The beauty and remoteness remains, but the American Indians are gone—that phrase doesn't exist anymore. The growing population, both religious and secular, does have one thing in common—radically anti-government. The secular includes Hedonists, Nihilists, Goths and Nudists. The religious are almost exclusively Mormon.

Vincent works in the lab with his team. All are dressed in what look to be white jumpsuits. Some are at their vid-screen consoles while Vincent and others watch the performance of the new propulsion engines through thick glass.

Above them on the second floor, Prophet Simon watches the tests through the observation windows with his two Counselors and one of the civilian military commanders.

"How are the tests proceeding?" the Prophet asks.

"We're ahead of schedule, sir," the Commander answers.

"This is such a drastic move on our part," the First Counselor says.

The Prophet says, "Even the Catholics in Texas are planning to leave the state. I never thought I'd ever see that in my lifetime. Texas Faithers fleeing rather than fighting. It can't be just us left in the Southwest."

"Our contacts say that the implementation of the government's Project Purify is imminent," the Second Counselor says.

"Are we fully certain that the general population will tolerate it?" one the officers asks. "Boggs is just one man."

"Boggs is just a man, but politics is a follower. Culture is what always leads. T. Wilson's administration exists because the people want it to exist, which sadly includes many anti-Resistance religious citizens. The ongoing Resistance-Registrant wars told us that with depressing clarity. Some people just like being a slave. The greatest generations to the worst in less than a century, and we'll never get it back," the Prophet says.

"But even non-religious citizens are rising up now," the First Counselor adds. "We should try to exploit that."

"Pagans?" the Prophet asks. "We can't put the fate of our people in the hands of Anarchists, Nihilists, Nudists, Drug Zombies, and Hedonists."

The First Counselor says, "I'm being as strong of a devil's advocate as I can be. We still have people in the Order with doubts."

"I know and I appreciate it, Mark. We all hate this. I'm sure our people were just as disturbed when they had to leave their homes in the Northeast and Mid-Atlantic for that strange land in the then-Mexican Territory called Utah. Now we can't think of any other place as our home, but we'll adapt. We'll always be Americans, even though America no longer is.

The Prophet turns to the Commander. "How's Vincent doing? I'm surprised that young man isn't running our civilian military yet."

"That's what we were grooming him for, sir."

"It's time we end the gray-haired gerontocracy we have in the Order." He smiles. "Let's at least lower some of our standards a bit and have a few leaders who are *starting* to go gray."

The Commander says, "We were, sir, but he and his wife went on sabbatical to start a family. It's only fair that they have their time."

"Who can blame him?"

"He's left his full-time duties from Military, but not the Project. He's been working on it in his spare time. He's even scaled back his class teaching. We're actually borrowing him from the Project for Exodus."

The Order's civilian equivalent of the government's Homeland Defense and Intelligence Agency is its own Civilian Military Services—simply referred to as Military—responsible for external paramilitary defense operations, and Control—responsible for intelligence gathering and internal security.

"Good." The Prophet looks down at the lab workers again.

"Do we really have all the financing we need for Exodus?" the Commander asks.

"There's one thing we can thank the Pagans for," the First Counselor says. "If they never started their man-made planetary climate change hysteria, fission power apocalypse hysteria, 'global burn up' and 'global freeze up,' we wouldn't have the bio-sphere and terraforming industries of today."

"Industries we've invested heavily in," the Second Counselor adds.

"Profits which will allow us to make Exodus possible. Our sales to Russian Bloc government parties will allow us to buy the protection we need in the short term. And short term is all we need for now."

"Everything is going perfectly as planned. Everything, for the last decade," the Second Counselor says.

Prophet Simon watches the lab workers engage the massive propulsion engines—colors going from white to blue, to yellow to bright orange, and finally neon green. "That's what I'm worried about. It's been going so perfectly for so long that I'm wondering when and how it will start to go perfectly wrong."

Dirty Ol' Tom

"Who's Brad Pitt?"
"Get me Brad Pitt."
"Get me someone like Brad Pitt."
"Get me a young Brad Pitt."
"Who's Brad Pitt?"
— The Hollywood Circle of Life

Sea of Japan, Russia Territory
7:52 a.m., 1 August 2096

The sea breeze is particularly strong this morning. Vincent opens his eyes and stares up at the ceiling. He can hear the waves crashing against the city-ship in his mind's eye, but that's not true. All living quarters of the *Pacifica* are along the inner circle of the city-ship, shielded from the ocean.

There's nothing like being in your own warm bed. He's back from the mission, but now the wife is out on one. The life of senior intelligence and military leadership in the Order is never dull and never quiet. The plan is to lie in bed for an hour or two. No. Under these warm covers, he can vegetate until well past noon. There's that feeling again. *Who's watching me?*

He glances at the open bedroom door and there she is—his youngest daughter, Cat, peeking in at him, with her hands on her hips. Unlike his other children, she wears horn-rimmed clear glasses, something many of the kids her age do to look older. Then when they do get older, they'll spend their entire lives trying to look younger. He immediately closes his eyes and throws the covers over his head. *Maybe she didn't see I'm up.*

"Oh, no you don't," she says.

The covers are pulled off his head. He lies there with his eyes closed, but he knows what's waiting for him. He opens one eye.

"It's time to get out of bed, Father," she says. "When you get out of bed, I'll tell you 'good morning.'"

God's cosmos can be a strange place. He can remember when he first saw the ultrasound of her, when she was brought home—all seven pounds of her, the first day she walked, the first day she talked—saying "momma" of course. Now she's a…big person, even at twelve years old, with independent thoughts and free will of her own.

Do all parents have these thoughts about their kids, or is it just me?

"I'm not done sleeping."

"But you're up."

"I'm about to go back to sleep."

"There's too much to do and the family is waiting for debriefing."

Vincent chuckles. He pulls the covers over his head again.

"Not so fast, sailor." She pulls the covers off his head again.

"Where's Mother?"

"Mother is on mission still."

Vincent rolls over in the bed onto his stomach. "Go away. I want to sleep one more hour." He covers the back of his head with his pillow.

"Thirty minutes only, Father," Cat says. "The family is waiting." She marches out of the bedroom.

Yes, general.

Pacific Ocean, Russian Territory
8:05 a.m., 1 August 2096

Mr. Varma waves as his silver speedboat, the *Moving Picture*, approaches. One of the three men standing on the deck of the yacht waves back. The name of the yacht is not visible. It digitally appears and disappears, as needed—a common practice for sea craft of Faithers and pirates, too. He's been to the *Honi* many times before. He pulls alongside it and sets anchor. The yacht belongs to the Mormon Order.

"Hello," he says.

"Good morning, Mr. Varma," one of the men pushes the ladder-bot against the side. Its ladder arms reach up and over the side into the speedboat. Varma climbs up the ladder with two bags in hand. The first man takes the first bag from him. A second man helps by taking the other bag as Varma steps into the yacht.

"A beautiful day today," he says.

"Yes, it is." The first man leads Varma inside the boat.

They go below to a group of men and women already assembled and waiting. They are happy to see him.

"Have some food, Mr. Varma," one of the women says as people greet him.

Faithers love their food at their meetings. "Oh, yes please."

"What do you have for us today, Mr. Varma?" one of the men asks.

Varma takes the two bags from the other men and sets them on the conference table. He is a traveling salesman among the Faither communities in this region, which include the Asian Consortium, CHIN territories and the Russian Bloc, almost thirty eight hundred miles. He also makes a trip to Australia every four months. Government post offices may have disappeared ages ago, but private shipping companies in the world have so many government rules and regulations to follow that no matter how private or independent they are, they are all extensions of the government. Faithers, regardless of country or specific religion, will have nothing to do with the government. An entire niche industry has arisen as a result—the personal courier—allowing people like him to carve out a very nice living.

Today he has an assortment of items from Asian countries such as China Proper, his native India, Singapore, Hong Kong, Hanguk Korea, and Taiwan. Varma begins to take the contents from the bags and displays them on the table.

"I also have some movies, too," he says.

Movies, vid-games, audio-broadcasts, etc. are all streamed from the Net and that's how it's always been in his thirty years of life. But the Net is also controlled by the government, which again, meant Faithers would have nothing to do with it. So the old tek of movies on physical discs returned to the world.

"What do you have?" a man asks.

"I have some Old Hollywood war movies this time. Classics." Varma finds the discs in the bag.

"Is there a hidden meaning in your selection, Mr. Varma?"

"None at all." Varma smiles. "Other than to recite my favorite movie quote: 'All of life's riddles are answered in the movies.'"

Everyone laughs. "A very good quote, indeed," says another man.

Even if Faithers did watch movies via the Net, they wouldn't, especially any from America. Today, with the legalization of prostitution, all narcotic drugs, and the general belief that all behavior is "normal," America's Hollywood basically merged with the pornography industry. Bollywood, the entertainment studios of India, not only became the main movie industry of choice for religious people, including all Muslim countries of the Caliphate, but most of the world. Even atheistic China, with its own thriving movie industry, loved Bollywood. Hollywood had become a curse word, except in the Americas, the Russian Bloc, and Australia.

It some ways India had become the new battlefield of cultural wars between atheist Indians and Hindu Indians. But unlike America, the religious were still the solid majority, and strangely, even atheistic China supported Hindus in India and not atheists.

Varma had met the Order years ago. Actually, he can't even remember when and where anymore, but it had to do with movies. He loved movies, and even if he wasn't from an entertainment family himself, with all his family working in Bollywood for generations, he would still be a movie evangelist like every other Indian.

"Old Hollywood? How long ago?" a man asks.

"Over a century ago," he answers.

He knows what they really want to know. What actors are in the movie? Jews will not watch anything made by certain Old Hollywood directors and actors. Catholics had a long list of actors and moviemakers that they would not watch, as did the Protestants, the Russian Orthodox, and even the reticent Shogun. Mormons had a long list too, but at the top of the list was actor-moviemaker Tom Hanks. He apparently made a movie that showed a sacred religious ceremony and, for that, even classics that Bollywood acknowledged would never be seen by any living Mormon. It even went so far with some Mormons in the Order, that "Tom" had become slang for "bastard." Everyone has their customs, even his fellow Hindus.

Varma takes his palm tablet from his bag and shows them the IMDB stats on of all the movies he has—ironically, a movie database created and still maintained by America. People glance at the stats casually, but he knows they are carefully reviewing them for banned names. They are satisfied and continue to inspect the other items.

Two women bring him a plate of food and a glass of juice.

"Oh, thank you."

"Mr. Varma, let's talk for a quick bit," one of the men says. "Bring your food."

The man is tall and very distinguished-looking with his gray hair and somewhat weathered skin. He is the typical "old salt," a longtime-seafaring captain who has been everywhere on the seas and has the stories, and scars, to prove it. Varma knows he is high up in the leadership, despite his casual dress, informal demeanor, and lack of *visible* security detail.

There is an important role for a traveling salesman like Varma, and that is of a courier of information. In Faither communities, information is the most important secular commodity there is—anything about mutual enemies and any possible threats.

He follows the man and a couple to a smaller conference room. The table has plates of food already there; they were eating before he arrived. They take their seats as Varma is directed to sit at the head of the table. Everyone eats.

"What do you think about the mess in the Russian Bloc?" asks the woman.

"It is sad. You think a nation is stable and nothing could ever shake it, and then unrest happens. They said the new president has had at least two assassination attempts."

"Every nation, no matter how advanced and civilized, is only a week or two away from total collapse," the lead man says. "We have millennia of history to tell us that. Destruction is so much easier to achieve than order is to maintain."

"Yes, my country knows that well," Varma says.

"Do you know what happened to the Russian Orthodox?" he asks.

"No, unfortunately I don't. I was supposed to be with them next week. No one knows what happened."

"Do you think it was the government?" the woman asks.

"I don't think so."

"But wasn't it their leader that tried to assassinate their president?—supposedly."

"Yes, their Pope Patriarch, incredibly, if it was really him. But that would have meant his execution or disappearance. Not half a million people, including children, including Jews."

"Why not?" asks the man. "It happens all the time in this part of the world. They don't care about women, or children, or anyone else."

"If it were any other religion, I would agree with you, but the Russian Orthodox? It's Russia. It's different when it comes to them."

"Even the Pennsylvanians in America declared war on their pacifist Amish," a woman interjects.

"True, but all my contacts say it wasn't the government. They're truly baffled. The Orthodox just…disappeared."

"Very disturbing," the lead man says.

"It is."

"Is this president of theirs really nicknamed the Leviathan King?"

"Yes and he really is a mobster, too."

"Why do you think he picked that as a nickname?" the woman asks.

"He has a tattoo of a giant squid on his back and over his body. I also heard that he was a longtime participant in some underwater extreme sports contest in Europa. It's actually called the Leviathan. I'm not sure what to believe. I can find out."

"Sure, if you can. Not a priority though," the lead man says.

Varma knows that he means just the opposite.

The man smiles and says, "So tell us about your latest adventures."

"Do you know I was actually in central China?"

"No way. How?" they ask.

"China is very restrictive on Indian travel in their country, even today, despite our great Chinese-Indian Alliance."

"We know. How did you get around the restrictions?" the woman asks.

Varma tells them all about his secret trip into the heart of China and throughout the CHIN territory and meeting with Faither enclaves to start business with them. When they finish their food, they rejoin the larger group in the main conference room. Everyone is fascinated by his stories and they end up buying all his items.

He waves goodbye from his speedboat. They wave back from the deck and inside the cabin. Both boats move off in different directions. The lead man watches the speedboat disappear in the distance.

"What should we do?" the woman asks.

"No one on the Twelve believes that the Russian Orthodox just disappeared. They were made to disappear. Their sub-city wasn't supposed to be operational for another year, but it's gone," a man says.

"We have to assume the Pagans know about Project Leviathan," the woman adds.

"This jeopardizes everything," the other man says. "We're using the same tek for the Project. We have to also assume the worst. The Pagans killed or imprisoned the entire Russian Orthodox, have their biosphere tek, and will be able to reverse engineer it. They might even be able to trace it back to us, despite everything we've done. We have to scrap the Project."

"No, we're not doing any such thing," the lead man says. "We also have no proof that anyone outside the Order knows anything about the Project. Anyway, we're too far along. We'll accelerate the Project instead. Assemble the Twelve on our return."

"Yes, Prophet," the other man responds.

The Pacifica City-Ship, Sea of Japan, Russia Territory
7:52 a.m., 1 August 2096

Vincent and his wife had their children later than most of their friends their age. Another one of the sacrifices made as leaders in the Order to protect their people—the Resistance, the Exodus from Utah, and the Exodus from America itself to the city-ships far from their ancestral nation.

"Channa?" Cat asks.

"Yes." Vincent reclines back in his living room chair with all his children sitting around him. His oldest son, Bear, sits closest, his eldest daughter, Dove, next. His other son, Seal, and Bee, his middle daughter, sit in front of him with Cat.

"Channa? As in Channa argus, Channa diplogramma, or Channa micropeltes?" she asks again.

"Stop showing off," Dove says.

"No, I don't mean the normal snakehead fish. I want you to find out if there are any other contemporary meanings for it."

"Father, maybe if you tell us where you encountered the name that will help us in our search," Bear says.

Vincent thinks for a moment.

"Father, we've never told anyone before," Dove says.

"That's not what I'm concerned about. You're my kids, not agents of the Order."

"We are agents of the Order," Cat says. "*Because* we're your kids."

"I don't think that reasoning would be appreciated by my boss, the Twelve, or anyone else I answer to."

"So…" Dove starts.

"So?"

"Father, you've never been concerned about allowing us to help before," Dove says. "Does this mean there's a possibility that you might—"

Vincent holds up his hand. "Please do not even speculate about any such thing out loud."

"Speculate about what?" Seal asks.

"Yeah, speculate about what?" Bee says. "Stop talking secret adult talk. Tell us."

"Father, we'll just ask Mom when she gets back," Bee says.

Vincent looks at her with a smirk. "Then you'll have to wait until she gets back."

The children laugh.

"Then tell us this Father," Dove asks. "Should we be expecting a special dinner guest soon?"

"Changing the subject," Vincent says loudly.

"Father, you're being very illogical," Cat says.

Vincent starts to laugh. "Changing the subject. Do you want to continue down this illogical line of conversation or…do you want me to tell you the story about the meaning of Channa?"

Every child stops talking immediately, sits up straight or readjusts their sitting positions, and eagerly waits.

"Okay then. I was diving in an undisclosed location and I was chased by an unidentified diver in a type of diving suit that I've never seen before. A suit that made him look like some kind of…Vampire." Every one of them perks up. "Our comm-intercept picked up his actual or code name: Channa. That's it. Go to work."

The children look at each other.

"We'll get to it right now, Father," Bear says as he stands.

The children rise from their seats and follow Bear to his room.

North Pacific Ocean
9:12 a.m., 1 August 2096

The mini attack sub looks like a giant manta as it glides through the ocean. Inside, a male crew of ten dressed in full black diving suits with only their faces exposed, wait for instructions. Their eyes are yellow, orange, or neon blue; and their faces are artificially pale white. These men are Vampires.

In the small private room, their captain sits in his giant pod-chair.

"Channa," the other man says from the vid-screen. "You failed."

Channa smiles, his multiple fanged teeth revealed. He stares back with his bright red eyes. "The setback is minor and doesn't change anything."

"Should we assemble the attack fleet?"

"Why? There are Russian subs everywhere and now CHIN and Caliphate subs are showing up with more frequency. There will be more subs and bots in the water than indigenous sea life. No. We can't let anyone know of our existence. It doesn't matter if the Jew-Christians know. They won't tell anyone."

"But they've seen us."

"None of that matters."

"The orders then are to do nothing."

"The orders are to wait. Let the Jew-Christians come to us. We know they will sooner rather than later. They come; we kill them, and get our plans on track."

The Pacifica, Sea of Japan, Russia Territory
2:22 p.m., 4 August 2096

Vincent sits reading in his pod-chair (simply called pods) on the family balcony. Pods are primarily chairs, but can be configured for any relaxation or entertainment purpose: bed, heat-massager, music player, auto-dispenser for food or water, pop-out interface for Net, or newsfeed access, etc. The family apartment is one of hundreds on the city ship's twelve levels, arranged in a giant oval design. The center is a self-contained, mile-long saltwater pool, currently filled with thousands of people swimming, reading or sleeping on aqua-beds, playing water volleyball and other games, or racing on kayaks, tiny sailboats or jet skis. Early in the morning and twice a week during the full day, the pool is set to "high-wave" mode for all the surfers.

"Father," Cat steps out onto the balcony.

"Yes."

"Apostle Aaron and another man are here to see you."

Vincent turns off his e-reader and hops up from the pod. "Thanks, Cat."

Two men are waiting in the main living room.

"Apostle, Mr. Thomas." Vincent shakes both of their hands firmly.

Aaron is on the Council of Twelve (the Twelve), the next-to-highest level of authority—the highest level of leadership being the First Presidency with the Prophet and his two Counselors. Aaron is, in fact, the President of the Twelve. He is always cheerful in his demeanor and, as with all the Apostles, wears casual suits in four colors only: black or navy for official duties, tan or brown for informal duties or fieldwork.

"Always good to see you, Vincent," Apostle Aaron says.

Vincent gestures for the men to sit on the couches around the center table.

"Your wife is still out on mission?" the Apostle asks.

"Yes. She returns tomorrow."

"The Twelve is still reviewing the report of your last mission. Before I cover that, may I ask…do you use your children on mission research?"

Vincent hesitates, but answers. "Yes, provided it's not restricted."

"Are they working on any research of your, this last mission?"

"They are, why?"

The Apostle is visibly concerned.

"They tried to access restricted information and—"

"Restricted information? They're doing a simple word search. Why would that be restricted?"

"They accessed restricted information and Control shut off all Net access for your family accounts."

Vincent is taken aback. He hasn't looked at Mr. Thomas at all, even when he shook his hand, but now glances at the man.

"I'm confused."

"Vincent, you're the authorized officer, not your children. I also understand this isn't the first time."

"Excuse me? Two of my children have already applied to the Academy and the other three will do the same when they're of age. Also, I am a scientist first, teacher second, soldier third. I encourage my children's learning at all times."

"Vincent, I'm not here to debate you, only to tell you that they accessed restricted information and that can't be tolerated by any officer, especially one of your rank. It's the same thing I say to all others. I understand the impulse; truly I do, both as a parent, grandparent, and once, a long time ago now, one precocious child myself. But as the adult, you must say no to children when it comes to mission business. These are dangerous times for us. You know that better than most."

"Unfortunately, your full Net access will be restricted for a period of time," Thomas adds.

Thomas is the Assistant to the Twelve. In lay terms, he is their collective Chief of Staff, the one who ensures their directives are carried out.

Vincent is visibly irritated. "Is there anything else?"

"The real reason I came by is because we will be moving you off the Leviathan Project."

Vincent leans back in his chair. "Excuse me?"

"Vincent, believe me, this has been in the works for some time," the Apostle says. "We need you elsewhere, especially with the turmoil in the Russian Bloc, and who knows what that could expand to."

"I am one of the founders of the Project, the chief scientist on the Project, and we are about to move to the last phase, and you're taking me off of it?"

"Vincent, we can't have you as both the Order's 'general' and the chief scientist on the Project," Thomas says. "We need your focus on one."

"Then I choose the Project. Promote someone else to my military role."

"You obviously are better suited for the military role. You even do dive missions still," Thomas says.

"Excuse me? Are you telling me you're removing me from the Project, which I've been on from the beginning as a founder for over a decade, because I still dive? I'm a diving instructor. That's what we do. I have to do dives to keep my rating."

Aaron says, "I can see this is upsetting to you, but this is the decision of the Twelve. We need our best people in the right places now. This is not punitive. It's not. We need you to accept our decision gracefully."

"Whatever is best for the Order," Vincent says mechanically.

"Also, please don't contact the Prophet directly," Thomas adds.

Vincent stares at him. "And why not?"

"Vincent," Apostle Aaron says softly. "This comes from the First Presidency and the Prophet himself. Again, this is not punitive."

"Am I going to be briefed on the data from the recovered Fish?"

"Vincent, that falls under Project business so it will be handled by others going forward," the Apostle answers.

Vincent suddenly stands up and walks out of the room.

"Vincent?" the Apostle says and looks at Thomas.

Vincent returns and hands a digi-card to the Apostle.

"What's this?" he asks.

"As of this second, I resign my commission."

The Apostle stands, stunned. "Please, Vincent, I will not accept this."

"Apostle Aaron, you can do whatever you want. When I was fighting the Resistance War against Boggs and the Pagans, I never did see you or Tom over there—"

"You will not use that tone with the Apostle," Thomas says angrily. "And you will not call me that word."

"Why? It's your name. Here you both are rearranging my life. Three decades of my life's work you arbitrarily throw out the window—"

"Vincent, that is not true," Apostle Aaron interjects.

"This is the most critical time for the Order and what do we get from you? Politics!" Vincent yells, "Cat!"

"Vincent, please," the Apostle pleads.

His youngest daughter appears.

Vincent glares only at Mr. Thomas. *Tom, I know you're the puppet master.*

"Cat, escort the Apostle and Tom out of our home."

Vincent storms out of the room. Cat looks at the men through her horn-rimmed, clear glasses disapprovingly. She puts her hands on her hips.

The Pacifica, Sea of Japan, Russia Territory
9:16 a.m., 5 August 2096

The White Seagull catamaran ship remains submerged as it cruises into the massive city-ship's underwater entrance, which goes to its internal ocean port. The city-ship *Pacifica* is listed as one of the many luxury city-ships on the open seas. Such vessels and stationary floating cities are especially popular with the super-wealthy, who wish to live out of jurisdiction of any one government, and uber-venture capitalist-backed scientists, who wish to conduct their research and development in the ultimate controlled environment.

The sea craft rises in the inner port of the *Pacifica* where dozens of other crafts of different sizes and types are docked. Doors lower to create a walkway and the crew disembarks.

Miri appears in a navy uniform with a turtle-shell suitcase in each hand. She is a fair-skinned brunette with hair down to her shoulders. She is visibly happy to be home, deeply breathing in the sea air.

"Miri," a woman calls to her, waving.

Miri sees her and smiles. The woman quickens her pace to her.

"Oh, let me help with that," she says as she takes one of the cases.

"Thank you, Linzee. What do I owe the pleasure of having an Apostle's wife greet me at the dock and help me with my bags?

The woman laughs. Linzee has very long blond hair tied in a ponytail. They actually grew up in the same ward (congregation) in America.

"How do you know we don't do this for all our people? Helping people is service, you know."

"Please tell my children that."

"Let me drive you home and we'll talk."

Linzee points to her transporter, the golf-cart transportation used by everyone on the city-ship.

9:40 a.m.

Miri walks through the front door to her smiling children. The daughters hug her even before she has time to set down her suitcases.

"Mother." Seal appears from nowhere and hugs her too. "Are you going to give us a good debriefing like Father?"

She and her husband started to do these "briefings" really more as a game when the children were small, but it only encouraged them. Now, they expect these family meetings to learn all about their missions, even the "secret" ones.

"I don't think it will be as exciting."

"Did he tell you what he saw?"

"Seal, let Mother get settled first." Bear appears and hugs her too. "Hi, Mom."

"Hi, oldest son." She looks at everyone. "Okay, Bee and Dove, take my suitcases to the bedroom. Bear and Seal, what food do you have for me to eat? Cat, where's your Father?"

Vincent sits in his pod on the balcony, reading with the light murmur of movie-soundtrack music playing from the speakers. Miri leans down and kisses her husband.

"You're back."

"I am."

"Anything exciting on the mission?"

"You'll have to wait for the family briefing like everyone else," she answers playfully. "But you and I have to talk before then."

Vincent turns off the pod's music. "Not out here."

"Why?"

"Not secure."

"Did you just say what I think you said?"

Vincent leads Miri off the balcony and into his private study, a room filled with physical books all along the walls. It has a large desk with an extended corner table. He uses the room for reading in general—Bible study, and research when he wants to get out of his home lab. They sit on one of the couches.

"Did you resign your commission?"

"News travels fast. Yes."

Miri looks up in the air. "Is this a reverse-psychology play to get a promotion?"

"No, I resigned."

"I don't know what you're up to, but you can't do that."

"Well I did."

"Vincent, you're not a normal person."

Vincent laughs.

"You know what I mean. Three of the Apostles will be retiring soon, and you're in line to be on the Twelve. Why are you doing this?"

"Miri, I've never ever wanted to be on the Twelve. I'm a scientist, not a pastor."

"Honey, outside of the Twelve, and even the Presidency, you're the most respected leader in the Order. You can't behave this way. You influence people. Why did you do this? Does this have to do with Mr. Thomas?"

"He has nothing to do with this."

"When, this century, are you going to tell me why you dislike him so much?"

"It doesn't matter."

"He's in line to be on the Twelve, too."

"That's why I dislike him."

"You really didn't like his late father either. Tomorrow, a few of the Apostles will be here for brunch. You're going to apologize and rescind your resignation. It will be as if it never happened."

"They talked to you already. Which wife did they send?"

Miri looks at him for a moment. "Vincent, there's healthy paranoia and then there's crazy-town. This is not Boggs, the Pagans, the Muslims, the CHINs, Anarchists, or someone else. This is us, our people. You've been making insinuations ever since we were back in America, dealing with those Vampires."

"That was seven years ago."

"That's when it started with you. What's going on?"

"Nothing is going on."

"Why do you even try?"

"Here we go. 'We've known each other since we were fifteen—'"

"We've known each other since we were fifteen. I know when you're not being truthful."

"Okay."

"And what did you have the children doing that the family would get flagged for restricted Net attempts?"

"Ask Tom."

"Don't call the man that. He's the Assistant to the Twelve and a senior leader in the Order. I'm asking you."

"The kids did nothing wrong. All they were doing is a word search for me. Nothing different from what they've done hundreds of times before."

"Vincent, you haven't been acting like yourself, and I'm not the only one who sees it. You've been antagonistic towards the leadership and you've never acted like that before. What's going on?"

"Nothing—"

"Okay, I'm going to unpack," she interrupts. "You can go back to the balcony and stay there. I'll be debriefing the kids about my trip."

"She leaves him alone in the room.

8:36 p.m.

Vincent is awakened from his light sleep. A pod can be so comfortable with its cushions and heat massagers. He pulls the earset from his chest pocket and places it in his right ear.

"Hello," he answers his phone.

"Mr. Vincent."

"Hi, Mr. Varma. How are you?"

"I'm sorry. Did I wake you?"

"Oh no, I still have a couple of hours before bed."

"I'm sorry anyway, for calling so late."

"How's the traveling salesman and movie connoisseur business these days?"

"Couldn't be better."

"Glad to hear it."

"I was calling because I wondered if you still have that movie I lent you the last time."

Varma never lent him any movie the "last time."

"Which one? You know the wife and I don't watch too many movies with all our work."

"It's one of the classics."

"All your movies are classics."

"They are. It's the one with Kirk Douglas."

Vincent and Miri's Quarters, The Pacifica
10:05 a.m., 6 August 2096

Vincent and Miri are sitting together on one couch. Facing them are Apostles Fisher and Lucius, to the side sits Apostle Aaron and Mr. Thomas, and on the other side is Linzee, the wife of Apostle Aaron, and one of the aides to the Twelve, Jenni.

"Vincent," says Apostle Fisher. "Let me start by saying that we deeply apologize for any miscommunication yesterday. You are far too important to the Order. We can't accept any resignation made in anger."

"I'm very sorry, Vincent," Apostle Aaron says. "It was my fault alone for not being clear. I can see now from your point of view no matter what I said, it did seem punitive. You're one of our leaders, Vincent. We could never do such a thing to you."

"We're all very sorry. Can we move past this?" Apostle Fisher asks.

Miri speaks first to prod her husband. "Of course we can. We can see the apologies are genuine and we apologize too, for this escalating to this point."

Apostle Fisher reaches out with his hand—Vincent's ID digi-card. "This belongs to you."

Vincent takes the card.

"We never accepted the resignation so there was no break in service. I personally spoke with Control and that whole Net-breach thing has been taken care of, too. There really wasn't any attempted or actual access of restricted information. That's what happens when you put algorithms in charge of systems instead of people. However, we do want your primary responsibilities to be with Military and not the Project. All we're doing is shifting our resources as we near the final phase. It is no black mark against you. You're the architect of the Project. Everyone knows it and will always know that. However, especially with the Russian situation, everyone is very concerned with security and especially with the data you secured from the recovery of our surveillance-bot. People are scared. We have a lot of good people, but you're far and away the best person to handle our external Order security. Does that make sense?"

"It does," Vincent answers.

"Without that security, there can be no Project. We need to be able to task our external Order security and know we have the person in charge to handle it, no matter what the situation."

Everyone looks at Vincent for any sign of resistance. They see none.

"Can I mention another issue?" Linzee asks. "Unfortunately, there is a rumor running rampant on-board, and all the other city-ships for that matter, that the Twelve actually fired Vincent from his post."

Everyone looks at him.

"Why are you looking at me? If people found out, it wasn't from me. I haven't been out of the apartment or talked to anyone since then."

"Before you say it, it wasn't Apostle Aaron or me either. But there was someone else in the room," Thomas says.

Vincent glares at him. "Are you really sitting in my house accusing my little daughter—?"

"Gentlemen," Apostle Fisher says quickly. "No one is accusing anyone of anything. Jenni, what are your recommendations?"

"That the Twelve publicly announce Vincent's change in post as a promotion, maybe a new or expanded title, additional duties."

"Yes, that's what we'll do. Is everyone agreed?"

Everyone nods.

"If I could talk to Vincent privately, please," Apostle Fisher says.

The crowd starts to rise from their seats. Apostle Fisher talks quietly to the other two Apostles. Everyone leaves the room as Apostle Fisher walks back to a seated Vincent; Miri stands to leave.

"You don't mind if my wife stays?" Vincent asks.

"Not at all," the Apostle answers.

Miri glances at him before sitting again. Dove pops into the room.

"Mom-Dad, we're seeing them out."

"Thanks Dove," Miri answers.

It's quiet now. Apostle Fisher looks at Vincent for a while with a slight smile.

"Vincent, Vincent, Vincent. I know it was you who purposely leaked the rumor that we 'fired' you. It worked. We got more calls in an hour than we'd get in an entire year. People were mad, truly mad. I got an earful when I was doing my evening walk yesterday. You're a popular man, Vincent. And you know it."

Vincent remains quiet.

"I still don't know what we've done to get on your bad side. I think I personally noticed it a few years ago. Not sure what it could be, but I'm here to say stop it. You're a senior leader in the Order. You're one of our leading scientists. You're one of our best military leaders. Stop it. You won't tell us what it is, to fix whatever it is. You won't tell anyone else what it is, to help. Then get over whatever it is, right now. Is that understood? No arguments, is it understood?"

"Yes."

"The Mormon Order is a tight-knit family. We can't afford to have any disturbances in the family, especially these days. My wife always says it's the 'end days,' the latter-days, but we've been saying that since humans were kicked out of Eden.

"You do know you're on the list to replace me, don't you? Of course you do. So behave appropriately now, not then." He looks at Miri. "Get your husband to stop it. Maybe he's told you what we did to get on his bad side."

"He'll stop today," Miri says. "You have my word on that."

"Vincent, the fish-bot you recovered."

"Yes?" Vincent is interested.

"We can guess why someone didn't want us to find it and why they disabled all the others. Before I say it, listen very carefully. No one can know. We have a very jittery population. We were driven from Utah, driven from America. This is something that could push people over the edge."

"My husband and I have never compromised confidentiality or security, ever," Miri says. "All of us do swear an oath to it—"

"Oh please, I don't want to get on your bad side too. It's just a formality. The Prophet says it to me and the entire Twelve all the time."

"Sorry," Miri says.

"It seems that there are several submerged structures near us.

They may very well be an underwater city of some kind. How long they've been there, who they are, and whether it is a coincidence that they are in the same waters we are in, we are unable to determine."

"How many people?" Miri asks.

"It could be hundreds or thousands of inhabitants. We don't know."

"My God," Miri says.

"How long have they been watching us, how many of our systems could be compromised, and what else they are planning? We have no answers. They also seem to have their own undersea fleet docked around these structures. We don't know the capabilities of their weapon systems either. From the Prophet himself, we need to do immediate reconnaissance of the structures and the surrounding area without being detected. That is the most important. Nothing in this region is stable. The Russian Bloc has outlawed all religion just like America. The Russian Orthodox has disappeared from the face of the earth, and the Order sits on top of the ocean like a helpless duck until the completion of the Project. Our only real defense is our cover story to the Russian authorities. We can't be detected by anyone on this recon. Vincent, pick your troops, pick your officers, and lead the mission."

Nosferatu Aquatus

*"In the ocean, no one can hear you scream," Cat, daughter of Vincent
and Miri, future President of the Twelve, the Mormon Order*

Vincent and Miri's Quarters, The Pacifica
5:05 a.m., 7 August 2096

Vincent jogs through the busy "war floor." Any threat to the Order
involves every adult man and woman, each doing their part. Non-
fighting personnel are in white, paramilitary troops are in navy.
Specific areas of the level are sectioned off from every other. The
closer to the actual "War Room," the greater the security becomes
and the more restrictive the access. People scramble in every
direction, control pods with their vid-screen displays are manned,
and the status lights on the wall are flashing "code yellow"—all in
preparation for this mission.

Vincent moves past the last checkpoint to be admitted into the "War
Room" by three guards. The room is unremarkable in appearance,
actually almost barren. Along the walls are personnel sitting in pods.
There are no vid-screens. The men and women in the pods read their
displays through their clear, virtual-image interface glasses. In the center
of the room is a large conference table where his "troops" wait. He is
immediately recognized by everyone; each one of them nods or smiles to
quietly greet him. Two people, a tall slender woman with black hair and

a shorter, lanky man with red hair, he does not know.

"Captain Vincent," greets a portly man.

Vincent says, "Hello, boss."

The man smiles back. "You report to me, but I'm not your boss. That task belongs to the Apostles themselves. And as of right now, you're officially *Commander* Vincent." He points to two men and one woman. "These are the captains of the *Bowhead,* the *Narwhale,* and the *Orca,* who you already know."

"He trained us, sir," the captain of the Orca says.

"Why am I not surprised? They will be under your direct command, along with the crew of your boat."

"Thank you, sir."

"Commander Vincent, I'm officially turning over the mission to you for execution."

"Mission accepted, Commander Glen."

"Here are your coded orders." He hands Vincent a palm tablet. "Also, Commander, you will have two observers on the mission."

Vincent quickly verifies he has full access to the mission specs of tablet and looks up to glance at the unknown duo. "Observers, sir?"

"Yes, they will accompany the mission on your boat."

"In what capacity, sir? Any specific duties?"

"Observation only. No other duties. They'll stay out your way and your crew's way. This is a paramilitary mission and they're civilians with no rank."

"Yes, sir. Anything else?"

"Nothing else, Commander, other than Godspeed."

"Thank you, sir." He looks at everyone. "Prepare for immediate departure."

Glen pats Vincent on the shoulder. The troops disperse, all walking out the door on the other end. The two observers wait and follow from the rear. It leads to the private passage to the city-ship's internal port. Vincent is the last to leave the war room. Out the door, through the hallway, and there she is, the flagship of the Order—the *Divine Providence*.

Sea of Japan to Pacific Ocean
6:01 a.m., 7 August 2096

Mormons own nothing in this region. In America, they had an entire state, but they gave all of it up in the name of safety to escape their own government, and especially the administration of four-term American President, T. Wilson. Now they live on the Pacific Ocean. But these are Russian waters, with Caliphate waters bordering on one side, and CHIN waters on the other. If anything goes wrong on the mission, there is no one to call for help. They're registered as "marine scientists" with the Russian Bloc government, but anything out of the ordinary could easily get them reclassified as spies. They are, after all, Americans, even if officially the Mormon Order, with all its members, has renounced their citizenship. The world is not as big as it once was for Faithers. Despite the risks, the unknown underwater inhabitants must be identified.

The *Divine Providence* cruises to the target location at a depth of one hundred feet. The surveillance data from the fish-bot, coupled with their own sea maps tells them where they need to look. The calmness of the waters is deceptive. Submarine activity in the Sea of Japan and all this region of the Pacific Ocean has exploded ever since the announcement of the death of Russian President Krutikov.

"Approaching target search area, Commander," a crewman says. "I like the sound of that, sir."

"It rolls nicely off the tongue, Commander," says another.

The crew laughs.

Vincent tries not to smile. "Be advised that there will be no other promotions today."

The craft moves into the search grid. The *Divine Providence* is a surface boat and submarine. On the surface, the command bridge is near the front of the main deck. Underwater it is one deck below; all main deck compartments mechanically folded down in the craft. Vincent sits in his captain's pod in the center of the command bridge facing the main front vid-screen. It shows the open sea. When they were closer to the surface, they saw numerous schools of fish. At this depth, signs of sea life are becoming less frequent. Three crewmembers are at their control stations to his left, and on his right are another three. Behind them are the steps to the lower deck. The two observers sit in pods near the front of the craft; taking turns watching the vid-screen and looking back at the commander and crew. Vincent pays no attention to them—or pretends not to.

"Contact!" yells one of the crew. "Starboard. Attempting to identify." He continues to look at his control station display. "Attempting to—sir, the contact has disappeared off sensors."

"How far away was it?" Vincent asks.

"Two thousand feet, sir."

"All stop," Vincent directs.

"All stop," answers another crewmember.

"Sir, sensors have it again."

"Where is it?"

"Fifteen degrees starboard, sir. Moving away at twenty knots."

"Do we have identification?" Vincent asks.

"Still working, sir."

"How can we still be working?" Vincent asks. "What is it? Russian, CHIN, what?"

"Sir, there is no database match for their configuration, possible pirate, sir."

"What's its heading?"

"Sir, it has a downward trajectory to the seafloor."

"Follow, but don't overtake," Vincent says as he looks at his display readings. He looks up at the vid-screen.

"Sir, it's disappeared off sensors again," a crewman says.

"All stop," Vincent says.

"All stop," the crewman answers.

"Plot likely course and prepare to fire tag." He counts to five in his head. "Fire."

"Tag launched, sir."

The mini-projectile is fired at the projected location of the unknown craft. If it's there, the device will be able to see it with its artificial eyes and will signal the coordinates back to the *Divine Providence*. Stealth-tek can fool sensors, but not line of sight scanners.

"Tag in range in five seconds, sir," a crewman says. "Four, three, two, scanning." He pauses as he watches his display. "Unknown craft relocated, sir."

"Move forward to intercept," Vincent directs.

"Forward ahead."

Vincent says, "Computer, screen magnify on contact and night-vision."

The blackness of the view turns to a light gray. In the distance, they see the grainy image of something in front of them.

"Magnify."

The image now takes up the entire vid-screen. It looks almost like a giant manta ray, but it is clearly a sea craft. The crew looks at Vincent—*there it is*—the manta-craft from Vincent's report.

"Multiple contacts!" another crewman yells.

"All stop," Vincent directs again.

"All stop," a crewman responds.

"Keep a lock on the target craft," Vincent says. "Identification of other contacts?"

"Three Russian attack subs, starboard. Closest one is ten miles away."

Everyone waits quietly. The craft hovers motionless where it is.

"Russian subs are doing a search pattern, keeping the same distance from us."

The stealth-tek of the Order's sea craft is the best. Pagans think Faithers are Trogs—quasi-Luddites with obsolete or barely functioning tek, but the reality is very much the opposite. But tek never stays the same. All sides are constantly improving both their means of evading detection and means of detection.

"Commander, what about our other boats?" asks the male observer.

"The captains of the other boats are following our movements exactly. They'll only act independently if in danger or directed by me," Vincent answers.

"Contact!" a crewman yells. "American recon sub. Ten miles, port."

"Why are the Americans here?" the female observer says with a half-concerned, half-disgusted tone.

"Where are the Russian subs?" Vincent asks.

"They're still moving in search patterns, sir."

"That means they have other subs nearby," Vincent says. "It's getting crowded down here."

"Isn't it strange, Commander," says a crewman. "American subs, Russian subs, CHIN subs, Caliphate subs, all the same to us now."

"It's been 'all the same to us' for a long while," Vincent says. "Where is our manta-craft contact?"

"No longer on sensors, sir. It's disappeared again."

Vincent looks at him. "Again? Where's the tag?"

"Contact!" a crewman yells. "Starboard. Contact! Port. More Russian subs. Ten miles away. Contact! Stern."

The crew glances at him, nervous. The observers watch the vid-screen, though it shows nothing more than open water.

"Commander, are we boxed in?" the male observer asks.

"Yes, we are," Vincent responds.

"What do we do in this situation?" he asks.

"Nothing."

"Nothing?"

"We wait. Minutes, hours, days, if we have to."

The observers look at each other nervously.

"Don't worry. Claustrophobia can't kill you." Vincent looks to his crew. "Are any of the Russia contacts moving to us?"

"Yes, sir," a crewman answers. "Closer to us, but not towards us."

"Contact! Fore. Moving to us!" The crewman rechecks her sensors. "It's the manta ray craft. It's moving to us, one thousand feet and closing."

They can disappear from our sensors at will, Vincent thinks to himself. *They can see us.*

"It's gone again, sir, the manta-ray craft," a crewman says.

Vincent watches the vid-screen, patiently. The crew watches their console displays, but also glance at their commander, looking for any sign of fear or panic. There is none. Soldiers feed off the emotional state of their leaders. He is calm; they're calm.

Everyone waits. No one talks; eyes are on their pod displays or the main vid-screen.

The first "one" appears. It looks like a sinister apparition with the vid-screen in night-vision mode. The diver's white helmet looks more like an emaciated head, with its antennas made to look like pointy ears, and its armless, legless body, looking like a long, ragged robe. Just like the one Vincent encountered days ago—the one chasing him.

Every eye is on the vid-screen. A second one appears, then a third and fourth. They float in place, looking directly at their craft.

Vincent glances at his display. Every other contact—the Russian subs, and the American sub—is moving off.

Another Sea Vampire appears on the vid-screen, much closer than the other. Its form takes up the entire screen. They can see its visor, running from one "ear" to another, and the three-claw attachment on the mouth area of its helmet.

Vincent glances at his display again. Not one of their boat's proximity alarms has been triggered.

Vincent works quickly from his console. He pushes a button.

I'm on the Highway to Hell!

Everyone on the bridge is startled. The music lyrics explode, but not from inside the craft, outside. They can feel the sound waves rippling through the ocean and the craft's hull.

The main Sea Vampire is as shocked as his fellow divers and they swim away frantically. The sound, however, is not with the *Divine Providence*. It follows the Sea Vampires. The manta-craft appears back on the vid-screen.

Highway to Hell. I'm on the Highway to Hell! Highway to Hell.

The divers disappear into the manta-craft and then, more concerned with escape than stealth, its full propulsion engages and it jets away.

"Contact," the crewman says more quietly. "Contact—multiple contacts. Russian subs. Seven of them."

In a few moments, they see one of the Russian subs move over and past them on the vid-screen after the manta ray craft. Two more appear and also disappear in the distance.

The crew looks at Vincent, smiling.

"Metallic rock as a military weapon. Good one, Commander."

Vincent says, "Make your report now."

"Yes, sir."

"I want all sensor data sent to my console."

"Yes, sir," answers another crewman. "Sir, can I work on figuring out a fool-proof way to track that craft? They seem to have the ability to intermittently disappear from our sensors."

"The loser cooks a family dinner for the winner. Any day we pick."

The crewman laughs. "Not a very bright bet, sir. Even by Mormon standards I got a huge family."

"Can't the computer do that?" the female observer asks. "I mean, figure out how to track the craft. It could do that faster than a human being."

"Maybe we should replace captains, crews, and *observers* with computers. Just like the Pagans," Vincent answers.

"No, that's not what I meant."

"We do verify with the computer," Vincent adds.

"Commander, how did you do that?" the male observer asks. "The music."

"A fish-bot can do a lot more than just surveillance," Vincent says as he types rapidly on his keyboard.

"Oh," the male observer says.

A couple of the crewmembers are visibly getting annoyed at the presence of the observers.

"Commander, can I make a suggestion—" one of the crewmen starts.

"Wait," Vincent says. He knows what he wants to say about the observers and looks up from his console. "Take two people with you and make sure there's nothing attached to the hull of my boat."

Everyone looks at him. The observers are scared too.

"Attached?" the observers say.

"Commander, sensors would have—"

Vincent stops typing and interrupts the crewman. "Seeing as their craft can fool our sensors and their diving suits didn't activate any of our proximity alarms, let's make sure. These are not dummies we're dealing with."

The crewman doesn't even have to pick volunteers. The three crewmen stand from their stations and go below.

"Commander, can we help—?"

Vincent interrupts the male observer. "I want the two of you to sit and not talk until I finish my work."

Both observers stay quiet.

Minutes later, the three crewmen return.

"All clear, Commander," one of them says.

Vincent stops typing. "Anything on the sensors?" he asks a crewman at their station.

"Nothing, sir."

Vincent finishes his typing. "Upload the new algorithm."

"Commander, I have one too."

Vincent smiles. "Verify with the system."

The crewman looks at his screen. "Three different versions."

"I still finished first, so I'll have my 'my people' contact 'your people' with what we want for Saturday lunch. Upload computer version," Vincent says.

The crewman laughs as he continues typing.

"Upload complete. There is a contact, sir." He turns to him. "It's them." He looks at the console again. "Five miles away from us, fully stopped."

"Is there anyone else nearby?" Vincent asks.

"No one, sir."

Vincent thinks for a moment.

"Commander," says one of his officers. "We need to abort the mission. This doesn't feel right. They know we're here and they're obviously waiting for us."

The male observer stands. "Commander, the mission is clear. That craft matches the description you, yourself, gave to Control.

We must find their underwater habitats and collect as much recon data as we can."

Vincent smirks. "Yes Mister, I do know how to read."

"Sorry Commander." The observer sits back down.

"Officers…" Vincent stands from his chair. "Follow me below." The two observers start to follow. "No, you two stay here on the bridge until we return. You can be the ranking officers."

"Ranking officers?" asks the female observer.

"Commander, we're not supposed to be directly involved in the mission," says the male one.

"We'll be back in two minutes." Vincent walks to the steps to the below deck, his four crewmen following.

"Contact!" a crewman yells.

The two observers look at each other.

"Who is it?" asks the male observer.

"Stern. Caliphate sub. Ten miles."

"Contact!" yells another crewman.

"My God, who is it now?" the female observer says.

"Starboard. CHIN craft identified. Ten miles," the crewman answers.

Vincent appears with his four officers. "Is the manta-craft still on sensors?"

"Yes, sir."

"Intercept." Vincent sits back in his chair. The other officers resume their stations.

"Commander, we've had both a Caliphate and a CHIN craft show up on sensors," a crewman informs.

"Ignore them. Get us to one hundred feet away from the manta-craft."

The *Divine Providence* descends and moves forward at a high rate of speed. The observers watch the vid-screen closely.

"Commander, aren't we moving too fast?" asks the male observer.

"Mister, how long have you been a submariner?" Vincent asks.

The male observer doesn't answer and returns his attention back to the vid-screen.

Their craft quickly closes the gap with the manta-craft. Soon its grainy image returns to the vid-screen.

"Commander, the craft is moving now," a crewman says.

The manta-craft nears an underwater mountain peak. As it nears the rock structure, it turns rightward to sail around it.

The *Divine Providence* continues on its intercept course. The observers glance back at the commander, who watches the vid-screen, ignoring them. They glance at the crew and they are all watching their monitors. But no one is speaking, not the pilot, navigator, any of the crew—this is strange.

The manta-craft disappears from the vid-screen as it goes around the peak.

The Divine Providence immediately dives and increases its speed forward. The observers are physically jolted and they look back at the commander. Vincent glances at them for a moment before looking back at the vid-screen.

"Why isn't anyone calling out commands?" the male observer asks.

The yellow threat lights turn on and switch from code yellow to bright red. Both observers are now scared.

"What's happening?" the female observer asks.

Five manta-craft appear on the vid-screen, all facing them and approaching at high speed.

Alarms sound. A dozen or more objects become visible, almost on top of them—*torpedoes!*

Explosions violently rock their craft. Something causes the torpedoes to detonate ahead of their target. The observers would have been thrown to the floor, if not for their chair's auto-engaged seatbelts. The craft is diving fast to the seafloor.

"Commander, what's happening? I demand—"

The female observer stops as they feel more explosions and see debris fill the entire display of the vid-screen.

"My God," the female observer says. "Is that our other boats? Did they destroy our other three boats?! Commander?!"

"Answer us, Commander!" the male observer yells.

Both observers look at the Commander. Vincent watches them coldly. The observers look at the other crew and every one of them is staring back at them. The observers are nervous as two crewmen rise from their stations and move toward them. They grab the couple from their chairs.

Vincent stands. "We're evacuating the craft."

"What?" the male observer. "What do you mean?"

Vincent looks at the two crewmen. "Put them in the escape pods."

"You're abandoning the boat? You can't do that, Commander," the male observer says.

The crewmen forcibly pull the observers away and down the steps to below. Two other crewmen join in to help them lift the observers, dragging them to the Escape Room. The observers are pushed into separate pods.

"No!" "Let us out!" "Stop!"

The observers are still screaming when the doors are sealed and their pods launch.

Their spherical escape pods race away through the water. The entire interior is wrapped in vid-screens, now in enhanced night-vision mode, giving the occupant the feeling of floating suspended within a transparent bubble.

They can both see it—the Divine Providence explodes!

Close Encounters of the Worst Kind

"Games lubricate the body and the mind." — *Benjamin Franklin,*
Founding Father of America (1706-1790)

The Pacifica, Sea of Japan, Russian Territory
12:01 p.m., 7 August 2096

They call it the "Shark Pit." The city-ship's marine life habitat and study tank is over three stories high and is as long as an American football field. The sharks—great whites, tiger sharks, makos, hammerheads, blues, threshers, whale sharks, etc.— seem to endlessly circle their artificial home, which is filled with many varieties of fish swimming in different groups, a jungle of large kelp in one section, underwater caves in another section, and crustaceans and aquatic plants on the artificial seafloor.

River stands in the large observation room, watching them. She has always liked sharks for some reason. The room is far from empty. For many residents of the city-ship it's a daily ritual to visit the Shark Pit and all the other smaller tank habitats featuring seals, sea lions, dolphins, mantas, octopi, etc.

She glances at her time-band and knows it's time to go. With her faux-leather portfolio in hand, she arrives at her office.

"River?"

She stops and turns as another woman runs up to her.

"Good morning, you."

"Good morning. Have you heard anything about the mission?"

"Mission?"

"Yes, we have four boats out searching for those secret underwater inhabitants near us."

River laughs. "I'm not a spy anymore. I don't follow all that unless I'm directly involved. I'm in boring construction these days."

When she worked within the American government, her codename was Ms. Crabtree. It was two decades ago now, but so many act like it was yesterday.

"Construction? Terraforming is a lot more than construction."

"Not terraforming. We're not on Mars. Simple biodome construction. So what about this mission?"

"I thought you might know something more than the gossip."

"Nothing wrong with gossip. It's almost always true."

"The Prophet isn't back yet and we have a lot of our officers out on mission today."

"What other officers?"

"Some of the Apostles are out, too."

"I didn't know that. Well, Kathy, if I hear of anything, I'll let you know."

"Sorry to be all chatty this morning. Some of us do have to work."

"Yes, we do."

River waves goodbye to her friend as they part. She nears the door of her office when a little girl comes around the corner, almost crashing into her.

"Whoa, what's your hurry?" River stops the near-collision with her hand.

"Oh, sorry."

"I know you. You're Cat, Vincent and Miri's daughter."

"Yes, I am. You're Mrs. River." She smiles. "You were one of my primary teachers."

"That's right. You were what—two years old?"

Cat laughs. "I wasn't in school at two. No one is. I was seven."

"How old are you now?"

"I'm twelve now."

"Soon you'll be able to drive submarines too, like your parents."

"Yes, I can't wait."

"Well let me get to work, Ms. Cat."

"Do you what it means by, '*The game is afoot*?' I think that's what I'm supposed to say."

"I think so too. Haven't heard that in a long time though."

Cat waves and runs off.

River watches her until she's gone. She turns to her office and the door auto-unlocks. As she sits down at her silver desk in the center of the office, the tablet console auto-engages and shows all her current emails and vid-mail. She just stares at the display as if it were blank.

This day was never supposed to have come. They were only supposed to be worst-case scenario games. Please God, hopefully it's a false alarm.

The Pacifica
12:01 p.m., 7 August 2096

Besides Military, the war floor also houses the Order's intelligence services. Control occupies the other half the same floor with its own separate entrances and all Control personnel wear black uniforms.

The section is arranged in small circular work areas of about five to a dozen personnel at pod stations or traditional desk consoles. Control's director stands at a seven-person work circle.

"What time?" Caleb asks them.

"Less than thirty minutes, sir. The number of subs has been

steadily increasing over the past hour. Caliphate, CHIN, and even a few Americans have been spotted."

"They want to be spotted."

"Sir?"

"They want to be spotted. Maybe it's to intentionally make the Russian Bloc nervous and commit excessive forces and resources to the sea. Other parts of the region would be left inadequately protected."

"Or sir, we could be heading to full-scale war. Maybe even World War Three."

"We need to present what's probable, not wild speculation. Assemble the analysis team, and I want firm recommendations within the half hour for me to brief the Twelve."

"Yes, sir."

"Any word yet?"

"No, sir. No word of any kind from our subs."

"Okay. Get me those recommendations."

His team goes to work. Caleb can see another officer wave his arms, motioning to him at the other end of the open work area.

"Make it twenty minutes from now," he says.

He leaves them and walks to the other man. The other officer is dressed in navy—Military services.

"Mr. Glen needs to see you right away."

"Lead the way," Caleb says.

The men leave Control. The officer leads him past the "halfway point"—the common name for the dividing line between the two sections into one of small conference rooms nearest the War Room.

A man is waiting. "Caleb," he says as he greets him with a handshake.

"Glen. I'm sure Military is glued to the monitors like we are."

"Everybody seems to be in the water. They want to see what the new Russian President will do about it."

"The man is a mobster. What do they think he'll do?"

"A mobster who was almost assassinated and is holed up in his deep, underground, presidential bunker. They're testing him. And there's no downside to them. If he's strong, they'll go home, if not, they'll see what territory or resources they can steal."

"We'll know soon. What did you need to see me about?"

"We've lost contact with Mission Tango."

"Commander Vincent is heading the mission, right?"

"Yes. We know you have two observers on the mission."

"Observers? We don't have any observers on the mission."

"What do you mean? Control has two people on one of the four boats."

"Control doesn't have anyone assigned on the mission."

"Then who authorized these two people, if not you. And now we've lost contact with all four boats."

"I'll find out right now."

"Please. I'll investigate on my end."

Each man walks out of the room and goes back to their areas. Both men are concerned.

Glen is in his work area when his vid-line rings. He answers. Caleb's face appears.

"Glen," he says. "You were right. The two observers are with Control."

"Then why didn't you know?"

"The observers were put on the mission directly by the Twelve. We didn't know. The notification just fell through the cracks."

"Okay. Are you in touch with them?"

"We've lost contact with them, too."

"Caleb, we have four boats missing. Four full crews."

"I fully understand the urgency. We're deploying a team of Fish."

"We already did that ourselves, hours ago."

"We have foreign subs in our vicinity and now our boats are missing."

"We may have another matter too."

"What other matter?"

"We've lost contact with the Prophet's ship."

"What? My God."

"You don't need to prepare any forces. The Twelve are already in the field with their own forces."

"Own forces? What forces?"

"They have two heavy attack subs already en route to the Prophet's last location."

"The Twelve don't go out on missions. And since when did they get their own attack subs? Did you know this?"

"I've probably said more than I should, but you and I are the ranking leaders on the city-ship with all of them on mission. You need to know everything I know. I recommend we go to code red, even though we're not under immediate attack. Do you concur?"

"I concur."

"Let's stay in contact."

"Yes, I'll keep you up-to-date."

"Same here. Out."

Caleb's face disappears from the screen. Glen turns. Not only is his team staring at him, but personnel in other areas, some not even in earshot, are watching him.

"Everyone, get back to work!"

People slowly do so.

He steps to one of his subordinates. "I want the war floor locked down now. No one in, no one out, and block all comms. We can't afford anyone leaking information until we know exactly what the facts are. One exception though." He looks at his other team member.

"I want you to immediately bring who I told you to my office."

"She's retired, sir."

"Get her."

"What if—"

"I don't care how you do it, just do it. You're authorized to share any information you need to, to get her here."

Hotel Residences, Neo-Orleans, Louisiana, America (Seven Years Ago)
5:30 p.m., 15 January 2089

The SUV coasts to a stop. Inside, Vincent sits in the passenger seat—dressed in a tan suit and holding a large astronaut helmet in his lap. One man sits in the driver's seat and another man in the back seat; both dressed in black suits. Next to the man in the back seat is River, monitoring the vid-screen displays of the hotel's surveillance feeds.

"We'll move in an hour," Vincent says.

"Do we need backup?" River asks.

"No. We'll deal with these Vampires alone," Vincent answers.

7:07 p.m.

The elevator opens and three people step out—Vincent wearing the astronaut's helmet, with its large mirrored front; and the two men dressed in black, wearing white frowning masks.

Hospital-Infirmary, The Pacifica
12:31 p.m., 7 August 2096

It's too late. Rumors of the loss of the Order's four subs have already spread through the city-ship like wildfire. Everyone knows. Everyone is saying that their four crews, thirty people in all, are dead.

River stares through the glass of the waiting room watching Miri lie in the bed, inconsolable, with all her children around her. Bear holds her hand and Cat lies on the bed with her, holding the other one.

River walks back to the nursing counter. A nurse looks up at her.

"Are you a family member?" the nurse asks.

"Family friend," she answers. "Has Medical Services heard anything more on the incident?"

"You probably know as much as I do. They say the boats were probably sunk by torpedo attack. Everyone is in shock. No Mormon has been killed in over a decade, since we left America, and now this. We're all in shock."

"Yes, we are."

"Oh, it looks like one of the family members wants to talk to you." The nurse points.

River turns and there is Cat watching from the other side of the glass doors of the patient rooms. The little girl opens the door and walks to her, but there is not sadness on her face, only anger.

"I was going to come back later and visit," River says.

"Did you know my father was going to be killed?"

"Cat, of course not. I've known your father long before you were born, before he was even married. We were soldiers in the Resistance. Let's talk privately." River touches the girl's shoulder and leads her away from the nurse. "What are you doing? You're supposed to maintain secrecy. I'm sure your father swore you to secrecy."

"My father is dead and I want to know why that man made me deliver that strange message to you. I liked playing 'secret agent,' but not anymore."

"The man you must mean is his friend. You should treat him as if it came from your father. Cat, do not tell anybody about the message. You have to promise me. Okay?"

"No, tell me. What does it mean?"

"I was a 'secret agent' a lot longer than you. If you were supposed to know, you would. Yes?"

Cat stares at her, unconvinced.

"Cat, this is very important. I think you have an idea of how important it is. Will you keep it all secret?"

"Why?"

"I'm not asking you to listen to me. I'm telling you to listen to your father who must have sent the man you're talking about. I don't even know who the man is, but he is your father's friend. Will you or won't you keep the secret?"

"I'm still thinking."

"That concerns me." River looks at her wristwatch. "I have to go and you have to stay with your mother. I will stop back later."

"When?"

"Later today."

Cat looks at her suspiciously. "I'm not sure if I like you anymore."

"Cat, please, please, follow your father's instructions. I can't say any more."

River walks away from her to the elevators. She glances back, but Cat is already gone; the glass door to the patient rooms is closing behind someone.

The elevator door opens and she walks out, her mind is miles away, thinking about so many things at once. As she walks out on the main deck, she stops for a moment to lean on the railing, twelve levels down to an open observation pool.

The silence is interrupted by a low beep as the elevator arrives. A man runs out like he's being chased. He's almost six feet away when he turns his head back, sees her, and stops.

"Ms. River?" he calls.

She stands up straight as he runs back to her. The man is dressed in navy and is breathing so hard that he has bent down with his hands on his thighs to compose himself.

"I kept missing you. First at your office, then the hospital. Don't you answer your phone?"

"Why should I? That's what voicemail is for. If I like your message, I'll call you back. And I don't believe in portable phones."

"You're joking, right?"

"I'm not."

"I need you to come back with me to Military."

"Why? I'm retired."

"Ma'am, I've been running all over the city-ship, and I can barely breathe. Can you show me a little compassion and just come back with me? I go back without you, I'll be sent back out to do it all over again."

"Standards must be slipping since my days there. We used to be able to run all day and not break a sweat."

"Yes, I'm happy for you super-soldiers. Gives us 'normals' something to strive for. Are you coming back with me, ma'am?"

Pacific Ocean
10:15 a.m., 7 August 2096

The escape pods had popped through to the ocean's surface almost simultaneously, hours ago. The pods had remained submerged until the foreign subs nearby were no longer on sensors.

Moments later, a mini-helicopter drone dives from the sky to hover closely above. The first of three hyper-speed yachts stops nearby, showering both pods with a wave of water. The two other yachts appear to form a triangle formation.

Now, the three yachts race across the water at well over two hundred miles an hour. At these speeds, the crafts are no longer making contact with the water, but coasting a foot above it. The drone follows them.

War Floor, The Pacifica
12:45 p.m., 7 August 2096

The heads of both Control and Military services quickly run to a War Room conference room. Security personnel, in navy and black uniforms, follow the men closely. At the center table are the two observers, sitting, obviously distressed, soaking wet, and wrapped in multiple towels.

The observers begin to instinctively stand, but Caleb raises his hand. "Stay seated."

Also waiting in the room is River with the officer sent to get her.

"I want this room vacated except for all requested individuals," Caleb says.

"I requested Ms. River," Glen says.

Caleb doesn't object. "You want to take the lead?"

"Yes, thank you." They walk back to the center table. "Do you need anything more to drink? Food?" he asks the observers.

"No, sir," the male observer says. "We're fine. Just need to get warm and dry. Sir, may I make a request?"

"Of course."

"I'd like to request that this debrief be of the highest classification, no one else but yourselves. Until, we know all the facts."

Caleb looks at Glen. "I agree."

River stands to leave with the young officer. All personnel exit the room until all that remain are the observers and the two division heads. Glen sits across from the two observers, laying his mini-tablet on the table.

He says, "Before we start the formal debrief, I have one question: where are my soldiers?"

Military Section, The Pacifica
1:47 p.m., 7 August 2096

River sits in the chair in front of Glen's desk. All offices on the war floor have glass walls, so officers can each view their teams at work. No one can hear them, but they are speaking quietly. Glen notices, and River turns her head. Outside the room, people on the floor are standing. A crowd approaches them, mostly men. The ones in the front are the Twelve.

A bodyguard walks ahead of them and reaches Glen's office. He opens the door. "If you can both step out here, please," he says.

Glen and River get up from their chairs.

The Order's Twelve Apostles stand before them. In the center is Mr. Thomas, the Assistant to the Twelve, but both Glen and River feel that the dynamic is all wrong. The Twelve seem to be subordinate to him somehow.

"You must have heard," Glen says.

"Yes," Apostle Aaron answers. "Any new reports?"

"No, sir. Nothing."

"My God," he says very distressed. "We haven't lost anyone in the Order for over a decade and now we lose four of our finest crews, four of our finest commanding officers. My God."

"Sir, we won't give up hope until we have positive confirmation of the deaths."

"Of course," Apostle Aaron says.

"You look familiar," Mr. Thomas says to River.

"Yes, sir. I used to work for both services."

"You're a teacher now?"

"I am, sir, only part-time. I'm also in construction services."

"Then why are you here on the war floor and in meetings with the head of Military Services?" Thomas asks.

"I called her in, sir, in a consultative capacity," Glen answers.

"During these crisis times, we're going to have to make a lot of changes," Thomas says.

Apostle Aaron adds, "We're sorry to say that this day is more of a crisis than you or anyone in the Order can imagine. The Prophet, the First Presidency, and all his crew have also been lost."

Glen and River audibly gasp.

"Lost?" Glen asks. "Dead?"

"We can be euphemistic when respect and decency calls for it," Thomas says.

"Yes, sir," Glen says.

Apostle Aaron adds, "There was no time for formalities or delay. Mr. Thomas, as of today, is the new Prophet of the Mormon Order."

"Yes, and we will not be losing any more members of the Order today or ever," Thomas says. "I will be instituting martial law."

The Long Game

Pacific Ocean
9:45 a.m., 7 August 2096

Vincent opens his eyes slowly. His crew and those of the *Bowhead*, *Narwhale*, and *Orca* are looking back at him.

"I'm sure the same phrase is running through all of your minds. What the hell just happened? I will explain all of it, but we must make sure the boats are secure. Find a safe harbor where no one will find us. We have to assume that others will be looking for us. We have to make sure not only that they don't find us, but that they don't even know where to look."

"Why would anyone be looking for us, Vincent?" asks the captain of the Orca. "That was such a display of trickery that you might have missed your calling. You should have been a movie maker rather than a scientist and soldier. Everyone thinks your boat is blown to bits and all our boats are also at the bottom of the ocean. But that's the problem. Everyone thinks we're dead, our spouses, our children, our family and friends, and our people. You said trust you, but if I knew you were going to do this, we would have thrown you into the escape pod, not the observers."

"You mean the spies," Vincent says.

"Spies? Vincent they weren't—"

"Yes, spies," Vincent interrupts. "When have any of us had an observer on a mission?"

"Vincent, you did this because you were offended Control or Military put observers on your boat?" another officer asks.

Vincent looks at him. "How long have you served with me?"

"Twenty-two years."

"Is it even remotely possible that my motives would be so petty and frivolous?"

"Vincent, leaders go crazy all the time."

"Vincent, you need to explain yourself right now or I'm taking my crew back to base," the captain of the Bowhead says.

"Vincent, if you don't explain yourself to my satisfaction we'll all be leaving," the Orca captain says.

"Even after all we've been through."

"Vincent, we're on a mission. This is not about friendship. You have tainted every man and woman involved. You have jeopardized all our careers. Do have any idea what my wife and kids must be going through right now? Your own wife and children? News that we've been killed and our corpses are at the bottom of the Pacific. What an act of cruelty to our loved ones. Vincent, compared to that I don't care that you saved my life during the Resistance wars."

"Fair enough, but you may regret that request five minutes from now."

Shogun Island, Philippine Sea
9:55 a.m., 7 August 2096

Japan is not one island, but over sixty-eight thousand. The four largest have ninety-eight percent of the nation. There are also dozens of man-made islands among Japan's archipelago. Shogun Island is south of the main islands, officially classified as one of the nation's natural reserves, but unofficially serves as the home of the ex-atheist, now Asian Christian Order known as the Shogun. They are sometimes called the Christian samurai of Neo-Asia.

A man in traditional Japanese attire, a black *hakama* (trousers) over his white kimono (robe), sits quietly in the tiny, beautiful garden of Gingko trees outside his meditation hall. His black hair is tied in a ponytail. He sips a small cup of saki with his left hand; a sheathed, two-foot sword lies at the fingers of his right hand.

A young woman nears him. She is dressed in the same attire as he, with her silky black hair in a ponytail.

"Kanji," she says. He looks directly at her. "Four submarines have requested permission for safe haven."

"Yes?"

"They are of the Mormon Order, but say they are hiding from the Mormon Order. The leader is Vincent. Do you know him?"

"I do."

"He is the one making the request. We have scanned them and their vessels completely. Their tek poses no issues. He says he will answer any questions if you wish, but would rather not. He says it is a grave internal matter that they have to handle themselves and that you would empathize with their situation."

"They can stay at the rock dome island."

"Should we notify the Continuum?"

"No. Let's see what unfolds."

The Pacifica
3:14 p.m., 7 August 2096

River has been through a few mass-panics in the Order. In the seventies when T. Wilson was first elected president, his Good Bible was mandated, and the Religious Registration initiatives were put into law, everyone was in panic. Then the Old Constitution was abolished and replaced with the Rule of Law, the Kansas Event, and the intra-civil wars of both the Jews and Christians. The Order was convinced that it wouldn't be long before the government came for them, as it had historically done in past.

However, this was worse than all of those panics combined. The Prophet is gone. Vincent is gone. The Order's flag ship is gone, as well as three of their best crews and boats—all in a single day. People are barricading themselves in their quarters. People are carrying long-barreled weapons. People are preparing for the end.

3:31 p.m.

River rings the doorbell. She has her rifle's strap slung over her shoulder.

The door opens. Miri stands there with a two-gun-holster on her waist and her son Bear holds a rifle.

"River."

"Miri."

"I was wondering when you'd show up. My daughter filled me in on the spy games."

"Are you going to let me in?"

"Why should I?"

"Let me in, Miri. We have a lot to do and not a lot of time to do it in."

River sits down on the living room couch. She lays her rifle on her lap. Miri sits across from her on another couch with Dove and Cat on either side. Bear and Seal remain standing.

"What's going on, River?"

"Miri, can we talk privately?—just you and me."

"No. I don't keep things from my children. And this has to do with their father so I definitely will not be hiding things."

River sighs. "Miri…I don't think Vincent is dead. I don't think any of the crews are."

Miri seems to be holding back tears; Bear and Seal slowly sit down, and all the children try to hold in their emotions.

"I'm not positive, but Vincent sent Glen a signal from his boat *while* he was on the mission."

"And?" Miri asks.

"You remember we did these things all the time during the Resistance. We had trigger words to set one action or another into motion. Vincent sent one of those trigger words for me through Glen. He also sent a trigger word for you through your daughter. The man who did is a friend. It was the same phrase."

"What do the trigger words mean?"

"The last time I heard it was over twenty years ago. I'm surprised I can even remember it. I guess the reason I do is because it was such a scary one, the meaning. Back then the Christians were dropping like flies, one denomination after another, the Jews imploding too, government collaborators were everywhere. Vincent put in place these worst-case scenarios. There was no Control or Military like we have now, back then. We were it, and we were making it up as we went along. Vincent was scared that it could happen to the Order, too."

"What could happen?"

"That the Mormon Order could be taken over by collaborators."

"River, that is so stupid. What would a collaborator do now? We survived the Resistance wars. We escaped America. That was the seventies; this is the nineties. We'll be in the twenty-second century soon."

"I agree Miri, but that's what these trigger words mean. You and I have known Vincent all our lives. Vincent is not a conspiracy person. He never was, even when all of us around him were. You remember his nickname before he was called the Astronaut."

Miri remembers. "The Vulcan."

"If he says it or thinks it, he can logically back it up. Miri, if Vincent is alive, we need to find him now. And we can't tell anyone. Not friends, not the Twelve, Control, Military; not even the new Prophet. If Vincent is alive, we need to find him."

Miri realizes something.

"What? What, Miri?"

"Vincent has not been acting like himself for years when…he is nice and respectful to everyone, even those people he doesn't like, but he was…he has been disrespectful to one person. It never made sense because that's not like him."

"Miri, what are you trying to say?"

"I'm not saying any more."

"Are you telling me that you know who might be a collaborator?"

"River, it's stupid. It doesn't make any sense. Collaborate to do what?"

"Maybe it's not collaborators, but conspirators. I don't know, Miri. You didn't answer me."

"No. My answer is no."

"Let me rephrase the question. Based on your husband's behavior, if you had to guess the identity of a collaborator or conspirator, would you be able to think of someone? Not based on your belief or any suspicion, but your husband's? Miri?"

"I don't know." She hesitates. "Yes."

Secret Island Hideout, Philippine Ocean
10:20 a.m., 7 August 2096

The secret cavern provides the perfect cover. The *Divine Providence*, the *Bowhead*, the *Narwhale*, and the *Orca* are docked together, tail to nose, to form one super-boat. The cavern is dark and secure. The only likely intruders here might be stray fish, but nothing more. The

Shogun may look like simple island-dwellers from the seventeenth or eighteenth century, but they have unique tek, rumored to be better than all Faithers, with the exception of the Magi.

The debate continues on the *Divine Providence*, but this time with the three captains and Vincent only. All four of them sit in Vincent's private but small quarters.

"We have to contact our families now. We have a secure location so why are we waiting?" the Narwhale captain asks.

"We don't have to wait," Vincent answers. "My people will contact us."

"You know something, Vincent," the Orca captain says. "People who look for conspiracies tend to always find what they're looking for."

"I thought I convinced all of you."

"You convinced us to give it all a second look. The one thing missing is motive. You never gave us motive. Why would anyone in the Order do this against the Order? That is the missing piece to your theory. That's what I'm having problems with, and I know I'm not alone."

"I don't know the motive yet. That's what we need to find out. First we need to get to the Prophet."

"What if he's involved in this grand conspiracy of yours?" the Bowhead captain asks.

"He's not."

"How do you know?"

"I'm not the only Watcher. So is he."

"The Prophet is part of your little 'watcher' group?"

"Yes, we came up with the plan back when he was the President of the Twelve, not yet the Prophet."

"Vincent, this is crazy. All of it," the Orca captain says. "What about our families?"

"I need two of you to help me with contacting the Prophet. The other two will work on contacting our families. Is that a plan all of us can agree to?"

The captains nod.

"This will all work out for us, I promise. Everyone is alive, and Prophet Simon will resolve all of this."

"Vincent, I just can't help thinking that while we're here playing games, we never did complete our mission. Those strange divers are still unidentified and the underwater habitats are still not found."

"The divers are identified, and I know where their habitats are. Those are not the questions we need to worry about."

"What do you mean you know where the habitats are and who the divers are? How?" asks the Narwhale captain.

"What we need to worry about is why their undersea city has been in constant contact with the *Pacifica* every day since I first came into contact with their first diver."

The captains look at him incredulously.

"I don't believe you, Vincent." The Orca captain is flustered. "You told us that these supposed observers knew the contents of your private mission orders and you showed us that they were sending out some strange beacon signals that these…strange divers and their manta-ships must have been using to track us. And we agreed that your boat's navigation computer might have been hacked and was being remote-controlled to take us straight to their ambush. We agree with you, but contact between the Order and them?"

"You're welcome to review the data on my console at anytime."

"How long have you had these suspicions of conspiracies?" the Bowhead captain asks.

"For years, but the disturbing information started coming in more than eighteen months ago."

"Why didn't you report it?" the Narwhale Captain asks. "Why?"

"Report it to whom? Who at *Pacifica*, exactly?"

"Vincent, don't tell us anymore until we directly talk to the Prophet," the Bowman's captain says. "I'm glad we're having this conversation privately and not in front of our crews."

"We have to contact our families," the Orca captain says.

"Yes," Vincent agrees.

"Why didn't you contact the Prophet with your suspicions? I think that's the most important question for me."

"You flush out conspirators with proof. If you don't have that, then you have to catch them in the act or it's nothing more than conjecture. I believe they've been at this for many years."

"Conspiracy to do what? What, Vincent? There's nothing for a conspirator to do," the Narwhale captain bursts out.

"Malign people forever without concrete proof. Sully their names when they could be completely innocent. No, I wouldn't do that. We know it's real now, but there is still no hard proof."

"Vincent, we've fought together, we respect you, but this is too much to take," the Orca captain says. "We're hiding from our own people. Don't tell us the names then. Tell us what you suspect."

Vincent answers, "I believe the plot is to seize the Leviathan Project and yes, that would mean the conspirators would have to be our own people and likely in leadership."

Pure Energy

"Jew-Christian dogma has absolutely no place in the scientific community and I'm proud of President T. Wilson's wholesale efforts to purge them from all levels of government. As a scientist myself, there is not a more glaring historical example of religious corruption of the fact-based, pure-science industry, than that of Al Gore and Margaret Thatcher on the issue global climate change being caused by humans. Both were radical Jew-Christians, the former, incredibly, an American Vice President, and the child of one of the chief proponents of skin-color segregation in Old America; and latter rose to office of Prime Minister in Pre-Islamic England—aren't Jew-Christian women supposed to stay home barefoot and pregnant?—a warmonger who used the full engine of government for this climate 'advocacy.' Aside from all the deaths, I'm glad the Muslims seized control of Western Europe, if only to end the cheerleading of the United Nations on this propaganda masquerading as true science. Gore made countless millions on data and claims of 'irrefutable evidence' and 'settled science' on this issue.

Typical behavior for a Jew-Christian and his mindless zombie followers—fake gods and fake science, of course, to the benefit of light-skinned America and Western Europe, and to the detriment of darker-skinned China, India, and Africa." — Newton Aster, Chief Science Advisor during first two terms of President T. Wilson administration

"Ironically, the battle over human-generated climate change, especially those disposed to the belief of impending global atmospheric apocalyptic scenarios, gave birth to the terrestrial and extraterrestrial biodome and terraforming industries—another wing of the government military industrial complex." — *Bloke, American civil rights attorney for Outland and Trogland*

The Pacifica
9:00 a.m., 8 August 2096

Mr. Thomas relishes being the new Prophet of the Mormon Order. He stands at the head of the regal conference table with a seated Council of Twelve Apostles, each man looking at him. The conference room itself has bodyguards lining the back, next to the main entrance.

He addresses the men. "The loss of the Prophet is something…it is something that the Order must overcome despite our grief and shock. We must put aside those emotions at the present time, but not forever, for the sake of the Order. Everything we do going forward must be to ensure the full safety of *Pacifica* and all our city-ships; we must identify our enemies; the military must be prepared for any possibility; and we must investigate fully those responsible for the killings of Prophet Simon, the former Counselors, and the four crews of our four best subs, with some of the best men and women in Military. All this must be done and accomplished with a greater unwavering determination than the Order has demonstrated on Exodus and even the Leviathan Project. The final phase of the Project will not be delayed—it will be accelerated. Gentlemen, let's pray for former Prophet Simon, the men and women we lost, and for God to reveal all our hidden enemies to us so we can bring true safety to our people. Let's pray."

Everyone bows their heads with their eyes closed.

Secret Island Hideout, Philippine Ocean
10:55 a.m., 8 August 2096

Vincent lies on his bunk trying to take a quick nap. There is a knock on the door of his cabin.

"Come in."

The door opens and the three captains slowly walk in and close the door. Their faces are so pale that Vincent sits up in his bunk and spins to the side so he can stand up.

"What wrong? What happened?"

It could be anything. That's the problem. There are infinite possibilities and from their expressions, it is bad—very bad.

"The Prophet is dead."

The shock puts Vincent right back down on his bunk.

"His yacht was lost and everyone aboard," the Bowhead captain continues. "The entire First Presidency."

"How?" Vincent asks.

"We don't have details."

Vincent looks up."How did you find out?"

"The Shogun notified us. The Order contacted the Continuum with the news. The new Prophet did."

"The new Prophet? Apostle Aaron?"

"No. Mr. Thomas is the new Prophet."

Vincent jumps to his feet with such a look of anger that the captains are caught off guard.

War Floor, The Pacifica
9:00 a.m., 8 August 2096

Mr. Varma remains calm even though three security guards stand behind him. Caleb sits at the same small table. Prophet Thomas is also in the room, standing in the back, watching from the shadows.

"Thank you for coming down so fast, Mr. Varma," Caleb says. "We appreciate your cooperation."

"Whatever I can do to help, I will. This is unbelievable. I am still in shock. I just saw him yesterday. I wish I knew something, anything to help."

"We know. If you think of anything more, please contact us immediately."

"How did it happen?" Varma asks. "You say the ship was lost. What happened exactly?

Caleb begins to answer.

Prophet Thomas steps forward. "We're keeping all those details private for now."

Varma looks at him. "I completely understand."

"May I ask a few questions?"

"Yes."

"Did the Prophet make any requests for information? I'm told you do that sort of thing all the time for us," Prophet Thomas asks.

"No, not this time. Nothing at all. I wish I knew something to help."

"It's okay, Mr. Varma. We appreciate it. Mr. Caleb, please escort Mr. Varma back to his boat."

"Yes, Prophet." Caleb motions to the security guards as Varma stands from his chair.

"Oh, one more question," Prophet Thomas adds. "Did you have any communications with anyone in the Order, the Mormon Order, here on *Pacifica*?"

Varma thinks for a moment. "Yes, that same day actually. I was in touch with a few people. I'll be in Australia next month, so I got several requests for items for when I go. I make the trip only four times a year."

"Who were those people?"

"All my calls to *Pacifica* are logged. Is something wrong with the logs?"

"No, but did you call anyone else not logged in, or did anyone call you?"

"Oh, no. No one. I'm a businessman. I always follow the rules or else I have no business."

"Thank you, Mr. Varma."

Varma nods and is led out of the room by the guards. They wait until he is gone and the door is closed. Caleb looks at Thomas.

"I want all business with Mr. Varma terminated as of today."

Caleb is surprised. "Why, sir? Did he lie about something?"

"Are we unable to find anyone in the Order to deliver useless trinkets to us?"

"He does far more than that, sir. He's part of our intelligence network and has been for many years."

"Terminate the relationship with him, and we'll figure out alternatives. I believe security has suffered within the Order because of our interactions with others outside the Order. I wouldn't be surprised that when the investigation is completed, we'll find that it was those interactions with outsiders that led to the tragedies yesterday."

Caleb stands. "Sir? What are you saying? Do you know more—?"

"I'll let Control uncover the facts."

"Yes, sir."

"I also want surveillance enabled on all the families of the missing boats, this Ms. River and—"

"Sir, we can't do that to the families of our heroes. Why would we do that?"

"—and Mr. Glen."

"I can't put surveillance on Military, sir."

Prophet Thomas moves closer to Caleb.

"Are your current duties going to be a problem for you? This is a critical time for the Order. A dangerous time, and I know that the stress might be too much for some. I can understand if you are one of those people."

"It is not a problem for me, sir."

"You were promoted into your post by Prophet Simon."

"Yes, I was, sir. Fifteen years ago, sir."

"I am not a 'sir.' I am the Prophet."

"Yes, Prophet."

"And?"

"I'll carry out your orders, Prophet."

The Pacifica
5:01 p.m., 8 August 2096

In the center of the *Pacifica*, a circular hole opens. A jet rises slowly, using its vertical propulsion, and when ten feet above the landing deck, jets away.

Underground Cavern
6:02 p.m., 8 August 2096

The jet rises from the water and flies forward as the cave wall seems to open like common double doors.

The pilot lands the craft. Thomas and Mr. Huntley sit in the middle section and two bodyguards sit in the rear.

"Prophet, if I'm to be your new head of both Control and Military, in light of crisis that we're in, these kinds of trips end today. Two bodyguards and a solo mini-flyer is not anything close to solid security measures. If you can't abide by my security recommendations, then you will need to appoint someone else."

Thomas smiles at him. "You will be an excellent choice."

Only the pilot stays with the craft. The other men don goggles and proceed into the entrance tunnel. It is completely dark, but with their night-sight goggles, they walk to the other end and stop. The "ground" descends.

The express walkway transports them further into the cavern's rock. Everything that they see in the dark with their goggles has almost a green glow. The wind rushes past their heads, and the trip seems to go on for miles, though Huntley glances at his wristband to show that only five minutes have gone by.

Doors open and then close behind them. The final doors open and the men are bathed in light. They remove their goggles and see three battle-bots are waiting. The robots' forearms, hands, and face turrets are pointing at them. The lead robot scans the men, and the robots disengage their guns and move to the side.

The men reach their final destination with a new robot walking with them.

"Report," Thomas asks.

"No intrusions from last visit twenty-five days, four hours, twenty-one minutes ago," the robot answers. It looks more like a scarecrow made of cables, except for its white mask-face and white elbow and knee guards.

Inside the Room, Thomas scans the contents—rows and rows of glowing white cubes, millions and millions of them. The cubes are stacked more than fifteen feet high. The cavernous room must be almost one hundred feet tall.

"So this is the Room." Thomas looks all around. "How much power do we have?" Thomas asks.

"We can power every vehicle, vessel, machine, and system for centuries," Huntley answers.

"And the Leviathan Project?"

"Without the renewing tek, one hundred years, but we do, so another fifty years."

"Our only limitation is where we go."

"Yes, Prophet. Are we still concerned about this Russian President having the exact same nickname as the Project? Many of us feel it may be the Pagan's way of telling us they know about it."

"They don't know about it. Not every coincidence is a conspiracy. But we will take extra precautions. I do agree that the disappearance of the Russian Orthodox had to do with outsiders. The wrong people probably found out about their Behemoth Project."

"If their Behemoth Project is in the hands of outsiders, then they have access to much of the same tek as we're using in Leviathan."

"No, they don't. It is several generations behind. Obsolete tek, as far as we're concerned."

"Are you sure?"

"I should know. I was in charge of the sale."

"How long do you want us to delay the sale to the others?"

"Indefinitely."

"But the Christians and Jews are expecting us to deliver their power cubes. Prophet Simon had already authorized the shipment."

"I'm the Prophet now and the others don't need them. I'm sure they have a larger stockpile than us."

"Prophet, the Shogun are Christians too, and we're relying on their help and cooperation."

"This is why we need to untangle ourselves from all of them. I'm not interested in the Order being a part of the herd. We will chart our own path."

Huntley hesitates. "Yes, Prophet."

"I'll pretend to be a part of their little Continuum until we're ready." He turns to the robot. "Prepare the Room for transport."

"Yes, it will be done," it answers.

"Amend your communication protocols. You are to address me as Prophet."

The robot's eyes instantaneously turn off and on, rebooting. "Amended. Yes, Prophet, it will be done."

The Pacifica
12:00 noon, 8 August 2096

River nears her offices and turns the corner. She stops—several men in black uniforms are waiting for her.

"Hello," she says as she walks past them. "What can I do for Control?"

"If we can talk with you inside, ma'am," one of the men says.

The biometric sensor opens River's door and she enters with the men following her. She throws her portfolio on her desk and sits down behind it. Four of the men seem to spread out to block the door and the three other men stand in front of her desk.

"Are all seven of you going to be speaking to me simultaneously? If not, then I want six of you to stand outside. You're making me nervous."

"Ma'am, I'm Mr. Huntley. I'm the Order's new chief of Control and Military."

"Control and Military are merged into one entity? How interesting."

"Interesting?"

"What do you want to talk about?"

"We had some background questions to cover?"

"Ask."

"Your husband wasn't Mormon, was he?"

"Are you joking? Why are you illegally reading my civilian file? What business is it of yours what religion my husband was? Whether

I'm equally yoked or not is not your business, snooper boy. Interfaith marriage is a crime now, is it? Why do you care? Do you want to make me a second wife?"

"Your jokes are not funny. Is that an answer to my question?"

"I don't know what this is about. Is this the new duties of the merged Services? The merging of Control and Military has been strongly rejected for years. I should know because I was one of the dozen or so of us who set them up. Didn't you read that too, snooper boy?"

"The realignment comes from the new Prophet, not this boy."

"Mr. Huntley, tell your men to leave my office and you can have a seat."

"My men will stay where they are until the interview is over."

"Interview? What interview?"

"The one we're conducting."

River stands up from her desk. "I am not doing any interview or interrogation. I'm retired from Control and Military, and I will not have anything to do with any men in black jammed into my office."

"Ma'am, that's offensive. We were men in black under the last Prophet. I'm sure you had no issue with our attire then. Weren't you one of the dozen or so who chose our uniform colors?"

"I was outvoted. The uniform's color reminded me too much of government stormtroopers and Vampires, but they didn't think primary colors would be appropriate. If they could see you, they would have voted with me for maybe a bright yellow or a hot pink."

Huntley smirks. "Will you be sitting for our interview?"

"No I won't—unless you're placing me under arrest."

"You're not under arrest, but if you don't cooperate with our investigation, that can be arranged."

"Then arrange it."

She grabs her portfolio from her desk. "Get out of my way!" she yells at the men in front of the door.

"Ma'am, is there a reason why you're hiding something?"

"Hiding something? Are we back to that? Dear citizen, you have to prove your innocence. There are plenty of dead Mormons in the ground from the Resistance wars who would object as violently as me. No, Mr. Huntley, you have to prove guilt, not the other way around. Again—get out of my way!"

Mr. Huntley motions to his men to step aside from the door.

River opens the door. "You frackin', wanna-be Boggs," she says under her breath.

"Excuse me, ma'am. I didn't hear what you said," Huntley says.

River is gone.

12:16 p.m., 8 August 2096

Miri sits at the living room table as Bear and Dove cook in the kitchen.

"What does it all mean, Mother?" Bear asks as he removes a skillet from the stove.

"I don't know," Miri answers. "I really don't know."

Bear stops. "I don't think Father is dead either."

"How do you know?" Dove asks.

"Mother, I agree with Bear," Cat says. "I'd feel it if he were."

"I wish we could all say that, but we don't know that," Miri says. "I've known many people who knew, could feel, that a loved one was in trouble or something bad happened to them. But I'm not one of them. We don't know."

The doorbell rings and they all look towards the door.

Bear opens the door and River stands there.

"Is Miri here?"

"Yes, why?"

River walks in past him. Miri is standing.

"Why are you back? Do you have news?"

"Miri, we have to leave *Pacifica* now."

"What? What are you talking about?"

"Gather up your children. We have to leave now. I thought we'd be able to do what we needed to do here, but that will not happen with this martial law directive and all the new changes in leadership."

"What changes?"

"Miri, we have to leave."

"I'm not going anywhere. If my husband is alive, he'll come back here, contact me here."

"If your husband is alive, he'll know exactly where to contact us. We have to go now."

"No."

River tries to convince Miri more forcibly. The doorbell rings again. The women look at each other.

Bear open the door again. A woman is led into the main living room—Haven, the wife of the late Prophet Simon.

"Mrs. Simon," Miri says with surprise. Both Miri and River walk over and they hug her.

"I'm so sorry," River says. "He'll be known as one of our greatest Prophets."

"He'll be known as the greatest husband, father, and grandfather," Haven says.

"What brings you here?" Miri asks.

"We need to leave, *Pacifica*."

6:00 p.m.

Haven Simon leads a crowd of people to one of the surface docks. She is flanked by her children and grandchildren, their families, Miri and her children, River, and several other families and officers. The dock guards stop her.

"Mrs. Simon." The guard is almost in tears as he recognizes her. "I'm so sorry. My family is still in shock."

"Thank you."

"We have you in our prayers, all of us do. If you need anything…"

"I know. Thank you and bless you for that."

"Where are you going, Mrs. Simon?" He looks at everyone with her.

"We are going to a special remembrance for my husband. Mr. Varma and some other friends of my husband are holding it for me and the family. I invited some friends to go with us."

"Mrs. Simon, it's dangerous out there and isn't too late in the day. The Russian Bloc could be going to war with the Caliphate and the CHINs. We're still in code red over the loss of your husband and our military boats."

"We will be guests of the CHIN government, itself. I don't think anyone will risk going to war with them."

"Guests of the CHINs?"

"Mr. Varma is a CHIN citizen. We'll be fine."

"But the Prophet—I mean the new Prophet. He has forbidden any departures or arrivals from outsiders."

"He cleared it for me before he left."

"Oh, you know he's not aboard."

"I do. Young man, I am the wife of a Prophet, and I will be leaving immediately. Is that understood?"

"Yes, Mrs. Simon."

She leads the group to the section of the dock with dozens of shuttle boats. Everyone loads into the boats, a dozen per boat, and begin to pilot out of the dock, one after another.

The massive doors of the city-ship's dock open and the boats head out to the open sea. *The Moving Picture*, with a smiling Varma at the wheel, appears. A larger yacht appears and pulls alongside his speed boat.

"Can someone tell me what's going on?" Miri asks.

"Not here," Haven says.

The shuttle boats stop next to both crafts. Haven and the others board either Varma's boat or the yacht, *The Yellow Brick Road*. Once aboard, the shuttle boats drive back to the *Pacifica*, each one is equipped with auto-pilot. *The Moving Picture* and the yacht speed away together.

"Mrs. Simon—" Miri starts to say.

"Haven. Please call me by my first name, Miri. You know my husband and I are very informal in that area. Yes, we can talk now."

"So something is going on," River says.

"Yes, something is and I don't like it. Mr. Thomas has been purging the Order of every leader appointed by, or supportive of my husband. He hasn't wasted any time seizing control of systems, and rewriting systems. And you, River, we need you because you've been working directly on Leviathan. You can tell me what he's changed. Mr. Thomas left for the Room an hour ago. He's properly already there, to do who knows what."

"Haven, why are we leaving? We should confront him," River says. "He sent a bunch of Gestapo-like Control agents into my office to interrogate me or arrest me. I don't know what."

"They know."

"Know? Know what?" River asks.

"They know we suspect them and know what they did."

Miri looks at River, then back at Haven. "What did they do?"

"I'm part of the Watcher group too. Your husband was in charge of it, Miri. Don't pretend you don't know what I'm talking about.

Your husband was the president and my husband was the president emeritus. He actually passed it on to your husband when he became Prophet."

"Are you saying we're leaving and we're not coming back?" Miri asks.

"Haven, we need to stay and confront them," River says.

"We can't do that, and I can't be objective knowing what I know."

"Know what?" River asks.

"Mr. Thomas and the men who are now his Twelve were out on their own special military boat, that incidentally no one knew they had, at the exact same time that my husband and his craft disappeared."

"What are you saying, Haven?" Miri asks.

"You know what I'm saying. I'm saying there's been a coup within the Order, and the new Prophet and his conspirators sent my husband and everyone aboard his yacht to the bottom of the ocean. Mr. Thomas killed my husband!"

Gatherings

"Entire ignorance is not so terrible or extreme an evil, and is far from being the greatest of all; too much cleverness and too much learning, accompanied with ill bringing-up, are far more fatal." — Plato, *Ancient Greek philosopher, writer, mathematician*

"I don't need to explain myself. I answer to God and me, not you." — *Prophet Thomas, the Mormon Order*

Sea of Japan
13 August 2096

Vessels, from tiny boats to gigantic cruisers, fill the waters with flags displayed high—the Supreme Islamic Caliphate or the CHINs. Japanese and Korean ships have scaled back their shipping weeks ago. Russian Bloc ships counter by stationing themselves to blockade any unauthorized entry into their territory and Russian Argus drones patrol from the sky.

Room of the Apostles, The Pacifica
1:03 noon, 13 August 2096

Prophet Thomas enters the executive room with Apostle Aaron. The other Apostles are already waiting.

"Prophet, this is not a meeting to take lightly," Aaron says. "The

Resistance may have been a ragtag team of religious civilians fighting any way we could, but the Continuum…they're not just an inter-Faither alliance sharing intel and having the occasional Net-meeting in dark cyberspace. They're a collective nation-state—a very dangerous virtual nation to actual or perceived threats. Be respectful of that, Prophet. Their leaders go back a long time with our leaders, like Vincent and Prophet Simon."

Thomas turns. "Vincent and Prophet Simon are dead, Mr. Aaron."

Cyberspace
1:13 p.m., 13 August 2096

There is darkness. A flashing green dot appears first, then dozens, thousands, and billions. The secret holographic Net-meeting in Freespace begins. The code becomes a room with several people standing in a circle. The same from the last meeting—Moses Atticus of the New Protestant Order, Tova Ben-Hurion of the New Jewish Continuum, Father Marcos of the New Catholic Order, Archibishop Masai of the African Collective, and Kanji of the Shogun Order. And one additional person, his figure glows to show he's speaking.

"I want to personally thank all of you for your condolences regarding the late Prophet Simon. He will be missed, and it will take many of us some time to fully recover," Thomas says. "But of course we must go on with life.

"There has been a dramatic increase in foreign craft in this area. The region is no longer safe for any of us, and that must be my primary concern. We will not be continuing our membership in the Continuum. Not to speak ill of the dead, but we will taking a different path, and there are security concerns that must be dealt with. I know you understand."

Another figure in the circle begins glowing.

"We do understand," Father Marcos says. "Will we be able to conclude our shipments? We, too, are moving resources out of the region."

Thomas's image begins glowing again. "We will. We're not sure of when exactly with these crises, but the delay shouldn't be too long."

"This is all quite unfortunate," Kanji says. "I can only speak for the Shogun Order, but there was no delay when we paid for our items. My council would like all monies returned until such time our shipments can be completed."

"That seems quite drastic," Thomas says. "The delay won't be long and—"

"Mr. Thomas—"

"Prophet Thomas."

"As you like. Prophet Thomas, in my culture, tragedy happens and a delay of a day or two is acceptable and common. A week however, when one man shakes another man's hand, when one Order shakes the hand of another, is not. An agreement with Prophet Simon was an agreement fulfilled. Will the era of Prophet Thomas be setting a new standard?"

There is a long pause before Thomas speaks. "We can't set an exact date because we don't know ourselves. The region is too dangerous."

Kanji's image engages before Thomas is even finished speaking. "My youngest son, when he was a child, used to play all kinds of mind games with me. He eventually grew out of it, but the lengths he would go to, the levels he would create. He realized one day that you can't play a game with people if they refuse to play with you."

Kanji's image disappears.

"What exactly is he implying?" Thomas asks.

"He didn't imply, Prophet Thomas. He stated it. These delays didn't start with the grief over the loss of your last Prophet, ten days ago. It began with you becoming the Mormon's new Prophet." The image of Moses disappears too.

The other Continuum members disappear and the Net-meeting room vanishes.

Thomas sits at a small table with a tall pyramid-like device on top of it. The connection has terminated. He looks at the Apostles and the guards around him.

"Transfer all the funds to other accounts, multiple accounts," Thomas says.

"I'll do it right now, Prophet." One of the Apostles activates his palm tablet.

Aaron wants to say something, but decides not to.

"Prophet…" The other Apostle on his e-pad looks up.

Thomas stands. "What is it?"

"The funds have already been reversed."

"The Shogun's?"

"No, all of them—Shogun, Jews, Protestants, Catholics. All of them."

He yells, "How can they have access to our account protocols? It's impossible for them to do such a thing in a few seconds. No one can. Not even the Magi."

"The transfer was made *before* the Continuum meeting."

Thomas and the other Apostles look at each other.

"Before?" Aaron asks.

"I know how they were able to do it."

"How?" Thomas asks. "No one has access to those protocols outside of myself and the Counselors."

"Or the last one."

"Those codes were erased immediately as soon as they were reported dead."

"And their wives?"

Thomas realizes the oversight and is enraged as he pounds the table with his fists.

"Who?!" he yells at the Apostle.

"The last Prophet's wife. Haven Simon."

The Pacifica
8:27a.m., 15 August 2096

Prophet Thomas walks through the hallway to the War Room. Huntley, the Apostles, aides and security follow.

The camera-bot is positioned right in front of him as he sits in a chair, his back straight, hands clasped slightly and resting in his lap.

"I know many of you are still grieving. I know many of you are scared. We've suffered great losses. Some of you are saying this is the end for us, the end of the world for us. But it is not. I met with the others two days ago, with at the Continuum. They expressed their fullest sympathies for our losses and the fullest confidence in my leadership of the Order.

"I know there are many rumors here on *Pacifica* and the rest of the city-ships. The rumors say there are invaders living underwater watching us, stalking us. Strange divers who pilot manta-like sea crafts, the ones who destroyed four of our best boats, with all hands, and obviously are responsible for the loss of Prophet Simon along with his crew.

"I am here to tell you that the rumors are true. They are after us. They did kill our people. But they will wish they never met us. The invaders are a group we are all very familiar with, from our days back in Utah. They are Vampires, like the ones Boggs sent back then to remove us from our homes, cities, and land in our own state. We had hoped the growing presence of foreign nations in the region would be blessing in disguise. Keep these invaders away from us. But that is not the case. The invaders continue stalking us, and it's only a matter of time before they attack.

"We are gathered here right now because we are not running away this time. We are going to war. I will be leading the battle against these invaders—these Sea Vampires. We will avenge our fallen. We go to war."

The wave of applause ripples throughout the room and every corner of the city-ship.

A Private Little Big War

"Those who make peaceful revolution impossible will make violent revolution inevitable." — John F. Kennedy, 35th President of the United States

"I was there. I saw them. I was a child at the time, but I saw them. They wouldn't leave us alone. All they did was start a war, a 'private little big war,'" — Matthias Simon, eldest son of Prophet Simon, The Mormon Order, Future "Sixteenth" Apostle for the Lost Ones

Before they sent stormtroopers, they sent the "compliance officers." Everyone knew the day would come. They had already "visited" Jewish and Christian enclaves. "Use religion against religion," the President T. Wilson had famously, or infamously, said, and not a single Faither had forgotten it.

Salt Lake City, Utah
2:35 p.m., 4 July 2083

"Die, you Nazi!" The brother and sister laugh, sitting on the floor in front of the family living room vid-screen. They watch the display as their white-gloved hands flitter all around—their players jumping, ducking, running, and shooting in the vid game.

Their mother appears. "What were you two shouting?"

"Nothing, Mom. We're killing Redcoats," the son says.

"I don't like these killing vid-games you kids play."

There are endless numbers of these shooter games. In this case, it's the Original Thirteen colonists fighting the Pre-Islamic Great Britain in the American Revolution. The kids made the case that they liked the game for "historical reasons."

"Mom, you played them too," the daughter says. Neither child takes their eye from the vid-screen. "And you played bigger ones than this."

The mother can't say anything. The vid-games she and her siblings played were full-body sensor suits with visors and full holo-view enclosures where they battled robots and aliens.

"I don't want any bad language in the house."

"Yes, Mom."

"And only one hour more."

"Yes, Mom."

"All that digital gaming rots brain cells and makes you stupid."

"Yes, Mom."

"And do your homework right after."

"Yes, Mom."

"And no more allowance, and you will cook all the meals in the house from now on."

"Yes, Mom. Wait."

"No, mom," the son says, laughing.

"That's tricking us mom," the daughter says.

"Oh so you can say something more than 'yes, Mom.'"

They both look at her laughing. "Yes, Mom."

She grins. "I'll be at the neighbors."

4:01 p.m.

The two siblings are at the kitchen table doing their homework. The sister is typing on her tablet. The brother is reading on his tablet, occasionally stopping to jot some notes with a stylus on another palm tablet.

The doorbell rings.

"I'll get it." The brother jumps up from the table and runs from the kitchen into the living room. "Door cam," he says. The vidscreen display on the door activates. The boy stops in his tracks. He sees the pale face of a man staring at the door—scary red eyes and fanged teeth, dressed in black.

"Who is it?" he yells at the door.

"Hello. Are your parents home?"

"Why?"

"I'm with the government. I'm here to help you."

**Brigham Town, Salt Lake City, Utah
5:05 p.m., 4 July 2083**

One of the Apostles stands in the town's meeting hall, waiting. News has spread fast and people continue to arrive from the back door. He looks at everyone's faces as they arrive—fear.

"They're in our town!"

"They're going house to house."

"We can stop them," the Apostle says, but his voice unconvincing. "We just have to stay unified."

"You said it would never come to this," one of the men standing next to him says. "Running from our own homes like hunted animals."

"The authorities will be here soon. We have to be patient," the Apostle says.

They hear them outside. The first Vampire enters the hall, a woman with shiny purple eyes, smiling with her fanged teeth. All the Vampires behind her, dressed in black, have similar sickly dental implants and colored corneal implants—red, yellow, ice blue.

"Are you leader of this town, sir?" she asks.

"I am one of the religious leaders," the Apostle answers.

"Oh good. My name is Ms. Elvira, no relation to the Elvira witch from TV."

"We don't watch TV."

"Oh, then you wouldn't have gotten my joke."

"Why are you here?"

"We are the compliance officers for this region."

"Compliance?"

"Yes, sir. The Religious Registration division."

"We don't get involved in politics. We avoid the public eye, stay to ourselves. We simply want to be left alone like every other religious American."

"Sir, if you live in America, then you have to follow America's laws. All religions have to be approved by the government to make sure all anti-hate, anti-bigotry, and all tolerance statues are followed and only sanctioned holy books are used. Religious people can't arbitrarily exempt themselves from following those laws."

The Apostle stands there. He is no longer making eye contact and seems to be having difficulty breathing. Everyone is looking at him, wanting him to say something, do something.

"What is your name, sir?" the Vampiress asks.

"Why?"

"No reason. Just for the record. Name?"

"Smith. John Smith."

She laughs. The Vampires around are completely emotionless. "You mean Thomas. Your name is Mr. Thomas, isn't it?"

The man says nothing, but looks down at the ground.

The main doors open and a man enters, dressed in civilian clothes, with four uniformed police officers with him. They move through the people at the door and stop in between the people and the Vampires. The man looks directly at the female Vampire leader.

"What's happening here?" he asks.

"Who might you be?"

"I'm the chief of police for this town. Who are you?"

"I'm Ms. Elvira, Senior Compliance Officer for the Office of Religious Registration. We are doing a field inspection."

"Field inspection?"

"Yes."

"Do you have any idea that your appearance is offensive? You're scaring our children."

The Vampire looks at the children in the room. One girl in particular looks to be crying as she hides behind her mother.

"I'm not the responsible for the religious bigotry of others."

"Bigotry, huh?"

"Chief, I'm not answerable to you. I work for Congress and the White House. I don't report to you, and I don't need your permission to conduct our work. This is a federal matter so I outrank everyone in this state, including your governor. You can either assist or go back home." She raises her hand and the other Vampires grab their weapons from their holsters.

Everyone in the hall gasps. Women stand in front of their children, and men stand in front of the women.

"Why did you do that?"

"Chief, you need to understand that we are going to do the job we were sent here for."

"You need to tell your people to holster their weapons right now, or I will arrest you and your four friends for endangering the public."

More people arrive. "What's going on?" a man yells from the door.

The new arrival is a tall man with white hair. Two police officers follow him.

"Mr. Mayor," the Vampiress acknowledges. "I feel special with all this attention."

"Why are there vehicles arriving in my town with armed federal police?" he asks.

People look at each other and go to the windows. SUVs and people transports filled with black-clad soldiers.

"Mr. Mayor, they are only for backup purposes."

"Your troops are surrounding my town. We got women and children here. Why are you here?"

"As I've already explained, this will be the third time; we are federal compliance officers here for a field inspection. Let's not play games. I'm sure all your men, women, and children are armed, which is why we have the federal troop backup so there are no misunderstandings."

"What's your name?"

"My name is Ms. Elvira and here, sir,"—she hands him a palm tablet—"is the authorization for our field inspection."

The mayor looks at it. He looks to the chief with a defeated look. The chief looks back with an expression of anger.

"We'll do our work and leave," she says. "If you don't like this country's laws, you can go live someplace else in the world. Now take me to your leader."

One of the other Vampires taps her on the shoulder. She notices the flashing red light on her wristband. First, she looks at the people and then turns to run outside to the backup troops.

She is met by a boy pointing a rifle at her. Elvira looks to the federal vehicles and every one of the soldiers are sitting on the ground with their ankles restrained and their hands cuffed behind their backs. Uniformed town police are everywhere with guns pointing at them.

The mayor and the police chief exit the building.

Elvira says, "You think you're the only Jew-Christians to try this. Let me tell you what's going to happen. We've been watching you for years. We'll use whatever force we need to, to do our work. You stop now and no charges will brought against you. You continue, and your men, women, and children will be arrested and deposited in the closest Supermax prison facility for a lot of years."

"Why are you doing this? Why?" the Mayor asks.

"I just told you."

"No, you gave me a speech. Why are we doing this? This is our state and you still won't leave us alone. You come in here looking like demons with your stormtroopers, with your guns, and to do what? Inspect our bibles? Make sure we're good little citizens? These are our families."

"You can tell Boggs where he can stick his registration initiatives—" the Chief starts to say.

"Who's Boggs?" Elvira asks, confused.

More residents arrive on foot and by vehicle.

Elvira laughs. "Your children will be in their eighties when they get out of prison. None of you will be so lucky. I will personally see to it."

"You know something, Vampire? Human beings are biological animals like all others," the Mayor says. "They will do anything to protect their offspring. I once saw a tiny momma mouse fight off a vicious cat to defend its young. Animals will do anything to protect their young."

"Well, sir, in your story, I'm not a cat. I'm a state-of-the-art, multi-gun turret, missile-loaded, fission-powered, gunship."

"In my story, I'm not a mouse." The mayor shoots the Vampiress point-blank in her chest with a gun she didn't even notice he had in his hand.

Sea of Japan
9:12 a.m., 15 August 2096

Prophet Thomas sits in the captain's chair of the sub. All he can think of is the history he will be making, the respect he will solidify within the Order. He has the title, but today he will earn it.

"Diving to one hundred feet, Prophet," says the sub's pilot.

"Very good. Proceed to target area."

The *Avenging Angel* was secretly constructed to be larger and faster than the Order's former Military flagship, the *Divine Providence*. It's nearly twice the size, has twice the payload of weapons, but it is stealthier than any sea craft in the fleet.

The lights are flashing "code yellow" and the entire crew of twenty is ready for battle. For this mission, Thomas is the general-in-charge. He tries to stop himself, but he looks anyway. A single vid-cam mounted on the overhead for everyone on *Pacifica* and the other city-ships to watch the battle to come live.

"We will launch, and I will lead the battle with a dozen of our best attack subs," he announced to the entire Order only forty minutes before. "We know where the Sea Vampires are and how many attack subs they have. Our attack will be swift and decisive. I know many of you are saying to yourselves that this mission is too dangerous. But that is exactly why we attack now—they won't be expecting it. Some of you are thinking this will be a very big war for us, but I don't think so. We have the power. It will be a very little war for us."

These waters are dangerous, both on the surface and below. Contacts are all around them, even now, but he's instructed the crew not to call them out with the vid-cam watching.

Huntley stands up and walks to him.

"Yes, Mr. Huntley."

"Prophet, should I brief the crew now?"

"Yes, please do. But do it privately, away from the camera. We want the public to see the battle. They don't need to know our strategy. Once you brief the crew, we will wait until all the Vampire subs return. Then we'll attack and destroy all of them at once."

The Pacifica
10:01 a.m., 15 August 2096

Onboard the *Pacifica*, people watch the live feed of the Prophet's boat. Some are gathered together in meeting rooms, others along the deck, some view with their families in their individual quarters, but everyone is watching.

The Twelve are gathered in the War Room with other agents and soldiers. The room is packed with people all looking at the giant vidscreen on the wall. Apostle Aaron notices the two observers that had been on Vincent's boat and put in escape pods; they are the only survivors from that tragic day. He thought they were civilians, but here they are dressed in black uniforms. He walks to them.

The two notice him. "Mr. Aaron," the woman says.

"It's Officer Sandee, correct?"

"Yes, sir."

"And I'm Douglas, sir."

"While we wait for the battle to begin, I did have a question for you both."

"Sir, we've been instructed by Mr. Huntley not to say anything to anyone, even our families, about the *Divine Providence* incident."

"I'm not anyone."

"Yes, sir."

"Especially when Commander Vincent and his crew saved your lives."

"Yes, sir."

"Obviously you were attacked by these Sea Vampires. How many were there?"

"Sir, we weren't attacked," Douglas says. "We made contact, but they were all other countries."

"But they put you in escape pods."

"They put us in escape pods to remove us from the boat, sir," Sandee says.

"Why?"

"We don't know, sir," Douglas replies. "But when the pods were a good distance away that's when the fatal attack happened and the boat exploded. They probably didn't even know what hit them. It happened so fast. I know it's insensitive to say, sir, so I would never say it publicly, but they caused their own deaths. If they weren't doing what they were doing against us, they would have been on the bridge and would have seen what was coming."

"Why did they do it then?"

"We don't know, sir. They wanted us off the boat."

The Avenging Angel, Sea of Japan
10:02 a.m., 15 August 2096

"Look at their underwater fleet," says a crewman.

The Vampires' underwater city is as many square feet as half of a city-ship, which means it is massive. A fleet of manta-ships is fully docked, one to a sphere. There looks to be over four dozen of the enemy sea crafts. If it were a face-to-face battle, they would still be outmatched, despite their tek. But many a war has been won by strategy and cunning, not superior weaponry or the size of the army.

The attack group hovers in the deep ocean at the three hundred foot mark, waiting. Prophet Thomas stares at the vid-screen, rubbing his chin. Stealth attack is standard operating procedure within the Order. Hide, wait, and destroy.

"Prophet, they're here," a crewman whispers. The lights are now flashing "code red."

The first manta-ship glides above them. Huntley is the only one on the bridge, besides the Prophet, who has seen the original feed of the one encountered by Commander Vincent. These manta-ships are much larger—more dangerous, meaner. Two more follow, then another five. The final two appear. The manta-ships move away, nearing the floating undersea structures.

One of the manta-ships glides to a stop.

There is no sound of any kind on the bridge. It's as if everyone is holding their breath as they watch the enemy on the vid-screen. The manta-ship continues forward to resume its course.

"Is the attack group ready?"

"Yes, Prophet."

"As soon as the last one docks with the structures, fire at will after a twenty-second delay."

"Yes, Prophet."

"Give me the countdown at ten."

"Yes, Prophet."

The view is magnified and they can see the structures clearly—a network of connected spheres; some aligned vertically, others horizontally. The manta-ships are fully docked. Moments pass.

"Ten," the weapons officer says. "Nine. Eight. Seven. Six. Five. Four. Three. Two. Launching."

The image of the structure seems so serene. The first torpedo hits and it seems as if the entire structure explodes with just one hit. A swarm of other torpedoes hit the target and the "fireworks" begin— a seemingly endless display of explosions. The crew cheers. When it's over, all that is left is a large sea-cloud of debris. The crew cheers again.

"Prophet, the big war we feared turned out to be a little one for us after all," says a still-applauding crewman.

"Take us home, pilot."

"Yes, Prophet."

"Good work, Prophet," Huntley says. "The attack was flawless."

"Yes, it was," Prophet Thomas says, smiling.

What the Frack!

"Half of the harm that is done in this world is due to people who want to feel important. They don't mean to do harm. But the harm does not interest them." — *T. S. Eliot, essayist, playwright, poet, literary and social critic (1888-1965)*

The Bombay Queen, Korea
6:17 a.m., 11 August 2096

Haven was the person to thank. No one would have minded, but she didn't want the families and the crews to have to reunite in a deep, dark underwater cavern. Instead, she rented two decks on an Indian cruise liner docked in Korea. No one could sleep the night before, and people were already dressed and ready to go on their respective boats, hours before the scheduled departure time. The crews of the *Divine Providence*, *Bowhead*, *Narwhale* and *Orca* were reunited with their families. The reunion lasted for hours—astonishment, tears of joy, and laughter.

The Bombay Queen, Korea
8:00 a.m., 12 August 2096

Vincent is emotionally exhausted, even though he did get a good night's sleep. He opens his eyes and sees it's not just his wife Miri in the bed with him. Cat is on one side, Dove and Seal are on the other side, all asleep.

Bear walks into the bedroom and opens the blinds of the bay windows to allow the morning light in. He stops to look at the bed filled with his family. A devilish smile appears on his face just before he notices his father is watching him.

"Bear," Vincent says. Miri wakes up. "Do not act on the thought that just popped into your brain. I was your age, too. Don't do it. You're a man now. Do not revert to a childlike state."

Bear ignores him and runs towards the bed. "Cannonball!"

His siblings all wake up instantly and his parents try to move out of the bed, but too late. Bear jumps and lands in the center of the water bed throwing everyone up into the air and to the floor. He cannot stop laughing.

"We're going to get you back bad, Bear," Seal says as he sits up from the floor.

"You're going to get it." Dove shakes her fingers at him.

Cat is already standing. "I landed on my feet because I'm a cat with catlike reflexes. You hear me, Bear?"

Vincent and Miri are lying on their backs on the ground. They look at each other as the kids continue their banter and go back to sleep.

The Kremlin, Moscow, Russia
10:00 a.m., 15 August 2096

The KGB Chief Zukov smiles for a moment as he looks at the private guest sitting in front of his desk.

"You look good, as always. I think it's being near the water so much that's good for the skin."

"You need to get out of the dungeons then," River says.

"I should, but my duties don't allow me to."

"I was disturbed to hear about your country copying America. Rounding up religious people and exiling them."

"We had a religious conspiracy trying to seize control of the government, behind at least two political assassination attempts. Either we did it, or the people would have done it for us in the streets."

"So when atheists do such things, it's okay, but when it's religious people, it's a conspiracy."

Zukov smiles. "Don't tell me you feel sorry for Witches and Vampires?"

"I don't, but it was everyone."

"We're not America or the CHINs. Most left the country voluntarily and those that stayed are no longer in Russia, but in Europa. They keep quiet, and they won't be bothered. They cause trouble again and they will be dealt with. I would remind you that these are the same rules for everyone living in the Russian Bloc, everyone, regardless of nationality, ideology, politics, biological designation, religious minority, or atheist majority—everyone. So what brings my ex-wife to Moscow?"

"You know."

"Yes, we spymasters know the answers before the question is even asked."

"I never thought of you as an atheist for some reason."

"I never was. I'm agnostic. I've always been. I'm not with either side. When I die, I'll know who's telling the truth and will make my decision at that time."

River laughs a bit.

"The Mormon Order has nothing to worry about," he says. "Actually your religion means nothing. It's your citizenship. Americans are not too popular with the Kremlin."

"Popular with your people, though."

"Ah, because Americans pay money for their popularity. The Russian Bloc is a very capitalistic country."

"Says the nation with big statues of Lenin and Stalin."

"America has statues of historical people too, who engaged in practices or had beliefs no longer shared by the majority. They are people of history, which is why we honor them. Nothing more. I was surprised when I heard you left your country. Dozens of generations of your people in one state, and you walk away."

"When we settled in Utah, it was not part of America yet. It belonged to Mexico, but then the Mexicans lost their war with America and America owned it. Everything seemed to be fine for a long time, solid citizens, until this century."

"You really are Americans. Russians would fight to the death rather than leave our land."

"We weren't afraid of fighting to the death. We were afraid of winning and becoming a people unrecognizable to even ourselves."

Zukov looks down at the table. He thinks of Igor.

"What about your boss?" River breaks the brief silence. "He's the President, not you."

"The President has no interest in a group of seafaring religionists on their way to destinations unknown. Your stay will be temporary, correct?"

"Yes. When we're done, we'll be gone."

"When will you get to the real reason as to why you asked to see me?"

"When will you tell me the reason you wanted to see me?"

He laughs. "Games, games, games. I'm surprised we didn't stay together longer."

"You remember why. You wanted more…'freedom.' Mormons don't do polygamy, and bigamy isn't a compromise position either."

"Yes, I do remember."

"You were also very anti-baby."

"You American religionists are very anti-progress. Why not have a domestic robot in the home to change diapers and clean nasty bottoms?"

River laughs. "I know you Pagans will never understand that most work is okay for machines, but some work must be done by people."

"Pagan doesn't mean the same thing here in the Russian Bloc as in America."

"Oh yes, I just accused you of being a druid witch-king. Sorry." She is ready to ask. "I want you to notify me of any danger that could impact my people until we leave, especially now. Private link between us only. Not to burden you, but just in case."

"I can do that. Actually, I was going to ask the same thing in a way."

"Really?"

"My boss is on a journey that…I feel at some point in the future he might realize he should never have gone down that path. If that ever happens, I want him to have options."

"Options?"

"Options to speak to people in your circle of friends."

"You're being very cryptic."

"I know I am. It will either happen or it won't, but I want the option to exist."

"Okay, I can do that."

Zukov pulls the tablet on his desk closer to him. "Now to business matters. Your people and our nation have done quite a bit of business over the years."

"Mutually beneficial business."

"Yes, I never got much into your internal religious beliefs and practices—other than knowing you have four holy books, Jews have three, and Russian Orthodox have two—but is it customary for members of your people to shoot at each other?"

"What?" River asks with a questioning look.

"Just because we've approved your people to be in our waters doesn't mean that our Argus surveillance isn't watching you. All of us are watched, always, even me. Some work is for people, other work is for machines. Machines are very good at surveillance; they never need to sleep."

"What exactly did you see?"

Zukov pushes the tablet to her and pushes the play button.

River stares at the vid. "What the frack…"

The Pacifica
12:49 p.m., 15 August 2096

The Avenger returns to *Pacifica*. The Prophet and crew exit the elevator on the main deck and a waiting crowd loudly applauds them. People rush up to the crews to shake the Prophet's hand. He stops to greet each person, each family.

Thomas arrives at the Room of the Apostles with the waiting fourteen Apostles. They applaud and greet him with handshakes, even the security guards join in.

"Welcome back, Prophet," Apostle Aaron greets.

"Thank you, gentlemen," he says and takes his seat the head of the table. "Let's get to business." The guards close the main doors. "It's time to move forward, gentlemen, with Leviathan."

"Do you think it's wise, Prophet," asks one of the Apostles.

"It is. Our immediate enemies are destroyed. We must be gone, before new ones show up."

"How long do you think it will take to be ready?" another asks.

"It's ready now," Prophet Thomas answers.

All the men at the table are surprised.

"When was it completed?"

"That's not important. The Leviathan Project is complete, and there's no reason why we can't activate it now."

"Prophet, there is one serious matter that does need to be addressed," Aaron says.

"Yes?"

"Mrs. Simon leaving *Pacifica* with the widows and families of the crew from the four boats we lost and dozens of others. We don't know why yet, and we have been unable to find them or contact them."

"So, why does that impact Leviathan?"

"Are you suggesting that we would leave them behind?"

"Mr. Aaron, this is not a cult. People can leave whenever they want. I left explicit instructions to everyone not to leave *Pacifica*. They knew that and left anyway. What their motives are is irrelevant. We must move forward. The Mormon Order isn't going to stand still and wait for anyone, even if it's the widow of our late Prophet. If they have no regard for the Order, then the Order has none for them. The lives of the many outweigh the lives of the few. Is there anyone at this table who disagrees with that axiom?"

No one answers him.

"I have as much affection for Mrs. Simon as any of you, but Leviathan must move forward without any more delays. I also must instruct all of you not to make any further attempts to contact her or anyone who left with her. If they return before we activate Leviathan, then we'll all be together again. If not, we have to go. We've been working on this for a decade. Time is up."

"What about the Continuum?" an Apostle asks.

"The Order is not subservient to the Continuum. We must do what's best for us. And no disrespect to the late prophet, but we will be charting a different path."

"If it were not for the others, we wouldn't have Leviathan," Aaron adds.

"That may be true, but it belongs to us. I already informed them that the Order would not retain its seat on the Continuum at this time, but we would reconsider in the near future."

The Counselors do a better job at hiding their concern than the Twelve.

"We've spent too much time being members of alliances and coalitions. It's time to leave the herd, not worry so much about what the other animals are doing, and strike out on our own. Look at the incredible things we can accomplish. This morning we destroyed an entire undersea city of Vampires bent on our destruction. All of us at this table can remember what those animals tried to do to us in the '80s in a state we controlled, right in our own cities, at our very own homes. We move forward, not backward. "

"But we still don't know what happened to the Orthodox," another Apostle says.

"That proves my argument. We have been getting entangled with others for so long that we worry about them rather than ourselves. I don't care what happens to the Russian Orthodox. I don't care what happens with their Behemoth Project. Even if their project was seized by the government, it has nothing to do with Leviathan. No delays. Leviathan will rise."

The Bombay Queen
1:02 p.m., 15 August 2096

The *Bombay Queen* is an Excelsior-class cruise liner manned by an Indian-only crew and staff. The nearly forty-year alliance forbids either country to display only their flag outside their borders. Here, flying high on the mast is the Indian flag with a tiny Chinese flag further down the pole.

They sit in one of the smaller conference rooms, but no less luxurious than any of the others. The captains of the four "lost" subs, other officers, agents, and civilian aides start to take their seats—the chairs arranged in a circle.

Haven talks with the Queen's captain before thanking him.

"Ladies and gentlemen, please don't hesitate to call us for any refreshments, drinks, or food." The captain nods and lets himself out, closing the door behind him.

"Is River going to join us?" Haven asks.

"She should be here," Vincent says. "Simply delayed."

"Do we know why she's gone?" Haven asks.

"We do," Vincent says. Haven smiles.

"Should we wait?" Miri asks.

"No, we should start," he says.

"Well, Commander, the stage is yours," Haven says as she sits. "I'm just the widow."

"You're a lot more than that."

"I'm still a civilian. You're the military officer and you've caused quite a situation here."

"Seems like we both have."

"Maybe we both need to explain to everyone what we know."

"I'm sure everyone here has already been trading notes. What do you want to do?" Vincent asks.

"I want you to lead an assault on *Pacifica* and arrest Mr. Thomas and the Twelve."

The sentence shocks everyone in the room.

"Why is everyone so surprised?" she says. "I'm a nice old lady, but I become something altogether different when people kill or try to kill the people I love. Vincent knows. He's seen my other side."

"Yes, I have."

"What do you have in mind?" she asks him. "I know you've

already thought about it, planned it, and are ready to go."

"Lead an assault on *Pacifica* and arrest Mr. Thomas and the Twelve."

Haven laughs, but no one else does. People stand to protest.

"There is no possible way we can do that," the Bowhead captain says. "What we need is proof. Proof that we can put before the people and have them take action."

"Thomas enacted martial law," Haven says.

"He'll never let us peacefully get anywhere near *Pacifica* or any of our city-ships," Vincent adds.

"Why not?" the Orca captain challenges. "You really believe they would kill us?"

"That's what they were going to do."

"None of us believe those torpedoes would have destroyed our boats," the Bowhead captain says. "Incapacitate yes, but not destroy us."

"So if we could go back in time, you would go back to your boat and let unknown ships fire torpedoes at you. You would say to yourself, 'They're only going to incapacitate us, not blow us to pieces and send us to the bottom of ocean?'"

"Obviously not, but what you're saying—"

"That's right. What you're saying is offensive." One of the aides is almost in tears.

Vincent looks around and notices that she isn't the only one.

"You are saying that our current Prophet murdered the old one to assume power. You have never liked Thomas, Vincent, never, or his father. Couldn't this be your own personal vendetta against him?"

"You're right. I don't like Thomas and never have and his father was a coward and a bum. But do you think I would sit here and make up things to accuse him of just for that. Jeopardize my career, my family…."

"Okay!" The woman composes herself. "You're right, but it still doesn't prove what you're alleging and Haven, how could you?"

"How could I what? What if I were to tell you that every person in a leadership position, in Military, in Control, connected with Prophet Simon, or Vincent here is being replaced by Thomas's people? It's called purging. I know the practice well. It's what President Boggs-Wilson did when he became Homeland Director for all of America and continued as President. Also, how did a man who is not even on the Twelve become the next Prophet? Seniority is the protocol, the oldest Apostle on the Twelve. I don't believe anyone not on the Twelve has ever been chosen. Aaron or Fisher were next in line."

"But what the Twelve did is not illegal," another man says. "It's not a democracy. The Twelve selects the next Prophet as a group. Their decision may seem strange to us, but we weren't part of the deliberation, and the Twelve are the same members as with Prophet Simon."

"Do none of you see what's happening?" Haven asks.

"We know," the woman says. "We see it, but what you're saying…even the charge…causing the death of…that would be outright murder. Even saying the words could tear the Order apart."

"We know that," Vincent says. He lowers his voice. "We had suspicions for a long time, but never acted, because we couldn't believe they would harm another member. And I didn't have the proof yet, but now I look back…my hesitation…and now Prophet Simon is dead!"

"What I'm hearing is that the case has not been made for action," Haven says in a calming voice.

"I'm not saying that all kinds of strange things have happened and are happening," an aide says. "None of us are blind, but there could be other explanations."

"I'm going to say what I said before to Vincent," the Orca captain says. "We all see the smoke, but we're not seeing the fire yet. If what you say is true, you're not talking about going anywhere and arresting anyone. We're talking about civil war, a civil war within the Order. I hate to say this." He looks sadly at Haven, shaking his head. "Even if you could prove what you two are saying, if it meant we'd have Mormons killing Mormons, I'd pretend the evidence never existed. I wouldn't be alone either."

"A murderer and conspirators running the Order?" Haven asks.

"I'd put it in God's hands. We are too vulnerable right now. And civil war is not an option—ever. You haven't come close to making that case for this."

"Until we find that proof, what shall we do?" Haven asks. "Any of you?" She asks the commanding officers in the room. "Vincent?"

Everyone looks at him. Vincent is typing on his e-pad.

"Please excuse me for a moment."

Vincent gets up from his chair and opens the door. River is standing in the hallway. She is fuming with rage.

"Why are you standing here? The meeting has started."

It only takes River a few seconds to activate the projector of her tablet and shine the drone surveillance vid on the wall. "Computer, dim lights. Again. Again."

They all watch the last moments of the crew of the Prophet's yacht—not what they thought they would be seeing. The gunfire exchange is loud and violent. It plays until the end and shuts off. Everyone looks at each other. Haven's mouth is open in shock.

Unknown Location
6:45 a.m., 16 August 2096

In the beginning, there was analog, then digital, then technology, and now tek. A world so dependent on that tek that without it, most human beings would cease to live—no one knew how to survive without tek and its machines. Those who can create them and maintain them are the true gods of society. Those who can hack into them and take possession of them from others are part genius, part artist, all criminal. Governments hunt these "tek-lords." They are perpetual threats to Tek World. The best ones, the legendary ones, are all Faithers.

The large cavernous room is filled with rows and rows of half-circle cubicles. Teks are hard at work typing and scrolling on their systems. No one has less than three vid-screens on their desk, some have as many as seven. Everyone is wearing dark glasses that allow them to view multiple pop-up virtual displays. No is talking in the room. There's too much work to do. And time grows shorter every day.

A tek enters the hallway to the Room. He is dressed simply and casually, with short, curly brown hair. The hallway is called the Skeleton Pass and the light has a very strange blue quality. The man enters the hallway. He is no longer a human being, but a walking skeleton. His skin is translucent. His bionic knees are clear. No external tek or devices are allowed in or out of the Room. He walks through a cloud of mist as he approaches the door. If there were any devices on him, they would have been rendered inoperable.

He opens the door and the skeleton is now a man again. No one looks up from their screens as he walks down an aisle. He sees the two men he's looking for.

The three men congregate in one of the empty mini meeting rooms. There's no need to sit; it won't take long. Goli is a giant of man, seven feet tall, and all muscle. His parents were of the Israeli Jewish Order. He belongs to the Conservative Jewish Order. Goli is one of those legends, a tek so brilliant, a tek-lord, that he has worked not only for Jews, but also other Faithers, for years.

The other man is quickly becoming a legend himself. NIS (his full nickname and what computers would probably call him if they could, is "Notoriously Invasive Species.") He is also known for his trademark circular eyeglasses that glow an intermittently neon blue. Some say the tek-lord single-handedly helped the African Collection Order bring the Christian-Islamic War ravaging Africa to a stalemate, which meant to the Islamic Caliphate's detriment. A former Catholic, he's now considered the Protestant's best tek.

The Room is not run by any one Order; it's run by the Continuum—the alliance of the Jews, Christians (Protestants), Catholics, African Collective (Catholics, Christians, Coptics, Armenians, Ethiopian Jews; various deists and agnostics of Africa), the Shogun, and the Magi. The two men oversee every tek in the Room, in addition to their own personal tek work.

"Who's the work for?" Goli asks.

The young man answers, "The Mormon Order."

"I thought they weren't on the Continuum anymore."

"It's complicated."

"Uncomplicate it," NIS says.

"The Mormons seem to be heading to a civil war."

Goli shakes his head. "This is the most critical moment for all of us in modern times. Why couldn't they have had their civil war ten years ago like the rest of us?"

"What's the name of ship you want us to hack into?' NIS asks.

The Pope and the Prophet

"I suspect that this whole thing began with the smallest notion of an idea, but grew in the mind to become an entity that would not be denied. It had enchanted and convinced its own creator that the idea was so righteous and necessary. It was plotted so carefully and quietly. It seemed foolproof in its execution and inevitable in its objective. Nothing could go wrong. But the prisons are filled with such master criminals," — Apostle Fisher, the Mormon Order

Unknown Location
11:45 p.m., 18 August 2096

The prison cell has no windows, only a small light on the nine-foot ceiling, but the room remains virtually dark. The man lies on a cot with his forearm covering his eyes. There is a toilet against the back wall and a sink on the opposite wall from the cot. There's nothing to do here, but sleep or lie on the cot.

Once a day someone comes with food. The cell door is never opened. The steel door has an opening that is slid open and closed after a tray is placed on the cold floor. Whoever is feeding him daily is probably not even human, more likely a rudimentary robot of some kind. It is always too dark to see clearly. He always puts the tray back by the door and after he sleeps and wakes up, it's gone.

He can't tell if he's at sea, but if he had to guess, he'd say yes.

There are noises all the time throughout the structure. He can hear people walking, doors opening and closing, beeping sounds, and sometimes alarm signals. Never has he seen the face of his captors. He remains in this cell in solitary with no idea of what will happen or how long he will remain here.

Something wakes him up. He looks at the main door in the near darkness and hears almost a sizzling noise. A yellow glow is coming from space between the door and the wall—intensifying in brightness, burning, melting the metal. The glow dims. The door is slowly slid open. He can see somewhat brighter lights in the outside hallway. A figure of a man appears.

"What's your name?"

"Simon."

The figure enters the cell cautiously, looking at some device on the back of his hand. The man is dressed all in black—black hoodie, black pants, and black combat boots.

"Mr. Simon, the Prophet of the Mormon Order?"

Simon hesitates for a moment. The man is also carrying a tek-gun in his right hand. He sits up on the cot. "You know me, but I don't even know your name."

"You know me too." The man enters the cell and reaches to his back to grab a small duffel bag. He pulls the sling over his head and throws the duffel bag on the cot. "Open it up. It's Christmas in August."

Only a Faither would use the word "Christmas." Simon opens the bag to pull out a collapsible tek-rifle. The man's voice is vaguely familiar, a Spanish accent. It would help if he could see his face.

"Do you know how to shoot?"

Simon smiles. "I do. Aim for the cheek." A common inside joke among Faithers.

The man smiles too. "There are more goodies."

Simon digs around the bag, an array of weapons: guns, grenades, knives, glove weapons, and brass-knuckle weapons. "You have quite a nice little selection here." He looks up. "I remember you now. We never met, but we talked on the vid-phone a few times. Father Marcos?"

"Of the New Catholic Order."

"I don't imagine we're in Mexico."

"We're not."

"Aren't you the leader of the Mexican Catholic Order?"

"I've been recently promoted, but we can chat about that later."

"So this is a prison break?"

"It is."

"I was with my crew when I was taken. I haven't seen any of them, but they must be here too, if they are still alive."

"They're alive. I already identified where they are. We'll release them too before the rescue team arrives, but we need to get ready. This is a proper prison break. Are you enjoying it?"

"Ask me after I get home."

"Then load up and let's go."

Prophet Simon cocks the tek-rifle. There's no functional reason for that movement in weapon anymore, but the manufacturers are smart enough to keep it. "I love that sound."

Father Marcos grins. "They were right about what they told me about you."

Nova Energy Island, Pacific Ocean
6:20 a.m., 19 August 2096

There are man-made islands are throughout the modern world—most are for relaxation and recreation, many named with some variation of the word *Atlantis,* others are for science and research. Some are for fish-farming or other food production, but the most important ones are for commercial or government energy production. They are known as "energy islands."

The Nova is smaller than most and it can sail anywhere in the oceans, albeit very slowly. Its domed roof canopy is completely covered with one-inch solar cells, millions of them. The island-city's buoy-like skirt rests on the ocean's surface and creates continuous wave power from the mechanical energy of the rising and falling waves. Underwater, the island is covered with upside-down windmill-like turbines wrapped in spherical meshes to prevent sea life from getting killed or injured by the blades. With solar, wave, and tidal power the island's life-support systems and basic utilities can run forever. But this structure has other functions.

The island's docking port and landing fields are on the one side of the island that is free of turbines and antennas. A beat-up silver submersible rises from the water as it drives into the open-air dock and then into the covered inner dock area. Three men exit the craft, each looking as dirty as their craft, with their faux snakeskin jackets, multicolored T-shirts, full body tattoos, and dark goggle-glasses. Two of the men have cigs in their mouth.

Channa walks to the pirates from the shadows. The men wait for the Sea Vampire to reach them.

"Why is it so dark in here all the time?" one of the men asks.

"We like darkness." Channa is in his diving suit, which out of the water looks like a big-shouldered robe.

"You Vampires need to play down the role a bit."

"So what god do Vampires believe in?" asks another pirate.

"Money and death."

The pirate laughs. "That's a good one. Me too."

"Do you have something for me?" Channa asks.

"The Contractor said there will be no further payments."

Channa stares at them with his cold, red eyes. "My interest is my *current* payment."

"Well, there won't be any. We decided to keep that too since they won't be paying anything more." The man giggles to himself. "You really don't scare us, and we know you Vampires are enhanced. We're enhanced too. With this jacket, I personally can bench-press a car."

"Do you know why Vampires are scared of True Vampires?"

"There are different kinds of Vampires? No, but you're about to tell us, right? Also, our men in our boat have their sights targeted on you right now, and our turrets are all open and ready to fire."

"Why did you come here if you were going to double-cross me?"

"We wanted to personally tell you what the story is. We didn't want you to think you were cheated by the Contractor. We wanted you to know it was us, and say goodbye. We got manners, you know."

"Have any of you personally met the Contractor?"

"No, but we know who it is. Some religionist, probably from the same group we snatched. See, all people are alike. A family member is more likely to knock you off than a stranger."

The men watch him closely.

"I'm going to eat your two colleagues first. That's why the general Vampire population fears True Vampires. We're cannibals."

The men pull their weapons.

Channa points. "Your boat is about to sink."

The man turns his head to look back at their craft only to see a bright flash of an explosion inside. The craft starts to sink.

Channa strikes while the pirates are distracted. He raises his hand and tiny projectiles are fired from the shadows, hitting each man in the back. Their bionic jackets start to violently spark, and the men seem to dance in pain. The Sea Vampire jumps at them and slashes all three across their faces with his one stroke of his claws. They fall to the ground, dropping their weapons, except for one man. Channa rips the weapon from his hand.

"Channa!" another Sea Vampire runs to him. "There are three heavy aircraft approaching us."

Channa looks at the bleeding pirates.

"The aircraft aren't ours," one of the pirates says, he is trying to touch his bleeding face, but the bionic jacket is dead and he cannot move his arms.

"The pirates came to destroy my island."

"No, we came to steal this island, and it's easier to have you let us in rather than having to break in."

Channa motions to a third Sea Vampire who appears with a large black barrel. The Vampire Leader grabs the edge of the barrel with his clawed hand and pulls it, spilling the contents on the deck—a bloody cocktail of body parts, fluids, and blood. "Human chum. It's so good." Channa reaches into the mess and grabs the piece of a head. "The diving commandos you sent to sabotage the island should have been more careful." He eats the flesh.

One of the pirates on the ground turns his head to throw up. The other winces as he closes his eyes.

"You freak!" the lead pirate yells.

From the darkness of the dock, more Sea Vampires appear and walk to them. All of them have strange, funnel-like objects on their right hands.

"Take only this one to the infirmary," Channa says to his men. "Keep him alive until we can interrogate him. Get the manta-ships in the water and prepare for battle."

"Channa, if we have a firefight, then our cover is blown and every nation around us will send in forces to investigate or board us."

"That can't be helped. Prepare the island for detonation and evacuation."

"And the prisoners?"

"Bring them with us for ransom, or for more chum to eat."

The Bombay Queen
4: 00 a.m., 19 August 2096 (Two hours, twenty minutes earlier)

Vincent's team is assembled and waiting—all dressed in camo fatigues, which are now appearing as full black.

"The Catholics are giving us one airship, the Protestants, another, and the Shogun are sending one of their kamikazes. We'll use our craft as the primary breach vessel. The others will provide cover and air security."

Haven is almost crying now. Vincent puts his hand on her shoulder.

"I just want all of you to come back safely," she says.

"We will. Our advance team is already there. They already signaled us. They're all alive."

Nova Energy Island
6: 25 a.m., 19 August 2096

Simon and Marcos sit in a storage room behind some shelves. Father Marcos looks at his wristband again.

"Which vid-game?" Prophet Simon asks.

"It's gross and highly inappropriate, but *Kill the Devil* is my favorite."

Simon laughs. "It's funny too. What do I do when I'm not doing Bible study and theological studies? Antique restoration. I like making the old seem as if it's brand new—old analog machines are the smallest in my collection, and classic pre-auto-drive-age cars are the largest. Almost three dozen. Some going back to the 1900s and all run perfectly. Classic motorcycles too."

"You'd be very popular in the Spanish Americas. We love those antique vehicles, the cars and bikes. Probably one of the only things people in the country and in the big tek-cities can agree on."

"How much longer do you think?" Prophet Simon asks.

"Any moment now."

"Wouldn't it have been better to go at night?"

"Your captives are—what's the word in English?—Vampires. We say *Vampiros*. We don't have many in the Spanish Americas. Apparently for them, night is like the day and during the day they stay indoors. When we start, we'll make a path to the main deck."

"Do they have any security machines—drones, robots? I hear berserker robot dogs are big in this region."

"I only saw maintenance bots, but let's assume they have it all. Unfortunately for this mission, we weren't able to do a full threat assessment because of time. That is why we'll be doing a lot more damage today. "

"So Father Marcos, I do feel special to be waiting in a storage locker with you, but even I know I'm not special enough to have one of the Catholic's major leaders do a prison break by himself. My people would throw me in jail for recklessness if I tried something like this."

"I was already in the area, supervising the roll-up of our Underground Railroad network. I got a call and I was the only one who could get here in such a short period of time. We had to move immediately. Besides, for years I did this all the time."

"I did all kinds of military actions too, but my people would never let me do them now. And the wife? Oh my God. I'd be grounded for months."

Father Marcos laughs a bit. "As you should be."

"It's sad though that it's all ending. The Underground Railroad is an amazing thing. There's no one to run this area in our place?"

"The Middle-East network will run it when we formally pull out."

"Who operates there? What Order?"

"It will be I.R.A."

"Are they even capable?"

"They'll have to be."

Father Marcos's wristband starts to flash.

"How are your people from Italy doing?" Simon asks.

"Very good, and we appreciate the help in maintaining our city-ships for the journey to Mexico."

"We were glad to help."

"I'm sorry to hear that your people had to leave Utah."

"It was inevitable. Just like the Texas Catholics had to leave for Mexico. We didn't feel safe. Maybe Utah and the Southwest should have stayed with Mexico."

"As a Mexican, you definitely wouldn't have wanted that. You'd be fighting the government *and* criminal cartels, and you'd be doing what you're doing now only five decades earlier."

"The Brave, New Tek World," Simon says. "That's what they call it."

"But there is nothing brave, new, or good about it."

"So true."

Father Marcos's wristband is now a steady blue. "They're here." He stands. "So let the Pope and Prophet go and do some violence, and get you out of here."

Prophet Simon cocks the tek-rifle. "Let's do it."

Nova Energy Island
6: 30 a.m., 19 August 2096

The tower surveillance eye does a continuous circle rotation of the surrounding ocean and sky, but there are no aircraft or sea craft.

"Where are they?" Channa asks the other Sea Vampires in the control bridge.

"They were on our sensors. The craft must be amphibious," one of them answers.

"Launch all manta-ships and get all our drones in the air. If it's these… Jew-Christians…they are as devious as we are, so assume the impossible."

"What would be the impossible?"

"They're already on board."

Nova Energy Island
6: 31 a.m., 19 August 2096

The alarms start blaring throughout the energy island, every corner, every level. Several Sea Vampires arrive in the prison section. The main door is already open.

"Channa was right," one of them says. He motions the others inside as he talks into his wrist-comm, "Channa, the holding area has been breached. He's escaped."

Channa listens from the control bridge. "Find them."

"Yes Channa," the Sea Vampire's voice responds.

Channa looks at his other men. "Is that pirate awake?"

"Yes, he is."

"Tell him that this is a one-time offer. Give me the name of the Contractor and we'll throw him overboard with a floatation device; otherwise, straight to the chum barrel. Go."

The Vampires quickly leaves the control bridge. The others remain behind.

"Channa, you're acting like we're definitely evacuating the island-ship. They're nothing. We can deal with them."

"Don't talk about it, do it. Activate the hounds now."

The Sea Vampires come out of the prison section.

"They're all gone," one of them says.

"How?"

"The doors were laser-cut."

"What about the sensors, the alarms?"

"None of them are working."

"Help me!" The scream startles the Vampires. It's close and it sounds like one of the prisoners.

The Sea Vampires look at each other. The leader motions to them to move out.

The floor slides open and a cyber-hound emerges from below. It is constructed out of black metal with glowing yellow visor eyes, hook claws coming out of its front paws, and retractable teeth. There are thirty of them assembled, waiting. Instructions received. The pack runs.

The Sea Vampires approach the area where the scream came from. All of them are pointing their funnel guns. All of them are wearing their faceplate helmets. They see a motionless body lying on the ground.

The lead Vampire doesn't wait; he starts shooting at it. The pulse bullets rip it apart. He stops and motions them forward. They slowly approach the bleeding body. One leans down to turn it over. The body flips over, sits up, and levitates to his feet. All the Vampires start firing at the android. Its body jerks around wildly, stops, and explodes.

The stunned Vampires pick themselves off the ground. Their helmet sensors start short-circuiting from the grayish goop from the android.

"Channa," the lead says into his wrist-comm. "Security is breached. They have androids aboard—"

Gunfire erupts from the shadows, cutting down the Vampires.

"Say again. Say again," Channa's voice says from the dead Vampire's wrist-comm.

A hand reaches down and removes it. Vincent stands up and hands it to one of his men, his *Divine Providence* second-in-command. They are all dressed in their camo-fatigues, which are the exact same color as the surrounding bulkheads, and carry weapon-packs on their backs. "This energy-island ship has five bridges. Track this back to the right one."

"Yes, sir."

Different alarms start sounding in the control bridge.

"We have a hull breach," a Vampire says.

"Where?" Channa asks.

"The prison holding area. Water is pouring in and flooding that deck."

"We have an entire army, but they're all outside the island-ship. Give the recall order now!"

Dozens and dozens of manta-ships are floating in the waters to protect the energy island. The order is received and manta-ships turn to start back to the island ship. At that very instant, an aircraft rises from the ocean and fires its missiles. Each missile separates into multiple mini-missiles and hits their targets in the air and in the ocean. Explosion after explosion, manta ships in the sea and the saucer drones in the air are destroyed.

"Launch! Launch!" Channa yells. "We're losing everyone."

More alarms start sounding. Multiple echoes now, increasing.

"Nothing is responding!" a Vampire has to yell to be heard above the noise. "The systems are not responding at all. We've been hacked!"

Channa and the Vampire bridge crew see a flash from the observation window and don't have time to react. The kamikaze jet is flying so fast that it fires at them—bullets shattering the windows, destroying all controls—and disappears before the sound wave of the jet arrives.

The crew is on the ground, wounded or unconscious. Channa is the only one unharmed and looks up now.

The first thing he sees is feet, then, looking up further, he sees a man in black with a mirrored faceplate helmet on his head—the Astronaut. All around him are other soldiers in black wearing white masks—open holes for the eyes, molded noses and smiling expressions.

The other teams converge on the control bridge. The captains of the *Orca*, *Narwhale* and *Bowhead* lead their teams, moving backwards as a group, as they shoot at the pack of cyber-hounds. The teams are not only well-armored, but electro-shielded. All pulse bullets of the cyber-hounds are deflected as the team quickly reduces the cyber-hounds to pieces throughout the hallway.

Two Sea Vampires try to torture the surviving pirate—the other two are dead and stacked in the corner—but every explosion distracts them and the pirate is so drugged that he doesn't fully understand what is happening.

"One more time," the Vampire says. "How do we know you told us the truth about the Contractor? You could be lying."

"The data is on our ship you destroyed, but you can still get it. Its black box is shielded to survive explosion." A black box is also the name of an ultra-secure, shielded data storage unit, often hidden in a vehicle, vessel, or building.

"What's the file name?"

"Black box." The pirate laughs. "You would never have guessed it."

Two shots and both Vampires fall to the ground. River enters the room with her team.

"Take him," she says. "And get a bot to the wreckage of their pirate ship and find that black box."

Two of her team unshackle the pirate and pull him away from his torture chair. One grabs a cylinder-like club device from his weapons pack and hits the man in the center of his chest. Something explodes from it and the pirate is 'shrink-wrapped.' They pick him up and carry him away.

Channa realizes that he didn't fear them enough. They cut through all his tek as if it didn't exist. All this time they were playing games with him. The Vampires never did have tek superiority over them. He lunges at the intruders.

Smart devices, smart cars, smart houses, and so on. Weapons too got smarter and better. Deadly weapons that could kill were endless, but there was no limit to the creativity of nonlethal ones. The Astronaut's skull seems to explode from the faceplate, and the helmet envelops Channa's head. The Vampire frantically tries to pull it off; his own claws cannot save him. He's helpless as his body starts to convulse and he passes out. Channa's head is fully encased in a silver cocoon.

The faceplate changes from mirrored silver to clear. "Take him," Vincent says. Two of his men drag the Vampire away.

Explosions rock the island-ship.

"We have everything?" Vincent asks, giving the control bridge a final visual inspection.

"We've stripped every atom of data from this vessel."

Vincent nods and leads the team from the bridge.

All the teams gather on the main deck under cover.

"When we're all boarded, blow it," Vincent says.

"The Vampires already set the island-ship's self-destruct. I'll change it from delayed countdown to manual control, Commander. To the bottom of the ocean, everything goes."

Vincent and the others wait as Father Marcos appears with Prophet Simon to them. There are smiles and tears of joy from everyone. Vincent hugs the man.

"We thought you were dead."

"You know better than that, Vincent. I've been dead before."

Vincent laughs. "Yes, I remember. The Pagans thought they had you that time." He looks at the tek-rifle in his hand and looks at Father Marcos. "He's a terror with weapons."

"Yes, I know," Father Marcos says. "He's upset he didn't get to shoot anyone."

"Thank you, Father. Thank you," Vincent says.

"It was my pleasure. Call us anytime," he says.

The kamikaze jet slows to a stop, hovering directly overhead. The other two aircraft rise from the waters.

"We have our temporary base in Singapore," Vincent says to Simon.

Simon nods.

"Why would a member of your Order do this to another? The person would have to have such a deep well of hatred or be psychotic," Father Marcos says.

Vincent says, "Or both. We know why he did it. Mr. Simon derailed his father from becoming Prophet."

"Vincent, no one becomes Prophet. God chooses us and our colleagues affirm or reject that selection," Prophet Simon says.

"Did God choose Thomas?" There is no response. Vincent continues angrily, "He did this to you. I want to personally lead the assault and grab him by the throat."

"No, we can't do that. It would be war. We're talking about an intra-Mormon war. That cannot happen. I'd rather let him remain

Prophet to avoid that."

The disagreement from the group is forceful and loud.

"The civil war is here," River says.

"He tried to kill you!" Vincent yells. "He and his conspirators."

River says, "Prophet, the Vampires were working for him! We have the proof on a data device. He must be brought to justice and I don't mean excommunication."

"Everyone, please," he says sadly, shaking his head. "If a civil war doesn't concern you, there is one thing you all are forgetting. Mr. Thomas has Leviathan."

Clash of the Titans

"One of the largest inter-religious battles ever to occur before World War Three took place in the Pacific Ocean. No one talks about it. It was never even given a name. It's almost as if it never happened. Obviously, it was overshadowed by another, more tremendous event, but that war was bad. It was very bad. We almost didn't make it." — *Prophet Simon, the Mormon Order*

The Bombay Queen, Singapore Strait
10: 35 a.m., 20 August 2096

The Asian Consortium—an alliance of all those Asian countries outside of Japan, Korea Prime, and the CHINs—has been led by the Singaporeans for over two decades. They signed a pact of noninterference with China, before the formation of the CHIN, and it has never been broken. It is a feat that neither Japan nor Korea could have accomplished because of historic tension with Beijing. The Singaporeans are often referred to as the "Jew-Christians of Pagans."

The Exiles. That's what they are calling themselves. Singapore is now their base, far enough away to be safe from, at the moment, their own Order. None of them have any intention of allowing "Exile" to become a permanent term, if only a civil war can be avoided.

The "private" conversation with Prophet Simon has turned into a standing room-only meeting in one of the large banquet rooms of the cruise liner. After almost ninety minutes of tearful hugs and stunned exclamations of "you're alive!" people call out questions.

"Most of you remember what it was like back then." Simon is flanked by his wife and his eldest children. "Whole denominations of the Christians were violently collapsing because of the Separatist Movement. The Jews had one violent internal civil war after another, even before the Fall of Israel. There was chaos in every Order, except ours. None of us should have found any of it unexpected. We were all civilians, and we found ourselves thrust into a war of persecution that none of us caused or deserved. We were just average people living our lives and raising our families. We may have become soldiers of a sort now, but we were never that. I think of the story of Rwandan Genocide of 1994. A simple hotel manager became a freedom fighter to save lives because of the extraordinary, horrific circumstances that he woke up one day to find himself in.

"Some of us, one night sitting around the meeting table, started to wonder. Were we really so unified, so perfect, that such a thing could never happen to us?—dissolution or civil war like the others. We concluded, after much back-and-forth debating well into the next morning, that we weren't. Why wouldn't it come to us too, sooner, later, who knew when? We had strong disagreements too, on how to fight in the Resistance, if we should even be in the Resistance, and every other political, social, and cultural matter.

"We decided to create an internal group that we enigmatically called the Circle whose whole purpose would be to put together a series of emergency protocols, in case such a thing ever occurred in our Order. Other Orders had been infiltrated by the government, and had government collaborators within their leadership or in their enclaves. More often, as we saw, the government didn't need to do anything at all. Just stand back and watch the Order rip itself apart. Everyone had been afraid of the same happening with us. But as time went on, the Separatist Movement became the new reality, the Resistance evolved into the Continuum. The protocols remained, but most of us had forgotten we had ever done it. Then there was Mr. Vincent."

Everyone looks at him standing with his family.

"He's my dad, and I'm not giving him up!" Bear yells, making the crowd laugh.

"Vincent seemed to take the whole thing a lot more seriously than the rest of us should have taken it, and started to notice a pattern. Tell us, Vincent."

"I created a computer program to do it for us," Vincent says. "It would monitor all our activities with the following question: Which separate actions or patterns, when taken together, could indicate with strong probability, an infiltration of the Order? In other words, it was programmed to assume everything was a conspiracy, not to determine if there was one. It also came up with a list of dozens of worst-case scenarios and I gave each one of them a codename from some classic movie actor. If a critical event was identified, and if I was unavailable, it would contact a primary designee to contact others. This is how Mr. Varma was involved. The program started to message me a few years back."

People look at each other.

Vincent acknowledges the group's surprise. "I was surprised when it did. I have to admit that it started to make me paranoid, but I kept it all to myself. It wasn't enough, and I knew that the real evidence may come too late, but that's the best we could do. I quietly investigated what I could. It became 'real' after my first encounter with the Sea Vampires and the program determined that they were in almost daily communications with the *Pacifica* itself. We were only reacting; I had to get ahead of events. We could have lost you, sir."

"Well you didn't. We're the good guys remember." Prophet Simon gives a genuine smile.

Everyone can't help but think how the man has bounced back so fast and completely, despite his ordeal.

"Mr. Simon," a man asks in the back. "When does the civil war begin?"

"Sir, there is still no change. No communications with *Pacifica* or any of the other city-ships are able to get through. Some of us had been able to secretly communicate with family members, but as of your rescue yesterday, everything is completely blocked. Thomas knows," an officer informs them.

Another officer says, "Yes, he does and as of this morning, an army of pirate ships is surrounding the *Pacifica*." People look at each with concern. "Also, all the other city-ships, as of this past midnight, left port en route to rendezvous with the *Pacifica*. Whatever we plan to do, he will have two armies, not one, in his control. We don't have one."

"He'll be the first Prophet ever to be excommunicated. Not even that. He isn't even legitimate," someone says.

"He'll never let us get near the people to let them know that."

"He will never *willingly* allow us to," Vincent says.

"We only have one play to make." Prophet Simon looks at his wife Haven. "We have a call to make."

The Pacifica
7: 35 a.m., 20 August 2096

These are international waters much further out from its previous anchored position in the Sea of Japan. The city-ship rests in a massive ring of vessels, surrounded by hundreds of boats, yachts, catamarans, hydrofoils, and every other kind of sea craft. They are manned by pirate crews, every last one of them—Anarchists and Goths, Vampires, Witches and Warlocks, Russians, Muslims and Asian natives, grungy Nihilists and half-naked Hedonists, well-financed cyborgs or mechanically-enhanced mercenaries.

Huntley watches from the observation windows. He is the only one with him in Thomas's private meeting room.

Prophet Thomas says, "Huntley, this is a game. The Russians, CHINs, and Caliphate are playing their own. Can the CHINs or Caliphate seize Russian or Europan territory? Can the Russian Bloc keep them away? They'll watch us, but they won't do a thing. They probably think the pirates have surrounded us to take our island-ships. That's what I want them to think."

"How are we paying all of these pirates, Prophet?"

"Is that really any of your business, Mr. Huntley?"

Huntley doesn't answer back.

"Please go check on the men. One of us must be there at all times."

"Yes, Prophet."

"How is my wife GlenDora doing in her new role?"

Huntley stops. "Very well, Prophet. She's a natural fit for Head of Morale. She's keeping everyone calm."

"Thank you. That's all."

Huntley leaves the room as Thomas looks out again at his pirate army on the sea.

Meeting Room, The Bombay Queen
8: 35 p.m., 20 August 2096

"Why can't we just get the Prophet onboard the *Pacifica*? Let the people see him," one of the captains asks.

"I love everyone's optimism, but if Jesus died and rose from the dead in 2096, everyone would think it some kind of android, holographic projection, or a clone. The Order has been told I'm dead. Many won't believe otherwise, even if they see me. They can subject me to every bio-scan known to humankind and still a percentage won't believe it's me."

"What's your plan then, sir? We still have to get you on *Pacifica* to stop them from accessing Leviathan," Vincent says. "You said we'll have an army."

"We will."

Cyberspace
11:55 p.m., 20 August 2096

The darkness is interrupted by a flashing green dot, followed by dozens, then hundreds, thousands, and then billions. The secret holographic Net-meeting begins.

"Unfortunately, the matter of the Leviathan Project now threatens our own Project Noah. Simon is no longer in charge of it, but this man Thomas. With the Russian Orthodox disappearing with Behemoth, Leviathan must not fall into unsanctioned hands. It is very probable that the Mormon Order may erupt in civil war. That being said, the Continuum is being asked to take sides between the factions. This is completely counter to the rules we set up in the days of our alliance, never to take sides," Archbishop Masai says. "But then we have to take sides."

Secret Stronghold, Wolf Point, Montana (Ten Years Ago)
7:00 p.m., 4 July, 2086

Ms. River leads the briefing. "What is Leviathan? It is the culmination of decades of advanced artificial biosphere tek—what some incorrectly term as terraforming, though the application could easily be modified for such use. Leviathan is a living city-ship capable of flight in any atmospheric condition, submerging to, until now, unimaginable oceanic depths, and even driving on land with its own network of morphing wheels. It creates its own power and air, and it is not only a "living" ship; it's a "living" weapon, capable of destroying any organic organism, or any inorganic weapon within a three-thousand mile radius in defense. It is programmed to protect those living organisms within its body and kill anything that threatens them."

"When will it be complete?" Prophet Simon asks.

"Projected completion is in ten years time—2096."

Parliament Men's Club, Moscow, Russia
11:35 a.m., 20 August 2096

Three men sit together on a mahogany bench, the air thick with steam, mixed with just a touch of drug vapor. Steam room spas remain a favorite place for lunchtime meetings among the political elite in Moscow.

"Does the President know what is happening around him? We hear he has never once left his bunker since being sworn in. People are questioning not only his courage, but his sanity," the Chairman says. He is the head of the Federation Council, the Russian Parliament's upper house.

"He is not insane and he is surely not a coward, Chairman. He is a mobster for Christ's sake," the new Prime Minister says. He is Russian President's number one in the government after him.

Young, topless men and women workers do a walk-through for stray towels on the floor or empty benches. Their uniform consists of red trunks and red peaked caps.

"*Was* is the key word," the Deputy says. "Was a mobster. But even so, mobsters are well qualified to deal with other mobsters, not superpowers with the power to destroy all life in a nation or on the planet." He is the chairman of the lower house of the Russian Parliament.

"The rumors are in all quarters. The Parliament believes that invasion of the Russian Bloc is imminent—by either the Caliphate or CHINs, most likely both," the Chairman says. "They are convinced he's weak and impotent. And from our vantage point, we don't see why they *wouldn't* believe that. Assassinations, chaos in our streets—even more now than before with this directive to expel all religionists from the nation, and a president hiding in his bunker."

"Do you know how many unauthorized foreigners are in our airspace, on Russian waters, under Russian waters, subs everywhere?" the Deputy asks rhetorically.

The Prime Minister leans forward with his hairy body and points at them with his fingers. "Listen to me closely. We are on the verge of the rise of the new Russian Bloc. The Leviathan King will send a message to enemies and friends alike that we will not be trifled with."

"What message?" the Chairman asks.

The Prime Minister leans back against the wall with a Cheshire Cat's, devious grin.

Presidential Bunker, Moscow, Russia
12 noon, 17 August 2096

President Ri Wen's face looks at him from the vid-screen with the perpetual calm and lack of outward emotion that he is known for. "President Aleyev, I, on behalf of the people of China and the peoples of India, humbly make your acquaintance. I look forward to when we will be able to meet in person."

"I look forward to that as well, President Wen. Thank you taking my call with such short notice," Igor says.

"I completely understand. I do not envy the strains that must be occupying your time. I do see you have made the wise decision of exiling religious inhabitants from your territories. My late father came to the very same decision more than thirty years ago when our nation had to deal with the Buddhist terrorist state of New Tibet, and he wisely exiled all religious inhabitants in our territories."

"President Wen, you are reading my mind. The Caliphate is attempting to test my resolve in protecting my nation. My intelligence services report to me that they have been planting agents on Russian and Europan soil and plan to use covert subs to invade our waters."

"That is shocking in its provocation, President Aleyev, but not surprising."

"Yes it is. I did want to notify you, as we are both neighbors equally threatened by the Caliphate. I will be sending a very strong message to them. The Russian Bloc will not tolerate such invasions of our sovereignty, now or ever. As a fellow President, I know you deal with this daily."

"Yes, I do. Thank you so much, President Aleyev, for kindly and personally notifying my nation of your justified action. May I ask what action you will take?"

"We haven't settled yet on the method, but it will make my point in a very simple manner. This is where my life as a mobster adds so much to my credibility when I say the following: Do not provoke the empire of Mother Russia."

Presidential Bunker, Moscow, Russia
12 noon, 18 August 2096

Emperor Al-Siddiq's face looks at him from the vid-screen. He is always in an affable mood, very quick to smile, whether he is going to give praise or order the execution of an entire province. "President Aleyev, I and the entire Islamic people are honored by your call. I know you were raised religious, so under the great eyes of Allah, we continue to mourn the passing of your predecessor. One day soon you and I will meet in person."

"I look forward to that as well, Emperor. And thank you for those words about our former President and my father," Igor says.

"Oh yes, your father. I miss my late father, too. You have much to occupy your mind, President Aleyev."

"Yes, I've had to make the reluctant decision to expel many religious terrorists and sympathizers from our nation."

"Yes, in my time I've had to expel many, many terrorist sanctuaries from our empire. People never seem to realize that the religious terrorist always kills more of the religious than the non-believer. We sent that message to the world when we removed Palestine-Israel from the face of the Earth, as if it never existed. Their constant insults and plotting against the Supreme Islamic Caliphate could not be tolerated anymore."

"Emperor, you are reading my mind. Threats against our people must not be tolerated. The CHINs are attempting to test my resolve in protecting my nation. My intelligence services report to me daily that they have been planting agents on Russian and Europan soil and using covert subs to invade our waters for this purpose."

"They've been doing the same with us for decades. How do you plan to deal with them?"

"Send a strong message. You've had to deal with them, which is why I wanted to notify you personally. We are both neighbors equally threatened by the CHINs."

"Yes, they think your nation and mine should belong to them."

"Yes, we must not tolerate invasions of our sovereignty, now or ever. I haven't settled yet on the exact method of our response, but it will make my point in a very simple manner. My life as a mobster adds so much to my credibility when I say the following: Do not provoke the empire of Mother Russia."

The Emperor laughs. "Very good, President Aleyev. I am glad to have a strong partner against our mutual enemies."

The Pacifica
7:02 a.m., 21 August 2096

The army of pirate ships has been moving their positions away from the *Pacifica* for the last hour to create an ever-larger ring of defense. They now see why—twelve other city-ships sailing to the lead city-ship.

Prophet Thomas watches from the main tower bridge with the other Apostles.

"This will be the first time all our ships have been in the same place since we left America," one of the Apostles says.

"And we'll never be divided again," Thomas adds.

"All troops are standing by," Huntley says.

"Good," Thomas responds. "Station squads of robo-soldiers on the decks of each ship as we've done here."

"Yes, Prophet." Huntley gets on his wrist-comm.

"We have a pirate army, a robot army, a human army," Aaron says. "Who are we expecting to attack us, Prophet?"

"This is to ensure that no one dares to. But if someone should be foolish enough to do so, then we can send them straight to hell."

The Bombay Queen
10:31 p.m., 20 August 2096

The captain of the Queen has granted every request they've had. Someone asked if he is related to Mr. Varma and the captain happily responded, "Mr. Varma comes from a very influential family in India, and they make movies everyone wants to see. *Everyone* is related to him."

Tomorrow it happens. It will either be a quick battle to stop a civil war, win or lose, or it will start one. Vincent will command and, despite loud objections, Prophet Simon is going as well. They wait on the main deck for their visitors.

Moses Atticus of the New Protestant Order arrives; only a few men accompany him to the main deck. He was given the title of "General" back at the Kansas Uprising in '76. He was the highest-ranking ex-military civilian present. The nickname stuck. He and his wife Emma (known by all as M) were founding members of the Continuum. He has dark brown skin and short black hair with touches of gray, the same as his mustache. He isn't just a "general," he's one of the best Faither fighters and respected leaders on the planet. He looks to be a man of his thirties, but he, Tova of the Conservative Jewish Order, and Vincent are all in their fifties—but then fifty is literally the new thirty in this age.

Shoshana, twenty years younger, is a member of the newest Orders in Judaism, the Shomar Order, but it's her founding and leadership of the Jewish Wolf Pack that she's known for by all. Jewish skinheads, both the men and women, always dressed in military fatigue pants and jackets, black combat boots, and black T-shirts with a Star of David in the center. Shoshana also wears a Star of David necklace. She arrives on the main deck with three male Wolf-Packers.

"The Shogun will provide any additional air-support we need, and the African Collective, courtesy of Archbishop Masai, has sent fifty Catholic Masai warriors," Moses tells them after everyone greets each other.

It's not lost on anyone that they are using only military terms. Has the war already started?

The Catholic Order's Sister Serena is also dressed in black, like Moses, when she arrives. The forty-something's flowing black hair comes down to the middle of her back. The first thing people notice about her when they see her is the black patch over her left eye. Her street name is Sister Cyclops. With bionic implant tek and body-farms, she could have a new eye at any time. She told them it's her daily reminder "Not to look where you're not supposed to, unless you're prepared to fight the person that looks back at you." She created the Central and South America network of the Underground Railroad with her two colleagues, the Twins.

"I figured you'd bench Father Marcos after our last encounter," Prophet Simon says to her.

Sister Serena smiles as she nods. "Yes, we did. We locked him in his room and took away his Johann Sebastian Bach music for risking his life like that. But he has an important ceremony to prepare for to occupy his time."

"This is your show, Vincent," Moses says. "We're only the backup. Prophet Simon has already said it. Your priority must be for the civil war to never get started. Take it from us. It starts and you can't even imagine the devastation your people will suffer. And no civil war ends when and how you expect."

"Exactly," Prophet Simon says.

Vincent says, "Then let's go to war…to stop a war."

The Pacifica
8:37 a.m., 21 August 2096

An officer runs to the control bridge. Prophet Thomas is speaking to Huntley and several of the ship's soldiers. Thomas notices him.

"What is it?"

"Prophet, it's the *Triton*. Apostle Fisher says it's urgent."

"Urgent why?"

"They have Continuum members aboard."

Thomas is furious. "How did they get on one of my city-ships through the blockade?"

The Triton City-Ship
8:38 a.m., 21 August 2096

Inside the ring of pirate ships, the city-ships are also arranged in a circle formation with the *Pacifica* in the center. The *Triton* is at the furthest outer point of the formation.

Apostle Fisher stands on the control bridge with armed personnel. A calm Haven Simon faces them.

"Is there some reason why I'm being treated like this Mr. Fisher?" she asks. "You have all thirteen of our city-ships in the open sea, vulnerable, in seas that are in striking distance of three hostile nations. This is an action that our Fifteen Apostles deemed as forbidden just a month ago, ever since we left America, or have you forgotten? And since when does the Order work with pirate criminals? Where's Thomas?"

"The Prophet will be here shortly," Fisher answers.

"I'm very disappointed in you, disgusted by you. I never thought you'd be a conspirator."

"I'm not a conspirator, Haven. I'm just an old man tired of fighting. I've been at it for fifty years, there's no end to it."

"It's called living. Why would that need to be said, especially a leader in the church?"

"I'm satisfied with my life. I tried to step down so Vincent could replace me. I'm just a follower these days. I follow whoever is in charge."

"Then where's your leader? Doesn't he know how to use a phone?"

"The Prophet will—"

"Prophet," she says with contempt. "He's not worthy to even be addressed as mister. Where's Thomas?"

The elevator opens and Prophet Thomas exits with Huntley and several more armed soldiers.

"It's about time," Haven says.

"Mrs. Simon," Thomas says. "What brings you back to the city-ships?"

"I thought I lived here."

"You and your party left despite my directive that no one could leave."

"Why have you been blocking all incoming transmissions?"

"Security reasons."

"Receiving a call is now a threat to the Order?"

Thomas ignores her and looks at Apostle Fisher. "How did she contact you despite the communications blackout?"

The man holds up a red brick. "They threw this onto the deck. It had her note attached and, of course, the deck officers helped her onboard from the boat."

"Which boat?"

"It was one of the pirate boats."

Thomas is angry. "No one was supposed to approach any city-ship. None."

"They said they didn't see it until it was there."

Thomas looks at Huntley.

"Don't worry, Prophet, the security perimeter will be strengthened."

"I was told that the Continuum was here," Thomas says to Fisher.

"That's what she said."

Haven watches Thomas with a smirk. He says, "They will not be allowed on any ship."

"Prophet," Fisher interrupts. "She said they insisted."

"I said no. Mrs. Simon, if you wish to return to the *Pacifica*, Mr. Huntley will clear you first. And then you'll be allowed to return to your quarters, but you will have to follow all my directives. Where are the others that you left with—?"

Alarms sound and a frantic bridge crew run to their station consoles.

"What is it?" Thomas yells.

"It's the *Pacifica*. Hostiles have seized the bridge, Prophet," a Triton bridge officer answers.

"Bring Mrs. Simon with us," Thomas directs.

The Pacifica
8:43 a.m., 21 August 2096

The mini-flyer touches down on the landing deck.

It takes only minutes for Thomas to return with Huntley and Military personnel. Two soldiers lead Mrs. Simon out of the bridge elevator.

"When we told you that we needed to see you, it wasn't a request." Moses stands in the center of their control bridge. He isn't alone. Several Catholic Masai soldiers stand behind him, the shortest one is six-foot seven. Two others, wearing fully black-clad uniforms and concealing helmets, also stand with them.

Outside on the main deck is Shoshana with dozens of her Wolf Pack soldiers. They have the path to the bridge entrance cut off and dozens of *Pacifica* Military soldiers at bay. Shoshana laughs, trying to provoke them. The Jewish skinheads are all very intimidating.

"I see the Continuum remains adept at sneaking around on other people's property. The Order is no longer a part of your organization, and since you've taken your money back from our accounts for our impending deal, we will be having no further business dealings. Now get off my ship."

One of the two unknown soldiers with Moses takes off his helmet—it's Vincent.

Thomas smiles. "Mr. Vincent has returned, too. You can also leave. Since you're here, I will give you a preview of what I will be disclosing to the people about you. Your gross dereliction of duty was directly responsible and allowed a population of Vampires to track the Order to its current location, and your 'disappearance' was your desperate attempt to throw suspicion off of you and your disgraced officers." He turns to Moses. "Are these the people that the Continuum has been listening to when it comes to the Mormon Order? No wonder your attitude towards us has been so deplorable."

"You know something, Mr. Thomas," Moses says. "I've known Vincent for a long time. We've worked together a long time. You, however, I've known only for a brief time. What I can say emphatically is that Vincent is good people, worthy of the respect and authority he has earned over a lifetime. You, on the other hand, are worthy of nothing, despite your title that I'm told by Mrs. Simon and others that you have trained your people well to mouth every five seconds."

"Mr. Moses, did you think that having the former Prophet's wife here would gain you some kind of special access? As you can see, it has not. Take your people and leave. Do not ever come back here or you will be met with by deadly force."

Moses steps closer to Thomas. Huntley and the city-ship soldiers raise their weapons, and so do the Masai solders.

"Tell me, Mr. Thomas, do you think, if you went to war with the Continuum, that you'd be victorious? I've been threatened by a lot of people, including the man we call Galerius and you call Boggs. We're still here. You should be very careful about who you threaten from your perch inside your glass house."

"Thank you for the advice, Mr. Moses. Will you be leaving now? Or do I have to have you all physically thrown overboard?"

"You're right. We should go." Moses steps back and motions to the Masais.

"And Mr. Vincent, you can take Mrs. Simon with you." He looks at her. "Know that I will begin official excommunication procedures against all of you. You will never be able to return to the Order."

"I don't think that will happen, *Mister* Thomas," Vincent answers back. "Do you know why I call you mister? Because the real Prophet, Prophet Simon will never let this stand. Did you tell everyone that your plot failed and he's still alive?"

Every Mormon officer and soldier on the bridge freezes, many with their mouths open.

"You're the one who will be excommunicated, Tom!" Vincent looks at the remaining, unknown soldier next to him. "Guess who's standing next to me?"

Thomas draws his weapon and fires point-blank at the unknown soldier. Vincent fires at Thomas.

The Atlantia
8:55 a.m., 21 August 2096

The outside firefight and explosions can be heard from every corner of the city-ship. Civilian and Military security personnel are running through the halls when the general broadcast vid-screens activate.

"This is River Petrov. Prophet Simon is alive. I repeat. Prophet Simon is not dead. Any Mormon who hears this message, you are to immediately apprehend and detain Prophet Thomas for the kidnapping, imprisonment, and the attempted murder of Prophet Simon. Prophet Simon has returned and is here on the *Atlantia*. Arrest Prophet Thomas immediately."

The security people are shocked as the message repeats. They look at each other.

Apostle Aaron's Office, The Atlantia
8:55 a.m., 21 August 2096

Apostle Aaron is frozen in place, as shocked as his security detail as the message replays on the general vid-screen.

"Sir, we have to get you to the secure room," one of the security men manages to say.

"I want the message terminated now," Aaron says, still agitated.

"Why would you do that?" a voice says.

A man in civilian clothes stands at the door. He grabs his neck and then pulls the whole Pretender mask off his head.

"Simon!" Aaron says, his knees nearly buckle.

"I'm surprised that all the access codes are still the same despite my supposed death." Prophet Simon walks to them. "Good to see you, Aaron."

"Simon, is that really you?"

"In the flesh."

"Stay where you are!" a female voice says.

Everyone one of them turns to the door to see GlenDora, Prophet Thomas's wife, pointing a gun at Simon. "I knew you'd attempt to make contact with Aaron first."

"GlenDora, what are you doing?" Aaron yells.

"It's a trick, Aaron. The real Prophet Simon is dead. This is an imposter. It's a trick."

"It's good to see you too, GlenDora," Prophet Simon says facetiously.

"GlenDora, put down the weapon," Aaron yells.

"I am taking charge if you won't," she says.

The entire city-ship shakes.

"What was that?" one of the security men. "Were we hit?"

"No," Simon answers. "That was a shot from the city-ship's heavy guns."

Aaron draws his gun and aims at GlenDora. The security men react. Half point their guns at Aaron, the others at GlenDora.

Simon looks at Aaron. "This cannot happen. Aaron, I'm not going to allow people to get killed over me. That's not why I came back. I came to put myself before the people and let them decide, not to take back the Prophet-ship. I'm going to raise my hands, interlock my fingers behind my head, and lie down face-first on the ground. Take me into custody and take Thomas as well, and then we can sort all this out."

The security men who were aiming their weapons at Aaron now point them at GlenDora.

"Don't you see what he's doing? This is a trick. He's not the real Prophet Simon."

"GlenDora, lower your weapon," Aaron says.

The city-ship shakes again as Prophet Simon does what he said he'd do and lies on the floor with his hands behind his head.

"Lower it!" Aaron yells.

GlenDora starts to do so. "I will not allow this." She flicks her wrist and fires her gun at Simon, but is shot by Aaron and the other guards instantly. She collapses to the ground.

"You tried to shoot him in the back!" a shocked guard yells and aims to shoot her again. Aaron slaps his gun hand away.

"You're going to shoot her when she's down on the ground?" Aaron pushes him in her direction. "Get her to the infirmary and keep her under arrest."

The city-ship shakes, but this time it is a continuous roll of about ten seconds.

Simon looks up from the floor.

"Get up, Simon," Aaron says.

Simon's face is very distressed. "We need to see what's happening."

The men run out of the room to the deck. As enter the hallway, there are gasps from civilians and security alike at the sight of Prophet Simon. The men find themselves being followed by almost everyone they pass. They bypass the elevators and run up the stairs.

They reach the main deck and run to the main railing. The men and everyone else is in total shock.

The first thing they notice are the flames. The ocean is littered with burnt out or destroyed smaller sea craft. There are people paddling in the water, trying to stay afloat, and yelling for help, but there are many dead bodies, too. The air is filled with aircraft firing at remaining sea craft, flying drones, and even some of the city-ships. In the blink of an eye, a missile hits one the city-ships and the explosion seems to consume the whole center section of the ship. It seems half of the city-ships are ablaze. City-ships fire with their heavy guns and missiles continue to fall, hitting the guns.

"My God," Simon says and turns to him. "Aaron, we have to stop this."

"How?"

"Contact every city-ship and take control. You're the President of the Twelve; they'll listen. I'll contact the Continuum and tell them to stand down. If you have to take control physically of each ship, do so. Take all the security you need."

"Get the control bridge on the line," Aaron yells at one of the officers.

Everyone on the deck is half-paralyzed by the sight of the fighting and devastation.

"We have to act now!" Simon yells.

"Yes." Aaron looks at a soldier. "Get every man and woman you can find. Half with me, half with the Prophet."

"Prophet Simon is taking back leadership of the Order?" an officer asks.

"No, we are going to make sure nobody else gets killed. We'll figure who the Prophet is later. Is that okay with you? Or do you want to just stand here while our people are getting killed? Our families and children are on the city-ships! All of us are!"

"I'm sorry, sir. Yes."

"At least Leviathan will not be activated," Simon says to Aaron.

"Simon, Leviathan went operational last week."

The Atlantia
8:57 a.m., 21 August 2096

River and her team are pinned down in one of the hallways. They are well-armed and well-armored, but the intense gunfire is coming from both ends of the hallway. Atlantian Military wants them dead—there's no doubt of it, even though they must know who they are. Her team stays close to either the walls or the ground, never taking their fingers off the trigger, not for a second.

"Do it!" River yells.

"We can't," the soldier yells. "We'll kill them."

"They'll kill us!"

River snatches the tek-launcher from him. "Watch out!" She fires a projectile down one end of the hall and wildly swings the weapon to fire another down the other end. The dual explosions are followed by complete silence.

River's team stares at her. Shooting at robo-soldiers and pirates is one thing, but human members of the Order is quite another.

"You can look at me all you want. We gave them every opportunity to stop this. Go and secure this level."

The soldiers get up from the ground and move out in teams. River feels a call coming in through her ear-set, but the tone is different. She touches her earlobe button. "Yes."

"Listen closely." It is her ex-husband's voice.

"Zukov? Why are—"

"I'm going to say this once and hopefully you are still intelligent enough to understand how serious this is. *Don't be where you are. Sixty seconds.*" The line disconnected.

A look of panic comes across her face. She jumps up. "Stop everyone!"

The two teams of soldiers stop and look back at her. She frantically motions them to come back towards her as she gets another line. "Call Vincent!" she yells into her wrist-comm. "Call Moses! Call Shoshana! Call Serena! Call Simon! Call Kanji! Call Abdalla! Everyone, I don't know what is going to happen, but we have fifty seconds to get away from this area as fast as we can or…I think we'll all be dead."

The Pacific Ocean
8:57 a.m., 21 August 2096

The American cruise liner sails the calm waters. On the main deck, the private party of senior male American executives continues—techno music blaring, wait staff serving plenty of glasses of liquid drugs, scantily clad sex workers hanging on the arms of the polyamorous male passengers, and the captain moving about, socializing.

At 9:00 a.m., the sky is consumed by a flash. Everyone's personal e-pad, tablet, Net-interface glasses, and devices stop. The ship's lights, power, machines, and systems stop. The entire sky rumbles as if a bolt of lightning came from outer space itself. Everyone looks around. People on the deck and the port windows watch it grow in the distance, many miles away—*a yellowish mushroom cloud, unimaginable in size, expands and rises higher into the sky, filling their entire view.*

The captain watches in horror. He can already see the ocean waters move away—the coming tidal wave is going to be beyond comprehension.

Smack! Something hits the deck only a couple of feet from him. He looks up and sees more. Birds, real and surveillance bots made to look like birds, fall from the sky, all around for as far as the eye can see.

"Abandon ship! Get everyone to the escape pods!" he yells to crew.

His eyes look out to the ocean horizon and he sees a wall of water rising. He whispers to himself, "We'll never make it."

He glances up again. So massive, so high, so monstrous—the yellowish, mega-mushroom cloud hangs frozen in the sky, above the "big blue."

Purge

"It was like a spiritual beckoning. I had an uncontrollable urge to be in its center, to become one with such colossal power." — The Siberian, world-famous Russian surfer, the first person to reach the impact point of the Russian Pacific Ocean Fusion Bomb Detonation of 2096 (also known as "Igor's Bomb")

The Pacific Ocean
8:58 a.m., 21 August 2096

In a flash, the "war" is over. The two sides were in a death struggle one moment, the next they were helping each other try to escape. The mushroom cloud is like a godlike Titan standing in the distance, but a new one rises. A killer tidal wave grows in size and power as it moves landward, blocking the view of everything behind it.

Most of the pirates are dead—or will be. Deck crew and soldiers scramble to get inside and below. Moses and his team jump from the *Pacifica* into the ocean. Shoshana and her team have already done so. Vincent and his team are the last ones to jump overboard. The Protestant, Jewish, and Catholic Continuum amphibious aircraft dive into the ocean. Two Continuum soldiers with rocket-packs have found their targets—Mr. Simon on the *Atlantia* and Mrs. Simon from the *Pacifica*; the four of them drop into the ocean. Sister Serena is the only one left in the sky. She turns her aircraft towards the killer waves that will reach them first and fires one last volley of missiles, before diving too. The missiles converge and detonate. The violent sonic blast is powerful enough to disperse the coming "smaller" waves of some twenty feet; buying just a little more time for the more damaged city-ships to submerge. The main tidal wave is as tall as a skyscraper and continues towards the coast, absorbing every floating human body, drone, sea craft, aircraft, debris, and all sea life in its path. To any eye, it looks like the entire ocean is beginning to stand up to walk towards the land.

Presidential Bunker, Moscow, Russia
9:30 a.m., 21 August 2096

The KGB head, Zukov looks up at his boss from the vid-screen.

"There was surprisingly little coastal damage considering the size of the tsunami wave. Japan bore the brunt of it, but they have the best tidal-breaker tek in the world. Their government wants to burn us at the stake and their newsfeed is wall-to-wall condemnations of us, but no loss of life among them, at all," he says.

Japan has the largest percentage of cyborgs in the world, mostly younger adults obsessed with having their bodies be part machine. However, the government is obsessed with external mechanization and using the nation's advanced robotic expertise. For coastal climate defense, underwater tsunami-breakers line its shores facing the open ocean. The giant moving mechanical walls are tethered miles off the coast and deploy after any severe seismic disturbance. Rising up from the ocean midway above the water line, they separate into multiple pieces to physically block approaching waves. More substantially, the breakers use powerful sonic blasts to disperse the wave energy of a tsunami. Modified over the decades, their effectiveness has increased exponentially, but this is the first time they were ever used against a fission-bomb-generated tidal wave.

Zukov continues, "Anything on the surface or under the water was another matter. Anything that could not get out of the path in time was either destroyed or picked up and thrown for miles. In fact, all the damage to the Japanese tidal breakers was due to boats, ships, and subs smashing into them. The bomb was strategically targeted close enough to be seen by all, but far enough away that we could deal with the waves.

"Mr. President, it was a brilliant stroke. Our Russian waters are free of all foreign subs, and free of all foreign bots. Sadly, our waters are free of all sea life too, so we'll be dependent on the Asian Consortium for our seafood for quite some time."

"The planet is far more resilient than any of the actions of its human parasites," the Russian President says. "The planet always survives and our tiny corner of the oceans will renew itself as it always does."

"Yes, Mr. President, the radiation was negligible. We Russians know more about radiation cleanup than anyone else on the planet. In a day or two, there will be nothing on the radiation sensors."

"Good."

"I imagine our tourism will take a substantial hit though. Our economy has already slowed, ever since President Krutikov's death."

"And tomorrow our economy will explode," Igor declares. "We are the empire that will do what is necessary to protect itself. No one will remember our weakness yesterday, only our strength today. The image of the mushroom cloud."

"Yes, sir?"

"Have Commerce start producing T-shirts and market them aggressively. Maybe a potential cash cow for our economy."

Zukov laughs. "What size should I get you, Mr. President?"

"I've been putting on quite a bit of weight. Just make me a large blanket with the image. I can wrap myself in it no matter what my final size will be."

Pacific Ocean, South of East China Sea
9:30 a.m., 21 August 2096

The *Pacifica* rises from the ocean with all its scars of battle—areas of blackened hull from fire or explosion, and punctures from missile strikes.

The charges were read aloud and transmitted throughout the thirteen city-ships for anyone who wanted to hear. "The great battle that we all thought we saw lead by Mr. Thomas against these Sea Vampires was staged. Their underwater city was a fake and the Vampires were never killed at the battle. They were working for him and were far away at an energy-island ship holding Prophet Simon and his crew. Mr. Thomas was in contact with them from at least the first time Commander Vincent encountered them. The Vampires' intent was to kill the Commander that very day. They also planned to kill Commander Vincent's four-boat team that very next day, tracking Vincent and his team by spies put on his boat by Mr. Thomas himself. Only Vincent's quick thinking saved all of them. Mr. Thomas apparently paid pirates as go-betweens, paid them huge sums of money—where he got it from we can only speculate—which is how he knew who to contact and why they responded so eagerly when he wanted to assemble his pirate army. Mr. Thomas was the one who had the Prophet's boat, the Honi, seized by the pirates in a sneak attack while he brazenly watched from his own secret warship just a mile away at the time, confirmed by Russian Bloc surveillance. He didn't even care others could see him. The only thing to be determined is how many of the Twelve were involved in the plot. Formal charges, including attempted murder with special circumstances, will be drawn up for public trial."

The medical staff treats Thomas's wounds with a topical surgical device. There are two gunshots to his body. If it were not for body-armor, he would have been killed. Now she applies bandage patches to the wounds. No one says anything. The staff thinks to themselves, *Did Prophet Thomas really try to murder Prophet Simon, should we arrest him?* Thomas thinks to himself, *Will someone detain me before I can escape?*

Huntley arrives on the medical floor with almost two dozen armed soldiers. He's bloodied and angry. A nurse greets them.

"Where is Mr. Thomas?" he asks.

"He just left, sir."

"Just left? Why wasn't he detained?"

"Sir, we're not getting involved in this. You want to detain him; then go do it. I'm a doctor, not a jailer."

"Which way did he go?"

She points.

War Room, The Atlantia
9:31 a.m., 21 August 2096

Apostle Aaron sits on a chair, looking defeated and distressed.

"Sir, all the city-ships have risen to the surface," a soldier informs him.

"Damage?"

"Sir, half of them need immediate repairs and half of those may need to abandoned, until that happens. We submerged and dove past the tolerance levels of each city-ship. We're lucky we were able to surface again."

"Do you have the casualty reports yet, from the battle?"

"No, but..."

"But what?"

"I don't think you'll want to see them."

Aaron covers his eyes with his hand to compose himself. "Where's Thomas?"

"We'll find out, sir," another officer answers.

The two officers leave him. Aaron turns his attention to the briefing. Caleb and Glen are back in control of their departments.

"The bomb was an older, modified hydrogen version," Caleb says to the assembled group of men and women in black, navy, or white uniforms. "We lost a substantial number of our sea craft because of how fast we had to dive and we lost all our aircraft on the decks. It was really the tidal breakers that saved us, besides the warning from the Continuum. The breakers shielded most of the tidal wave-fall from us. The bomb's EMP also did substantial damage to some of our systems. Thankfully, our life-support systems are an easy fix, but our weapon systems are gone, and we've lost all our fish-bots in the Pacific—all. If there were any subs in the vicinity of the blast, they and their crews are at the bottom of the ocean."

"Were there any subs in the bomb's vicinity?" someone in the group asks.

"We don't know and probably will never know. If there were foreign nations in Russian waters, they were there illegally. It's unlikely that any of those nations will acknowledge their existence."

"How many people do you think were killed?"

"We may never know."

"How many of our people were killed?" a woman asks.

Glen takes the question. "We'll have numbers in a couple of hours, but we have to secure all the city-ships. That's the priority."

"And Mr. Thomas?" someone asks.

"He will be detained."

The man who asked the question looks at Aaron.

"Shouldn't you be detained, too?

Aaron stands. "I knew nothing of the plot and most people accept that, but if that's what you all want, then I'll cooperate."

"Where did the Prophet go?" Caleb asks.

"He was whisked off the deck by Continuum members wearing jet packs. They flew away so fast and all of us….all we could see was the tidal wave coming. I was snatched off the deck as the city-ship was diving."

"So he's fine?"

"Yes."

Another man asks, "Can someone tell me how the Order found itself in this hellish position? Decades of detailed planning and preparation, day after day, and then in one day, one battle that should never have happened, it's all undone."

"It's not undone," Aaron says. "Others have suffered greater disasters than this. They recovered, so will we. We'll be fine."

"You don't look fine. And I don't think we do either."

The Kremlin, Moscow, Russia
10:37 a.m., 21 August 2096

Zukov arrives for the impromptu meeting. Five men are waiting, who immediately stand to their feet as he enters the room. He walks to the chair at the head of the table and sits. They take their seats, too.

"Am I to understand that we have foreign subs in the area again?" Zukov is angry. "How many bombs must we drop?"

"The subs are civilian, sir. Only civilians."

"Are you sure?"

"Yes."

Another officer says, "Sir, we may have gotten all the foreign military subs out, but it's swarming with civilians now."

Zukov looks at him. "Why?"

"People want to know what it's like to swim through radioactive fallout."

Zukov looks at them incredulously and starts laughing. "Seriously?"

"Yes, sir."

The officer hands Zukov a tablet to review the report.

Zukov starts to laugh again. "Is this for real?" He rereads a paragraph on the report. "There are flash mobs going to the area to have sex."

The men start laughing, too. One of them answers, "Yes, sir. It seems that we've inadvertently created another tourist attraction."

"Sir, this could be a great idea. Let's leave them there and tax them for use of the area, or charge a fee for being in the fall-out area. I can see it now: sex under the mushroom cloud."

"Silly people. Too bad there's not enough radiation left to cause them any harm," Zukov says. "I'm tempted, but no. It wouldn't be long before the tourists would actually be foreign spies. The President wants the area free of subs and people." Zukov wipes the smile off his face. "Gentlemen…" They can see he's very serious and stop the laughing and joking. "We want the media to talk about the strength of the Bloc under our new president, our show of force against our foreign enemies, not horny naked people flocking to area. If we allow them to choose the story to cover, we know what story the media will choose. Issue a directive and keep people out of the area for the next ninety days."

"Yes, sir. We'll get them all out of there."

"Gentleman, we also must not forget that the danger is not over. Our enemies are watching us from the shadows, looking for any sign that this was an act of desperation, rather than a decisive display of our resolve. Our enemies would have joined forces to overrun us a long time ago if it wasn't for the fact the Caliphate wants the whole world to be Islam and the CHINs want the whole world to be Chinese. We can't afford for anyone to see through our poker face. We, and every other person in this region, could find ourselves in the middle of the proverbial World War Three, if we're not careful. Never forget that. Leak multiple reports to the media, as many as we need to, to show that there is 'catastrophic' radiation in the region. Scare them, scare everyone."

The men nod.

"I know many of you are scared of the President. Even the new Prime Minister is scared of him, though he puts on a brave face. You hear the rumors, the scientists from the Zone he had brought to him, who have never left there either, rumors of inhuman screams down there. I know I'm the only one left comfortable talking to him regularly. I personally do it so he has a true human connection, despite what he is doing. I'm glad you're scared of him. Take that emotion into the public. If you are scared of him, then our enemies will be *terrified* of him. Ultimately, it is that, your fear, not the bombs that will keep Russia and Europa safe."

The men nod in agreement again.

Zukov remains quiet for a while before looking at the tablet again. "Now, what is this report? Some massive air-and-sea battle before the bomb blast, between civilians and pirates in the middle of the Pacific? Thirteen city-ships?"

The Pacifica
12:15 p.m., 21 August 2096

As prisons go, this is a nice one. The Twelve are confined to an empty apartment with guards stationed at the door in the hallway. They sit at the large table eating their lunch. Some look as presentable as always, others look like they went through a battle—and they did.

The two men stand outside the room. "We have to ask them," Caleb says to Glen. "Most of our sensors are out. We're blind, deaf, disabled, and floating helpless in the ocean. He could be hiding in a closet for all we know, and there's over ten thousand closets on each city-ship times thirteen. We have to see if they know anything."

"As if they'll tell us." Glenn is less than enthused.

Caleb and Glen enter the room. The men stop eating and look up.

"Apostles, sorry to interrupt, but we have further questions," Caleb says.

"You can't find him," Apostle Fisher says.

Caleb gives him a suspicious look. "Why do you say that, sir?"

"Just a guess."

"Do you know something?"

"No, I'm a prisoner. How could I—"

"You're a traitor," Glen snaps at the man. "You're lucky no one threw you and the rest of you overboard."

"Mr. Glen," Apostle Aaron speaks up. "Please, remember that we weren't all involved in the plot. Or have you already judged all of us?"

"Yes, Mr. Glen," Fisher says. "Neither of you can judge us, only the people."

Caleb holds an angry Glen back. "If you had succeeded in killing any of my soldiers—" Glen starts to say.

"Okay, okay," Caleb says. "This is not the trial. Nothing will be resolved in this room. Mr. Fisher, I'm going to ask you again. Where's Mr. Thomas?"

The Open Sea (Over Two Hours Earlier)
9:45 a.m., 21 August 2096

The one-man sea craft jets through the ocean at incredible speeds, two hundred feet below the surface. Thomas is determined to get there first, no matter what the risk to his life.

The War Room, The Pacifica
1:00 p.m., 21 August 2096

Both Control and Military officers watch the vid-screen of Vincent.

"Commander Vincent, is Prophet Simon okay?" Glen asks.

"He and Mrs. Simon are fine," Vincent answers, but his tone quickly turns angry. "I am personally adding a charge of murder to the list with special circumstances."

"Vincent, he shot an android."

"He didn't know that. He thought it was Prophet Simon."

"Vincent, he'll never see the light of day. That's already determined, so we don't need to add anything else to the list. We need to find him first."

"Commander, I suggest we get Prophet Simon to address the ships," Glen says to Vincent. "Maybe he can convince whoever is hiding him to turn him over."

"He'll do that," Vincent answers. "Maybe he killed himself. That would be the honorable thing to do."

"Vincent, he wouldn't have gone to the infirmary if that was his intent, and we still would have found a body."

"Also," Caleb continues. "When will you and the others be returning?"

"We'll return for the trial."

"Why? Are you concerned about Huntley?" Caleb asks. "I can assure you, he's extremely motivated to find him to clear his name."

"So you say. What I remember is that a lot of people I've known all my life tried to kill me and my team."

"Vincent," Glen says. "I agree with Caleb. That's unfair. They thought you were responsible for Prophet's Simon supposed death and were attempting to seize the city-ships by force."

"I'm sorry." Vincent pauses.

"What are you thinking, sir?" asks a War Room officer.

"Where's Leviathan?"

Everyone nervously looks at each other. Caleb and Glen exchange glances.

"Vincent, I know what you're thinking," Caleb says. "It's

impossible. One single person cannot activate Leviathan, let alone run it."

"Are we positive?" Vincent asks.

"Vincent, you were one of the founding teks. You probably know more about its systems than we do. It's impossible."

"Could it have been changed?"

Caleb looks at his officers in the room. "Well?"

"Impossible, sir," one of them answers. "Mr. Thomas isn't a tek. He wouldn't even know what to do if he got access to it, but he never did. And even if he did have access to it, he couldn't have accessed and changed it in a few weeks. It is quite impossible."

"Is anyone monitoring its location?" Vincent asks.

Caleb says, "That system remains inactive until Leviathan is activated, to prevent anyone from tracing the link."

"Vincent, our priority now has to be repairing our city-ships and getting out of this region as quickly as possible. People are scared we could be in the flash zone of another world war with the Russian Bloc dropping H-bombs just to "clean out" its territorial waters."

"I'll get a team over to you to help."

The Bombay Queen
1:00 p.m., 21 August 2096

Mr. Simon knocks on the door of the makeshift private vid-transmission room, one of the smaller quarters of the cruise liner.

"Come in, sir," Vincent says sitting in front of a tablet in vid-cam mode for the meeting. He turns off the device.

"Where's Thomas?"

"Still missing."

"Do you really think he's hiding in a closet?"

"No, but he's somewhere plotting his next move."

"Do really believe a single person could activate Leviathan?"

Vincent sighs. "He couldn't."

"Based on your questions to them, you don't think so."

"They all said it's impossible for him to access Leviathan."

"Vincent, things haven't been going our way this month from the start. And it's not even over. Something I learned from the Magi is there are a lot of things that are impossible in the world, but then you go into a world where they are. Is the *Divine Providence* operational?"

"Yes. All our boats are."

"If we want to independently determine whether it's active, how would we do that?"

Vincent hesitates. "We can't. I already checked. It's been moved from its holding location."

"Then let's see if we can get ahead of events for a change."

"If the impossible is possible, then there wouldn't be a damn thing we could do to stop him. He could kill every one of us before we got anywhere near him, and as we've personally seen, he doesn't have a problem with that."

"Vincent," Simon says with a smile. "We're the good guys. We can be pretty smart when we put our minds to it."

The Pacifica
12:00 noon, 24 August 2096

Mr. Thomas is being broadcasted on every general vid-screen on all thirteen city-ships. Frantic Control officers try to cut off the transmission from their stations. Caleb tries to help them.

"How is this happening? How is he getting in?" Caleb asks.

An officer looks at him. "Someone onboard had to give him the current access codes."

"Good afternoon everyone. As you can see, I am very much alive. I am not here to answer the falsehoods that have been spread about me or to defend myself against illegitimate charges filed against me. I am here to retake my position as the true leader of the Order. For every man and woman, every Mormon hearing the sound of my voice, you are to leave the derelict and obsolete city-ships that we have been pathetically calling home and join me on our new home, waiting for you right outside now, on…Leviathan."

The Pacific Ocean
12:05 p.m., 24 August 2096

The lone fish-bot stops its forward motion. All of the Order's surveillance bots were destroyed first by the attacking Continuum forces, and then, finally, by the fission bomb blast. This is one of a few dozen, hastily constructed to provide some kind of security perimeter net until the city-ships could be restored to full capabilities.

Something is rising from the ocean depths. It is so large that the bot's ocular sensors cannot determine its size. It is too far down to see clearly, but it is rising fast. The Fish remains in place as another form rises and upon impact, the bot goes dead.

The thirteen city-ships are anchored in a circle formation when the first sign of it is visible. A mile away, something peeks through the surface. The Leviathan continues to emerge. At first it seems to be a city-ship itself, but then points, in a vast wide circle all around it, start to rise from the water—a circumference larger than all thirteen city-ships combined. And it is still rising.

It stops its ascent; two-thirds of its mass is still underwater. All the thirteen city-ships combined are equivalent to a hand in comparison to a whole human body. The Leviathan looks like a curved upside-down cruise ship made of a translucent, shimmering blue material.

The ocean is filled with hundreds of shuttle boats approaching the single open mouth-like port of the colossal ship. Shuttles dock and people exit onto the port deck. Cable-like tentacles pick up empty shuttles to place them on giant shelves near the dock, each shelf emitting cushions of air. People follow the lighted walkway in.

The destination is a large, cavernous auditorium. Thomas waits, already surrounded by Huntley and a small army of soldiers. The "room" fills quickly with a steady flow of people.

"Mr. Thomas," Caleb walks in with his own team of soldiers.

"Mr. Caleb," Thomas answers. "Is this your welcoming committee?"

"Yes, it is. Are we going to be able to hold the trial here?"

"Actually, Mr. Caleb, that's exactly what we're going to do. However, please be careful about how you hold your weapons. The Leviathan is very protective of its master."

"You're the master now?"

"I am."

Caleb looks at Huntley. "I see you're back where you belong." Huntley says nothing, but keeps his hand on his gun belt.

One of Caleb's men touches his shoulder and he looks back at him and quickly notices it too. Baseball–sized drones are surrounding the men as cable-like tentacles rise from the floor. The cables wrap around their ankles securely, but give them enough slack to move about.

Thomas smiles at Caleb.

At 12:55, Prophet Simon enters the room with his wife, Haven. Thomas's wife GlenDora is at the entrance, smiling as she greets people when she sees them. Haven walks right up to the woman.

"Mrs. Simon," she says nervously.

Haven punches her in the face. GlenDora falls to the ground and after a few seconds, starts to cry.

Mr. Simon takes his wife's hand and leads her in.

Mr. Thomas has already seen him. The hum of noise in the room from many thousands of people immediately stops. Prophet Simon lets his wife's hand go and walks within inches of Prophet Thomas's face. Simon makes no hostile movements towards him. Thomas stares back, but maintains the slight smirk on his face. No one makes one sound in the cavernous room. Everyone watches to see what will happen.

People cry out. The men look at the door. Vincent runs up to Thomas, pulling a gun.

"Vincent," Simon commands. "You are to holster that weapon immediately."

Huntley and his men point their weapons at him. Caleb and his men point their weapons at Huntley and his men. Miri appears behind her husband and points her gun at Huntley's forehead. The commotion of the crowd grows; no one knows what to do.

"Vincent! Holster that weapon now," Simon tells him again.

"Vincent, you should listen to him," Thomas says. "You had your chance. You shot me twice and couldn't kill me."

"I wonder if I shoot you in the head this time, if I'll be more successful," Vincent snaps.

"Thomas, shut up," Simon yells. "You are not helping. Vincent, lower that weapon. Do you really want it to go this way? You shoot him, his men shoots you, his men and our men shoot each other, you go down, me, your wife, everyone. Is that what you want?"

"At least he'll be dead and won't have Leviathan."

"It's not worth it." Simon walks to him and grabs his gun. "Vincent, no more. You know better than me, that as long as he stands on Leviathan, he's untouchable. We lost this round. Enough of our people have been killed over all of this. No more."

Vincent reluctantly lowers his weapon.

Everyone else, as if on cue, does the same. The crowd calms down and a few of the Apostles appear and stand between the two factions to calm things more.

"This is how it has to be," Simon says to Vincent. "Sometimes you just have to submit to the situation as it is and let the God sort things out."

"God expects us to act."

"That's exactly what we're doing."

The Bombay Queen (Three Days Earlier)
8:00 p.m., 21 August 2096

The Continuum members stand together with their drinks (alcoholic or not) in hand around the unique open firepit in the private bar. Simon and his wife Haven are the main guests.

"Mr. Simon, I'm glad to see you again," says Tova of the Conservative Jewish Order.

"Thank you."

"Which ship are you staying on?" someone asks other members.

"The *Trinity*," Moses answers.

"You mean the *Godhead*," Simon says with a smile.

The men and some of the others start to laugh.

"Some of us missed the obvious inside joke," Tova says.

"Every Order has inside jokes with other Orders. You can write a book on it."

"So what will you do?" one of the Continuum members asks Simon.

"My people here and I will make the decision by midnight."

"Whatever it is, this must be resolved in our favor," Tova says. "Time is too critical."

"Do you know something more?" Simon asks.

"We've all been assuming the Russian Orthodox disappeared due to the government or other external forces," Tova continues. "What we've gathered from our investigation suggests that their disappearance may have been triggered internally, without the knowledge or consent of its people."

"That being said," Moses says. "If Mr. Thomas was somehow able to get control of Leviathan, and the longer he goes without being found, the more likely we think that possibility may actually exist. The Continuum would have to intervene *by any action necessary* to safeguard that tek. There's not a superpower or nation in the world that would be willing to kill a lot a people to get their hands on it."

The Leviathan
1:18 p.m., 24 August 2096

Thomas raises his hands to focus the crowd's attention on him and loudly says, "I am glad Mr. Simon is here, because there will be no public trial. No one will be detained and arrested. No one will be imprisoned or executed. Choose!"

No one among the thousands of people quite knows what he means. But Simon does.

"Today, you choose your Prophet. Choose Mr. Simon, then leave. Take your families with you and go. The thirteen city-ships are yours. Choose me, and you live here, on Leviathan, and we will make a new life away from danger, away from the Resistance—that's what they are, no matter what name they call themselves today—away from this fallen world and its fallen people. So everyone choose now!"

No one in the crowds moves at first. No one knows what to do.

Vincent raises his hand. "If you don't want a murder and conspirator as your Prophet, come with us and Prophet Simon away from this place. Don't let him confuse you into thinking that you can only be safe here under his martial law. Don't let him think that what he did was anything but evil. The only fallen person here is him!"

"Choose!" Thomas yells. "I'll make it simple."

All Thomas has to do is think it—the Leviathan's brainwave-reading tek activates it—and a partition, at the midpoint of the enormous room, starts to close slowly. People hesitate at first, but then act and start to move to their chosen "side."

Simon stands quietly with wife, Vincent and Miri next to him. Apostle Aaron and his family join them and, unexpectedly, so do Apostle Fisher with his family. Two more Apostles join them, but the others remain with Thomas. Caleb at first stands on Simon's side, but his wife and family stare at him, until they move over. Glen, his family, and most of the Military stay on Simon's side. Half of Control remains with Thomas. In the general population, three-fourths remain with Simon. Vincent is visibly disturbed that so many people are staying with Thomas. The partition closes.

The partition wall becomes transparent and Thomas walks to it as he waves back the crowd from him on his side. He stands opposite Simon—just the two of them, staring at each other.

"There we are, Mr. Simon," Thomas says.

"There it is, Mr. Thomas."

"Since we will never speak again in this life, I just wanted you to know. August fourth was the day. That's the day I started my grand plan, at the funeral. You caused my father's death. You so disgraced him that he had to leave the Fifteen—people calling him coward, rejecting his leadership. He knew he'd never be Prophet, after you came back like some folk hero—you and your puppy, Vincent, from your Resistance battle. Father died soon after. He hid it from everyone, except us, his family. We saw him die a bit every day, shriveling up from grief of his disgrace, until he was dead. My mother followed soon afterwards; she could not live without him. It was at his funeral that you had the audacity to show your face at, say words over his grave, my father, that's when I said I'd make you pay."

"Mr. Thomas that is not what happened to your father, not even close. You were a child at the time and you're a hateful child now, personally responsible for the deaths of our people by the scheme you set in motion."

Thomas ignores him. "As of this day, you and all of *your* people are excommunicated from the Mormon Order. Leave Leviathan immediately and do whatever it is you Exiles plan to do."

"Thank you Mr. Thomas. Looks like this is the last time we will ever see each other."

"Yes, it is. You have five minutes to be off my ship before we launch."

Simon turns and gathers Haven and Vincent. The two of them have such looks of anger that they would probably reach through the transparent wall to kill Thomas if they could. Simon moves through the crowd to the front to lead everyone off the part-city, part-weapon, "living" AI city-ship.

"Mr. Huntley," Thomas says. "Prepare for departure."

"Yes, Prophet."

Thomas looks at the other Apostles and says, "The First Presidency and the Twelve have to be remade. I want a list of names of who we should bring on."

2:28 p.m.

Simon's group makes it back to the inner port to find all the shuttle boats waiting for them. Vincent is deeply disturbed. Simon notices.

"I'm so ashamed," Vincent says.

Simon puts his hand on his shoulder. "Don't judge them too harshly. People just want to be safe and secure for themselves and their families."

"How could they follow that Tom? What he did! What he tried to do!"

"They were run out of their home state, run out of their home country, don't know what really went on between me and him, went through a deadly battle against the alliance they thought they were a part of, saw a fission-bomb detonated near them, their city-ship had to dive so quickly and recklessly into the deep sea—possibly never to return, to avoid a killer wave. Vincent, be a bit more forgiving. They're all just average, simple, God-loving people."

Vincent sighs. "I didn't think of it like that." Miri hugs him.

Their boats emerge from the Leviathan's inner port. Simon points to the Apostles with him, Vincent, Miri, River, and Haven. "Have everyone get to their ships and pack up everything they want in one travel case. We're abandoning the city-ships. They must do it as quickly as humanly possible."

"Abandon?" Aaron asks.

"Abandon," Simon answers back.

Thomas exits the elevator with his bridge team. The Leviathan's bridge is a huge curved room and unlike anything they've seen before—hover-pods with full consoles, shimmering blue walls and floors, a lighted silver ceiling, and tiny baseball-sized drones hovering in the air.

He sits in the captain's chair as the entire wall reveals itself to be a vid-screen, showing the bridge a view of the shuttle boats making their way back to the city-ships.

"Tell anyone who wants to risk going back to their quarters to get belongings that air shuttles will depart in ten minutes."

"Thank you. Most of the people will want to do that," one of the Apostles says.

"Monitor everyone closely and when the last person gets back, we launch."

3:09 p.m.

Huntley returns to the bridge from the elevator and walks to Thomas.

"It's done, Prophet. Our people have their things and the others are..."

Thomas looks at him. "What are they doing? We can see them from the screen."

"They're abandoning the city-ships and they're moving all their shuttle boats together."

Thomas laughs. "They can do whatever they want. I don't care in the least bit. The warmongers can go their way, and Simon, who disgraced my late father, can lead them to hell if he wants. Prepare for departure."

The bridge crew prepare as Huntley hands Thomas a palm tablet.

"The full codes."

Thomas smiles. "To think Leviathan is only one-third operational and to feel its power."

"You'll have permanent control of all its external weapon systems and its propulsion matrix," Huntley says. "Reset the system by voice command for the authorization upgrade."

"System," Thomas calls out. "Recognize Prophet Thomas H. Thomas, Temporary Shepherd. Access 459 Tango Lima Zulu. Permanent Shepherd Reset."

The computer voice responds, "Listed. Prophet Jonathan Q. Simon."

"System, erase and permanent delete. Recognize Prophet Thomas H. Thomas, Permanent Shepherd."

Every one of the thirteen city-ships is abandoned. People are huddled in shuttle boats, one suitcase apiece, crowd together in the sea. No one knows why. No one feels anything but despair. They've been purged from their own Order.

The Leviathan slowly rises from the ocean into the sky. The air vibrates and people wince from the power of its monstrous propulsion engines.

"Infestation identified. Purge commencing."

The Leviathan hovers fifteen feet above the water surface. A little boy is shot out of the colossal craft, screaming as he plunges into the water. A girl, two women, a man, several people, dozens of people—all are shot from the ship.

Simon and all the others watch from their shuttle boats in shock as the Leviathan "expels" *everyone* from itself. Hundreds, thousands, tens of thousands of screaming, terrified people plunge into the sea.

The vessel seems to physically "cough" and what seems to be debris shot out are actually the personal belongings, large and small, of this "city's" people. It moves in the air above Simon and the others and countless cable tentacles shoot out from its bottom hull. Each tentacle reaches down, and gently wraps around each person. They are all pulled up in unison into the craft. Smaller cable tentacles follow and reach down to grab suitcases and belongings back into the craft. All bottom hull doors close. The Leviathan automatically starts to rise higher into the sky.

Inside Simon, Vincent, Apostles and officers exit the elevator.

"Recognize Prophet Jonathan Q. Simon. Access 007 Tango Alpha Omega," Simon calls out to the system.

"Recognized and accepted. Welcome home, Mr. Simon," the computer voice says.

The ocean is littered with people paddling to stay afloat or swimming for the empty shuttle boats. People are crying, screaming, or paralyzed in near hysteria. Thomas is in complete shock too as he treads water.

People are yelling at him. "What happened?!" "What's happening?!" "Help!"

He cannot speak or look at anyone, including his wife who is having a panic attack next to him, slipping under the water. His eyes are locked on the Leviathan. The engines blast as it continues to rise into the sky. It powers up and jets away leaving them all behind—forever.

Shogun Island, Philippine Sea
12 midnight, 25 August 2096

Kanji sits on a bench in the outside patio of his personal hut. Both Magi heralds, Top Hat and Wings, sit with him. Even from this distance they can see the Leviathan resting on the coast.

"Outsiders will be looking to hydrospace rather than outer space," Wings says. "And vice versa later, as orchestrated. Plenty of confusion for our needs, to last for ages."

"Was Project Leviathan ever in danger?" Kanji asks.

The Magi smile. "No," Wings says. "It is and has always been part of Project Noah."

"How many Leviathans are complete?"

"*One hundred thousand as of today.*"

Top Hat never speaks and holds up her left hand. A glowing white "Y" appears in the center.

"Why?" Kanji asks. "With the disappearance of the East

Orthodox, no one can be left behind, so there is a situation the Shogun must attend to. Project Noah will not be delayed by our part though. I fear that the balance of power on this planet is only beginning to unravel. I believe that the Russians have started the dominoes falling. The late Krutikov planted the seed in the minds of non-superpower nations that they could be ones too, and in the superpowers, that status quo is not forever. It all would have happened anyway eventually. There are many who want a global war…*to reconfigure the world.*"

"Then we must bring an end to the beginning before they bring the beginning of the end," Wings says. "The division before the decimation."

Twenty-nine years until the first attack of World War III. The AFTER EDEN saga continues in Book Four: ***RED HALO***.

Thank you for reading!

Dear Reader,

I hope you enjoyed *Rising Leviathan*.

Can You Write Me a Review?

If you enjoyed *Rising Leviathan* (After Eden Series, Book #3), I'd greatly appreciate a review on one or more of the following sites:

Reviews are the best way for readers to discover good books. My writer's motto is simple: "Readers Rule!" Thanks so much.

Always writing,

Austin Dragon

CONTINUE THE ADVENTURE

Get Your Next *After Eden* Book!

<u>**The After Eden Series (Chronological Order)**</u>

Thy Kingdom Fall (After Eden Series, Book #1)
Stars and Scorpions (After Eden Series, Book #2)
Metal Flesh (After Eden Series: Tek-Fall, Episode I)
Hell's Menagerie (After Eden Series: Tek-Fall, Episode II)
Rising Leviathan (After Eden Series, Book #3)
Pure Conspiracy (After Eden Select Novel)
Red Halo (After Eden Series, Book #4) Coming Soon!

<u>**The After Eden Series (Group Order)**</u>

Main After Eden Series
Thy Kingdom Fall (After Eden Series, Book #1)
Stars and Scorpions (After Eden Series, Book #2)
Rising Leviathan (After Eden Series, Book #3)
Red Halo (After Eden Series, Book #4) Coming Soon!

After Eden: Tek-Fall Companion Novels
Metal Flesh (After Eden Series: Tek-Fall, Episode I)
Hell's Menagerie (After Eden Series: Tek-Fall, Episode II)

After Eden Select Novel
Pure Conspiracy (After Eden Select Novel)

ABOUT THE AUTHOR

Austin Dragon is the author of the *After Eden* **Series**, including the *After Eden: Tek-Fall* mini-series, the classic **Sleepy Hollow Horrors**, and the new cyberpunk detective series, *Liquid Cool.* He is a native New Yorker, but has called Los Angeles, California home for the last twenty years. Words to describe him, in no particular order: U.S. Army; English teacher; one-time resident of Paris; political junkie; movie buff; campaign manager and staffer of presidential and gubernatorial campaigns; Fortune 500 corporate recruiter; renaissance man; dreamer.

He is currently working on the next books in the *After Eden* Series, and new books and series in mystery, fantasy, YA dystopia, classic horror, and more science fiction!

Connect with Austin on social media at:

Website and blog:
http://www.austindragon.com

Twitter:
https://twitter.com/Austin_Dragon

Pinterest:
http://www.pinterest.com/austindragon

Google+:
https://google.com/+AustinDragonAuthor

Goodreads:
https://www.goodreads.com/ADragon